Collected

Jessica Thorpe

Mother Bard Books, LLC.

To Jonathon and Charlotte.

Contents

Chapter One

Emmitt clutched the wheel. His knuckles were white, and his fingers were pins and needles. He made a mistake, but there was no escaping the consequences. He had driven here, after all. He promised to be here. Emmitt inhaled deeply, held it, and let out an audible sigh.

"Mindful breathing." Andrew stared forward with a neutral expression, barely acknowledging Emmitt. It wasn't a question. Andrew knew he was nervous. He always knew, but knowing was never enough. Andrew had to let Emmitt know he knew.

Emmitt quieted his breathing. *Asshole*. He wasn't sure if he was directing the sentiment toward his brother or himself. As Emmitt silently contemplated who the asshole was, Andrew remained still, with his eyes fixed forward.

When he spoke again, his indifference was so cold it was almost frigid. "It's good to confront your irrational emotions. It means you're aware of your flaws and on the path to becoming a more perfect you. The next step is getting out of the car. Can you handle that?"

"Yes," Emmitt snapped, shooting a sideways glare at his passenger.

Andrew refused to meet his eyes. "Let's go, then."

Emmitt hated being patronized. He hated when Andrew defaulted to his rehearsed motivational lines to communicate with him. He especially hated how effective it was. Emmitt, unthinkingly, had successfully pried his fingers from the steering wheel, opened the car door, exited the car, closed the door, and walked halfway across the street. By the time his indignation had fermented into a quiet fury, Emmitt was nearing the sidewalk. Pausing at the pavement, he considered, briefly, that he might rationalize it as an act of defiance. *Maybe I'm reversing his reverse psychology. I'm using reverse reverse psychology on Andrew.*

He smirked bitterly at how ridiculous it all was. Ultimately, he was where Andrew wanted him to be. Where Andrew had asked him to be. He allowed the mea culpa to slip into his mind, acknowledging that no one had coerced him. Emmitt certainly expressed several reservations, but those reservations hadn't stopped him from taking part in this "opportunity to manifest your dreams into reality" (as Andrew had put it).

A bead of sweat trickled slowly down the back of his neck. With knots in his stomach and his notebook in hand, Emmitt reached the edge of the property and looked around.

The property was sizable, even enviable, yet it was smaller than Emmitt had expected. Tall hedges created a fence around the house, obscuring it from view of street traffic and snooping neighbors. An imposing security gate closed off the driveway, leading to further concealment. It was a suburban fortress. Only the roof and chimney were visible from the sidewalk, which led Andrew to suggest, aloud, that the house was probably one story. No shit, Emmitt thought. Andrew then said that the single story meant the house was "California ranch-style." Emmitt rolled his eyes and kept his mouth shut. Andrew continued to fill the air with his calm, detached tone, stating that he liked the amount of privacy the hedges provided. Emmitt again disregarded his brother's words. To Emmitt's growing displeasure, it was becoming increasingly clear that Andrew either didn't comprehend or didn't care he was on the receiving end of the silent treatment.

Frustrated by his unsuccessful attempt to irritate Andrew, Emmitt promptly changed tactics. He would drop the silent treatment, but only if he had something clever to contribute. Emmitt often ruminated on the fact that Andrew had the annoying ability to state the obvious while eliciting fawning agreement from everyone in his presence. No one was here to agree with him now. Emmitt figured it wouldn't take too long to come up with some biting, cynical retort to one of Andrew's insipid musings. The cogs in Emmitt's mind were already turning. It was a petty decision, determined by an internal conversation that Andrew would never be privy to, but it eased Emmitt's frustration for the time being.

With a clearer mind's eye, Emmitt reluctantly pried himself away from his thoughts and looked closer at the hedges. A small wooden gate embedded in the immense shrubbery had been unlocked and partially opened. Andrew walked nearer and opened it fully. As his brother stepped toward the opening, Emmitt grabbed at the first thought that entered his mind, impulsively seizing the opportunity to one-up his brother's unremarkable observations.

"You know, this gate is a convenient way to protect the house from intruders, while still offering access to guests," Emmitt said cheerily. "It's just so ... what's the word I'm looking for? Functional. This gate is really functional, and it's a great addition to the property. Just think, without a gate, we'd have to struggle to climb over the twelve-foot privacy hedges." He smiled wide, bared his teeth, and tilted his head toward Andrew.

"Ten feet."

"Pardon?" Emmitt's teeth clenched harder. His smile faded.

"The hedges are only ten feet tall."

"Bullshit."

Andrew finally made eye contact. His gray eyes burned into Emmitt, but his tone remained calm. "I'm six foot two. If I put my arms up above my head, I have a little over eight-foot standing reach. Look." Andrew lifted his muscular arms above his head and placed his back against the hedge. "Does it look like two feet or four feet from the top of the hedge?"

Emmitt hesitated, then resigned himself to defeat. "Two," he grumbled.

"Exactly. And you shouldn't use unprofessional language. We aren't far from the house. You should act in private ..."

"... how you *conduct* yourself in public," Emmitt finished. "If you're going to quote Mom, you could at least get it right. '*Conduct* yourself in private how you *conduct* yourself in public.'"

"It's good advice for building better habits," Andrew replied calmly.

"It's meaningless." Emmitt mumbled the words, defeated by the exchange and angry at himself for initiating it.

Andrew shook his head, finally breaking eye contact. He sighed, walked through the open gate, and led on. Emmitt followed.

Once inside, Emmitt noticed that the lawn and garden were well-maintained. Two mature oaks caught his attention. Emmitt knew from their own childhood home that oak trees were messy, shedding nightmares, but someone had cared enough to clear the barbed leaves from this yard. There wasn't a stray leaf on the lawn. Various planters with pruned rose bushes and rounded topiary hedges lined the house. The grass was trimmed and impossibly green. The long summer hadn't scorched it yellow, and the nascent autumn weather hadn't faded it to a dull beige gray. An image of himself and Andrew playing pirates in their backyard as children while picking prickly leaves out from between their toes flashed into Emmitt's mind and softened the edge of his mounting bitterness. He briefly considered sharing the thought with Andrew, but ultimately kept it to himself. He risked a scolding for attempting to reminisce with his brother. Worse, he'd be branded, once again, as unprofessional.

It was difficult for Emmitt to hide his agitation when so much was unknown. Andrew seemed to know almost as little as Emmitt, but unlike Emmitt, Andrew remained unbothered by his own ignorance. Dissatisfied by his brother's lack of curiosity, Emmitt researched the family before their first visit to the house. Aside from a few notable individuals making public fools of themselves, the rest of the family remained private. It was a particular blow to Emmitt to have to rely on the crumbs of information the family had given Andrew.

After prodding desperately, Emmitt had discovered that this was their fifth house. The family had been evicted from the previous four houses, and Emmitt suspected they were in danger of losing their current residence if their circumstances didn't improve. It was too little to satisfy Emmitt, but it was the reason Andrew and Emmitt were here now. More precisely, it was why "Drew Key" was here. Emmitt was an afterthought. An assistant. If he was honest with himself, he would have to admit he preferred it that way. At least he wouldn't suffer the blame if things went wrong. Drew Key was an active participant by nature. Emmitt Key was an observer.

With a limited knowledge of the family's finances, and a compulsive habit of acting underwhelmed, Emmitt couldn't suppress the growing disappointment that occupied his thoughts. The house itself, as Andrew had confidently stated, was only one story. Somehow, a "California ranch-style" house (albeit a very large "California ranch-style" house) didn't quite fit his expectation of the Yates family. Perhaps the passive-aggressive fight with his brother had influenced Emmitt's surging dissatisfaction. Then again, the Yates name was the definition of American royalty and old money: hotel chains, real estate investments, and probably a railroad or two. The Yates Museum and Botanical Gardens, established two generations prior, was located only five blocks away within the quiet, affluent Santa Teresa neighborhood. The museum was a converted estate with multiple spiraling staircases and a hundred rooms. The gardens sprawled with forking, winding paths that took hours to walk. This house was a mid-century mansion. Emmitt had expected a palace. He'd expected something grand to contrast with the grotesque he assumed lay within. *That would be something to write about.*

This juxtaposition was a prepared topic. A foregone conclusion. A shower-thought-turned-thesis for his book. Emmitt reflected on his pettiness regarding the imaginary slight. *How could I suffer betrayal from a family I've never met? And don't I plan to exploit their situation?* He didn't like to think about that. The prospect of publicly embarrassing anyone who wasn't Andrew made Emmitt uneasy, and he worried his very presence in the house would cause offense. If his presence wasn't enough to draw the ire of the Yates family, his impetuous tongue might be enough to get them both kicked out of the house. Emmitt couldn't predict how Andrew would react if he allowed his unedited thoughts to slip nervously out of his mouth.

His thoughts didn't settle as he continued to scrutinize the house. Emmitt grew more disappointed the longer he looked. The house was neither dilapidated nor pristine. There were no visible holes or cracks. The paint wasn't chipped or faded, and he didn't notice any cobwebs. Conversely, there weren't any marble statues. No golden trim. No oversized fountains with cherubs holding grapes and harps. It was a worst-case scenario: It was boring.

The siding was brown, the ledgestone veneer that covered the chimney and part of the exterior was brown, the shutters and door were a slightly darker shade of brown, and every visible window had bland beige curtains draped inside. Emmitt had never been claustrophobic, but the sight of the heavy curtains blocking every window made his chest tighten at the thought of entering.

As they walked closer to the front door, Emmitt glanced over at his brother. He wondered if Andrew had also expected more from the Yates' house. Emmitt caught a slight furrow in his brother's brow. The corners of his mouth turned down, and his nostrils flared. Andrew must have sensed Emmitt's eyes on him. He settled back into his baseline of calm confidence as he quickened his pace. There was a hint of smug superiority in Andrew's carefully curated expression, but he kept his mouth shut and his eyes fixed on the house.

As they stopped at the front door, Emmitt tried to mimic Andrew's relaxed composure. "You ready? Or do you need a minute?"

Andrew paused and seemed to ponder the question carefully. "I need a minute."

Andrew looked squarely at Emmitt with a wide grin, took in a long, audible breath, held it, and let it out with a loud sigh. With a radiant smile of pearlescent veneers, and a twinkle in his cool gray eyes, Andrew announced he was ready and rang the doorbell.

"Asshole," Emmitt mumbled.

"*Conduct* yourself," Andrew replied.

Chapter Two

At first, nothing happened. Emmitt stood quietly and tilted his head, listening for any sign of life inside. There were no audible footsteps. No voices yelling they would "be there in a minute." No dogs barking. Nothing. He widened his eyes and looked at Andrew, who stood motionless in front of the door.

"Ring again?" Emmitt asked in a hushed voice.

"No. They're here. There are two cars parked outside the garage, and they left the gate open for us. It may take some time for one of them to answer the door. We don't need to rush them." Andrew's annoyance was palpable.

Emmitt sensed his brother's irritation, but he wouldn't keep his mouth shut. "I saw the cars. Maybe they didn't hear the doorbell. Or maybe they heard it, but they think we're Jehovah's Witnesses, or a package delivery. Or maybe they think we're trying to sell them solar panels."

Andrew exhaled sharply. "Sybil is expecting us. We set up a time to meet. We'll look desperate and unprofessional if we ring twice. Be patient."

They waited for an eternity of five minutes. Andrew remained fixed in place, while Emmitt stirred anxiously, shifting his weight from one leg to the other. Emmitt darted his eyes to avoid the stony glare emanating from his brother. As he continued to scan the front of the house aimlessly, a slight disturbance to the otherwise static scene caught his eye: slowly and silently, a woman's hand appeared in front of the bland beige curtain that covered one of the large windows at the front of the house. The hand, decorated with long, mint-colored acrylic nails, pulled back the curtain just enough for Emmitt to make out one large hazel eye bordered by the bushiest eyelashes he had ever seen.

Emmitt cleared his throat and tried to gesture inconspicuously to his brother. Andrew narrowed his glaring eyes at Emmitt. Emmitt continued to look at the cyclops staring back at him, forcing Andrew to follow his gaze. With both brothers staring at the eye that was staring back at them, the curtain opened wider to reveal the head of the woman.

"Oh my God! You're here! Stay there. Let me get to the door. It'll just take a minute. Stay. There." The disembodied head of the woman beamed up at them, then quickly disappeared from the window.

"I told you we just had to be patient," Andrew said with a satisfied grin.

After a short time, the front door cracked open. The head, with body fully attached, slid through the opening to greet them. Emmitt tried to sneak a glance at the interior of the house, but the slight opening of the door and the quick exit of the woman made it impossible.

As the wide-eyed, bushy-lashed, barefoot bombshell in the form-fitting pink sweater and tight white cutoff shorts blocked their entry, Emmitt felt himself instinctively step back. There was an agitation to her excitement. Emmitt glanced at Andrew, who calmly fixed his eyes on Sybil. Drew Key didn't seem fascinated or frazzled by the woman. Drew Key remained placidly professional.

"Oh my God! Drew Key is at my house! I told everyone all about you. If anyone can help us with our problem, it's you, Drew. Thank you so much for coming … Who's this?" She tilted her head and turned her hazel eyes toward Emmitt, gaping at him with a mixture of surprise, confusion, and something else. Emmitt was sure it was contempt. It was almost imperceptible, but the toothy smile she flashed at him showed a subtle line of tension running down her jaw to the base of her neck. "I'm Sybil, but you're probably already aware of that," she said in a breathy, condescending tone, as she reached her hand out to Emmitt.

Emmitt stiffly shook her hand and introduced himself calmly and politely. It was impossible to avoid knowing about Sybil Yates. She was famous, but not in the same way she used to be. Nothing justified the arrogance that bubbled out of her as she introduced herself to Emmitt.

After shaking hands, she turned her attention back to Andrew. To Sybil, he was Drew Key: Life Coach. She looked at him with awe and wonder. The admiring eyes fixed eagerly on her new motivational mentor. Drew Key: Transformation Strategist. Drew Key: Savior.

Without warning, the woman with the frenzied smile started crying. Emmitt took another step back and watched cautiously, confused by the sudden shift. She wrapped her arms around Andrew's waist, sobbing and struggling to catch her breath. Andrew held her silently and let her weep. Emmitt stood frozen in place, waiting for it to end.

He avoided looking at his brother, afraid that he wouldn't be able to hide the eye roll he was trying to hold back. An eye roll would be unprofessional. Emmitt contented his mind with the image of Sybil's makeup imprinting on Andrew's white designer polo shirt, fabricating a pseudo-celebrity Shroud of Turin painted with a heavy layer of cosmetics. As Emmitt allowed himself to drift, Sybil's meltdown came to an unnaturally abrupt conclusion. To Emmitt's immediate disappointment, Sybil's makeup and Andrew's shirt remained flawless when she finally pulled away.

Sybil apologized for her meltdown, composed herself, and brightened her face with the wide eyes and beaming smile she had affixed at the beginning of their encounter. Her mascara wasn't streaking, and on closer inspection, Emmitt noticed there were no tear stains on her cheeks. Not even a sniffle remained. It was an unnerving transformation. Andrew remained silent and waited for Sybil to speak.

"How embarrassing. Yuck!" She giggled nervously, gently patting her dry eyes with her acrylic mint-tipped fingers. "Is my nose red?"

Andrew studied Sybil's face seriously. "No. If you're worried about your eyes swelling, you can try massaging ..."

"The Cheng Qi pressure point," Sybil excitedly interrupted. "I've read all your mom's books ... oh and yours too, of course. But her book on acupressure, especially the Cheng Qi point, has been a real game changer for me."

Andrew smiled. "I knew we had compatible energies when you first opened the door. This is really going to help with the process. My brother and I are ready to get started. I would say 'whenever you're comfortable,' but I think you know ..."

"Comfort is the adversary of change," Sybil finished.

Emmitt's unease grew as the conversation circled back to Andrew and their mother. Emmitt hoped Sybil wasn't a sycophant, but her fawning disposition wasn't encouraging. The last thing he wanted to hear was Sybil Yates parroting the self-help one-liners of Drew Key and Serenity Rivers-Key. One Drew Key was enough for Emmitt. One Serenity Rivers-Key was one too many.

"There is one thing I need to get out of the way," Andrew said. "As you know, I like to be direct, and I wanted to confirm that your family—meaning you, your mother, and your sister—are all willing to be featured in my new book. That's why my brother, Emmitt, is here. He'll be aiding us in the process and taking notes—"

"Do I get to sign off on pictures?" Sybil interrupted. "Drew, I trust you completely, but I need to make sure you're capturing my best self." Sybil batted her eyelashes and smiled sweetly at Andrew.

Andrew offered Sybil a polite smile in return. "I spoke to your uncle. The book won't include any pictures. We've updated the waiver to include his additional terms. I want you to know there won't be any embarrassing anecdotes included. No blame. No shame. I firmly believe we will succeed. I have the updated waiver available for signature whenever you're ready."

"Yeah, that's fine." Sybil's enthusiasm waned at the mention of the waiver.

Emmitt noticed her flirtatious smile falter into a glazed-over expression.

Slowly, her eyes looked off to the side sheepishly, as though she remembered something important. "Drew, I want you to know that I'm absolutely willing to be featured in your book ... but my mother and sister aren't as open about this as I am. Renata is desperate for me and Mom to fix our issues, but she's also very private. Oh, and she hates it when I do things like this. She thinks anything involving self-help is a scam." Sybil smirked impishly and shrugged her shoulders.

Andrew's smile broadened. "Sounds like Renata might get along with my brother."

Sybil twirled her hair absentmindedly. "I doubt it. She's shy. You probably won't even notice her. We're not alike at all."

"What about your mother?" Andrew asked.

Sybil continued twirling her hair while occasionally looking up at Andrew. "My mother? She's stubborn, but I think if you can get Renata to sign off on the book, my mother might consider signing. Just don't mention her rooms, or where she sleeps, or the 'h' word, or my Uncle James ... and definitely don't mention my dad in front of her. Hmm ... what else ...?" Sybil trailed off in thought as she bit the tip of a mint fingernail. "Oh, I should probably also mention that Mom hates self-help too."

With two-thirds of the family against them, and Sybil only interested in Drew Key reciprocating her overt advances, Emmitt wondered why he and Andrew were at the Yates' house at all. He tried to stay silent. He fidgeted with his notebook and then folded his arms to stop the fidgeting, but he couldn't restrain his growing irritation.

"Do they have any idea that Drew is planning on incorporating your story into his next book?"

Emmitt could sense Andrew watching him closely. He locked his eyes on Sybil and waited for an answer.

Sybil grimaced at Emmitt, then slowly confessed. "Not ... entirely. I'm sure I mentioned some of it, but I guess I didn't tell them it would all be written and published. Is that going to be a problem?"

"It's not an issue." Andrew had turned his attention away from Emmitt and looked encouragingly down at Sybil. "We can figure this out together, and everything will work out. I believe everything will work out for the best. Do you?"

Sybil looked up dreamily at Andrew. "I do. Now that you're here, I really believe everything will work out."

Chapter Three

As Sybil slowly opened the door, Emmitt controlled the urge to lean in and peek inside. Emmitt knew Drew Key should enter first. He shifted his weight as his fingers tapped rapidly on his notebook. *Open the door*, his mind commanded. Another stony glance from Andrew made Emmitt freeze in place. Sybil opened the door halfway before pausing and glancing back them.

"That's as far as it goes." Sybil giggled. Her overly lashed eyes moved from Andrew to Emmitt, then settled back on the narrow opening. "It may be a bit of a squeeze."

"We'll fit," Andrew said. His eyes twinkled, but his pearly veneers were concealed.

Andrew's face was as affectionate as it was imposing. Emmitt had always envied that look. Drew Key commanded respect in the way he carried himself. He inspired adoration. He was effortlessly captivating. Sybil Yates had clearly fallen prey to Drew's charm. It was obvious to Emmitt that Sybil was attempting to force a reciprocation.

She glimpsed back at Andrew from the doorway with a demure smile, then slid through the partially opened door, tilted her head and sighed at him with a sweet, breathy apology. Her hazel eyes glittered through her impossible lashes.

Andrew followed slowly and deliberately. He turned sideways to fit his broad shoulders through the door and inched his way into the maw of the house. When only one large, tanned, veined hand held the door open from the inside, Emmitt finally proceeded.

He managed, with ease, to slide smoothly through the gap in the door; for although he and his brother shared their father's imposing height, Emmitt was lean and agile, while Drew Key had crafted himself into Apollo to fit within his brand. It was hardly an accomplishment, but doing anything better than Andrew, no matter how small, boosted Emmitt's confidence. Once inside, Emmitt quietly closed the door behind himself.

Prior to this very moment, Emmitt had expected, and even prepared himself for, a stench. He thought of the worst things: rotting garbage, mildew, cat urine, vomit. For weeks, he had imagined these smells. He deliberately strolled past dumpsters behind the alley of his apartment building. He volunteered at an animal shelter, and even stopped rinsing and cleaning his dishes for three weeks to breathe in the rancid air in his too-small apartment, hoping to develop a tolerance. Emmitt had been ready to show off his extreme fortitude by not dry heaving the moment he entered the house. He imagined a quiet gratitude and admiration from the Yates family. A lesser part of him gleefully envisioned Andrew holding back his six-egg omelet and black coffee breakfast while running out of the house to escape the putrid air. This fantasy had played out so vividly in his head that, when Emmitt entered the house, the lack of stench dismayed and upset him. The air was musty and thick. It was like walking through an old library or an antique store: stale and stuffy, but ultimately inoffensive.

Emmitt bit down on the soft flesh in his cheek. His over-prepared-ness was pointless. His efforts were wasted. Andrew had said not to bother. It was a little thing in a string of other little things, but it stung Emmitt sharply. *It's nothing. Stop getting angry and focus.* He realized that even the voice commanding him in his own head was Drew's. Emmitt was spitefully determined. If Drew Key could remain composed, Emmitt Key could too.

Looking around the entryway, he could see the columns of stacked boxes that barred the door from opening fully. Sybil slipped further into what Emmitt guessed was the living room. He could make out the top of a brick fireplace, extending at least seven feet wide, which would have dominated the large room had it not been hidden by the Yates family's possessions.

Emmitt carefully scanned the surrounding space to steady himself. Two sofas appeared to be arranged in an L-shape, with what might have once been a coffee table between them. In a cleaner room, the sofas would have made the fireplace the focal point. With all the clutter, however, nothing and everything drew his attention. His eyes darted wildly, trying to take it all in. The two presumed sofas had been piled so high with blankets, clothing, books, and overflowing moving boxes, it was impossible to discern the shape, color, or material of what lay underneath.

Two large grandfather clocks stood shoulder to shoulder between one sofa and the coffee table. A white bed sheet had been partially draped over the standing clocks. *To protect them?* Emmitt wondered who would bother to protect a grandfather clock from dust, when he could see ceramic vases, a crystal decanter, and a four-foot-tall bronze statue of the Virgin Mary lying haphazardly on top of framed photographs, embroidered pillows, and over a dozen rolled rugs on the floor. Mismatched armchairs, ottomans, and side tables had also been covered and piled with miscellany. Loose papers, unopened sets of floral stationery, and unused holiday gift bags were strewn alongside expensive-looking antiques. Emmitt knew he was unqualified to distinguish between the valuable artifacts and the worthless trinkets, but what was *valuable* to the Yates family? He suspected his understanding of the word would differ from their perception of it.

Although the room had been filled nearly to bursting, Emmitt noticed a mostly unobstructed, narrow trail that led further into the house. A memory of a family trip to the Grand Canyon wormed into Emmitt's mind. He remembered his mother insisting Emmitt face his intense fear of heights, and Andrew smugly siding with her while reassuring Emmitt that, "It'll be fine. Look, little kids are walking down the trail, and *they* aren't crying." He could see his dad, gritting his teeth and silently following behind as his mom and Andrew grabbed Emmitt's arms and forced him down the precarious, winding path to face his fears.

As the memory festered in Emmitt's mind, he noticed a tightness rising in his chest. His face flushed and his fingertips tingled. He took in a long, silent breath and stood completely motionless, hoping to avoid Andrew's attention.

Emmitt slowed his breathing. Gradually, the tightness and tingling subsided. *No more daydreaming, Emmitt.*

He forced his eyes to focus on the cluttered room. Despite the explosion of items that lay in piles around the house, most of the hoard was contained in storage bins and moving boxes. Everywhere he looked, there were stacks of black, gray, and clear plastic bins packed alongside buckling, overstuffed cardboard boxes. Some stacks towered almost as high as the eight-foot ceiling.

As Emmitt shifted nervously on his feet, he felt the rolled sleeve of his button-up shirt brush against the skin of his brother's bare arm. Like Emmitt, Andrew hadn't moved since entering the house. He didn't seem to notice how near Emmitt was to him. Emmitt dared to lean slightly forward to glance at his brother. There was a look of wide-eyed curiosity Emmitt hadn't expected to see.

Perhaps it was a look Andrew didn't *want* Emmitt to see. Immediately sensing Emmitt's eyes on him, Andrew briefly pressed his lips together, fixed his gaze ahead, and moved down the makeshift path toward Sybil. Emmitt remained still, gaining distance from his brother and waiting for Sybil to lead them further into the house.

Sybil waved an arm dramatically toward the living room. "So, this is our house. We've lived here for ... let me think ... about two years? Three? Yeah, I think it's been about three-ish years. We've always lived in this neighborhood. We just kind of hop into a new house when we're forced out of the old ones. The neighbors hate us, since we never really go away." Sybil spoke without grief or shame. She smiled and joked as though their evictions were nothing more than trivialities. "I can give you a full tour of the house, if you like, but it might be difficult to get through some areas. You may have to squeeze into some pretty tight places." Sybil smirked as she eyed Andrew's well-built frame.

"We can manage," Andrew said. "I'd like to see a bit more of the space. It'll help us develop a clear plan going forward."

"Of course! I'd love to show you more," Sybil gushed. She tiptoed toward Andrew and whispered, "My mother is probably sitting in her usual spot. I'll introduce you to her, but I can't promise she'll be nice."

"I'd love to meet your mother," Andrew said.

Sybil turned and led the way. Andrew followed Sybil, and Emmitt followed Andrew. They walked in single file along the path that weaved through a maze of boxes and furniture, toward the sound of an unfamiliar voice. The voice was deliberately hushed. Another unknown voice answered the first, but Emmitt couldn't discern any words from the conversation.

Sybil walked further into the living room and through an open archway to a formal dining room. Andrew and Emmitt halted outside of the room.

A dimly lit chandelier illuminated a large table, which was covered with several tablecloths, piles of unopened envelopes, prayer books, and a dozen family photo albums. Four mismatched hutches lined the back wall. The hutches contained valuable glassware, delicate china sets, painted porcelain dolls, decorative vases, and a litany of statues of the Virgin Mary and other saints. One or several of the Yates women must have hand-picked the items that filled the china cabinets, but Emmitt was certain he'd passed by equally valuable treasures scattered on the living room floor.

What is valuable to them? He couldn't get the thought out of his head. The rationalizations captivated his attention. Why were certain items beautifully showcased, while others were left dangerously prone in piles or buried under clutter?

While further surveying the room, Emmitt spotted a paper attached to the glass of a hutch. In prominent lettering, the sheet read, "A Prayer to Saint Anthony: Finder of Lost Things." Emmitt smirked at how hopelessly appropriate it was.

Turning his attention away from the hutches, Emmitt's eyes moved to the room's occupants. Two middle-aged women sat on cushioned dining chairs at the table. Sybil stood behind them, gripping one hand on the back of each chair and smiling at Andrew. The strong family resemblance was enough for Emmitt to conclude that one of the older women was Sybil's mother. The other was a large nun, dressed in a brown habit. She had a wide, freckled face and a wider smile directed firmly toward Andrew and Emmitt.

Emmitt looked at Andrew, who seemed genuinely surprised.

"It's nice to meet you, Mrs. Yates." Andrew began. "I'm Drew Key. I spoke to your daughter and brother about helping—"

"I know," Shannon coldly interrupted.

Shannon Yates was a thin, stern figure. Her graying blonde hair was pulled back neatly in a bun. Her dark-blue eyes narrowed and creased at the edges. In all but her eyes and un-augmented frame, she could have been a time traveler: an older, harder, sadder Sybil.

The woman lifted her head as she glared at Andrew. "Sybil is capricious. I've given up on trying to decipher her whims." She offered a grimacing smile as she gently patted Sybil's hand while keeping her eyes fixed on Andrew. "And my brother does many things without consulting me. Do you know how many times my brother has heartlessly evicted me?"

Andrew stared at the hard woman while Emmitt promptly chimed in. "Four times. This is the fifth house you've moved into, and you've been here for about three-ish years."

It was impulsive, but Emmitt knew the answer, and he felt an irrational pride and pleasure saying it before Andrew could get a word out. Despite the innate charm that Sybil Yates had been instantaneously allured by, Shannon Yates appeared to be immune to Drew Key's charismatic persona, which made Emmitt instinctively eager to gain her favor.

"Who are you?" Shannon demanded.

Andrew quickly reasserted himself. "This is Emmitt ... my brother." There was a curtness in his voice as he uttered Emmitt's name. Andrew course-corrected to his usual affable confidence and continued. "Emmitt will assist me as I assist you in your family's journey."

Shannon's eyes were daggers on Andrew. The corner of her mouth turned upward into a snarl. "Do you understand how hurtful it is to hear someone tell me they plan to guide me on a 'journey' when my family has been forcibly removed from our home four times? *My* home—what I considered my home—was taken away from me thirteen years ago. We've been vagabonds. Homeless. Living at the mercy of my brother ever since. How maliciously tone-deaf are you?"

Andrew's eyes widened, while Emmitt grinned fiendishly as Shannon Yates scolded his older brother.

After a long pause, it was the nun who broke the silence with an uncontrolled burst of laughter. "Shannon! Jesus ... Mary and Joseph ... you are too much." The nun gasped for breath between her roaring chuckles. "If you would've laid it on any thicker, Satan himself would be begging on his knees for your pardon."

Shannon glanced over at the laughing nun. Her face stiffened momentarily, then softened, yielding to the nun's overpowering levity. The creases faded from her face, but she remained formal. "Perhaps *homeless* is hyperbolic, but I was never consulted regarding this self-help nonsense. I don't mean to turn my ire on you, personally, Drew Key ... or Emmitt." When she spoke his name, she shifted her attention to Emmitt and continued. "We have had others come in and try to help. There were professional organizers, clinical psychologists who specialize in hoarding, social workers, city workers … Sybil once brought in some nondenominational youth pastor to 'exorcise the clutter demon' after I informed her that Catholic priests don't perform exorcisms on houses. It smelled like burnt lavender for weeks. Apparently, sage only works for expelling the negative energies of normal spirits."

The nun interjected with a broad smile on her freckled face. "You should be thankful that hoarding demons aren't repelled by garlic."

"Yes. Thank you for looking on the bright side, Sister Eugene. I'm always appreciative," Shannon replied dryly. "Sister Eugene is a licensed counselor. She visits me every week, as a friend. I'm not her patient, but that fact hasn't stopped her from taking me to task for certain choices I make that may be interpreted as … faults." The last word caught in her throat as she forced a strained smile. "At every turn, I seem to be forced into help that I don't want, and frankly, it's help I really don't think I need."

Emmitt nodded solemnly as she spoke. When she finished, his eyes wandered, finally settling on the far corner of the room. The clutter had been swept away, creating a clean radius around a shrine. Dried funeral wreaths were propped on plant stands, while an oversized portrait of a man in his forties hung on the wall in an ornate gold frame. Smaller family photos adorned the seat of an antique-looking Windsor chair, which functioned as an altar for the memorial. Lit votive candles emitted a soft glow on the floor around the chair.

Off limits, Emmitt thought. He was curious just how much of the Yates women's lives would be off limits. Unsure of how to proceed, Emmitt was grateful when his brother finally spoke.

"I understand you're frustrated, and I won't try to change your perspective," Andrew began calmly. "Sybil has asked for my help. If you aren't interested, I'll respect that, but I still want to continue with Sybil ... and Renata, if she's interested. Will you allow my brother and me to help your daughters?"

"Renata isn't home right now," Shannon snapped. "While I can't speak for her, you should know she keeps all her possessions in her rooms. None of *this*," she gestured her thin arms widely, indicating the hoard that lay before them, "is hers to throw away or donate or move. Sybil has her own mess. You're free to help her, but Renata doesn't need any help." Shannon was emphatic.

Sister Eugene barged into the conversation. "Now, Shannon, you should let Renata decide if she needs help. It's good that the Key brothers are here to offer assistance. It would be better if you tried to work alongside Sybil with the decluttering. Perhaps you could offer her support—"

"So that I can learn to clean up my own mess? I know what you're implying, and I do not want to be roped into yet another cleaning effort that devolves into an intervention, where I lose my valuables and have to move into yet another property." Shannon had lost most of her composure. Her mouth twisted into a grimace, and her eyes were wide and wild.

"You said you're at the mercy of your brother, Mrs. Yates. Has he threatened to take away your current home?" Emmitt asked. Once again, his curiosity overtook his better judgment. There was no risk in remaining silent, but if the job was going to end prematurely, he was willing to pry.

Surprisingly, Shannon answered. "My brother is constantly threatening to take away my home. I never know if the city is involved, or the HOA, or if he's just being malicious. He's full of excuses and lies, so I never know what to believe. He says we could face another eviction if we don't clear the house soon. But James is our landlord. He'd be the one to evict us!" Shannon's voice had risen, and her pale face flushed pink in frustration.

"How much time did he give you before evicting you from the previous houses?" Emmitt pressed gently. He sensed Andrew's eyes on him once again.

Shannon took a moment to calm down and gather her thoughts. "Usually? A week. Sometimes two, but it's never enough time. It's always the last minute, and there is always a rush to get it done his way. No one concerns themselves with *my* wishes. They scold me. They tell me I'm in the way. And they always blame me." Her eyes held a deep, bitter pain as she remembered.

Emmitt looked at her sympathetically, and again, nodded his head.

"We were kicked out of the second house two days after the city sent a notice," Sybil chimed in cheerily. "Well, two days after we *noticed* the notice. They dumped just about everything that time. We could only fill four moving trucks. Uncle James held onto the most expensive stuff, like the antique furniture and Great-Grandma's jewelry. He kept it all in the museum's storage until we got to the next house."

Emmitt dared to continue before Shannon could interject. "What if we work at a slower pace? Any progress is good progress, and if Drew puts all his energy into working with Sybil, it might lessen the pressure on you. If your brother sees Sybil's progress, it's possible he'll let up a bit on the threats. That gives you more time to decide if you want to join in. No matter what you decide, I promise we'll stay out of your way, and we won't move—or even touch—your possessions without your permission. We can't control how your brother reacts, but we might be able to draw his attention away from you by focusing on Sybil's efforts. He'll probably still be angry if you don't participate. But it still gets to be your choice, Mrs. Yates."

"I don't plan to participate." Shannon was firm, but she had calmed down considerably. "I won't stop you from helping Sybil or talking to Renata, as long as you keep your word and don't attempt to pressure me."

"We can agree to that," Andrew said.

Eager to turn the focus back on herself, Sybil spoke up. "Okay! Let's keep the tour moving. If we just head through this archway behind me, I can show you the kitchen and Renata's rooms."

Shannon bristled at the suggestion. "No. It isn't right to barge into her rooms when she's not here … and don't even think about leading them into my rooms."

Shannon's eyes darted past Emmitt to a darkened hallway that opened into the living room. Emmitt followed her eyes and peered over his right shoulder to see the ominous entry into what must be Shannon's section of the house. The path was narrower, and the hallway was so packed with boxes, it would have been arduous for Emmitt to squeeze through … and impassable for Andrew.

Emmitt's curiosity faltered as he once again felt a tightness rising in his chest at the thought of being wedged between a wall and the massive mountain of boxes. As Emmitt glanced at Andrew, he noticed his brother's tightening jaw and ruminating stare as he fixed his eyes toward the hallway. Andrew appeared to be equally grateful for Shannon's forbiddance, which only made Emmitt more aware of the disquieting pattern of synchronicity. He didn't expect Drew Key to feel the same trepidation he felt. Drew Key was supposed to remain aloof.

Sybil rolled her eyes and let out an audible groan. "Ugh. Fine. I guess the house tour is over. If we go back the way we came, I can take you through the hallway that leads to my rooms."

She hurried back to where Andrew stood and eagerly grasped his hand. With Sybil taking the lead, they backtracked through the perilous trail. Emmitt gave a quick nod to the two women at the table and silently trailed behind his brother.

Chapter Four

Sybil led Andrew down the path and past the entry, through a narrow hallway lined with boxes stacked along one wall. Emmitt lagged further behind them, unsure of what to do. He thought he should remain silent, allowing Andrew to take full control. That was a reasonable short-term solution. Sybil certainly wouldn't mind. In her eyes, Emmitt was nothing more than a third wheel. A nuisance. Shannon Yates was different. Shannon had shown open contempt for his brother, and Drew Key would likely have a similar effect on Renata Yates if Sybil's warnings were to be taken seriously.

Shannon had said that Renata didn't have a hoarding problem. If Renata was as shy and disinterested as Sybil asserted, they might never meet her. Shannon was also determined to distance herself from the cleanup efforts, so it was plausible that Sybil would be the only member of the Yates family willing to work with them. Sybil was the only Yates that Andrew's publisher showed any interest in, so it seemed reasonable for Emmitt to assume he could stay silent in the long-term, as well as the short-term. He wanted to be happy at the prospect of fading into the background while Drew Key worked his motivational magic on Sybil, but his thoughts kept drifting back to Shannon Yates.

The adrenaline that had peaked during his conversation with Shannon had finally subsided. A new terror took hold and twisted in Emmitt's gut. He risked everything when he opened his mouth to speak to her. It was only a matter of pure luck that kept Shannon from kicking them out of the house. Wasn't it?

As Sybil stopped every few steps to point out a treasure or trinket to Andrew, Emmitt continued to replay the encounter in his head. While looping the conversation and considering its conclusion, the panic eventually dulled, and he allowed himself to concede the possibility that it wasn't pure luck. Perhaps partial luck, or predominant luck. But pure luck? Had Emmitt remained silent, could Drew Key have calmed Shannon? Could he have reasoned with her? Then again, would Andrew have *needed* to calm her down if Emmitt hadn't flippantly inserted himself into the conversation to begin with?

Emmitt's conscience prickled. He couldn't decide if he should be proud or ashamed of himself. What was the overriding motivation for his actions? Was it pride in taking charge of a tenuous encounter? Or sympathy for the woman who seemed so displaced and miserable while sitting on a trove of treasures? Was it spite? Mercifully, Emmitt had calmed the woman down, but he didn't know Shannon Yates. It had been a stupid risk to take, and he expected to get an earful from Andrew later. Still, he couldn't figure out why he had taken the risk.

As he inched nearer, to close the widening gap between his brother and himself, Emmitt resolved to keep his mouth shut for the rest of the visit.

Sybil had released her grip on Andrew's hand to press herself closer to him and wrap her arm tightly around his. Andrew didn't complain, but he didn't appear to be enamored either. Drew Key continued to conduct himself professionally. Sybil's clawing grasp caused them to sidestep through the long hallway to the door of her bedroom. When they finally reached the room, they stopped at the doorway. Sybil's hoard had pinned the door open from the inside. Emmitt quietly maneuvered behind Andrew and Sybil in the hallway. He inched closer and craned his neck, peering over Sybil to see inside.

Like the living room and hallways, Sybil's bedroom contained towers of moving boxes and plastic tubs of various sizes. Emmitt couldn't spot a bed from where he stood, but he could look over smaller stacks of boxes and bins to see several clothing racks standing side by side. Dresses, blouses, sweaters, skirts, and jackets filled the racks. Most of the items still had tags attached to them, but all the clothing appeared to be hung neatly on the racks. Unlike the rest of the house, he didn't notice a clear path to enter or exit the room. Getting in or out would require shifting stacks of boxes onto other stacks of boxes, and Emmitt doubted Andrew could squeeze through the gaps. He doubted even Sybil could squeeze through, leading Emmitt to wonder where she slept at night.

From where he stood, Emmitt could see three standing jewelry cabinets and a large built-in vanity littered with lipsticks, perfume bottles, makeup brushes, and a mountainous stack of magazines. The bookshelf that framed the oversized vanity held books, trophies, framed certificates, and a dozen clear plastic makeup cases filled with beauty products. Although Sybil's bedroom was better organized than Shannon's living room, both were equally overwhelming.

As Sybil explained her situation to Andrew, Emmitt backed away from the pair, opened his notebook, and quietly took out his pen.

"Controlled chaos is what I've been calling it," he heard Sybil say. "But it's more chaos than controlled right now, and it makes me feel, I don't know ... anxious, I guess. I'm usually good at focusing on my mindfulness, and I'm trying to level up my frequencies. I can tune it out most of the time, but when reality hits, it really hits. Is it normal for my frequencies to fluctuate?"

Drew Key answered, "Sometimes a person operating at a high frequency will come into contact with a low-frequency person or object, which could cause fluctuations. I would say this room is an extremely low-frequency space. Sometimes our living areas can be a metaphor for our innermost selves. It would make sense for your highest self to experience a few inner blockages when exposed to a literal blockage of this magnitude."

"You are *so* right. Sometimes, I can feel the chaos building up inside of me, and it really does manifest itself physically." Sybil clutched at her throat with her free hand and whispered, "Just looking at my room makes me feel a little dirty."

"Mhmm," Andrew said with a sharp nod, ignoring Sybil's seductive tone.

Emmitt pressed his pen tightly against his lips and tried to keep from snickering.

Sybil lowered her hand and pouted. "Drew, I just don't know what to do to create harmony and balance in my life. My room should be my sacred space, but it's just ... well ... hell."

"When did this chaos start? Have you had trouble keeping your space clean in the past, or is this level of collecting a new manifestation?" Drew asked.

"Oh, I've always been messy." Sybil giggled. "We had maids that would come in when I was a kid, so I never really had to clean up after myself. I was too busy performing. I wasn't home most of the time, and when I *was* home, my mom didn't expect me to clean up. In my defense, I was working ten hours a day, sometimes six days a week, when I was only five years old! And it wasn't like my mom was tidy either. Cleaning was always more of Daddy and Renata's thing. Daddy seemed to enjoy it, and Renata was always his shadow. When it got really bad with my mom, the maids stopped coming. Safety hazard, or something. Daddy was already dead by then, and Renata couldn't keep up with the mess. So, we got evicted. Over and over. We just kept moving, and everything kinda got out of hand ..." Sybil paused, thought for a moment, and continued. "So, do you think I'm collecting all this stuff because I didn't have a childhood ... or my vibrations are off ... or because the lack of discipline in my childhood morphed me into a messy adult?"

Messy? Emmitt considered whether it was a deliberate understatement, or if she was honestly delusional.

"I can't analyze you," Andrew said. "But I can look at habits and behaviors and invalidating thoughts that are impeding your progress. You said the chaos started as a child, and just kept building to an unmanageable level. Is that a fair summary?"

"Yes," Sybil said confidently.

"Then we just need to work on controlling it, little by little. We'll deal with the chaos as it presents itself. Have you thought of any goals you want to accomplish while we work together?"

"Like, other than cleaning? I was thinking cleaning was my goal," Sybil replied uneasily, still clutching Andrew's arm. "Is inner peace a good goal? Or should it be more specific, like going through a certain number of boxes?" Sybil seemed desperate to determine Drew Key's opinion on the correct answer.

To Emmitt's surprise, Andrew apologized. "I'm sorry if I put you on the spot. I should clarify that I'm here as a facilitator. My greatest aim is to help you clear your life of obstructions, so that you can better commit yourself to reaching your goals. Ultimately, Sybil, you get to decide what we work on together. You set the goals, and I'll help you achieve them. We can start with a set number of boxes, then eventually move forward to clean the room completely. After organizing your personal space, you may slowly achieve a sense of inner peace. There isn't a right or wrong goal, and you may find that a lot of smaller goals coalesce, allowing you to have a greater sense of accomplishment as we progress."

"You really don't have to apologize. I just don't want to disappoint you. I know how valuable your time is, and I also know my mom and I haven't been committed to the process in the past. I really, really want to make a big change this time." Sybil gently ran a finger up Andrew's forearm, as her voice lowered. "You know, Drew, you're so authentic. You really understand me. I know that our compatibility is the thing that's finally going to help me fix this annoying problem. You said before that our energies match up perfectly. Are you a Scorpio, by any chance?"

Sybil's cloying tone made Emmitt close his notebook. She may be genuinely smitten or grateful, but it sounded disingenuous. *Is this really who she is?* Emmitt almost wished he had stayed back with Mrs. Yates and the nun.

Andrew also seemed unsure of Sybil's doe-eyed golly-gosh charm. He maintained his composure, but Emmitt noticed the back of his neck and shoulders stiffen, and his tone became slightly less affectionate. "Aries, actually. Sybil, do you think you could come up with a list of goals? We'll start small, with things that can be relatively easy to achieve: going through a single box, or a dresser drawer, or one pile of magazines. That will give you a chance to think about what you want to accomplish, to visualize it, and commit to it. The list can be as long or short as you need it to be."

"I can do that." Sybil's voice wavered. "So, do you want to see my other room? My office is less cluttered than the bedroom, and it's where I run my business, so I think that room should be my first priority ... or do you think we should start with the bedroom first?" The desperation slipped back into her voice.

"I think coming up with a list of goals will allow you to figure out what your top priority is. Again, there is no right or wrong order. If you commit to achieving your goals, we should be able to accomplish everything on your list. We'll leave it at that for now. I have no intention of overwhelming you on the first day." Andrew spoke with a tender firmness that left no opportunity for argument.

So that's it? Emmitt had expected a full day with Sybil. He was grateful for a reprieve from the disingenuous chatter of the former child actress, but he wondered why Andrew would stop the tour so abruptly. Drew Key was a master of self-help. Drew Key was collected. Nothing fazed him. Was Andrew recoiling from Sybil's advances, or was he merely adjusting the appointment to suit his client's needs? Emmitt doubted Sybil would view Drew's sudden retreat as anything other than a sign of rejection, but what did Emmitt know about self-help?

Sybil's smile faded. "Oh. I was ready to get started now, but if you think it's best to hold off, I guess we can wait."

"It's best not to get ahead of ourselves. It is a process, after all. We'll have plenty of long days ahead of us. Emmitt and I will be back in two days, and we'll get started on your list of goals. I'm looking forward to working with you, and hopefully, your family as well." Drew patted his large, tanned hand over the small hand with the mint nails that still held tight around his arm.

Sybil's face brightened. "Okay. I'll be ready with a list when you come back. Let me show you out."

With Sybil still gripping firmly onto Andrew's arm, they side-stepped their way back to the entrance of the house, with Emmitt leading the way. At the entry, Sybil yelled to her mother that they were leaving.

Shannon Yates walked to the archway and offered a curt goodbye, which relieved Emmitt, who had no desire to wind all the way back to the dining room for a formal parting. Emmitt was an expert at inconspicuous exits and neglected goodbyes, and he was glad Shannon didn't expect a handshake or pleasantries.

Drew Key, who was adept at pleasantries and formal partings, stopped momentarily, almost as if he was unsure of how to proceed. It was like a glitch, barely noticeable to anyone but Emmitt.

Finally reaching the door, Drew Key turned to face Shannon and announced, "Goodbye, Mrs. Yates and Sister Eugene. It was a pleasure to meet you."

The booming voice of Sister Eugene called back from the table, "Goodbye, Drew and Emmitt! God bless you for your help!"

Shannon sneered and quickly disappeared from the archway.

Once outside, Sybil hugged Drew goodbye, with one last giggling "thank you," and a fervent promise to compile her list of goals before their next meeting. She gave Emmitt a half-hearted smile as she limply shook his hand and then slipped back into the house.

Chapter Five

Twenty minutes of silence passed in the car. Emmitt stretched his neck, turning his head to the right to glance at his brother, hoping to make eye contact. Hoping Andrew would break the silence. Andrew, who had spent the first fifteen minutes in the car checking messages from clients and texting responses, was now staring placidly ahead.

Emmitt was restless. A torrent of thoughts, concerns, and speculations flooded his mind as he struggled to maintain a pretense of decorum. Andrew preferred silence to Emmitt's often chaotic, aimless ramblings. Andrew spoke with purpose and politeness. Emmitt's conversations were prone to veer off course. Once he started on a tangent, he wouldn't cease until he caught himself clumsily plodding through presumptions or tangling himself in trivialities. Even then, it was hard for Emmitt to stop. And Andrew was the only person Emmitt could talk to right now, owing to their proximity and current confinement in the car. His brother would argue that they were also bound by professional discretion, so Emmitt had no one but Andrew to confide in. He was nearing to burst, and if this was a game to see who would break the silence first, Emmitt could live with losing.

"So," Emmitt said, not knowing where to start, "the rental is nice."

This was a lie, but Emmitt thought it might be better to ease into a conversation, rather than lead with his thoughts on the Yates family. Andrew didn't like to gossip. Emmitt realized, just as the words slipped out of his mouth, that his innocuous comment may also be a powder keg. When conversations between the two of them exploded, Emmitt always lit the fuse.

"Yes, it is," Andrew said.

"I'm surprised you went through the trouble to have me sign as an authorized driver. And I'm more surprised you actually wanted me to drive it. I know I wouldn't trust myself renting a car like this."

"You should have more self-confidence. I trust you."

Emmitt rolled his eyes. "Any stops before we get to my apartment?"

Andrew shook his head. "Why don't you just drop me off at my house. You can keep the rental tonight."

"If I was cynical, I would suspect you only wanted me here to act as your chauffer."

"It's a good thing you're not cynical," Andrew said. "It's a practical decision. Having you drive gives me more time to check in with my other clients. This is a big job, Emmitt."

"So, you're making sure your other clients don't get jealous?"

"No," Andrew argued. "Not exactly."

"'Not *exactly*?'" Emmitt repeated. "So, they are a *little* jealous."

There was stiff formality in Andrew's tone. "Some of them maneuver within the same social circles as Sybil. And Sybil isn't shy about letting people know we're working together. My other clients know about her … reputation. Some require assurances. And I have to be sensitive to their concerns. They need to know they won't be neglected."

Emmitt barely listened. He nodded his head until Andrew stopped speaking. "And what color did you say it was?"

"Silverback."

"Looks gray to me."

Andrew remained silent. Emmitt couldn't.

"I still think we should have used my car. It would have saved you money, which you probably need since your car is being worked on again."

Conversations with Andrew always tilted Emmitt toward provocation. When he noticed an opportunity to dig into his brother, he usually took it. Emmitt reasoned that, if Andrew would just argue with him like a normal brother, he wouldn't have the urge to poke at him as often.

"The rental is a better option. It's exotic. It fits within the Yates' neighborhood. We'll be back in my car when it's fixed. It should be ready by tomorrow." Andrew knew he was being baited.

Emmitt was only sorry he wasn't better at hiding his childish glee when teasing his older brother.

Emmitt attempted one more go at Andrew before shifting topics. "How many times have you needed to replace the brake pads? Or is it engine trouble again? Andrew, did the ass-warming function stop working? You quote Mom all the time, but I remember Dad used to say, 'luxury doesn't always mean quality.' You should take his advice more often."

"Dad's always been cheap. He doesn't understand the value of a good first impression. You're a lot like him."

"Thank you." Emmitt knew it wasn't a compliment, but he liked the comparison.

"You're welcome," Andrew said flatly.

"I just think my station wagon is far more reliable than your luxury SUV with perpetual organ damage."

"It's possible. But I can afford to fix my car."

"Fair enough," Emmitt said.

He felt the sting of Andrew's jab and realized he had pushed just far enough to spare himself from a full reprimand. Emmitt could bear a few blows to his ego, and he relished a good argument, but a lecture from Andrew was too much to endure.

"Anyway, that's not really what I wanted to talk about." Emmitt smirked as he tapped the wheel and glanced teasingly at his brother.

"What a surprise." Andrew sighed.

"Look, when we were at the house, with Mrs. Yates … I guess I got carried away and took over the conversation …"

"You saw an opportunity. You took initiative. You kept us in the house and allowed us to continue the process with Sybil. If you're trying to apologize, don't."

"Yeah, but it could have gone horribly wrong." Emmitt wasn't sure why he felt the need to explain himself, especially when Andrew didn't appear to be angry. Why was Andrew so calm? Emmitt didn't want to be scolded, but he expected—and possibly deserved—a warning for his impetuousness.

Emmitt glanced at Andrew and asked, "Hypothetically, what would you have done if it hadn't worked?"

"It *did* work, so we don't have to worry about it. I've told you before, there are no failures, only opportunities to learn and grow. I don't deal with hypotheticals. I deal with reality. You successfully handled a tense situation. You should take pride in your success instead of focusing on an imaginary scenario."

Emmitt had been hoping to speak with *Andrew*, but all he could hear were the words and smug intonation of Drew Key.

"Okay, no hypotheticals." Emmitt had no interest in being both praised and admonished by his brother in the same breath, so he shifted topics again. "Practically speaking, then, how are we going to convince the mom and sister to sign off on a book about hoarders?"

"It isn't a book about hoarders. It's a book about growth and transformation. And you should use their names, Emmitt," Andrew chided. "You don't want to depersonalize Shannon and Renata, or you risk turning them into subjects in a book, rather than people in need of help."

"But they *are* subjects in a book. At least, that's what they're supposed to be. And if none of them sign off, we don't get to write the book, and I don't get published. I'd like to have some assurances that my time won't be wasted. Anyway, what about professional distance? That's a thing, right?" Emmitt fought to conceal his bitterness as he challenged his brother.

Andrew immediately grasped the source of Emmitt's poorly hidden hostility. "You're getting paid for your efforts. We'll each get paid for working on the cleanup for three months. If it takes longer, or they never sign off on the waiver, I'll compensate you myself." Andrew's firm, reassuring tone may have soothed Sybil, but it incensed Emmitt.

"I don't want *your* money!" Emmitt seethed. "I just want to be sure that I can write about this. What's the point of taking notes and following you around the house if they don't sign off on the book? Sybil was supposed to work that out before we arrived. It's one thing if Shannon and Renata don't sign, but Sybil hasn't signed either. How 'committed to the process' is she if she didn't follow through on the one thing you asked her to do? You asked her, right?"

"Yes, Emmitt. I asked Sybil to have a conversation with Shannon and Renata, but it isn't fair to consider it a simple request. Sybil signed the original waiver, but I had to update the form. I understand you're angry, but you can't blame Sybil. Hoarding is a complex problem, and every member of her family is suffering because of it. We've already seen how resistant Shannon is to change, and Renata might have left the house to avoid interacting with us. Sybil has a lot to prove before her family can reasonably trust her commitment to decluttering, and they love her enough to try to protect her from public embarrassment."

"I get it," Emmitt groaned.

Andrew ignored Emmitt and continued. "Have you considered that their family dynamic may be dysfunctional? And perhaps asking for too much, too soon, might derail any attempts to help the Yates family? Perhaps you're not aware of a concept known as *patience*, that, when employed, can be extremely beneficial when dealing with scenarios similar to the one we are currently experiencing."

Emmitt could finally recognize Andrew's voice in Drew Key's words. It was comforting to know that, deep inside the carefully curated construction of the aspirational Adonis, beat the fuming heart of a condescending older brother. It was far better than a fully automated, know-it-all, self-help guru.

Emmitt wanted to press further. He wanted to fully excise the persona from his brother, but he stopped himself from carving further. There was a balance to maintain. He had already presented his own worst qualities to pull Andrew out of Drew's clutches. Any sign of life would have to suffice as a victory for Emmitt.

Emmitt relaxed the tension in his face and managed a half smirk. "I understand what you're saying. It's just a shame they can't be as forthright and functional as we are."

Emmitt turned to look at Andrew. Though his brother continued to look ahead, Emmitt could see he was smiling.

"Tomorrow we'll meet with Shannon's brother, James. He should be able to give us more information about Shannon, Sybil, and Renata. My priority is helping the Yates family. The book is a secondary concern."

A new tide of rising fury struck Emmitt. "You said—"

"I know what I said, and I intend to keep my promise. I will repeat: I don't believe in failure. These obstacles are opportunities. We may need to work a little harder than expected, but we will succeed. Sybil signed off once, and she's already agreed to sign the new waiver. Sybil Yates has never turned down an opportunity for exposure. Regardless of what happens, you will get paid for your work—and before you say it—it won't be pity money from your big brother. We will work, we will create our book, and our book will be published. You need to cultivate a positive mindset, Emmitt. You're too pessimistic."

"Okay, fine. I'll drop it." It was exhausting trying to argue with a perpetually positive thinker. At that moment, another thought occurred to Emmitt. "James Yates, right? He's Shannon's brother?"

"Yes." It was almost a question. Andrew didn't seem sure where Emmitt was going.

"So, Shannon's maiden name is Yates, and she kept it?"

"Lots of women do that. What's your point?" Andrew asked.

"But both the daughters are also Yates. That sitcom that Sybil was in ... *Raising Rosie*, right?" Emmitt paused as he tried to envision the little blonde girl with the curly pigtails and pink overalls posing with a plastic smile, as the obnoxious theme song played during the opening credits. "Sybil Felicity Yates. It was back when all the child stars used their full names. It's possible that her dad died either during filming or after the sitcom's cancelation, since she remembers him cleaning the house while she worked as a child star. Shannon must have been married to the man. There's a shrine to him in the dining room. Shannon has a cathedral's worth of Catholic paraphernalia around the house, and her best friend is a nun. She had to be married to him. You're the name expert. What was the guy's name?"

"I don't know," Andrew said.

"It's weird, though, not being able to talk about Mr. Whatever-his-name-is. I won't say anything to Shannon's brother. I'm just thinking aloud ... but you're not even a little curious?"

"There's probably a boring explanation. There's no sense getting worked up over it. Dad's Catholic, and it didn't keep him and Mom from getting divorced."

"Yeah, but Dad isn't a practicing Catholic. He had some passing anecdotes and advice carried over from the Jesuit prep school and university he attended, but he kept his Bible and catechism stored in a box in the attic when we were kids. Then again, they were the first things he loaded into the truck when he left: Bible, catechism, some prayer books, family photos, and his and Mom's wedding album." Emmitt frowned as he remembered, then another memory rose and lit up his face. "Do you remember the time we went to that baptism, and Aunt Kathy found out we didn't know how to cross ourselves ...

and the look on her face when Dad told her he hadn't even bothered to baptize his own kids? Uncle Rich had to hold her back to keep her from retrieving the emergency holy water she kept in her car. Dad nearly had a panic attack when he had to explain how furious Serenity would be if she found out you and I had been emergency baptized. You know, I sometimes wish Aunt Kathy would have succeeded, just to see the horror on Mom's face when we came home."

"Emmitt," Andrew sighed.

"I get it, I'm rambling. Even if we ignore the name, the secrecy that surrounds Sybil's dad is strange. We don't have any personal information about him. You've promised not to mention him. They have an altar dedicated to his memory. There were candles, for Christ's sake. They're risking their lives to keep a couple of candles lit for him!"

"His story isn't our business."

"Look, this is just between us. I'm asking you personally: do you think it's a little weird they have a shrine to a man who appears to be erased from their family history? I've read the news articles, and I've seen the interviews to prepare for this. Sybil never mentioned her dad. Never. All we know from Sybil is that the man liked to clean and died before they started moving. Isn't that something that may be important to look into in order to help with 'the process'? It seems like it might be crucial for us to find out more about him."

Andrew refused to entertain the question. He glanced icily at Emmitt. "Shannon and Renata Yates aren't in the public eye. Some people value their privacy more than others. It isn't right to speculate."

"But Shannon and Renata exist, Andrew! They're both listed in the museum directory. There are public relations articles highlighting the philanthropic work of the Yates family. Renata and Shannon are both mentioned in the articles. Apparently, Shannon used to organize endowment dinners and other charity functions. Renata works at the museum. They may be private, but they exist."

To Emmitt's dismay, Drew Key had heard enough. "We were hired to help the Yates family complete a specific task. This isn't a fishing expedition or an exposé. Our task is to facilitate goal-setting and work toward achieving those goals. We are single-focused. Anything outside of our purview is inconsequential."

"Shit, Andrew, I was just asking for your opinion. I promise I won't make that mistake again."

Andrew breathed out deeply. "Don't make promises you don't intend to keep, Emmitt."

Emmitt grinned unapologetically as he pulled the car into Andrew's driveway. "You sure you don't want me to leave the rental with you? I can call a service to drive me back home."

"Keep it. I'm not going anywhere, and I'll need you to drive in the morning while I finish catching up with clients. I'll see you tomorrow, Emmitt." Andrew opened the door, exited the car, and closed the door firmly. He gave a brisk wave as Emmitt pulled away.

Emmitt's curiosity remained unfulfilled. It itched in his mind and preoccupied his thoughts. He drove to the nearest shopping center and parked. He pulled out his phone and searched articles, obituaries, interviews, and the Yates Museum and Botanical Gardens website to find any information regarding the mysterious father and husband. Emmitt focused on the screen, searching for a name or a face that matched the portrait hanging in the Yates' dining room.

As the bright yellow light of a streetlamp lit across his lap and onto his phone, Emmitt finally looked up. Glancing back at the screen, he noticed it was almost seven o'clock. He had spent four hours searching. It was four hours wasted. No name, no face, no obituary. He knew no more now than when he started his search. The man was still a mystery.

"He liked to clean, and he died before they started moving," he rasped to himself.

Emmitt tossed the phone onto the passenger seat. He yawned deeply and twisted from one side to the other, stretching his stiff back, then turned on the ignition and headed back to his apartment.

Chapter Six

After a restless night, Emmitt dragged himself out of bed, showered, brushed his teeth, and readied himself for the day. The only scheduled task was to attend an informal meeting with Andrew and James Yates. "Informal" was the word Andrew used, but Emmitt didn't quite know what he meant, and he was disinclined to seek clarification. Even if Andrew provided a definition, Emmitt's wardrobe might not meet the requirements. In this instance, it was easier to choose ignorance. *Another button-up shirt and dark-wash jeans, I guess. I should probably iron them too.* Whether formal or informal, the meeting would center on a singular topic: the hoard.

Emmitt grabbed one of two button-up shirts still hanging in his closet (the third lay crumpled on his bathroom floor from the previous day). He tossed the shirt onto his unmade bed, along with the jeans he had worn to the Yates house the day before. He pulled out the iron from a kitchen cupboard and plugged it into the outlet next to his bed. When he had finished, his jeans were free of wrinkles, but he had ironed two large creases in the arm and back of the charcoal-gray shirt. He tried ironing again, but the lines only etched deeper into the fabric.

"Shit," he groaned. "Roll up the sleeves, Emmitt, and face front at all times."

There wasn't time to try ironing again. He was already running late, and he didn't want to waste the only clean button-up shirt he had left trying to fix his mistake. Drew Key could have perfectly pressed shirts and flawlessly folded cuffs. Emmitt Key was a fashion nonconformist.

He quickly dressed and haphazardly rolled the cuffs to his elbows, attempting to hide the conspicuous wrinkle. He turned to look through the open door and examined himself in the bathroom mirror. Emmitt bitterly tugged at the unevenly folded sleeves as he stared at his reflection, but his adjustments only accentuated the disparity. He stopped and took a long look at himself, shook his head, and walked over to the kitchen table to pick up his wallet, phone, and keys.

"That's as good as it gets," Emmitt sighed as he walked out the door.

While driving in the car to pick up Andrew, Emmitt's mind had time to wander. He knew his curiosity was antithetical to Drew Key's modus operandi. He also knew Andrew walked a fine line of giving advice without pathologizing. Despite knowing these limitations, Emmitt wanted more. He hoped he could uncover some interesting bits of information to pepper throughout the book. He wanted to find some way to differentiate this work from every other Drew Key publication.

Although Emmitt had been tasked by his brother to write the bulk of the book, Andrew's niche was in the self-help world. These kinds of books were mostly puff pieces meant to elevate the guru's influence over potential clients. They served as little more than an advertisement for their practice. Emmitt grimaced every time his mother or brother used the term "practice" to speak about their businesses. While both would openly admit they weren't affiliated with any medical field, the wording was intentional. It was a trick of yoga instructors, hypnotists, psychic mediums, Reiki healers, and self-help gurus to establish a psychological alignment with clinical professionals. To Emmitt, it was grifting. Now that he was involved in it, what did that make him?

Emmitt wanted to write, and Andrew offered him an opportunity to be published. His name would be on the cover. Alongside Drew Key, Emmitt reminded himself. The thought continued to ring in his mind.

Sometimes, he could justify his decision. One glance around his tiny, mostly barren apartment would allow Emmitt to say, "I need the money." Or, reflecting on his job, he would argue, "I need to challenge myself. Take more risks." There were days when deep reflection had been pushed aside for pragmatism. Today would not be one of those days. He had so many questions he couldn't ask. What he wanted to write about would never pass Drew Key's standards of sanitized, generic positivity. Emmitt was beginning his writing career as a hack.

"Nowhere to go but up," he mumbled shamefully to himself as he pulled into Andrew's driveway.

With Andrew in the car, Emmitt resigned himself to silence. After speaking to two clients, Andrew's phone accidentally synced to the rental's speaker system. Andrew attempted to fix the problem, tapping on his phone, then leaning in to examine the car's touchscreen. Failing to succeed, Andrew made Emmitt pull over and turn off the car, while he turned off and restarted his phone. It was useless.

After that, as Andrew called client after client to explain the circumstances, Emmitt was surprised at how shamelessly willing they were to continue their sessions, knowing Drew Key's younger brother was listening in. Emmitt drove wordlessly, while Andrew provided daily aphorisms, listened patiently to blubbering excuses, reset "manageable goals," and even led a ten-minute guided meditation, which relaxed Emmitt so completely, he nearly missed the freeway interchange. Without shifting the rhythm or tenor of his soothing instructions, Andrew sharply jabbed Emmitt's arm to startle him back to reality.

As the interchange looped Emmitt off the interstate, he took his left hand off the wheel to rub his sore arm and glanced over at his brother. The tranquil words continued to exit Andrew's lips through an arrogant smirk, and his steely smiling eyes darted to fix teasingly on Emmitt.

After the guided meditation, the calls continued in quick succession. Emmitt had to force himself to suppress laughter when a client burst into tears after relaying to Drew Key that her pug's psychic revealed her beloved dog would prefer to live with her ex-boyfriend. Losing primary custody of little Seraphina had undone all her progress: she started smoking again.

"But, only two packs, so far," she assured Drew, "and I've already made an appointment with my hypnotherapist on Monday."

As Drew Key complimented her initiative, Emmitt pinched his own leg to keep from snickering and tried to tune out the distraction.

He focused his thoughts on the events of the previous day as he drove mechanically to the café. There was so much that needed to be done, and Shannon Yates had already refused to participate. Conversely, Sybil seemed a bit *too* eager to spend time with Drew Key. Even Andrew bristled at her fervor. The other one didn't even bother to show up.

Renata Yates, Emmitt remembered. *Wouldn't want to depersonalize Renata.*

Worst of all, none of the three had signed off on the book. The whole point of accompanying his brother was to publish his first book. And to help, Emmitt forced himself to concede. But that was assuming he or Andrew *could* help. Four previous houses and the lack of progress from various professionals made that prospect seem unlikely.

"Only four moving trucks," Sybil had said, as if the cost of such a move was negligible.

The jewelry and expensive items had to be kept in the museum's storage. What does she consider expensive? Or cheap, for that matter? What is valuable?

The Yates family's assets were incomprehensible to Emmitt. How were the finances allocated? Shannon said her brother was her landlord. Did he own all her houses? Did she have any money?

Emmitt hoped that meeting James Yates would reveal more, but he suspected James would be as resistant and suspicious as his sister. There was a ubiquitousness to the Yates patriarch. Emmitt didn't know if it was prompted by a sense of care or control, but it was an inarguable fact that the man was fully enmeshed in his sister's and nieces' lives. James had contacted Drew Key on behalf of his niece, James allowed Drew and Emmitt to work with the family, and James would be the one to pay them for their cleaning efforts. Emmitt didn't know why he was involved, or why he was the one paying them. There was a good deal Emmitt didn't know, and every vague answer only prompted more questions.

Despite his ignorance regarding the inner workings of the Yates dynasty, Emmitt understood why James would be willing to facilitate any effort to declutter. It was an undeniable fact that the Yates women were terrible tenants. Because of the family's affluent estate, it wasn't clear how much of a financial burden Sybil and Shannon created, but the embarrassment they caused was obvious. Even if Shannon wanted to hide in her house and drown herself in her treasures, Sybil had been more than willing to take part in interviews. She was an unapologetic fixture in tabloids, with many accusing her of actively courting bad press with her antics.

There had been an independent short film years prior that was meant to chronicle an ordinary day in the life of Sybil Yates. Instead, the film acted as an infomercial for a wellness company Sybil had been promoting. The company dissolved after numerous hospitalizations were linked to the supplements she endorsed. Most victims suffered from insomnia and tremors. One woman developed a heart condition. The company's founder went to prison. Sybil never apologized.

She continued to shield herself with her hoarding disorder and eventually participated in a reality show called *Celebrity Psych*. Emmitt recalled a rumor alleging "gross professional misconduct" between patients and staff, which led to the cancelation of the show's second season. After the cancelation, Sybil was spotted in the Bahamas, rolling around in the sand with the married acupuncturist featured on the show. While Drew Key could be arrogant and egotistical, he wasn't a public nuisance. Emmitt's family could be *embarrassing*, but they weren't *an embarrassment*.

Still, as much as he studied and scrutinized Sybil's past, Emmitt couldn't find any information about her father. Sybil said nothing about him during her interviews. She never mentioned her mother or sister either. Not in interviews or in her reality television appearances. Perhaps it was a positive side effect of being egotistical; Sybil was so full of herself she couldn't imagine talking about anyone else. Or perhaps she wasn't categorically evil and wanted to protect her family. Emmitt had certainly known about Sybil's issues before Andrew approached him, but he wasn't aware that her mother was a hoarder, or that she had a younger sister, or that they all lived together, until Andrew had spoken to him about the job.

After a final call to calm down a client who had broken her water fast after five days, only to binge on everything in her refrigerator and pantry (including a bottle of steak sauce, a wedge of gorgonzola cheese, and a jar of pickled onion juice), Andrew silently put his phone down and stared ahead.

Then Andrew surprised Emmitt by initiating the conversation. "We're not too far from the café. You ate before, right?" Andrew asked.

"No. Am I not supposed to eat at the café?" Emmitt wasn't particularly hungry, and his nerves would keep his stomach in knots until the meeting was over, but he didn't like the idea of Andrew telling him what he could or couldn't do.

"You can get a coffee. I'll feed you after."

Emmitt lifted an eyebrow. "Are you sure you want to risk coffee? What if I burn my mouth? What if I spill? Oh God, Andrew, what if I drink too much and have to piss?"

"Don't be crass," Andrew scolded. "We need to be prepared for this meeting. After yesterday's introductions with Shannon and Sybil, we should be ready for unpredictable behavior."

Emmitt grinned as he teased Andrew. "So, which way do you think it'll go? Do you think James will scream at you for being insensitive or clutch at your arm and ask if you're a Scorpio?"

Andrew's eyes fixed icily on Emmitt. "This isn't a joke. James Yates could refuse to work with us, just as easily as Shannon did. We don't know the Yates family. We need to present the best possible versions of ourselves to him."

Emmitt grumbled, "I know that. I wasn't planning on eating, but you don't have to forbid it. Seriously, I know you have a high estimation of your own professionalism, but it's not like I'm planning on adjusting myself or picking my nose in front of him. I know how to *conduct* myself."

"This is important, Emmitt." Andrew furrowed his brow. "And don't think I didn't notice the crease on your sleeve. Folding the cuffs up to your elbows isn't distracting from it ... and how is it so difficult for you to fold them evenly? It's the cheap fabric that sets in that kind of crease. It won't matter how many times you try to iron it out. And I know those are the same jeans you marinated in yesterday. Wash your jeans, Emmitt. You're not doing all you can to project professionalism."

Emmitt flushed. He bit the inner skin of his lower lip and mumbled, "I'm working with what I have."

Andrew breathed out heavily and softened his tone. "Alright, listen ... I'll let you borrow some of my shirts: polos and button-ups. I'll take you back to my place after we drop off the rental. They're already pressed and dry cleaned ... just don't pile them on the floor after you wear them. Get a laundry basket. I'll hire a service to pick them up, clean them, and press them for you until the job is done."

"I can't accept—"

"They're a loan, not a gift," Andrew asserted while staring ahead, ignoring Emmitt's glances. "You're not taking anything from me. I'll want them back. And don't stretch out the collars. I've got about thirty pounds on you. If I can keep the collars from stretching, it shouldn't be a problem for you."

"Fine." Emmitt hated ironing slightly more than he hated Andrew's charity, and he could console himself with the fact that he was only going to borrow the shirts. Andrew wasn't giving him anything. "Thanks," he mumbled.

"Mhmm," Andrew nodded back stiffly.

Emmitt could never quite overcome the misery of being chided mercilessly for minor failings. Andrew could tell him he was poor, stupid, or vulgar, and it wouldn't penetrate as much as his nitpicking. A biting reprimand over a creased shirt sleeve or a forgotten name cut deeper than a dig at Emmitt's beloved hand-me-down station wagon or a painful jab to the upper arm. Worse, Emmitt's unmistakable embarrassment had resulted in an equally awkward overture from his older brother.

Emmitt fixed his eyes on the road as a bitter shame built within him. He wanted to show Andrew he could be serious. He wanted to prove he could behave. Mostly, he didn't want Andrew to pity him.

Emmitt swallowed and forced himself to ask seriously, "If I'm going to be professional, to your standards, can I clarify something that's been on my mind?"

"Only if it isn't a joke," Andrew said.

"It's not. Does James Yates know about the book? I won't bring it up when we meet him. I'm just curious if this is a secret between Sybil and us."

Andrew's tone was sharp. "It was never a secret. It was part of the agreement. I told James about the idea for a book the first time I spoke to him. He didn't have any objections, as long as Shannon, Sybil, and

Renata agreed to it. Sybil signed off on the original waiver I sent to her ... but her uncle and his attorneys had additional stipulations they wanted to include. I won't hold Sybil to the terms of the original agreement if it causes friction between us and the rest of her family. And it really isn't wise to anger the man who'll be paying us for the job. He had certain conditions that needed to be met, and I gave him the original waiver with Sybil's signature as a sign of good faith. When I explained my intention was to uplift the Yates women and focus on their progress, he sounded optimistic. And you saw yesterday just how excited Sybil was to get started."

Emmitt fought to stifle a rising surge of laughter as he said, "Sybil was way too excited ... please, Andrew. Please admit it. I'm not being dramatic or imagining things. She was practically throwing herself at you."

"Yes," he admitted. "She was too excited. That's why I cut the day short. I figured she would cool off if I gave her some goals to work on and left her to focus on herself for a couple days." Andrew paused before continuing. His voice was determined and bore an edge of antagonism. "We're not hiding anything from anyone, and we're not apologizing for having our own project. I was honest with James Yates. If he changes his mind, that's on him, but I'm not ashamed of what we're doing. It's a mutually beneficial arrangement, and I was more than accommodating to the Yates family's requests."

"Quid pro quo, I get it." Emmitt wanted Andrew to be right. He wanted to be confident in Drew Key's ability to succeed, regardless of the odds. Emmitt tried to sound supportive. "Look, if you want me to be quiet, I'll order my coffee and stay silent. Not serial killer silent—with the wide eyes and dead stare—I'll shake hands and answer questions directed at me, but you can lead the conversation. I won't butt in."

Emmitt's attempt at deference didn't elicit the response he expected. Instead of gratitude, Emmitt noticed Andrew was nearing exasperation.

His jaw tightened as he stiffened his posture in the passenger seat. "I don't want that," Andrew growled. "I asked you to be a part of this. You're not here just to follow me around and take notes. I don't know why you seem so determined to act like a kicked dog. I want you to be here. We're a team, Emmitt. If you have something to contribute, then do it. We share our victories and our failures."

"I thought there were no failures. Only opportunities." Emmitt winced as he uttered the words. He hated himself for saying them. His brother was trying to treat him as an equal, but Emmitt was a dragging, sinking force, eager to pull Andrew under. Emmitt always had to prove Andrew right. He was unprofessional. Callous. Pitiable.

Andrew shook his head and sighed. He pointed mechanically out the passenger window. "There's the café. Turn in here."

Chapter Seven

Inside the café, Emmitt scanned the room. He didn't know what James Yates looked like, but there were only two occupied tables, and he guessed that the three teenage girls with their whipped cream-topped coffee shakes and the white-haired geriatric man sitting alone with his newspaper, coffee, and croissant were probably not him.

Turning to his brother, Emmitt whispered, "Where should we sit for the fullest professional impact?"

Seemingly unaffected by Emmitt's snide remarks in the car, Andrew motioned to a corner table nearest to where they stood.

"Take the chairs facing the door, so we can see when he comes in. It's far enough from the others that we can have some privacy, but near enough that he doesn't have to walk the entire length of the café to get to us. You sit, I'll order."

Despite his guilt, Emmitt couldn't help but smile as he reached the designated table. *Of course, Andrew has a strategy on where to sit.* Emmitt sat and waited.

It wasn't long before Andrew came back with coffee. Emmitt shifted uncomfortably and kept his eyes fixed on the door.

"Don't stare," Andrew ordered. He was calm, but firm. "The door has a bell, and there are windows everywhere. You can even see the parking lot from here. We won't miss him, and he won't catch us by surprise, so calm down."

"You don't actually help when you do that," Emmitt whispered.

"Do what?"

"When you deliberately point out my anxiety, it messes with my head. It makes everything worse … like now I'm worried I look unnatural, like I'm sitting weird or something."

Andrew scanned Emmitt from where he sat. After a long pause, he smiled and said, "Yeah, I see what you're saying. You *do* look weird and unnatural. But you've always looked like that. You should focus on the things you can control. For instance, you could stop bouncing your right leg up and down."

Emmitt stilled his shaking leg. "You know, you're the one who's making me feel self-conscious. And that wasn't a very mature thing for you to say. Professionalism, my ass, Andrew. Do you make it a habit of telling your clients they're awkward and ugly?"

"None of my clients are awkward or ugly, and I didn't call *you* awkward or ugly. You said your anxiety made you sit in a weird and unnatural position, and I agreed. You should be grateful for my intervention. Look, your leg stopped shaking, you're not hunching your shoulders, and you aren't even doing that jittery tapping you normally do on your coffee cup. You don't notice it, but you're habitual with your nervous tics. I made you aware of it, and you stopped." Andrew's smile grew wider.

Andrew was right. Emmitt had momentarily forgotten his anxiety and transformed it into ire against his brother. Even now, Emmitt's annoyance far surpassed his nerves. He wasn't sure if this kind of transference was ultimately helpful, but Emmitt was relieved that his stomach was no longer tied in knots.

The respite was short-lived, however, as Emmitt heard the little bell chime. The door opened, and a stout, middle-aged man entered the café.

The man wasn't alone. A younger woman was standing next to him. *His daughter? Wife? Personal assistant?* It was the young woman who confirmed the man's identity to Emmitt. He focused his eyes on her and immediately noticed the unmistakable resemblance—she looked like Sybil. She wasn't a carbon copy, but the slight frame and delicate facial features were similar enough for Emmitt to presume her identity.

The man's eyes met Andrew's. He smiled with a slight nod in their direction and made his way toward the table. Emmitt and Andrew stood in unison to greet the pair.

"Drew Key? I'm James. Good to meet you. This is Renata, my niece and Shannon's daughter." James had a tight smile and a firm handshake.

"I'm happy to meet you in person, Mr. Yates. And Renata, I'm especially pleased to meet you. This is my brother, Emmitt. He's here to help as well. Can I order anything for either of you? A coffee or something to eat?"

"Oh, coffee sounds good, but I'll pop over to the counter and get it myself. Renata, honey, can I get you something?" James asked.

"No, thank you." Renata's voice was soft and wavering. Her eyes fixed downward.

"You sure, honey? Even a cup of water? Or tea?"

"No, but thank you for asking."

"Alright, I'll be back in a second."

As James left, Renata's eyes followed him. Emmitt noticed her hands tightly gripping the back of her chair.

Emmitt wasn't accustomed to being near someone who was more nervous than himself. It buoyed his ego, though he hated to admit it. Andrew must have sensed it too. Emmitt wondered if Andrew would call her awkward and tell her to stop clutching the chair.

"Renata?" Andrew said. "I apologize for being rude. I never asked if you would like to have a seat." Andrew gestured to the chair that Renata still clutched.

She relaxed her grip and slowly sat down.

"It's good to see you. I'm glad we're meeting face-to-face," Andrew said with a smile as he seated himself on the wooden chair. Even his gray eyes softened and sparkled.

Renata didn't notice Andrew or his sparkling eyes. She wrung her hands and gave a few side-eyed glances, awaiting her uncle's return. Emmitt caught himself staring and quickly sat down. Renata hadn't bothered to look in Emmitt's direction, but Andrew shot a suspicious glance at his brother before looking back at Renata.

"It's nice to meet you. Thank you for helping." The almost-whispered response from the young woman was perfunctory. She finally settled her gaze on the table.

As he cautiously studied her, Emmitt was surprised at the close resemblance to her sister. If Shannon Yates inhabited a future form of Sybil, Renata was an unpretentious iteration of her older sister. Her dark, ash-blonde hair cascaded in soft waves down her shoulders and arms. Her makeup was soft, her face hadn't been plumped, tightened, or lifted artificially, and her nails were short and unpainted. She wore a loose, cozy, cream sweater tucked into her jeans, along with a delicate gold watch she would occasionally glance at.

Emmitt wanted to say something to her. He wanted to commiserate about their shared social anxiety, but, unsurprisingly, was too nervous to start a conversation, fearing he would say something insensitive or embarrassing.

Andrew continued to be conversational, without pressing the shy woman. "We had a productive day yesterday, and Sybil is looking forward to getting started." He paused, waiting for a response. When Renata remained silent, he continued. "We're going to take things slow, and I don't want to overstep. Are there any areas in the house you want us to avoid?"

"No," Renata said.

Andrew again left a long pause before continuing. "That's good to know. Are you living in the house? I was told you were living with your mother and sister, but living situations can change, and I don't want to assume something that isn't true."

"Yes."

Another pause from Andrew. He continued, patiently, "You certainly have a lot of clutter to contend with. From what we've seen, it can't be comfortable for you to live in the house in its current condition."

Renata remained silent, avoiding eye contact.

Andrew tried again. "The process will be rewarding, but difficult. Of course, you're already aware of this. You probably understand better than anyone the difficulties we're going to face. We're committed to helping, and we'll be by your family's side as long as it takes. Do you think you would want to be involved in the cleanup effort, or would you prefer to be left out of it?"

"I don't know. I …" Renata began, then sighed. "I just don't know."

"Not a problem," Andrew said. He sat upright with his hands folded on the table, and an unwavering smile directed at the woman who refused to look at him. "I didn't intend to put you on the spot. I'm sorry if it came across that way. This is a complex problem, and you don't have to commit to anything. If supporting you means giving you space and trying not to disturb you while we focus on your sister and mother, then that's what we'll do."

Renata sighed again. She pressed her lips together tightly and looked off into the distance with glistening eyes, as though she was struggling to find something to say … or struggling to maintain her composure.

Emmitt didn't know what he would do if Renata started crying. He wasn't sure what Andrew would do, either. Renata wasn't Sybil. Emmitt was fairly certain that, if Renata started crying, she would produce actual tears. He briefly pictured Renata burying her face in his chest while he wrapped his arms around her, then quickly forced the image out of his mind. Unprofessional, he thought to himself.

James Yates finally broke the silence as he returned with his coffee. "Alright," he said confidently, while taking a seat next to his niece. "What did I miss?"

"I was telling Renata how committed we are to assisting Sybil and Mrs. Yates. We're ready to help them clear and organize their clutter," Andrew said, turning his unwavering smile toward James.

"Hoard. Let's call it what it is." James Yates took a deep breath, flared his nostrils, and tightened his jaw. "Look, I'm appreciative that you're both willing to help, but Sybil ..." He paused, furrowing his brow and shaking his head. "Sybil likes to make plans and lists, but there's never any follow-through. You're not the first to try to help, and—not to question your capabilities—I don't think you'll be the last. Sybil is ... mercurial. I will say, to your credit, she seems especially confident in you, Drew. Certainly, more than any other professional she's asked me to hire. I'm just not confident that Sybil and Shannon will change. I think it's only fair for me to warn you: you're wasting your time."

Andrew's smile faded, but he remained determined. "I understand your frustration—"

"Let me be blunt," James interrupted. "Most families have financial constraints. They may not be able to stop a person from hoarding, but they don't have the resources to ... what do they call it ...?"

"Enable," Renata said.

"Enable. Thanks, honey." James smiled at his niece and continued. "If someone's grandma or brother piles up enough newspapers, prescription bottles and broken furniture to get the city involved, there are real consequences. If they don't change, they end up homeless or living in a nursing facility. Most families can't handle the financial burden. But it's different with our family. There will never be a financial rock-bottom for Sybil or Shannon. Even with the measures we've been able to put in place, they will always have money to spend on junk, and they will always have a house to live in. Shannon may hate me, but she knows I'll never leave her homeless."

Andrew persisted. "I'm aware of that. Most of my clients are wealthy, and many have bad habits that are intensified by their financial abundance. I believe any attempt is worth the effort. If you leave things the way they are, you'll only continue to build upon your anger and frustration. When my brother had a conversation with Mrs. Yates—"

"She spoke to you?" Renata interrupted. Her voice was subdued, but her dark-blue eyes fixed firmly on Emmitt.

Emmitt flushed, and stammered, "Well … I mean, it wasn't a long conversation, or anything like that … but, yeah. She was worried and upset …" Regaining some composure, he continued steadily. "I didn't really accomplish anything. She didn't tell us to leave, but she refused to participate. Andrew … Drew convinced her we would take our time working with Sybil first. May I ask, out of curiosity, are there any deadlines to meet with the city? Mrs. Yates seems convinced she's going to be kicked out of the house soon."

"No … God, she never listens," James fumed. "I repeatedly warned her she was heading toward the same outcome as her last eviction. I won't sugarcoat the truth. Her hoarding is worse than it was when she had to be vacated from the other properties. It's a miracle the city's board of health hasn't come in and condemned the place already. I made sure the house provided additional privacy so the neighbors couldn't look in. It has more square footage than the other houses. I've hired gardeners to come every week, and I've told Shannon that anything left outside is forfeit. I've tried to protect her, and while I have cautioned her, I have never threatened my sister. The city imposed her previous evictions. She couldn't continue living in a condemned house, but she was never willing to do the work to keep the properties from being condemned to begin with. The cycle just continues, and I move her into the next house. And the next. And the next."

"It sounds like you really care about your sister ... but maybe it would ease her anxiety if you didn't warn her so often," Emmitt said.

Renata's eyes widened at Emmitt's words. She looked at her uncle to gauge his reaction to Emmitt's impertinence.

James Yates cocked his head at Emmitt and smirked. "Well now, perhaps I could do that. You are the expert. Or is your brother the expert? I'm not sure what either of your qualifications are."

"Neither of us are medical experts," Emmitt admitted. "Drew has helped a lot of clients. I'm more of an assistant ... but I do have experience with a caring brother who wants what's best for me and isn't afraid to tell me all about my personal failings. He means well, but I don't always appreciate his advice. Sometimes I'm obnoxious just to spite him. I'm guessing you're the older brother, right?" Emmitt snuck a glance at Renata, whose eyes twinkled as she placed a hand over her mouth to hide what appeared to be a smile.

"Yes, I am," James said. "I never thought caring for Shannon would be a problem, but I suppose I can refrain from giving brotherly advice to my little sister, if you truly believe it will help." There was a twinge of condescension in his tone that reminded Emmitt of Shannon.

"Honestly, I'm not sure if it will or won't help, but anything that lessens her stress is worth trying. If she's stubborn—or sick—then it doesn't really matter how correct or convincing your arguments are. You're only wasting your own time and sanity trying to get through to her. Drew is focused on a stress-free declutter. He has the patience to work with Sybil, even if it's just one box a day. If there aren't any deadlines hanging over her head, maybe Mrs. Yates will see the progress Sybil is making and decide to work with us." Emmitt tried to mimic the confidence of Drew Key. He hoped to convince James Yates, abate his brother's concerns of incompetence, and impress Renata.

"There is no time frame unless the city gets involved," James said. "I can't control that, other than paying off fines, but if they come in and condemn the place, there isn't anything I can do to stop them. We agreed to a set fee for three months of work, plus whatever you make from your side project."

"What if it takes longer?" Emmitt asked.

James's eyes narrowed on Emmitt. "Are you already asking for an extension?"

"No. That wasn't my intention," Emmitt said. A flush of heat rose to his face, but he willfully pressed forward to maintain the momentum he was building. Andrew trusted him enough to speak, and he was determined to conduct himself professionally. "Like I said, I'm not an expert, but I've done some research, and there are dangers in pushing too hard, too fast. We don't want to make things worse for your family, and it would be wrong for Drew and me to over promise and under deliver. We'll work within the time frame, but I don't think we should pressure either of them to finish cleaning by a certain date."

"Emmitt makes a good point," Andrew said. "It may be beneficial to measure your expectations against the expectations of Sybil and Mrs. Yates. Mrs. Yates is currently unwilling to participate, and that may or may not change within three months. Sybil will work with us, but she only has two rooms to clean. It would be wrong for us to promise a spotless house within three months. What would you consider as a success?"

"Any progress," Renata said. She glanced at Andrew, then looked down at her fidgeting hands that lay on the table.

James smiled sympathetically at his niece. "Yes. Anything is better than nothing. If you can survive three months, and still want to soldier on, that might be enough to grant an extension. I won't make any promises now, but I'm open to negotiating in the future. Renata will know if progress is being made. Poor thing has to put up with both of them, and she's well aware of their antics. No professional has lasted more than a few weeks in the house with those two." James paused, thought for a moment, and continued. "I will say it is admirable for you to try to help. You've been surprisingly courteous … and candid. And the sheer audacity of this one," he said, wagging his finger at Emmitt, "may just plow through all of Shannon's defenses. But I still don't think it will work. I won't stop you. Maybe you can help, maybe you can't. Sybil, at least, seems willing to try."

"We're committed to the process. As long as Sybil is willing to participate, we'll make ourselves available to her," Andrew said.

"I'm sure you will," James said with a chuckle.

Emmitt noticed Renata smile at her uncle's remark. It flashed brightly on her face, then vanished.

James looked squarely at Andrew and clapped his hands together tightly. "Now, getting back to the side project. Your book idea? That will be up to my sister and nieces to sign their consent. You've been in contact with our lawyers, right? I've heard you agreed to the stipulations they wanted to include."

"Yes. I have the updated consent forms. I'm willing to wait to see if Mrs. Yates agrees to sign off … and if you're not comfortable, Renata, you don't need to be included in the book. I understand you value your privacy, and I'll respect your decision. Sybil has already agreed. I just need to give her the new form to sign." Andrew smiled at Renata, but she had lost interest in the conversation. She stared out the window with a solemn expression.

"Well, those were my thoughts." James shrugged and stood up. "I've warned you of the futility of trying to help Shannon and Sybil, and I told you not to get your hopes up regarding the book. Don't get me wrong, if Sybil has already agreed, she'll be a wellspring of material. She signed once without bothering to look anything over, so I doubt you'll have an issue getting her to sign again. That girl always has a story to tell, and she has no trouble oversharing or embellishing. Hopefully, that will be enough for your book. Anyway, I had better head out if there's nothing else. You have my number, Drew, if there's an emergency?"

"Yes, Mr. Yates. It was nice to speak with you again," Andrew said.

Andrew and Emmitt stood and shook hands with James.

Turning to Renata, Andrew cupped both of his large, tanned hands around hers. "It was a pleasure to meet you, Renata. I promise to do everything I can to help your family."

With startled eyes, Renata managed a small "Thanks."

She looked up with a restrained smile and nodded to Emmitt. Emmitt smiled without restraint and nodded back. She held his gaze for a moment longer, then turned and followed her uncle out the door.

Emmitt waited for the little bell to chime before he dared to speak to Andrew.

"Did that go well enough for you?" Emmitt asked. "Because, right now, it seems like we're treading water. We haven't sunk, but I'm not sure if we've gotten anywhere either."

"It went well enough. Anything that isn't a 'no' is a foot in the door. We're still on track for tomorrow, and Renata didn't say she wouldn't sign."

"Renata didn't say much of anything, Andrew."

"A victory is a victory, no matter how small."

"How'd I do?" Emmitt asked.

"Surprisingly well," Andrew said. "I don't know how—"

Emmitt's stomach released a roaring rumble before Andrew could finish his thought.

"Thank God that didn't happen in front of James and Renata. What are you feeding me, Andrew? I've got a new theory on the Yates mystery. We can talk about it over lunch."

"I'm sure I don't want to hear it, Emmitt," Andrew said.

"Too bad. My new theory is that James Yates is Sybil and Renata's dad. Like a Hapsburg thing. They have a family bush, which makes it easier to keep their wealth intact. The portrait of the guy in the dining room? Not a real person. It's all a ruse. They live in shame, which caused the hoarding to manifest. They're building physically metaphorical walls to keep people from discovering the truth."

Emmitt saw Andrew stifle a grin. "Emmitt, that's sick ... and slanderous. You've already pointed out the shrine. They clearly love the man in the portrait. No one would risk their house burning down to light votive candles for a man who never existed. The Yates name is historical. It's a legacy. He probably just dropped his last name and took Shannon's. If Sybil was an actress and Renata works for the museum, it makes sense for them to maintain that legacy. More doors open with the Yates name."

Emmitt pointed at Andrew. "So, you've been thinking about it too! Let's get some pizza and talk about it."

Andrew shook his head. "I won't gossip, and I don't eat bread. Anyway, it's only nine thirty. It's too early for lunch. Why don't you just order something here?"

"Nah. You kept me waiting too long. They only have croissants and muffins, anyway. There's no protein for you here, Andrew. Let's go to Gigi's Diner. They have omelets, bacon, sausage … and thirty varieties of pie."

"Isn't that near the beach? It's forty minutes away, Emmitt."

"I'm driving. Hey, you can talk to more clients on the way … and I'll pay."

Andrew frowned. "I don't know. We still have to pick up my car and drop off the rental."

"We can do it after. Come on, Andrew. You promised to feed me. You didn't specify that I had to eat here."

"Alright." Andrew let a small smile escape as he walked past his brother and toward the door. "But I'm paying."

Chapter Eight

As Andrew pulled up to the Yates house in his luxury SUV with cup-warming function, virgin vegan leather upholstery, and new brake pads, Emmitt had to admit he was less anxious than he had been the previous two days. He experienced a rare night of peaceful sleep and woke without an immediate fear of meeting Andrew's impossible standards for dressing professionally. Emmitt was now in possession of a closet filled with clothes borrowed from Andrew, and he was currently sporting one of the dozen freshly pressed, designer polos his brother had hand-picked for him. He downed a thirty-two-ounce cup of cold brew, which was more cream and sugar than coffee, and Andrew had barely protested when he ordered an apple fritter for breakfast. To Emmitt's relief, there had been nothing more from Andrew than a passing comment about "empty calories." Full of sugar and caffeine, Emmitt was energized and eager to start the day. He exited the passenger side of the SUV and made his way across the street to the Yates house.

At the gate, Emmitt stopped to let Andrew enter, then followed closely behind. He had glanced down briefly at his notebook, attempting to flip to his notes from the first meeting, when he ran into his brother's back. Emmitt staggered while Andrew remained upright, staring ahead.

"Jesus, Andrew!" Emmitt blurted, trying to steady himself. He looked up and saw what Andrew had been staring at. "There must be twenty boxes blocking the garage door," he said in disbelief. "You think Sybil already started to move stuff out on her own?"

"No." Andrew was stiff. He didn't look angry, but his jaw clenched, and his body seemed cemented in place.

Emmitt leaned closer to Andrew and whispered, "Do you think one of them is messing with us?"

"I don't know," Andrew said hesitantly. He must have heard the doubt in his own voice. Andrew's muscles tensed as he snapped, "We shouldn't speculate. Let's go in and figure out what's going on."

"After you." Emmitt motioned for Andrew to lead and fell back behind him, using his brother as a shield.

Emmitt was relieved he wasn't leading. His neck and shoulders tensed at the recent development, and Andrew's uneasiness only intensified Emmitt's agitation. Perhaps he was a coward. It was, after all, his choice to hide behind his older brother. When in doubt, Emmitt could defer to Andrew's authority. He had the freedom to speak whenever it suited him and remain silent when conversations became stiff and uncomfortable.

Emmitt tried to soothe himself with the idea that Andrew enjoyed being in charge. Even as kids, Andrew always took the lead.

If it's anyone's fault, it's his fault for conditioning me to either follow him or stay out of his way.

This wasn't the whole truth, but the sudden bitterness the thought produced was enough to make Emmitt set aside his guilt for the moment.

Andrew rang the doorbell. Sybil opened the door.

"Drew! I'm so happy you're here! I came up with a list of goals, and I took action. I have a surprise that I think you are going to love!" Sybil was energetic and animated. Her lack of control made Emmitt wonder if it was possible for a person to bubble out of their own skin.

Before Andrew could speak, Sybil slid out the door, grabbed him with her mint claws, and pulled him back toward the driveway.

When they arrived in front of the row of stacked boxes, she stopped. "Ta-dah!" she cheered, clearly expecting a positive reaction from Drew Key. "It's a complete organization solution system in rose gold. It's got everything: shelving units, mounted cabinets, a rolling garment rack with matching velvet hangers … I think they even threw in a label maker."

Emmitt and Andrew could only stare as they confronted the boxes again. It felt like a punishment.

"I love your enthusiasm," Andrew began slowly and deliberately. "I just wonder if buying an organization system *now* is in alignment with your current goals."

"You don't like it?" Sybil pouted. "You weren't here when I was setting goals. I thought I was doing what you wanted by taking initiative for myself." Sybil's voice was unsteady. She frowned and sulked. "I just wish you were here when I was making this decision. I genuinely thought you would be proud of me, but I guess I just can't trust my own judgment at all."

"It's only a minor misunderstanding. I should have been clearer on the point of setting goals," Andrew said. "Would you be willing to return the boxes? It would save time if we didn't have to find a place to store them, and you can reorder the unit when we've made more progress in your rooms."

Sybil hesitated. "I understand what you're saying, Drew, but it was a final sale ... and it was fifty percent off ... and the rose gold is so pretty ... and I'll need it after everything is cleared out of my office. It has filing cabinets with dividers that I really need for my businesses. Oh, Drew, if you could just imagine the aesthetic, you would agree that this is the perfect way for me to organize everything. I suppose I should've waited to order it, but I look at it as a goal for myself. This is my reward for all my hard work, and an incentive to finish quickly. But if you really, really think I should get rid of it, I'll do it for you, Drew."

Sybil's mouth pouted, but her eyes were unreadable. Perhaps she was toying with Andrew to see if he would let her have her way, or perhaps she wanted Drew Key to assert authority over her and force her to get rid of the boxes. Either way, it seemed like a game to her. Sybil was almost coercive in her argument, but she remained pleadingly deferential to Drew. Emmitt had to admit she could be seductive and persuasive, but she was also melodramatic, and possibly delusional. He couldn't figure her out. *We need to be careful around her*, Emmitt thought.

Andrew's eyes remained fixed on the stacks of boxes. "If you have a place for them, we can help you move the boxes. I only ask that you keep in mind, whatever you choose to bring in will ultimately add to the problem we're trying to fix." Finally prying his attention away from the new obstacle that further complicated an already overwhelming task, Andrew looked at Sybil and asked, "Do you think you can refrain from acquiring anything else from this point forward?"

Sybil nodded eagerly, then stopped abruptly and scrunched her nose. "Yes … but … well, I still need to purchase stock for my businesses. I have a very enterprising spirit, and I refuse to stagnate. I know I need to slow down so I can finally take time to focus on myself, but I can't ignore my work responsibilities. So many people depend on me, Drew. You understand, right?"

Sybil tilted her head and flashed her hazel eyes at Andrew. Her hands released their grasp on Andrew's arm to clasp them childishly under her chin in a mock *pretty please* gesture.

"I won't tell you what to do with your work," Andrew said. "You know what you need to run your businesses, and I won't interfere." He paused before adding, "I also think it's important we don't confuse goals with rewards. Do you, by chance, have your list of goals? I'd like to see what you've come up with."

"Of course!" Sybil bubbled. "Let's go inside, and I'll show you what I have so far."

Sybil grabbed Andrew's arm once more and led him into the house. Emmitt followed behind. Inside the house, Sybil led them down the path to the dining room and motioned for them to sit. Sybil's mother was nowhere to be seen.

Emmitt couldn't help but ask, "Where's Mrs. Yates?"

"She's at the convent, visiting Sister Eugene. She heard you two were coming today and just bolted." Sybil giggled. "Renata's here … somewhere …" She let the last word trail off languidly. "Stay here. I need to go find my list."

Sybil bounced out of the room and hurriedly maneuvered back along the trail. When she was out of sight, Emmitt looked at Andrew with an exaggerated stare. He lifted his eyebrows, shook his head, and let out a subdued sigh. Andrew returned Emmitt's stare and managed a tight smile as he shook his head in silent accord.

When Andrew had briefly explained the Yates women's hoarded house to Emmitt after proposing they work together, Emmitt thought he could intellectualize the challenges they would face. He took a seat at the dining table and shifted his chair slightly to look back through the archway into the living room. As he carefully scanned the room, Emmitt realized experiencing the hoard was far different from envisioning it. There was no right way to determine where to begin. He would become captivated by certain items, then quickly lose interest as soon as something else caught his eye. It was impossible to focus. There was no space to think clearly. No place to sit and sift through the clutter. The sensory overload was almost paralyzing. It was undeniably overwhelming. As Emmitt shifted his chair back to face the table, he looked at his brother and frowned. Even Andrew—the great Drew Key—seemed slightly frazzled by the experience.

Emmitt glanced over at the shrine and felt a surge of disappointment. He could never ask about it. He pried his attention away from the portrait of the man in the dark navy suit with dusty brown hair and smiling hazel eyes, and sulked at the mystery that would remain, for him, unsolved.

His gaze slowly wandered past the shrine and settled on a hundred eyes of wood, bronze, and alabaster saints staring at him from the filled antique hutches. Like Andrew, they all seemed to pity him. The dozens of eyes of the Virgin Mary were the most sympathetic to

Emmitt. There was compassion in every countenance, which stirred an undefinable anguish in his chest. His father once called her "Blessed Mother." He wondered if she was perpetually sorrowful. So many children. So many disappointments. She had to watch the good one suffer for the benefit of all the fuckups. But she still had to love them all, didn't she?

Emmitt took a deep breath, straightened his posture, and settled his eyes on the notebook he had placed on the table. He hadn't bothered to move the stack of woven placemats that lay beneath it, fearing Shannon Yates would return and notice the items were repositioned. He and Andrew waited in silence until Sybil returned.

She fluttered into the dining room and sat next to Andrew at the head of the table. "Got it! Oh ... my ... God. You wouldn't believe how long it took me to find it," Sybil said breathlessly. "I swear, I thought I put it on my cot in the office. Nope, not there. I threw all my blankets on the floor for nothing! I checked my dressers, the bookshelf ... then I remembered. Yesterday, I had a video conference with my team. They know me better than I know myself, so of course, I asked them to help me with my goals. I can't believe I forgot the list was on my desk!"

"I'm glad you found it," Andrew said. "What did you come up with?"

Sybil looked down, unfolded the sheet of paper and read, "Number one: get an organization system. Done!" Sybil giggled. "I certainly didn't have the reaction I was hoping for—and you wouldn't believe the added cost for an overnight, early morning delivery—but at least I can check it off my list."

Sybil made an exaggerated motion with her sparkling pink pen as she checked it off the list. "Number two: clean my bedroom. I really struggled with this one, Drew, because I wasn't sure if I wanted to clean my bedroom or office first. My girls convinced me that the bedroom should be first. It has to be a sanctuary to ease my mind and lower my cortisol levels. If I'm less stressed, I can sleep better and have a better balance of energy to flow into my passions. You don't know how uncomfortable that stupid cot is! I want to sleep in my bed again."

"You really sleep on a cot?" Emmitt asked. Sybil didn't seem like the type of person who would endure any level of discomfort. Emmitt had to admit, though, that he didn't know Sybil well enough to discern anything about her. They were only slightly more than strangers. "When was the last time you slept in your bed?"

Sybil glared at Emmitt with a tight smile. "Ladies never tell. Besides, who wants to focus on a minor inconvenience?" Sybil couldn't keep her eyes settled on Emmitt. They leapt restlessly on Andrew. "I'm convinced it's why my mother is so cranky all the time. We can't even crack the doors to her rooms, so her cot is stuck in the hallway on the other side of the house."

Sybil shifted her eyes and pointed to the dark hallway leading to Shannon's section of the house. A morbid fascination turned Emmitt's head to view the treacherous passage once more. As he studied the opening a second time, Emmitt's mind conjured an image of Shannon imprisoned and unable to move in the constrictive corridor. He shuddered and twisted his head back toward Sybil, who perceived his wide eyes and twitching mouth. She flashed a smirk that dripped with malevolent joy.

Emmitt felt Andrew's cool eyes on his face as he fought to regulate his terror-stricken demeanor.

Andrew's eyes didn't rest on Emmitt for long. He turned his attention to Sybil and asked, "Does the path open up, or are the boxes packed tightly along the entire length of the hallway?"

Sybil's face softened as she addressed Drew casually. "I've never gone through it, but my sister squeezed herself in once. She said the cot is wedged between the wall and Mom's boxes. She had to climb over piles of Daddy's old clothes to get to it. There was one section where she had to crawl *under* boxes ... I don't know how my mom managed that marvel of engineering. Renata was terrified when she came back out. She offered for her to sleep on the couch in her sitting room, but our mother was too stubborn and proud to accept. Of course, Renata didn't bother to offer her couch to *me*, but that's just how she is." Sybil kept her gaze on Andrew as Emmitt's heart sank at the realization.

Sybil looked down at her list with a superficial smile and continued. "Number three: clean and organize the office. That's where I run my businesses. Number four: install organization system. See Drew, I told you I had a plan for it!" The smile on Sybil's lips remained, but her tone was more critical than cheerful.

"Number five: two fawn-colored French bulldogs. I want a boy and a girl, and I'm going to name them Louis and Antionette. So cute, right? Once I clean and organize my rooms, I can adopt the puppies and give them a safe place to live. Number six: ... hmm ... I wrote 'global entrepreneur.' By this point, I'd had a few glasses of wine, and we kinda got sidetracked watching dog videos on the internet. I'm not sure how I'm going to accomplish this goal. I may get back into acting, if the right role presents itself, but I'm not waiting around for opportunities. I'm currently building my reach and reputation by focusing on aspirational marketing and my bankable, bubbly personality. Honestly, if Melody Boutroux can sell those creepy living baby dolls and ugly cat sweaters at three a.m. on the shopping channel, then there's nothing stopping me from building *my* empire ... Oh, that reminds me. Drew, didn't you used to date Melody?"

"Yes," Andrew replied with a hint of surprise as Sybil mentioned the name.

"What happened?" Sybil displayed a look of dramatic concern that prickled the skin on the back of Emmitt's neck.

"Cat allergies. Melody has a kind heart and takes in foster cats that are difficult to rehome. It's a shame that things didn't work themselves into alignment," Andrew said frigidly.

Emmitt knew Andrew had once loved Melody. Years ago, their relationship was serious enough for him to fly with her to visit their father. Andrew *never* visited their father. Emmitt liked her. Melody was eccentric, but she was also warm, friendly, and fully aware of her own idiosyncrasies. She was also funny. She could make Andrew laugh openly and uncontrollably, which was a nearly impossible achievement.

In the end, though, she wouldn't sacrifice her collection of cats, and Andrew wouldn't sacrifice the trajectory of his career. He had told Emmitt the antihistamines were causing him to be too lethargic, and the red nose and dark circles under his eyes were damaging his image. This had been after a long conversation with their mother, who always urged Drew Key to focus on his career rather than his relationships. Emmitt had called him an idiot. Andrew didn't argue, but didn't change his mind, either. Emmitt was confident Andrew's sudden coldness wasn't directed at Melody.

"Oh, my God, her cats!" Sybil mocked. "She must foster a dozen at a time. Drew, I just don't know how you could stand it!"

"Not so many as a dozen," Andrew said. "She only ever had four or five at a time. It was always amazing how quickly she could find them permanent homes. They would come in scraggly or matted or missing an eye, and she would wash them, clip their nails, and set up a professional photoshoot to capture their 'true beauty.'" Andrew's tone softened as he smiled.

Then he caught himself and redirected his attention toward Sybil. "But that isn't important. What's important is that you've made a list and set reasonable goals, while also giving yourself more complex goals ... and rewards ... to work toward in the future. You've done an amazing job, Sybil." Andrew kept the softness in his voice, but his smile was less sentimental. "And I suppose I should commend you for already accomplishing your first goal. We can get started on your second goal, if you're ready?"

"I'm ready," Sybil said eagerly.

Emmitt wasn't sure why Sybil would not-so-casually steer the conversation to Andrew's ex-girlfriend, but it made him uneasy. Drew Key and Sybil Yates lived in a smaller world than the rest of the planet, but Andrew and Sybil weren't friends. Sybil seemed desperate to snag Drew Key as her personal guru—or lover—but Drew Key was professional to a fault. He would never date Sybil.

With an uncharacteristic urge to protect his brother's honor, Emmitt attempted to shift the topic further away from Melody. "You mentioned Renata was here. Will she be helping us?" Emmitt asked. "Should we ask her, or leave her alone?"

Emmitt was impatient to see the shy woman again. He wondered if she would be more comfortable and willing to talk when she was at home. He was also curious about the dynamic between her and her sister.

Sybil side-eyed Emmitt. "Renata!" she screamed, loud enough for both brothers to wince. "You wanna help me clean my room with Drew Key and his brother?"

There was a pause. An unseen door opened and closed, and Emmitt could hear the faint sound of footsteps approaching. Renata poked her head out from a smaller archway that opened into the dining room from a dark, undiscovered area of the large house.

She spoke quietly and briefly to her sister. "Not today ... sorry." She nodded her head at Emmitt and Andrew, acknowledging their presence without making direct eye contact. Then she disappeared.

"Figures," Sybil said. "But I'm used to it."

Sybil's contrived dejected tone, combined with her calm narration of Renata's distressing experience in Shannon's hoarded hallway, turned Emmitt's annoyance into a quiet anger. He felt the urge to say something, but promptly bit his tongue. His eyes shot a quick fiery glance at Sybil, but neither Sybil nor Andrew noticed.

"It was worth a try," Andrew said. "We're more than willing to welcome her help whenever she's ready."

"Drew, you ... and your brother," she said, narrowing her eyes at Emmitt, "are so sweet to encourage my mother and sister. Sometimes, it seems like I'm the only one willing to fix things."

"That must be difficult for you," Emmitt said flatly, holding Sybil's gaze.

"Yes, I'm sure it is difficult for Sybil," Andrew asserted. He shot a freezing glare at Emmitt, then swiftly shifted his attention back to Sybil, radiating a deliberate warmth to counterbalance Emmitt's chilly remark. "We're hopeful Renata and your mother will come around. Until then, you have our undivided attention. Let's get started."

Emmitt noticed Sybil brighten at the mention of Andrew's "undivided attention."

"I'm so ready to get started. Follow me, boys." As they wound their way to Sybil's bedroom, she added, "I was thinking we could start with the first four bins that are closest to the door."

"That works for us," Andrew said.

Emmitt doubted there would be enough space to sort through boxes in the cramped hallway, but he decided to stay silent and leave the logistics to Andrew and Sybil.

At the door, Sybil positioned herself uncomfortably close to Andrew, and leaned even closer to apologize for the cramped surroundings.

Andrew surveyed the area and finally noticed the first problem that needed addressing. "We'll have to move the boxes to another location. There isn't enough room for us here. It'll be a tight squeeze, but Emmitt and I should be able to grab these bins and move them somewhere else. Is there a place where we can start sorting? Maybe outside?"

"I don't want to do it outside. It's cold, and I don't want my stuff to get damp or dirty." Sybil looked up at Andrew and smirked. "But my sister's rooms are clean ... and spacious."

Emmitt considered that Sybil might be attempting an act of aggression against Renata. Andrew sensed it too.

"Renata was clear that she didn't want to help today," Andrew said.

"She doesn't have to help," Sybil countered. "She can stay in her bedroom or in the kitchen while we work in the sitting room. It really is the best place for us to organize."

Emmitt's irritation was mounting. He tried to reason with Sybil. "You care about vibrations and energies, right? Don't you think intruding into Renata's private space might make her upset and throw off your ... frequencies?" He struggled to find the correct terminology. "It can't be good for the organizing process if the air is filled with her negatively charged particles ... right Drew?"

"Emmitt makes a good point," Andrew said. "It doesn't help you or Renata to make use of her space without her consent."

"Then why don't you get her consent, if you're so bothered about what I do?" Sybil snapped. Her words were in response to Andrew, but her eyes were trained on Emmitt.

Sybil's sharp outburst startled Emmitt, but he refused to shrink back from the diminutive bully. He stood taller, knowing he had been right to question Sybil's earlier affectations. Piercing through Sybil's façade bolstered Emmitt's courage.

"Alright. I'll ask Renata, but what if she says no?" He looked down at Sybil for an answer.

"Then we're done for the day." Her tone was callous. Her eyes still burned into Emmitt.

Emmitt held her stare without flinching. Sensing her lack of effect on Emmitt, Sybil tore her eyes away from him and shifted back to Andrew, relaxing her face and posture. Emmitt noticed her lip quiver as her voice wavered.

"Drew, this is getting so stressful. I just need a place to sort through my things. I don't know why my sister would do this to me ... I ... I just want to get better."

Unbelievable. Selfish. A barrage of even less charitable words washed over Emmitt, but he tried to let them slide out of his mind. *Remember, you're trying to help. You can't hate Sybil. You don't have to like her, but you can't hate her. Sybil is sick.* Emmitt kept repeating *Sybil is sick* in his mind, hoping it would overwhelm his hostility.

Andrew patted Sybil gently on the shoulder and tried to calm her down. "This is a lot for you. You're doing well, and I'm proud of your resolve to make positive changes."

Sybil's demeanor altered once again as Drew Key spoke. Shannon Yates said Sybil was capricious. James Yates had called her mercurial. Emmitt looked at Sybil feasting on Drew Key's approval and saw an addict getting her fix. He wondered if Andrew was genuinely proud of Sybil, or if he merely understood what motivated her.

It didn't take an exceptional intellect to figure out what motivated Sybil. Sybil sought satisfaction through constant, concentrated attention and unwavering admiration. Drew Key was being paid to care, but it wasn't fair for Emmitt to view his brother's words and actions as wholly opportunistic. Despite Emmitt's contempt for the guru Drew Key, he knew *Andrew* Key liked to help people. He wanted to help Sybil. Even if Andrew was playing into Sybil's ego, he was only appealing to it in order to encourage her. He didn't do it maliciously; he was a practical problem-solver. Drew Key didn't scheme; scheming was their mother's talent.

It was difficult for Emmitt to coalesce the compassion required for the job with the fact that this was, ultimately, a job. Emmitt was unable to shake off the self-loathing he felt for profiting off of Sybil's hoarding problem, but he could never match Andrew's patience or attentiveness, and he wasn't interested in making an effort to empathize.

He didn't dislike Sybil because she was rich; Renata, Mrs. Yates, and James Yates were wealthy, and he didn't hate them. It wasn't her pseudo-celebrity status or her inflated ego, either. Drew Key had a following and an ego, but Emmitt found him more irritating than abhorrent. There was something fundamental about Sybil's personality that was loathsome to Emmitt. Sybil wanted everyone to concede that she was special and important. She wanted to rewrite reality to force people to see her exactly how she wanted to see herself. She wanted unconditional adoration, regardless of how she treated others.

And there was something else. There was something about her that reminded Emmitt of his mother. Emmitt didn't want to give Sybil any affirmations to boost her already-inflated sense of entitlement.

Emmitt begrudgingly acknowledged that he himself was prone to hyperbolic one-sided grudges, and he knew he needed to conduct himself at a higher level of professionalism, as Drew Key often scolded. He didn't like Sybil, but he had to admit that she didn't deserve his hatred. More importantly, he didn't want to let her win. She wouldn't sabotage their efforts without a fight from Emmitt; and, in this case, fighting required a gentler approach. If he intended to move forward, he would have to be more covert in his disdain.

As Sybil continued to whine to Drew about how maligned she felt, how much she had to overcome, and her family's inability to support her in her time of need, Emmitt relaxed his face and waited patiently for her to conclude her woeful list of grievances.

When she had finished, and Andrew had once again comforted her, Emmitt finally spoke. "I'm sorry if I was being rude," Emmitt said, looking at Sybil. "I'll speak to Renata and see if she's willing to share her space to help you organize."

"I forgive you, Emmitt." Sybil was calm, but her face glowered at him. "Thank you for taking accountability. I'm used to people hurting my feelings and never apologizing for it. Owning up to your mistakes is really going to help us build trust."

Emmitt controlled his tongue and tried to smile as he forced a measured tone. "Do you have any advice to get your sister to agree to let us use her room?"

"No. We're just too different to get along with each other. I've made my peace with her negativity, so I've done my part. If she could just, for once, see things from my perspective, Renata might just stop hating me so much. Her quiet animosity is one of the major crosses I bear." Sybil's mouth tensed as she smirked at Emmitt. "You should really be careful around her."

"Well, then, wish me luck." Emmitt turned and wandered cautiously down the hallway toward the unknown.

He realized he would have to avoid any direct conversations with Sybil if he hoped to stifle the growing contempt he held against the heiress actress. He clutched his notebook tightly in his right hand and balled his left hand into a fist.

As he stepped toward the dining room, he kept whispering the mantra, "Sybil is sick."

Chapter Nine

Emmitt walked past the entry and wound back to the dining room. He passed the shrine and stopped at the narrow archway where Renata had previously made her appearance. As he peered into the room and tried to discern its function, he realized the dining room he now stood in was only a breakfast nook.

Emmitt inched further into the darkened room. He glanced to his left and saw several tall towers of boxes stacked in multiple rows extending from the wall, then turned his head to the right to see his reflection staring back from a mirrored wall behind a cluttered wet bar. Pressing ahead, he encountered an enormous dining table. The elaborately carved wooden table could have easily seated twelve people, but like the rest of the furniture in the house, it was piled high with boxes, blankets, papers, and collectibles. Countless boxes and containers had been packed tightly underneath the table, which left no space for the formal dining chairs. Some of them had to be placed under the counter of the useless wet bar, while others were surrounded by mounting piles of miscellany or wedged between other pieces of inaccessible furniture. One wall had two matching, tufted, Victorian sofas pushed against it, along with several additional antique hutches.

Emmitt considered whether he should try to knock on the wall of the room or call Renata's name from the archway. He didn't want to risk startling her by screaming her name.

Slowly, he walked past the wet bar and noticed a closed door near the end of the large room.

He knocked softly and called her name as quietly as he could. "Renata?"

There was nothing but silence.

Emmitt called louder. "Renata? It's Emmitt Key ... I'm sorry to bother you."

He had no intention of barging through the closed door, but he wasn't certain if Renata would ever answer him. Emmitt always remained still and silent when solicitors came to his door. Why should he expect a different response from her? She already said she wasn't interested in helping.

After wrestling anxiously with what to do, he finally decided he would knock and call her name one more time before resigning himself to defeat.

Emmitt knocked louder and raised his voice, being careful not to yell. "Renata? It's Emmitt Key. I have a request from Sybil. Can we talk for a minute?"

Leaning in close, Emmitt tilted his head and pressed his ear against the closed door. He stilled his breath and listened. After a minute, he heard a faint stirring from the other side. He leaned his head back as the door opened slowly. Renata kept her hand on the knob as she stood within the doorframe.

Emmitt could see a large kitchen behind the small woman. The marble counters were cleared, and there were no boxes or bins on the white tile floor. It was immaculately clean, and Emmitt could detect a fresh scent of lemon.

"This must be your part of the house," Emmitt whispered in awe.

"Yes," Renata said quietly.

She loosened her grip on the doorknob and opened the door fully. Her eyes shifted as she turned and moved further into the room, positioning herself behind the large kitchen island and creating a barrier between herself and Emmitt. She turned to face him, but her eyes fixed on the countertop, as though she was studying the faint gray veins in the white marble.

Emmitt unconsciously rubbed a hand along the back of his neck as he looked at the woman who couldn't—or wouldn't—look back at him. "I'm sorry to bother you. I think I made your sister angry, and I've been sent to ask if we could use one of your rooms to sort through her boxes. We're stuck in the hallway right now, and she refuses to work outside." Emmitt waited anxiously for a response.

Renata didn't look up.

Without realizing, Emmitt had shifted his weight toward the island and began tapping his fidgeting left fingers on the countertop. He looked down, noticed the nervous tic, and quickly clenched his fingers into a fist.

"Shit ... I mean, shoot ... sorry." He lifted his eyes to see Renata still staring at the marble counter, though he noticed the corners of her lips raised slightly in response to his outburst.

Emmitt gently placed his notebook on the counter and tried to force a smile to hide his embarrassment. "I have a hard time controlling my fidgeting ... and my language. I realize this isn't a great second impression. Sorry for that."

"I get nervous too. Don't worry about it." Renata finally raised her head to look at Emmitt. She studied his face with her deep-blue eyes. "How did you make Sybil angry?"

There was a new sensation rising in Emmitt's chest as he straightened his posture and tried to calm himself. "Our personalities conflicted ..." Emmitt hesitated, then started again. "I'm not naturally upbeat or supportive. I wasn't completely rude, but I also wasn't encouraging. Sybil was expecting more sympathy from me. It's just ... well, it's exhausting being around someone who constantly needs to be at the center of everything. You already know that. You live with her. That can't be easy. I thought Andrew was bad, but Sybil ..." Emmitt stopped himself as a sudden realization dawned. He feared he was being too honest with Renata.

"Sybil only cares about Sybil," Renata finished.

"Yeah." Emmitt sighed, relieved by Renata's response, and eager to continue the conversation. "I'm pretty sure she's trying to sabotage the process by demanding your involvement. Andrew and I tried to ask her to leave you alone, but she's threatening to end today's cleanup if you don't allow us to use your room."

"Either way, she wins," Renata said. She pressed her lips together and looked away.

Emmitt swallowed a lump of self-contempt that caught in his throat and tried to apologize. "I shouldn't have bothered you. This isn't your problem. I'm sorry I tried to make you participate. I'll go tell Andrew we're done for the day."

"No." Renata breathed deeply. "She can sort through her boxes in my sitting room, but please make sure whatever comes in goes out. Sybil ... takes advantage."

"Does she try to guilt you into storing her things?" Emmitt asked.

Renata looked back at Emmitt and furrowed her brow. Her face became animated as she huffed, "No. She doesn't ask, she just does it. I'll come home and notice boxes stacked in a far corner or hiding behind a sofa. She ignores me when I ask her to remove her things. She thinks she's being cute. And it's never junk. She knows I won't throw away her old pageant trophies or her communion dress. I just end up moving it all into the dining room ..." Her eyes welled with tears. She sniffed them back and lowered her voice. "Everything gets shuffled around the house. Nothing ever leaves. And Sybil doesn't care."

"Shit. I'm sorry," Emmitt said.

Renata tried to smile. "It's okay. Well, it's not okay, but it's not your fault."

"Are you sure you want to help? I know I wouldn't be so accommodating if it was my brother making demands on me."

"Is your brother a narcissistic hoarder?" Renata asked with an embittered smirk.

"No. Not a hoarder, anyway." In truth, Emmitt didn't believe Andrew was a narcissist either, but he didn't feel a pressing urge to clarify. "Has she been diagnosed? As a narcissist, I mean."

"No. One doctor said she has OCD, then another one said OCPD. The doctor on a reality show said both diagnoses were wrong, and Sybil has a problem with impulse control—ICD—but he lost his license to practice medicine after getting too involved with his patients. Maybe he had ICD too."

"The doctor *and* the acupuncturist? Wow."

Renata rolled her eyes and shrugged her shoulders. "Maybe she's not technically a narcissist, but she charms people. Even professionals

... not the good ones, but the good ones are usually the first to be dismissed. The ones that stick around are more than willing to tell Sybil what she wants to hear ... but Sybil gets bored easily. Even the most devoted professional will eventually lose her interest. That's why Uncle James was so blunt with your brother. Sybil is Sybil. She'll never change. She runs hot and cold, and it's nearly impossible to gauge her commitment to anything. Sometimes, I feel like I'm the only one who notices the depths of her selfishness."

"I noticed." Emmitt asserted the words with such unwarranted confidence, it prompted a surprised cackle to burst out of Renata's mouth. She hurriedly clasped a hand over her lips to stifle her laughter.

Emboldened by his effect on Renata, Emmitt leaned further onto the kitchen island and whispered, "I think Andrew knows something's off too, but he won't admit it. She is a client, after all. And it's not like he could diagnose her, even if he wanted to. But there are times she makes him tense up, and he's usually unflappable."

Renata seemed amused by Emmitt's honesty. "I'm glad you noticed, but I'm not sure your brother would appreciate your candidness. He probably thinks I'm a client too."

"You're right ... I didn't consider that." Emmitt flushed with embarrassment. "I guess I should be more professional. I am curious though ... Do *you* consider yourself to be a client?"

Renata thought before answering. "Not really. Mother and Sybil have similar issues, but I don't think I need help with anything." Renata shifted her eyes before resting them back on Emmitt's. She smiled nervously and wrung her hands. "I want to help. I want things to get better, but I just don't know how much I can handle."

Emmitt bit his inner lip, realizing the weight of suffering Renata endured. Nothing was simple. Emmitt was foolish to think everything would just work out. Once again, the good one had to suffer so the fuckup could benefit. Renata was accommodating and kind, but her kindness allowed Sybil to trample her mercilessly.

And why was he here? To help? To stand up to Sybil? Those reasons may have fortified his resolve, but they weren't what motivated him. Emmitt wanted to see Renata and speak to her again. But he hadn't considered Renata might not want to speak to him again. Was she angry that he was standing in her kitchen? There was no way for Emmitt to know. She'd be too polite or shy to say, even if he asked.

One of Emmitt's fingers tapped aggressively on the marble counter as he struggled with what to do. Emmitt didn't want to bully Renata with Sybil's selfish demands. He fixed his eyes steadily on her face. He couldn't see any hatred or distress directed at him, but he couldn't be certain.

"Are you okay?" Renata asked.

Emmitt's mind flashed back to the eyes of the Virgin Mary statues locked in Shannon's hutches. All concern and sympathy. No malice. It was too much for Emmitt to take.

"It isn't fair for me to force your hand with Sybil. I don't want to make things worse for you by helping her. I'm going to go back and tell them you said no." Emmitt grabbed his notebook, turned, and took a step to leave the kitchen.

"But I've already agreed to help," Renata said.

Emmitt halted and turned back to look at her. "I don't want to force you—"

"You're not," Renata interrupted. Her smile was sweet, but her tone was firm. "Sybil put you in a difficult position. Besides, it's only your first day of cleaning, and I should be more charitable. Even Sybil deserves some grace." Renata glanced past Emmitt and settled her eyes on the open door. "You can bring the boxes in through the kitchen. Sybil hates to wait, and I've already talked too much."

"I don't think you've talked too much. Honestly, this is the first enjoyable conversation I've had today. I haven't wanted to slam my head into the wall once." Emmitt relaxed as the anxiety subsided. Renata didn't hate him. Not yet, at least.

"Do you say all the things that pop into your head?" Renata asked. Her eyes glistened with fascination.

"Not all the things. I've had to keep a lot to myself with Sybil. You're easy to talk to."

Renata grinned as she pointed to the door leading out of the kitchen. "I'll leave the door open for you and Andrew ... or Drew. Which does he prefer?"

Emmitt shrugged. "He's always been both. And he's not particular. I prefer Andrew, but you can call him whatever you want."

Renata nodded. "Well, you and ... Andrew will have to be careful. It's a tight fit, and my mother is vigilant and unforgiving. If things are knocked over or rearranged, she'll notice. I get an earful every time I put one of Sybil's boxes in the dining room. Mother always knows."

"I promise, we'll be extra careful. Thanks, Renata," Emmitt said.

Renata's smile faded as her eyes fixed on Emmitt. "Do you think you and your brother can help Sybil?"

Emmitt hesitated. His eyes widened as he struggled to maintain a measured tone. "We're going to try. Andrew is determined to keep her focused. I hope we can help. I realize—hearing myself—I don't sound hopeful, but that's more of a personal failing. It's one of many personal failings. You'll probably notice a pattern after a while."

Renata attempted to stifle another giggle. "I didn't mean to put you on the spot, but at least you're being honest."

"Andrew and I will do whatever we can to help your family, Renata."

"You really should get back to him, Emmitt," Renata said.

Emmitt enjoyed hearing his name spoken through her lips.

"Right. I'll be back. Thanks, again." He set his notebook back on the counter, flashed Renata one last smile, and turned to leave the kitchen.

With a burst of accomplishment, Emmitt walked back to Andrew and Sybil and shared the good news. Andrew smiled and lifted the first bin. Sybil's wide eyes and long lashes examined Emmitt. Her surprise seemed more suspicious than pleasant.

Andrew interrupted Sybil's stony stare with an enthusiastic, "Lead the way, Sybil."

Snapping to attention, Sybil quickly softened her face and led Andrew toward the kitchen. Emmitt grabbed the next bin on the stack and followed.

Navigating along the trail was difficult. Emmitt's anxiety heightened as he inched slowly past the precarious towers of Shannon Yates's boxed treasures. He urged Andrew several times to "go slower" and "be careful." Andrew ignored Emmitt as he maneuvered effortlessly through the rows of boxes and mountainous piles. *Show off.*

They walked through both dining rooms, past the kitchen, and finally stopped in Renata's sitting room without leaving an avalanche in their wake.

"One more time." Andrew smiled at Emmitt as he set down the first plastic bin and turned to walk back through the kitchen.

Emmitt let out a small grunt as he lowered his first box. He turned and wordlessly followed Andrew while Sybil and Renata looked on from opposite ends of the room.

On the second trip back from Sybil's bedroom, Emmitt let out an audible puff of breath as he felt the beads of sweat trickle down his back.

"You need to work out, Emmitt," Andrew said, as they walked down the hallway. "You're lucky to have a fast metabolism, especially considering all the junk you eat, but it won't last forever. I'll get you a gym membership, so you can build more muscle and stamina. We can go together."

"Not ... necessary ... I'm good," Emmitt panted. "Hey ... does your cleaning service ... remove pit stains?"

"Yep," Andrew said cheerfully. "They'll remove any stains. I picked the best. I had to account for the fact that you would be wearing my shirts."

Emmitt smirked as he followed his brother back to the room. Once they finished placing the boxes in the den, which Renata called her "sitting room," Emmitt could fully appreciate the contrast of the family's living arrangements. Each of the Yates women appeared to have their own designated spaces. From what they had experienced in the living and dining rooms, Shannon Yates's sections contained an overgrowth of items. The hoard swelled and spread until entire portions of the house had to be abandoned. Despite everything, Shannon persisted in trying to establish a way to reach her possessions. There was little organization other than the filled hutches and curios, and the only cleared space surrounded the altar to her husband.

Sybil Yates built literal walls to blockade any potential visitors. There was a semblance of organization, but there were barriers that made her bedroom completely impregnable. Shannon, at least, had paths that led Emmitt and Andrew throughout the house. Accessing Sybil's bedroom would require a complete dismantling of her defenses.

While surveying the sitting room, Emmitt was certain that Renata's inner sanctum could be featured in a magazine. The kitchen was hers, and it was pristine. The sitting room was also clean and organized. One green velvet sofa and two floral armchairs were arranged on a large, ornate rug. The curtains were the same deep green velvet as the sofa. Renata kept them open and tied back with heavy golden cords, letting a burst of sunlight into the room. Emmitt realized this was the first time he had seen sunlight in the dark and claustrophobic house.

There was a functional brick fireplace and a built-in bookshelf that was half-filled with books. The open shelves displayed vases filled with fresh-cut flowers. There were almost a dozen potted plants placed throughout the room, adding an abundance of life and color to the already vibrant space.

The only display of excess hung on the walls. Artwork filled every bit of wall space in Renata's sitting room. Framed family photos and portraits hung alongside oil and acrylic paintings of various sizes. Emmitt's eyes surveyed the works of art. He wondered if they were valuable or merely sentimental. He guessed the former but knew it would be rude to ask.

Andrew turned to Renata, who was standing by a closed door on the opposite side of the room. "Thank you for allowing us to use your room, Renata. We appreciate your kindness and understanding."

Renata nodded silently. She moved closer to the door. Emmitt wondered if she was attempting an exit.

Sybil stopped her before she could grab the handle. "Where are you going, sis?" Renata froze as Sybil questioned her. "Since we're already here, why don't you stay? It's your room, after all. No need to hide in your bedroom. Sit with us. Be social." Sybil smiled sweetly at Renata.

"It's your decision, Renata," Andrew said. "We'd love to have you join us, but I understand if you don't want to be involved today."

Renata looked over at Emmitt, who stood behind his brother and Sybil. Emmitt smiled mischievously and rolled his eyes. Renata looked back at Andrew with a hesitant smile and agreed to stay. She walked slowly to one of the floral armchairs and sat, quietly studying the brothers and Sybil. Emmitt could feel her eyes on him as Drew Key took over.

"Alright, Sybil, we'll set aside three areas: items to keep, items to donate, and items to toss." Drew pointed to three spots on the rug. "We'll need a few trash bags. Sybil, do you know where we can find some?"

"No ..." Sybil said. "That's not something I do. Renata? Do we have trash bags?"

Renata was already up and nearing the open door leading into the kitchen. "I'll get some," she said.

She disappeared into the kitchen, reappearing within seconds. She handed the bags to Andrew and walked to Emmitt to hand him his notebook.

"You left this on the counter," she said. "I thought you might want it back."

"Thanks," Emmitt whispered.

Sybil pestered Renata. "Did you have a peek inside? What did he say about me?"

Renata frowned at Sybil and shook her head. "I didn't look inside. That would be intrusive."

Sybil let out an exasperated sigh. "You're no fun, Renata."

Emmitt silently contemplated the efficacy of taking notes during the cleanup effort. If Renata had been intrusive, she would have seen that his notes on Sybil were wholly uncharitable. Worse, she would have discovered that he had taken notes on her too. He had jotted down his first impression of Renata as he ate a slice of pumpkin pie at Gigi's Diner with Andrew the day before. He hadn't been vulgar, but his descriptions were pretentious and poetic. *Mortifyingly* pretentious and poetic.

As they worked with Sybil, Emmitt's involvement would require a strong emphasis on performing physical tasks. Moving containers and boxes meant putting down his notes. If Emmitt was going to risk Sybil stealing his notebook, he either needed to be more clinical and polite in his note taking, or he needed to drop the notebook entirely and focus on cleaning and organizing. He knew the safest option was quietly hauling boxes at the Yates house while keeping his notes safely hidden in Andrew's car.

Emmitt watched Renata walk silently to the armchair and sit. Andrew thanked her for her help and turned back to Sybil.

"Here we go. First bin." Andrew opened the lid, and Sybil peered inside.

"Hmm. Where to start …" Sybil reached in slowly and pulled out a curling iron.

"Keep, donate, or toss?" Andrew asked.

Sybil paused and looked at the curling iron. She turned it over in her hands, studying it. "Well, I'm not sure. I've had this forever. I remember using it for some animal charity event in Santa Barbara … dogs or birds or something. It gave me perfectly beachy waves. It's all the tabloids talked about for a week."

Andrew put a hand on her shoulder. "Sybil. Keep, donate, or toss?"

"Keep? Is that okay, Drew?" Sybil asked.

"It's important for you to decide, Sybil," Andrew said.

"Keep." Sybil handed the curling iron to Andrew, who placed it on the rug in the designated spot.

Sybil continued. She reached in and brought out another curling iron. "Oh, I can't get rid of this one. I took it with me on a trip to Bali, and even with the humidity, my curls held all day. So, keep." She handed it to Andrew.

Sybil pulled out another curling iron. "You guys," she giggled, "this is getting embarrassing, but I can't get rid of this one either. On my last trip to Paris—"

"Excuse me, Sybil?" Emmitt asked, hoping to sound deferential. "When was the last time you used any of these curling irons?"

Sybil tilted her head and gazed upward. "Hmm … maybe a couple years ago."

"Six years." Renata's voice was gentle and cautious. "That was the last time you went to Paris. We went to Bali with Mother twelve years ago. The charity event in Santa Barbara supported an exotic bird sanctuary, and that was eight years ago."

"But I didn't remember where I put them," Sybil whined. "Everything gets jumbled around every time we move. Now that I know where they are, I can use them again. Anyway, Drew said I get to decide, and I want to keep them."

Drew intervened. "I think what Renata and Emmitt are getting at is the fact that you can clearly maintain a professional and glamorous appearance, even without access to your older hair styling tools. Did you use a curling iron this morning?"

Sybil nodded as she bounced some of her blonde curls in the palm of her hand. "Yes. I used a tapered ceramic curling wand for this look."

Andrew continued. "So we know you can look effortlessly captivating without the older products."

Sybil's face grew radiant as she soaked in Drew's compliment. "Thank you for adding some perspective, Drew. And thank you for noticing my hard work. It may seem effortless, but I am very regimented when it comes to maintaining my glamorous exterior."

"I'm sure you're talented enough to make any styling tool work. And I see that you have no shortage of quality products. Would it be fair to say that, as you've experimented with different curling irons, you've gotten better at picking out quality tools that work for you?"

"Yes," Sybil asserted confidently.

"Then perhaps these older curling irons are unnecessary in the new life you're cultivating. You should be confident in your own abilities and talents. These are just tools ... You're the artist."

"Drew, you are so right! I never thought about it that way."

Sybil rifled through the bin. She picked out dozens of curling irons, straighteners, and hairdryers, and placed them all in the "donate" section on the floor. She took the Bali curling iron and tossed it on the pile. Looking at the final one, she hesitated.

She looked up at Drew. "I loved my beachy curls. Can I keep this one?"

Andrew crouched down next to Sybil. "I can't answer that for you. I am curious, though, did you love what it did to your hair, or did you love the way you felt when you were featured positively in the tabloids?"

"Both," Sybil said, without hesitation or introspection.

Emmitt put his hand over his mouth to suppress a growing urge to laugh. Renata noticed his internal struggle and offered him a small smirk in solidarity.

Unaware of the silent interaction between Emmitt and Renata, Andrew addressed Sybil. "Then I think you have your answer. And look at the progress you've made! The first bin is almost empty, and there's only one item in the 'keep' pile. You've done amazing work, Sybil."

"Thanks, Drew." Sybil blushed. She glanced at Emmitt before turning to look at her sister. "And Renata and Emmitt ... thank you for your help."

After a brief, stunned silence, Emmitt recovered enough to mutter, "Yeah, no problem ... You're making good progress, Sybil."

Renata sat frozen in astonishment as Sybil continued to work.

Chapter Ten

After two hours of sorting, Sybil reduced her kept items to two bins. With additional pressing, praise, and flattery, Drew Key convinced Sybil to halve her kept items once again. Having parted with three-quarters of her first four bins, Sybil was radiant and giddy. Drew Key continued to heap embellished compliments onto her. It was hyperbolic, but it was effective.

Andrew encouraged Sybil to continue. Emmitt entrusted his notebook to Renata before helping Andrew bring in two bins, then four, then two again. As Sybil sorted, the donation and trash piles grew. By the end of the day, four empty bins were stacked neatly in the corner of Renata's sitting room. Five bins were filled with donations, and only three bins were carried back to Sybil's room.

As Andrew moved Sybil's kept items back into her bedroom, Emmitt gripped his notebook under his right arm and helped Renata carry five trash bags to the outdoor garbage bins. Emmitt piled up the bags and pushed down on the lid of the overstuffed bin, then looked back and saw a slight smile on Renata's face.

"What do you think of the progress?" Emmitt asked.

"It's good," Renata answered.

Emmitt wanted to press further, but he was tired. Renata must have been worn out too. She'd had no interest in taking part in the cleanup. Emmitt had pushed her to participate. Renata could have sulked, as Emmitt reasoned *he* would have done, but she didn't. She helped. Renata bagged trash with Emmitt, placed sorted items back into bins, and brought in bottles of water as they worked.

Renata, like Emmitt and Andrew, patiently listened to Sybil tell stories about every item she touched: the custom boar bristle hairbrush she borrowed from a stylist during a photoshoot in Sydney, the pink compact mirror with painted poodles she brought with her to Paris, the gold embroidered *omamori* charm she bought from a twenty-four-hour convenience store next to a Shinto shrine in Osaka. Everything was significant.

If Shannon is like Sybil—if we're forced to go through each item individually—how long will it take to clear the house? Emmitt allowed the distressing thought to dissipate as he looked back at Renata.

"What do we do about the boxes?" Renata whispered. Emmitt wasn't sure if she was addressing him or merely talking to herself.

Which boxes? He thought for a moment, then considered the stacked boxes in the driveway. "Sybil's new storage organization system ... in rose gold ... with the label maker?"

Renata remained serious. "Yes. I don't want the boxes in my sitting room, but if she keeps asking ... and whining, I'll have a hard time saying no. I can't just wait and move them into the dining room like I normally do. They're too heavy for me to lift, and there are too many of them. And you and Andrew couldn't put them anywhere in the house without crushing whatever they're stacked on top of."

"So, you don't want them in your room, and we can't pile them on top of the other clutter in the house. Can we just leave the boxes in the driveway for now?"

"I don't think so. We usually keep the driveway gate open during the day. Even if we close it to hide the boxes, people are curious, and the neighbors already know who we are. Keeping the boxes outside too long might cause someone to call the city. It's happened before. Not here ... not yet."

Emmitt nodded. "And if some nosy neighbor calls the city to say they're concerned about the state of the house, we're finished before we've made any noticeable progress."

"Exactly."

"And your rooms are the only clean rooms left?" He already knew the answer. Emmitt was stalling, hoping an idea would come to him.

"Yes. I could call Uncle James ..." Renata frowned as she spoke. "I wish I didn't have to bother him over this. He does a lot for us already."

Emmitt briefly considered offering his own apartment to solve Renata's dilemma, but immediately recognized it was a terrible idea. It was unprofessional, as Andrew would say, impractical, and too presumptuous. They didn't know each other, and Renata might interpret the offer as an awkward overture. Emmitt knew he would have meant it as an overture, though he would never state it outright. He liked Renata. He felt drawn to her, and he suspected she wasn't entirely put off by him. Renata was easy to talk to. She was attractive, and she hated Sybil's antics more than he did. Emmitt knew offering his apartment as a storage unit would be nothing more than an embarrassing attempt to garner Renata's favor, and he was determined to keep silent on the matter.

"Do you think I should?" Renata asked.

Emmitt, still lost in thought and not entirely paying attention, attempted to channel the words of Drew Key. "Do *you* think you should?"

Renata's deep-blue eyes and soft voice penetrated Emmitt. "That doesn't work on me. I'm immune to self-help rhetoric. I'm asking for your opinion."

"Well then, I guess I should stop trying to guide you toward ascendancy," he smirked. "Sorry for that. I got distracted trying to think of a solution, but I couldn't come up with anything."

Renata grinned at Emmitt. "My uncle. You met him. I can call him … I'm asking if *you* think I should call him."

Emmitt considered the question seriously. "Would he be mad? Day one of cleanup, and we need to call him over to haul twenty boxes away … It seems like the kind of thing that might make him upset, but you certainly know him better than I do."

Renata shrugged. "He would do it for me. That isn't the problem."

"What is the problem?"

"I don't know how serious Sybil is."

"And if Sybil isn't serious?" Emmitt asked.

"Then I've embarrassed myself trying to help her. I hate feeling like I'm being fooled or taken advantage of."

"You shouldn't feel embarrassed if it turns out Sybil lied to you. It wouldn't be your fault if she betrayed your trust."

"It *would* be my fault. I know what kind of person she is. I know I shouldn't trust her. If my uncle is stuck with a warehouse full of Sybil's boxes at the museum, that would be on me." Renata crossed her arms and gazed downward, studying a long crack in the concrete.

Emmitt tried to be encouraging. "You brought up a legitimate concern about the city being involved. There isn't room in the house to store the boxes, and Sybil refuses to return them. You can let your uncle know Sybil made steady progress today, but you can't say for certain if she can keep it up."

"That doesn't sound convincing," Renata said, looking up at Emmitt.

"It's the truth."

Renata sighed. "Alright. I'll call."

"Good luck," Emmitt said, then paused. "Do you need me to stay out here for moral support? Or should I head inside? I'm here to help guide you on your journey, after all. Tell me what you need me to do." Emmitt couldn't help himself. He grinned shamelessly at Renata.

She smiled and tilted her head down slightly as she looked deeply into his eyes. "Emmitt, could you dial the number and hold my phone for me?"

Emmitt's grin faded as he let in a quick breath and tried not to flush. "If that's what you want …"

Renata's innocent expression instantly faltered as she broke into laughter. "No. I was only joking. I'm not quite as needy as Sybil. You can go inside, Emmitt. I think … if I concentrate, I can make the call myself."

Emmitt let out a loud cackle. "Alright," he said as his laughter waned. "I deserved that. But you can still yell for me if you end up needing my help to dial the number. I won't judge you."

Emmitt turned and walked through the back door into the kitchen. As he entered Renata's sitting room, an idea occurred to him.

"Andrew?" he called as he walked into the room. "Do you think it would be okay if I moved the donation bins into the back of your car? I mean, only if Sybil's ready for me to pack them." Emmitt smiled at Sybil, realizing it was her permission he needed.

Sybil smiled back. "They're ready to go."

"What's the rush?" Andrew asked.

"Renata is asking her uncle if he can store the boxes that are in the driveway until we clear Sybil's office. I thought, if he could visualize what … *Sybil* accomplished today—" Emmitt caught himself before saying *we*, "—he might not see this as a setback."

"If Renata's calling, he'll help," Sybil said, rolling her eyes. "He'll do anything for her. And why wouldn't he? Renata is such an angel." Sybil's insincerity dripped from her lips.

Emmitt couldn't understand what caused Sybil's altered demeanor until she glared at him and addressed him directly.

"But why would she talk to you about my boxes? Are you two conspiring? And who called it a setback? Is that what you're calling it, or is that what Renata said?"

Emmitt cursed himself for ever opening his mouth. He reeled from the sudden violent shift and wondered if there was any way to correct course and calm Sybil before Renata returned.

"I … I …" Emmitt stammered, still unsure of what to say. "I said setback … Renata never said setback … I misspoke. I'm sorry. Renata is worried someone in the neighborhood might see all the boxes in the driveway and notify the city. We weren't conspiring. She wanted to help."

"Hmm." Sybil lifted her eyes in thought. "So, you think I suffered a setback? Why?" Sybil's entire face twisted into a pained expression. She lowered her brow and grimaced.

Emmitt realized he had genuinely hurt Sybil with one innocuous word. "I'm sorry, Sybil. I didn't know what else to call it. There are a lot of boxes out there—"

"I said I had a plan. My organization system is necessary for my eventual metamorphosis. Do you care if I turn into a butterfly or not, Emmitt?"

Emmitt didn't dare laugh. Sybil may have sounded ridiculous, but Emmitt was finally witnessing an honest reaction from her. It was fascinating and terrifying. He needed to tread lightly.

"I want you to be a butterfly, Sybil. I'm sorry I hurt your feelings."

"Emmitt didn't intend to upset you, Sybil, but he doesn't always think before he speaks," Andrew said, finally joining the conversation. "'Setback' was the wrong word to use, right, Emmitt?"

"Right," Emmitt said in a low voice. He still wasn't sure if Sybil would let it go, but he was grateful to have Andrew step in.

"Can you forgive Emmitt, Sybil?" Andrew asked.

"Yes, Drew," Sybil said. "Eventually."

"Would you allow Emmitt and me to move the donations and empty bins into my car?"

"Yes," Sybil sighed.

Emmitt breathed in, relieved that the conversation seemed to be, for the moment, over. With Sybil's approval, they loaded the four empty and five full containers into Andrew's SUV. Emmitt kept his notebook tightly pinned under his arm until he reached Andrew's car, then tossed it on the floor of the passenger seat with a silent vow to never take it back with him to the Yates house.

Back in the sitting room, Emmitt, Andrew, and Sybil waited for Renata.

Entering the room, Renata's eyes darted at the three faces that stared at her. They finally settled questioningly on Emmitt. Emmitt wanted to explain himself. He wanted to apologize, but he didn't want to embarrass Renata.

"Did your uncle agree to store the boxes?" Emmitt's face burned with guilt.

"Yes," Renata replied slowly.

"Great," was all Emmitt could say.

Sybil leaned back on Renata's couch and propped her feet on the coffee table. A small grin formed on her face as she slid into the conversation. "Why, of all people, would you call Uncle James?"

Renata frowned wearily at Sybil. "You left boxes in the driveway ... there's nowhere else to put them."

"Isn't there?" Sybil gazed exaggeratedly around Renata's room. "Really, Renata? No space at all? Interesting." Staring at her sister, Sybil continued. "You know, Mom doesn't want to deal with Uncle James. She doesn't want him on the property. She was clear ... Wasn't she clear, Renata?"

Renata's jaw tightened. Her eyes burned on Sybil.

Sybil smiled and looked at Emmitt. "And bringing Emmitt into a private family discussion is inappropriate. The poor thing was running around frantically trying to clear away bins and fill Drew's car with donations, just to help *you*. What did you do to him, Renata?"

Renata shrunk back into the doorframe as she glanced at Emmitt. She was more in the kitchen than in the sitting room. Her face flushed crimson, but her mouth stayed shut.

Emmitt felt a fury rise within him, but it was Andrew who spoke.

"You've made excellent progress today, Sybil. You had an admirable amount of energy and initiative, but also a good deal of support from your sister." His gray eyes wandered to Renata, who flushed an even deeper red. "This house belongs to three unique individuals, who all need to feel supported." Andrew looked back at Sybil and smiled. "We're creating a sanctuary for you, Sybil. But Renata has her own sanctuary she wants to maintain. For her to do that, she needs your uncle's support. Renata has come up with an idea that keeps your organization system stored away until you need it, and she may have given us more time to work with you and your mother without the interference of city officials. She's ensuring Emmitt and I can continue to come over and assist you."

Sybil softened. "Of course. Right again, Drew." Emmitt noticed her top lip twitch. "Sorry, Renata. I guess I got carried away when I found out you were discussing family matters with Emmitt. If you wanted to discuss my organization system, you should have talked to me. Like Mom said, you don't need any help, so there really isn't a reason for you to discuss anything with him." Her gaze had shifted. Her mouth was smiling, and there was no hint of anger in her voice, but her eyes were daggers on Emmitt. "Are we done, Drew?"

"We've made good progress today," Andrew said. "Emmitt and I will wait outside to help your uncle load up the boxes, then we'll swing by the donation center to drop off your items. We'll be back in two days."

Renata led them out and stood apart from them in the driveway. When her uncle arrived with a large white box truck, Emmitt and Andrew worked in silence. They loaded the boxes onto the truck, then shook hands with the quiet, scowling man.

The sun was setting as Emmitt entered the passenger side of Andrew's SUV and clicked his seatbelt. Looking across the street, he could see Renata speaking to her uncle with a red face and gesturing hands. As the car pulled away, Emmitt watched as Renata's uncle drew his arms around her to comfort her as she sobbed.

Chapter Eleven

Renata was quiet and withdrawn the first two weeks after her uncle arrived at the house with a moving truck to pack Sybil's organization system. Though she avoided speaking to Emmitt, she continued to provide water and began ordering lunch for the group as the workdays extended from mornings into late afternoons. She still helped Emmitt move Sybil's sorted clutter into donation boxes and trash bags, but she no longer accompanied him when he left the room to throw out Sybil's garbage. Sometimes Emmitt would catch her looking at him, and sometimes she would smile or laugh at his jokes. Though her silent treatment was mild and polite, Emmitt was determined to leave her alone and let her decide if she would ever speak to him directly again.

At the beginning of the third week, Emmitt's hope stirred. As they passed through the kitchen, they noticed Renata baking a new cookie recipe and wondering aloud if someone would try them to determine whether they were worth making again for various upcoming holiday dinners and museum functions. Andrew remarked on the delicious aroma, but he regretfully declined a taste due to his self-imposed dietary restrictions. As a small frown set on Renata's face, Andrew quickly pointed at Emmitt, explaining that he was the dessert expert of the Key family.

Sybil trailed into the kitchen behind the brothers and immediately insisted that she also needed to adhere to unspecified dietary restrictions and refused to sample a cookie. Emmitt, who had never refused an offer of food, enthusiastically offered to taste them. He ate one, complimented Renata's baking abilities, then asked if he could eat Andrew's and Sybil's cookies as well. Despite her lukewarm grudge, Renata's face lit up as he asked to take a few more into the sitting room to snack on. By the end of the workday, Renata had neatly packed a half-dozen cookies and handed them to Emmitt with a silent smirk.

Now, as the third week was ending, Emmitt found himself again at the Yates house, sifting through Sybil's boxes in Renata's sitting room. They had sorted three boxes worth of items into the usual piles.

As Sybil opened the fourth box, she let out a small squeal. "Oh," Sybil gasped. "I have to keep these. I can't get rid of anything from this box."

She lifted a small object wrapped in pink tissue paper and carefully removed the wrapping. Inside the pink paper was a white teacup made of bone china. The rim and handle of the cup were trimmed in gold, and large yellow roses with dark-green leaves decorated the outside and the inside of the cup.

"It's beautiful, Sybil," Renata said. Her tone was as despondent as it was dreamy. "I'm glad you found all your tea sets."

"Me too." Sybil's eyes fixed in hushed rapture. She let out a satisfied sigh and gently stroked the gold trim of the cup with her finger. As she continued to examine it, she said absently, "Didn't Grandpa get you the same tea set, Renata? Where's yours?"

Emmitt noticed Renata's neck tense at Sybil's question. "You don't remember?" Renata asked.

Sybil momentarily pried her eyes from the cup and looked up in thought. They flashed in remembrance of something. It didn't seem to be a pleasant memory. "Oh, right … It happened so long ago, I had nearly forgotten. Never mind."

Having seen the box of old treasures, Sybil became enraptured. Andrew clearly sensed a standstill and proposed they break for lunch.

While Sybil continued unwrapping cups, saucers, trays, and teapots from various sets, Emmitt, Andrew, and Renata placed donations into empty boxes and filled trash bags with broken and unusable items. Andrew lifted one of the filled donation boxes and left to load it into his car, while Emmitt grabbed two trash bags and exited through the kitchen door to throw them into the outdoor garbage bins.

As he turned back toward the house after tossing the bags, he noticed Renata had followed him outside. He stood frozen as she walked nearer to him.

"I'm angry with you." She was now standing so close that, as she shifted her body, she nudged her left arm and shoulder gently into Emmitt's side.

Emmitt thought she looked more hurt than angry. It was like looking into Sybil's face when he called her organization system a setback. Emmitt hadn't forgotten that look.

"I'm sorry. I got too excited, and I guess I didn't account for Sybil's reaction. I should have kept my mouth shut and let you handle it." Emmitt looked down at Renata as she studied his face.

Renata sighed deeply. "It doesn't matter who told Sybil. She would've reacted the same way if I told her … possibly worse. It's not like I could have kept it hidden. The boxes needed to be removed, and Sybil needed to be told. I just don't like being surprised. I hate being singled out and stared at, and I hate when Sybil tries to embarrass me. When I panic, I can't get any words out. I looked like an idiot."

"I don't think you looked like an idiot. I think Sybil looked like a bully. Anyway, I should have stepped in and said something to Sybil when she put you on the spot," Emmitt said. "I should have done something."

Renata smiled, but she appeared doubtful. "That probably wouldn't have helped. I think your problem is the opposite of mine. You say too much when you're flustered. I can tell when Sybil gets on your nerves. You tap your fingers and shift in the chair, and then you make a joke ... usually at Andrew's expense. Sometimes at Sybil's, when you know it'll go over her head."

A rush of warmth filled Emmitt's cheeks. Renata had watched him. She noticed his habits.

He struggled to remain composed. "I thought I had done a pretty good job of controlling myself the last few weeks. I have been trying ... and failing, apparently."

Renata shook her head. "You're not the only one who's failing. I kept trying to work up the courage to talk to you. I was sure I'd be able to do it last week, but I kept chickening out. So now I'm angrier at myself for being a coward."

"You're not a coward," Emmitt insisted. "I wanted to say something, but I seem to put my foot in my mouth whenever I speak."

"Well, I'm glad you're still here, despite your *setback* with Sybil."

Emmitt groaned. "God, she told you?"

"She was pretty worked up about it. No one can have a moment's peace if Sybil is restless. She has to let everyone know how victimized she is."

"I'm sorry," Emmitt said. "I didn't even think when I said it. I didn't realize she would be so angry."

"You couldn't have known. But Sybil has finally calmed down, so I've been able to calm down, and I don't want to be mad at you, so I won't ignore you anymore."

"I missed our trash talks," Emmitt said.

Renata laughed. "Me too."

"So ... since we're talking again, can I ask you something?"

She lifted an eyebrow at Emmitt. "You want to know about the tea set?"

"Yes, please," Emmitt said sheepishly, shifting his eyes away from her.

Renata smirked. "Eventually, you'll need to learn restraint."

Emmitt glanced back at Renata and grinned. "I'd prefer if I didn't have to learn that lesson today."

"Fine." Renata sighed. "We each received a tea set from my grandfather when we were little. I was five, so Sybil would have been eight ... possibly nine. You saw Sybil's. Mine was the same design, but it had pink roses instead of yellow. Grandpa had accidentally mixed up our favorite colors, so he gave Sybil yellow and me pink. Sybil thought we should trade, but I didn't want to. She didn't think it was fair. She broke my pink tea set ... the cups, saucers, and teapot. Dad tried to glue all the pieces back together—he was always good at fixing our broken things—but it was impossible for even him to repair it."

"Why didn't you want to trade?"

Renata stared at Emmitt in surprise. "Are you defending Sybil?"

"No," Emmitt said. "I didn't mean to defend her ... but you said your grandpa mixed up your favorite colors. Why wouldn't you want the yellow one?"

"Because Grandpa didn't give me the yellow one. He gave me the pink one. It would have been rude to trade. We should have both been grateful and kept the one that he gave us."

"I won't argue," Emmitt said. "It was shitty for Sybil to break your tea set."

"Yes, it was. You don't think it would have been rude for us to trade?" Renata asked with a look of bewilderment.

"It depends, I guess. What kind of person was your grandpa?"

Renata smiled. "Grandpa was everyone's favorite person ... even Sybil's. He and Grandma would always have tea parties with us when we visited their house. We'd watch old cartoons together, and he'd buy a gallon of ice cream, and get three spoons, and we'd eat until we were nearly sick. He and I would watch Sybil rehearse her lines, and we would plant roses and vegetables in his garden."

"He sounds like a great person," Emmitt said.

"He was. I guess he was also the kind of person who wouldn't have minded if Sybil and I traded tea sets."

"You didn't want to risk hurting his feelings. You're considerate."

"Maybe," Renata said. "We should probably go back inside. I wouldn't want Sybil to get curious and demand to know what I was doing to you behind the trash bins."

"Yeah." Emmitt breathed out, trying not to flush at the thought.

Emmitt walked to the kitchen entrance and opened the door for Renata. As they entered the sitting room, Sybil continued to occupy herself with unwrapping her tea sets. She had already taken four sets out of the box and arranged them neatly on the coffee table: yellow rose, navy and white striped, mint with pink cherry blossoms, and lavender floral chintz. Pink tissue paper littered the floor surrounding the box. Andrew sat on the green velvet sofa, looking at his phone. Emmitt assumed he was reading messages from his other clients.

He looked up and smiled as they entered. "I'm ordering lunch today. What are we having?" Andrew said.

Sybil paid no attention to Andrew. She was attempting to find the matching pieces of an embellished silver tea set.

As Emmitt looked at Sybil's childlike tenderness toward her beloved possessions, a thought leapt into his mind. "What if we had a tea party today?"

Sybil stopped what she was doing and twisted her head and shoulders to look at Emmitt. He could feel Renata's eyes join her sister's suspicious glare.

"Are you making fun of me?" Sybil scowled.

Emmitt shook his head. "No. I mean it. You can drink out of those cups, right? I mean, we might have to wash them first … or are they just for decoration? I don't have experience with this kind of thing."

"You're serious?" Renata asked.

"Yeah. Andrew can order sandwiches—and a protein wrap for himself—and, if Sybil wants to pick a tea set, we can brew some tea … or do you steep tea? Look, if it's a stupid idea, we don't have to do it." Emmitt quickly realized his ignorance of basic tea party etiquette.

"I don't think it's stupid." Renata turned and looked at her sister. "Sybil?"

"Hmm." Sybil looked carefully at the various sets lovingly laid out on the coffee table. "It's an informal occasion, so we can use the lavender chintz for lunch ... but I'm not washing anything. I've already worked hard today."

"I'll wash them," Renata said.

"That's fine," Sybil replied. "Just don't let Emmitt help wash. It's not that I don't like you, Emmitt. I just don't trust you. No offense."

"None taken." Emmitt smirked. "Am I allowed to drink tea from the cup once it's clean?"

Sybil sucked her teeth and narrowed her eyes at Emmitt. "Only if you're careful. Can you be careful, Emmitt?"

"I'll be careful."

One corner of Sybil's lip curled upwards. "I don't know if I believe you. Do you believe him, Renata?"

Renata looked at Sybil as she reached down to grab the lavender chintz cups. "Yes. I think Emmitt can be careful."

Andrew looked up from his phone and glanced at Renata as she moved toward the kitchen.

Renata smiled at Andrew and said, "Sybil is very protective of her tea sets."

Andrew grinned and nodded, then shifted his attention back to his phone.

Sybil continued. "You don't seem like the type of person who has a gentle touch. I'm not saying you're clumsy, but I think you might be careless. Some things don't deserve to be broken. Some things are too exquisite to be cracked by your carelessness, Emmitt." Her eyes shifted and held on the back of Renata, then darted across the room and fixed on Emmitt. Emmitt finally understood. Sybil wasn't being protective of the tea set. "Swear that you'll be careful," Sybil demanded.

She knew. Why hadn't she said anything? Why hadn't she been more explicit with her teasing? The more time Emmitt spent with Sybil, the more confounding she became. For as bitter and jealous as she was, Sybil still had the desire to safeguard her sister. And despite hating Emmitt, she wasn't stopping him from pursuing Renata.

Emmitt let his eyes wander to Renata as she walked through the kitchen door, then turned his gaze back to Sybil. "I swear, I will be very careful." He fixed a determined look on his face as he held Sybil's stare.

"Good." All the tension melted from Sybil's face. She lifted the lavender chintz teapot and giggled. "Let's have a tea party!"

Chapter Twelve

Emmitt sat at his kitchen table with his laptop open. He stared at the screen while his mind wandered. As he sipped his coffee and crunched his buttered toast, his thoughts repeatedly returned to the Yates sisters.

Andrew and Emmitt had visited the house more than a dozen times over the past month. Drew continued to encourage and praise Sybil, Shannon continued to be absent, and Renata continued to allow Sybil to use her sitting room to rummage through bins and boxes. Although her office remained untouched, Sybil had made progress by clearing half of the hoard from her bedroom. She was a slow sorter, and her pace had continued to decline with each visit from Andrew and Emmitt, but she remained determined. Sometimes, Emmitt wondered if she was purposely stalling.

Sybil would still bat her impossibly long lashes at Andrew, while Andrew remained politely detached. To Sybil, every generic platitude uttered from Drew Key's lips was life-changing, inspirational, or thought-provoking. Andrew's attention continued to fuel Sybil, but Emmitt sensed Sybil was acutely aware of his brother's underlying disinterest. Perhaps she thought she could wear him down, or perhaps she was punishing Andrew by dragging her feet. Emmitt didn't mind the sluggish pace. The more time Sybil spent sorting, the more time Emmitt could spend with Renata.

Emmitt both relished and dreaded the thoughts that entered his mind when he reflected on his time spent with the younger Yates sister. He knew he had cracked open a door that should have remained shut. Andrew's words clanged in his head. *Unprofessional*. But was he unprofessional? They had done nothing but talk. Whatever Emmitt felt was irrelevant; there was no sign Renata felt the same way. They joked and confided and commiserated. Nothing more.

He had listened to Renata complain about Sybil's excess and criticize her mother's lack of participation. The two had even shared stories about their older siblings' weird habits: Renata told Emmitt that Sybil went to bed every night with a full face of freshly applied makeup, and Emmitt told Renata that Andrew snored so loud that, as children, their parents had to move him into the downstairs guest bedroom so the rest of the family could have a night of uninterrupted sleep.

After telling her about Andrew's snoring, Emmitt had to pause and reflect. Andrew was still his brother, and if Emmitt was going to embarrass him, he figured he should also be honest about himself. So, Emmitt had admitted to Renata that, as a young child, he used to have night terrors. He would run into his parents' room, breathlessly crying, only to be scolded by his mother for his lack of focus during the meditation sessions that were meant to teach her sons to lucid dream. She maintained that, at six years old, Emmitt should have been capable of guiding his nightmares to a peaceful resolution. Night terrors were for toddlers.

He remembered her words and relayed them to Renata in the same tone that dripped with his mother's sweet condescension. "I'm doing this for your benefit, Emmie. I'm carving out time I don't have in my schedule for you, and I need my sleep to recover from your demanding antics. My clients expect me to be my best self, but I can't be my best self if I have to take care of you all hours of the day *and* night ... Drew never had these problems."

His father would take Emmitt back to his bedroom and tuck him in, whispering, "I'm sorry. I'm so sorry." The defeated look, coupled with the quiet, lamenting apology, scared Emmitt almost as much as the nightmares. It scared him more than Serenity.

Once his father left his room, Emmitt would tiptoe downstairs to Andrew. His brother would gently reprimand him, but he would always let him crawl under the covers next to him. Despite the roaring sound caused by Andrew's deviated septum, Emmitt could always sleep through his snoring. In the morning, his father would pick him up and carry him back to his own bed during Serenity's morning run.

When Emmitt told this to Renata, she looked solemnly at him, then smiled. It was like Sybil's smile, except hers reached her eyes and lit up her entire face.

She teased Emmitt with a tenderness that caused him to question his professional resolve to remain platonic. "You love your brother."

He flushed and nodded his head. "Yeah ... but he's still a pain."

The thought of the encounter brought a subdued smile to Emmitt's face. He caught himself drifting and tried to nudge himself back to reality, but he continued to stare blankly at the screen. *She pushed her whole body into me to get my attention. She joked about what she'd do to me behind the trash bins. She sent me home with cookies. Even when she was mad at me, she was kind. Does any of that mean anything?*

It was foolish for Emmitt to fixate on trivialities. He forced himself to turn his attention back to his work.

It was work he had neglected for the last month. Although Emmitt was self-employed, his accomplishments couldn't match the achievements of his family. Drew Key ran in pseudo-celebrity circles, and his influence had continued to escalate over the last five years. Serenity Rivers-Key (who hadn't bothered to drop her married name after the divorce) was a genuine celebrity and a household name. She owned her own wellness magazine, she opened a chain of yoga studios in dozens of major cities across the country, and she manufactured her own brand of essential oils.

Tommy Key was a partner in one of the top corporate law firms in Michigan. Emmitt had begged to move in with him after the divorce, but his father argued there was more stability for nine-year-old Emmitt to stay in his childhood home, attend the same school, and be near Andrew (who, even at twelve, had refused to visit their father after he moved out of the state).

After graduating from college, Emmitt was aimless. His mother had offered him a job as a literary critic for her magazine, but three consecutive one-star reviews—and the impending threat of a fourth—had caused Emmitt to be brought in for questioning. After explaining that he had circled the word *manifesting* three hundred twenty-five times, *authentic* two hundred forty-seven times and *self-actualizing* one hundred thirty times within the first nine chapters of his mother's recently released self-help book, Emmitt was directed to Serenity's office.

When Emmitt refused to take a seat and loudly proclaimed that there was no difference in the messaging and persuasion techniques among motivational speakers, psychic mediums, hypnotists, magicians, FBI interrogators, and network marketing scammers, Serenity fired him. It was the worst week of his professional life, but at least he had humiliated Serenity. He never regretted that.

As a smug smile lifted his lips, Emmitt once again caught himself drifting. He stared past the letters on the glowing screen. This was his job now. It barely paid the bills, but every month he earned slightly more than the month that preceded it … except this month. This month, he had been busy with the Yates family.

He forced a glance at the paperback that laid unopened next to him on the table: *The Man Who Had All the Luck*. Emmitt sighed and looked back at his laptop.

He had established his own literary study guide website, where he provided broad overviews and chapter summaries of novels. For an additional charge, he would offer premade outlines for term papers. In Emmitt's mind, it was an ethical step above writing the papers outright.

Emmitt also posted long-form video essays of literary classics on the internet. His viewership was steadily growing as he continued to film and post his dissertations. He never revealed his face or name. Emmitt preferred anonymity. Andrew once suggested that seeking anonymity indicated some sort of underlying shame or guilt over his chosen profession. Emmitt wasn't ashamed, but he wasn't proud either. He enjoyed writing scripts and filming videos, and he appreciated his growing audience, but he still hoped for more.

"I can't do this right now." Emmitt sighed deeply and closed the laptop.

He tapped the table and finished his coffee, wondering what to do. As he sat for a moment, an idea came to him. He quickly grabbed his phone and dialed. After a few rings, a woman answered.

"Is Henry still there?" Emmitt asked.

"Yes, Emmitt. He's still here. Did you want to visit him?" the woman answered.

"Yes, please. I can be over in about ten minutes."

Emmitt hung up the phone. He hurriedly washed his breakfast dishes, put on a light jacket, grabbed the paperback off the table, and headed out the door. He walked three blocks to the facility.

When he opened the door, the woman at the counter smiled and gestured down the hall. "He's where he always is, Emmitt. It's unlocked for you."

"Thanks."

Emmitt quickened his pace down the hallway to Henry. When he reached the third stall, he opened the fence to greet him.

"Hey, Henry. I'm sorry it's been over a week since I visited ... I've been busy. Do you want to read with me?"

The old dog looked at Emmitt with sad eyes and nudged his hand for a pet. Emmitt crouched down and gently stroked the dog's head with his hand. He sat on the concrete floor, and the old mutt laid his head on Emmitt's lap.

As he read to Henry, Emmitt finally settled his restless mind. He read for thirty minutes, then talked to the dog about his recent conversations with Renata.

After an hour passed, Emmitt finally raised himself from the floor. "Bye, Henry. See you in a few days, unless someone finally realizes what a good boy you are. It'll happen soon, buddy."

He wished it could be him, but his apartment wouldn't allow dogs, and he barely had enough money to keep himself afloat. *Hopefully, the book will change things.*

Emmitt gave the dog a final scratch behind the ear and reluctantly turned to leave.

Chapter Thirteen

Another two weeks of cleaning had passed when the brothers were called back to the Yates' house for an unscheduled visit. Andrew received a call from Sybil the night before, saying she had an impromptu vacation planned for the rest of the week, and today was the only day of cleaning she could fit into her schedule. When Emmitt received the call from Andrew, who explained Sybil's plans, Emmitt reminded his brother that impromptu, by definition, meant unplanned. Andrew sighed at Emmitt's attempt to play a game of semantics and told his brother he'd be at his apartment by seven sharp.

They pulled up to the Yates house by seven thirty.

As Andrew reached to unfasten his seatbelt, Emmitt tapped his arm and leaned in, as if to whisper. "We're past two months," Emmitt said.

"Yeah."

"Do you think we can finish before the deadline?" Emmitt asked anxiously.

"Possibly."

"Are you going to ask for an extension?" Emmitt couldn't hide his growing annoyance at Andrew's one-word responses.

"Only if it's necessary. We have a few weeks left, Emmitt. There's no need to rush to ask for an extension."

Emmitt wished Andrew would share in just one of his many concerns. He wanted reassurance that they could continue their work. Emmitt was invested in the book … and Renata. Sybil was important too, he supposed, but her interest had waned. They had spent less time at the Yates' house over the previous two weeks, and there were days when Emmitt couldn't make an excuse or find an opportunity to speak to Renata privately.

"Emmitt." Andrew's voice startled him. "I asked if you were ready."

Emmitt thought for a moment longer, then asked, "Do you think it's a good idea to praise Sybil for doing the bare minimum? She's slowed down a lot since the first couple of weeks. We're lucky if she gets one box sorted before she's bored or distracted. And how many times has she claimed to have an important meeting with her team, which ends up cutting the day short? Three times? Four?"

Andrew looked at Emmitt. "Sybil is a client. We made a commitment to help her. It's part of our job. It's also part of our job to not interfere with her other responsibilities."

"We have a set schedule. It hasn't changed," Emmitt persisted. "She always waits to see how the day is going before she makes an excuse. She was fine working all day when she had you bending over and lifting boxes to make a pathway to her clothing racks, but just last week she stopped twenty minutes in. You were only gone for a couple minutes, but she pouted every second you ignored her … I'm just grateful she didn't ask me to bend over."

"There wouldn't be much to look at," Andrew joked. "But I shouldn't have taken a call from another client. He's new, and I wasn't sure what he considered an emergency. Turns out it was only a small fire I had to help put out, but it was an emergency to him." Andrew steadied his eyes on Emmitt. "It's the same with Sybil. What you or I measure as the bare minimum is not the same as Sybil's bare minimum. You've seen the house. It's chaos. It's unlivable by any standard. Sybil deserves praise for the effort she's made, even if it has slowed down a little."

"It's just …" Emmitt paused and considered his words carefully. "Sybil already has a high opinion of herself. Sometimes she terrorizes Renata for fun. She brings up Melody, for no reason, other than to mock her. And how the hell does she even know about you and Melody … and how is *your* personal life any of *her* business?"

Emmitt felt a tangent rising. He stopped and took a breath before pushing himself back to the point. "Sybil likes to think that she's owed more than she already has. She's completely self-involved, but she also sees herself as a victim, despite all her excesses. Does any part of you think that constantly piling on compliments will make her a worse person instead of a better one?"

"Do you think someone with a high opinion of themselves would constantly need to put others down? And do you think I like hearing all of Sybil's snide remarks about Melody … how she lives in a kennel, or how her house is haunted by all her dolls, or how crazy she is because *one* time she wrapped her phone in tinfoil after one of her brothers told her it would keep the government from spying on her? Melody and Sybil have known each other for a long time, and Melody has always been kind to Sybil. You like to complain about Sybil, but you haven't received half of the cruelty that she's hurled at Melly … Melody." Andrew appeared to be fighting his own rising tangent. He sighed deeply and continued. "I don't mind complimenting Sybil's progress when it's warranted. I don't force you to praise her." Andrew gave Emmitt a smirk and stared at him with his cold, gray eyes. "And didn't you call Melody my crazy cat lady before you met her?"

"That's different. We're brothers. I'm supposed to make fun of your crazy cat lady girlfriend and her weird doll collection. But I like her. I like how weird she is, and I like the conspiracies. I liked the two of you as a couple, and I still think you're stupid for not figuring out a way to get back together. She made you happy, Andrew. Sybil's a bundle of misery, and I don't trust her." Emmitt bristled at the sound of his childish petulance.

"I'm not trying to date Sybil." Andrew had a gentleness in his voice that further agitated Emmitt.

"I know you're not trying to date Sybil," Emmitt snapped, "but Sybil seems to be pretty interested in you. I know you take clients as they are, and you don't do any research that might give you a negative impression of them—"

"I certainly don't read tabloids, like you do," Andrew snapped back.

Emmitt groaned. "I know. You're a better person than I am. If you want me to concede that point, I will. I just want you to look at things from my perspective. Just once, see things from the point of view of your hyper-critical, cynical younger brother and accept that Sybil acts in her own best interest, and sometimes, there are victims of her selfishness."

"If you're trying to defend the reality show staff from *Celebrity Psych* or that con artist, Felix Bryson ..."

"I'm not. Those assholes were supposed to be professionals ..." Emmitt hesitated as the last word resonated. He pushed the thought down and began again. "You saw Renata shrink away when Sybil teased her. Sybil continues to attack Melody for no reason. She assembled her employees to come up with the list of goals she was supposed to compile herself. And Sybil has a history of affiliating with get-rich-quick schemes. I know you don't have a problem with them, but a lot of people lost a lot of money because of her. Ninety-nine percent, statistically speaking. Sybil profited from their losses and moved on to the next scheme. She's still doing it. She might do the same to us." Emmitt was breathless and exasperated.

"She might," Andrew said.

"She might," Emmitt mocked. "Seriously? Just 'she might,' and that's it?"

"Yes. That's it. What do you want me to do? Get angry?"

"Yes! Get angry … or, at least, tell me you have a plan if she tries to slip her hand down your pants or fire us right before the job is done and claim she did it all herself!"

"I'm fairly confident I can physically stop her if she tries to stick her hand down my pants." Andrew waved his hands in a sideways chopping motion directly above his crotch, which forced a cackle out of Emmitt, shattering his scowling face.

"Stupid," Emmitt said, trying to suppress his laughter.

"And Sybil may fire us at any point, for any reason. It happens. We can't control it." Andrew looked soberly at Emmitt and patted him firmly on the shoulder.

Emmitt lowered his voice. "Just … for my sake … please, tell me you see how manipulative Sybil is."

Andrew sighed. "Emmitt … I see it."

"Good," Emmitt said.

"Are we good to go?" Andrew asked.

"Yes ... no," Emmitt said. His thoughts turned back to his own hypocrisy. He couldn't hold the words in. "I have one more question. It's not related to Sybil. It's more of a hypothetical."

"You say a lot without actually getting to the point, Emmitt." Andrew checked the time on his phone and let out a long breath.

"I'm complex. Layered. Sophisticated." Emmitt laughed nervously.

"You're a convoluted windbag." Andrew smirked. "You know I don't like hypothetical questions."

"Fine," Emmitt said, trying to hide his anxiety. "I was wondering, if Renata doesn't need help, and she doesn't want to be featured in the book ... is she a client?"

Andrew's smirk faded. "Yes. It's not professional—"

"Got it." Emmitt sighed. "Just verifying."

"Emmitt ..." Andrew began.

"I get it. Forget I said anything."

"Has she said anything to you? Are you two ...?"

"No," Emmitt said firmly. "I already knew the answer but figured I might try asking anyway to see if you'd surprise me by telling me what I wanted to hear. I've talked too much. We don't want to be late."

Before Andrew could respond, Emmitt released his seatbelt, bolted out of the car, and shut the door behind him.

Chapter Fourteen

Emmitt rushed to the front door and rang the doorbell before Andrew had walked through the opened driveway gate. As Andrew quickened his pace to reach the front of the house, Sybil opened the door. Her blonde hair was tied up in a meticulously messy bun, her makeup was thick and flawless, the short sleeves on her pink tee shirt were folded into cuffs, and her light wash jeans were skintight.

"Don't look at me, I'm a total mess right now!" she giggled, playfully attempting to shield her face from them. "Packing is so hectic. This team-building retreat was sprung on me last minute … can you believe it?" Sybil didn't wait for a response. She immediately turned and gestured at Andrew and Emmitt to follow her into the house.

As he followed behind Andrew, Emmitt wondered if anyone had ever seen Sybil without makeup. Renata had told him that even when Sybil suffered from kidney stones, she still had to apply a base coat of foundation, blush, and lip gloss before she would allow Renata to drive her to the hospital. Was it vanity, or insecurity?

Emmitt had never put much energy into his own appearance. One of the few compliments his mother had given him was when she once commented, "At least you can fall back on my honey eyes and Mediterranean complexion and your father's thick hair and strong jawline. There wouldn't be a hope for you if you were unattractive." That was four years ago, when he had called to wish her a happy Mother's Day. Emmitt assumed she wanted to motivate him to better himself. She wanted him to build on a firm foundation, as Andrew had.

Serenity's words didn't motivate Emmitt, but he held on to the fact that, despite his many failings, at least his spiteful and disparaging mother believed he was handsome. The thought produced an unexpected twist of sympathy for Sybil. Perhaps her beauty was the one thing she could cling to. The one constant in her life. When it came to the art of self-presentation, Emmitt had to admit that Sybil's bare minimum was at a far higher level than his.

Emmitt was driven out of his thoughts by the sound of a familiar voice. It was the laugh that gave it away.

"Is Sister Eugene here?" Emmitt asked Sybil.

"Oh, yeah," Sybil said. "And I may have forgotten to tell my mom that I changed the dates around. She didn't know you two were coming today." Sybil turned toward the breakfast nook. "Mommy!" she shouted. "Drew Key and his brother are here!"

Shit, Emmitt thought. He was sure Sybil was reveling in the melodrama she was attempting to manufacture. Emmitt knew it wouldn't be easy to keep Shannon Yates calm if they were forced to confront her, but part of him was impatient to see her again. There were lingering questions he hoped to ask. He hadn't encountered Shannon since their first meeting. Her absence offered Andrew the ability to focus on Sybil—and Emmitt the opportunity to focus on Renata—but Emmitt remained curious about the Yates matriarch. Sybil's penchant for creating chaos could be an opportunity for Emmitt to scratch his own itch. Perhaps Emmitt wasn't entirely unlike Sybil in that regard. Sybil was already leading them through the living room to greet her mother, and while Emmitt was anxious, he also felt a sudden exhilaration rising in his chest.

"Mommy, say hi to Drew and Emmitt." Sybil's sing-song request sounded forcefully innocent.

As Shannon came into view, Emmitt could see her disappointment. She glared at Sybil, then turned her attention to the unwanted guests.

"It's good to see you again," Sister Eugene's voice boomed. "And congratulations on the progress you've made so far. Sybil showed me her bedroom. It's incredible."

"Thank you," Sybil responded.

Emmitt flashed a broad grin at Sybil's back. Sister Eugene noticed.

"And, I suppose, I should also congratulate Drew and Emmitt for assisting in Sybil's success." The nun smiled back at Emmitt with a wink that Sybil was too distracted to notice.

Sybil's eyes shifted to stare intently at her nails just as Sister Eugene's focus shifted away from her.

Shannon's face was stiff, and her tone was sharp. "Are we done patting ourselves on the back?"

"No one's patting you on the back, Mommy," Sybil said absently, still staring at her nails. "You haven't done anything."

Shannon glowered at her daughter, but Sybil didn't bother to lift her head.

Sister Eugene kept her cheery disposition, unfazed by the brewing tension between the mother and daughter. She gestured to Andrew and Emmitt and addressed them directly. "I suppose you two can relax and enjoy a bit of a vacation while Sybil is out of town. Two weeks is quite a break.”

“Two weeks?” Andrew couldn’t hide the surprise in his voice.

“Yeah …” Sybil said, finally looking up. “I thought I told you the trip was extended … but I guess it just slipped my mind. Like I said, it’s been so hectic. But I’ll notify you the day I get back. Promise.”

“Of course,” Andrew said. “It’s not a problem. We already agreed to work within your schedule, and you obviously can’t neglect your career.”

“Obviously.” Sybil bobbed her head up and down in dramatic agreement.

Sister Eugene playfully nudged Shannon with her elbow. “You know, Shannon, it could be an excellent opportunity for you to get a start on tidying up other parts of the house. You would get the undivided attention of these two young, strapping men while Sybil’s away.”

Shannon bristled at the suggestion. “I’m not interested.”

“Well, now. You haven’t given them a chance. They’ve been patient with Sybil—”

“I said no.”

The nun shook her head as she looked at Emmitt. “I tried.”

“I would prefer it if you stopped badgering me,” Shannon grumbled.

Andrew watched as the conversation collapsed. Emmitt kept his eyes fixed on his brother’s stoic expression and heard Andrew’s voice cut through the growing tension. “We aren’t pressuring you to participate, Mrs. Yates. If you change your mind, Sybil can give you my number. You can contact me anytime, but for now, our plan is to continue working with Sybil. If you don't want us to visit while Sybil is on her trip, we'll stay away until she returns."

"Good," Shannon said.

With the potential crisis averted, Sybil seemed to sense the fun was over. She swayed out of the breakfast nook, sighing, "Drew, let's go. I only have a couple of hours to work today."

Andrew followed Sybil. Emmitt took a step to follow Andrew, then stopped. He took a deep breath, then turned to face Shannon.

"Mrs. Yates," he began. His throat was tightening, but he knew he might never have another opportunity to speak to her. It had to be today. "Do you consider yourself to be a hoarder?"

Silence filled the room. Emmitt noticed Andrew and Sybil stop and turn in unison to stare at him. He tried to block them out as his eyes held on Shannon. Shannon froze as Emmitt's words penetrated. Her face reddened as she struggled to compose herself.

"Wha—" she started, then blew out the remaining air in a sharp, audible breath. "What right do you have to ask me that question?" Her voice quivered in anger. "You don't know me. I have been perfectly clear that I want no part in this. You have no right to ask me that."

"I'm sorry," Emmitt said. He was sorry, but he was also determined to get an answer, regardless of Shannon's discomfort.

He didn't quite know what possessed him, but he knew he had to ask. It was important. If admitting to the problem was the first necessary step to spur Shannon into action, Emmitt wanted to know if there would ever be a chance for her to confront her disorder. He was also curious for his own sake. He couldn't say which reason drove him to press further, but he wasn't going to stop.

"I'm trying to understand. I've been trying to understand since I first entered the house with Drew. Sybil has a deep connection with her things. I've never experienced that kind of connection to an object, and I wonder if you have that same level of attachment. Does it give you a sense of comfort to be surrounded by your treasures, or does it feel like a prison to you?"

Shannon fumed, "I'm not interested in giving you any personal details about my living situation, just so you can exploit me in your book."

"I won't," Emmitt said. A sense of inexplicable calm washed over him. "I couldn't, even if I wanted to. You haven't signed the waiver giving us permission to include you in the book. Your brother had lawyers involved to make sure you would be protected. Drew has no interest in embarrassing you. He wants to help your family. I just want to know if you think you're a hoarder."

Shannon kept her eyes narrowed on Emmitt as she spoke. "One of my sisters married a duke. Her estate is twelve thousand square feet, not including the guest house, which has six bedrooms ... each with an en suite bathroom attached. Their guest house is larger than this house. They also own a villa in the South of France, where they live during the summer months. She has eight walk-in closets to hold her wardrobe, and separate closets for her shoes and purses. She buys more trinkets than I do, owns more artwork, more furniture, and two dozen sets of fine china. Each set could easily feed a dinner party of eighty guests. If Mary tried to fit every item from her estate and villa into her guest house, it would burst at the seams and overflow acres in every direction."

"Respectfully," Emmitt argued, "if you tried to fit all the items from your formal dining room into my apartment, you would have the same effect. I understand what you're saying, Mrs. Yates. I guess the terminology gets complicated when accounting for square footage and multiple properties. From what I read—which, admittedly, isn't much—there seems to be a lot of consideration regarding the suffering caused by the accumulation of items. I don't think there's a specific number of items that would automatically flip the switch from avid collector to hoarder. It doesn't seem fair, but if your sister can walk comfortably through her house—or villa—without the fear of being crushed to death, and without the risk of being trapped if the house caught on fire, then it isn't a hazard or a hoard … but I'm not confident about the technicalities … or generalities, for that matter."

Shannon only stared at Emmitt, before she continued. "Well, my other little sister, Grace, runs a large breed dog rescue out of her farmhouse. She's currently fostering eighteen of them. They roam freely inside and outside the property. She could easily afford to buy a facility to keep them, but she insists they need her constant love and care. Great Danes, Great Pyrenees, Saint Bernards … they rule the roost. There are stains all over her hardwood floors from their excrement." Her nostrils flared as she sneered in disgust. "Most of her furniture has been torn up or worn out by her dogs. There's hair … everywhere. Her youngest, Logan, had a severe asthma attack because of all the pet dander in the air. That didn't faze our Gracie. She strapped a CPAP machine to her child and took in two more dogs. Her house is in worse shape than mine. It's more hazardous than mine. Most people would choose this house over the disgusting barn she lives in."

Emmitt remained calm. "I believe you, Mrs. Yates. You certainly surround yourself with a lot of beautiful things ... but you're still comparing two less-than-ideal scenarios. If you take out the dichotomy, most people would consider both houses unlivable."

"Fine." Shannon wasn't ready to concede. "But my brothers ... Lucas overfills the studios and galleries of his closest friends with his unsellable artwork ... and James, the eldest, is in charge of the family trust. If he wasn't so stingy, I could have kept my house and rented storage units for the excess." Shannon's anger had diminished. She was now pleading her case to Emmitt. "James is the head of the museum board. He has access to warehouses ... and not just a few little units. There are two large warehouses on the museum property, and two converted airplane hangars for extra storage off-property ... and he has plans to expand."

Shannon frantically rifled through piles of paper on the table and picked up a brochure for the Yates Museum and Botanical Gardens. "Three new events for members: an egg hunt for children during Easter, a summer concert series, and a harvest festival in the fall. Renata says they've also expanded their Christmas decorations this season. They're adding a Dickens Christmas Village with costumes and carolers, which means more items to buy and store ..."

"Are Renata and James buying decorations for their own benefit, or for the benefit of the families who come to visit the museum and gardens?" Sister Eugene asked. Her voice was gentle. She laid her large hand on Shannon's angular shoulder.

"Both, I think," Shannon replied quietly. "And why stop with my siblings? Some might call the museum a hoard. My grandfather was the one who established it, but his parents and their parents before them were collectors. They were fortunate enough to have the space to contain their treasures. I don't have that luxury."

"I don't disagree with what you're saying," Emmitt began, trying to sound supportive while gently steering the conversation back to his original question. "So, do you think it's just a matter of space? For instance, if your house was twice as big as this one, do you think everything you own would fit comfortably inside?"

Shannon paused and considered. Still seated, she looked into the living room and around the breakfast nook. Her eyes finally settled on the portrait of her late husband. "Perhaps not," she whispered.

"Do you think your life would be better if you could walk through your house freely? Wouldn't you like to sit on one of your sofas with a blanket and a good book, or entertain guests during the holidays in your formal dining room?" Emmitt asked.

"No."

"Really?" Shannon's answer shocked Emmitt. "Seriously? You're more comfortable being confined to a dining chair?"

"Yes." Shannon had apparently regained a bit of her original anger and defiance. "And if I am a hoarder, then I am only one of many in the Yates family. Perhaps they hide it better than I do ... or perhaps their hoarding is more socially acceptable. I don't know and I don't care. I'm not interested in your help, and I'm frustrated that my family continues to treat me as a villain, all while they refuse to acknowledge their own hypocrisy."

"So, all the Yates siblings are hoarders ... including you." Emmitt could also be defiant. "I'm willing to agree that you aren't the only one with a problem. It's possible you're not the one with the *worst* hoarding tendencies, either. But you acknowledge you're a hoarder, right?"

Shannon sighed. "I suppose I can acknowledge it, if it puts an end to this conversation. You, at least, seem willing to listen to me, and you've recognized my siblings' failings … but you are tiring, Mr. Key."

Emmitt flashed a broad and dazzling smile at Shannon. "So are you, Mrs. Yates … and I don't think you're a villain, for what it's worth."

Sister Eugene chuckled. She slapped her knee as Shannon rolled her eyes. Emmitt nodded and turned to face Andrew, but as he took a step toward his brother, he noticed Renata poke her head out of the archway that led into the formal dining room.

"Emmitt," she said in a voice that was just above a whisper.

All eyes turned to her. She blushed red with embarrassment.

"Um, well …" she began. "Since Sybil will be gone for a couple weeks, I was wondering if you … and Andrew … would come over to help me organize a few things. It should only take a day … probably only a few hours …" She trailed off.

Emmitt answered, without hesitation. "Of course. What day works for you? Do you need my contact information, or do you already have Andrew's?"

Shannon's eyebrow raised in curiosity. "What have I missed? Renata, what could you possibly have to organize?"

"Emmitt and Andrew have made a lot of progress with Sybil. I have a few boxes in the garage I can sort through, and some of the art on my walls …"

"Which ones?" Shannon snapped. "The art in the den—"

"Is yours, I understand," Renata softly reassured her mother. "I won't remove anything that's yours. But the art in my bedroom is mine … and I'd like to declutter a bit."

Andrew stepped closer toward Emmitt and addressed Renata directly. "We're happy to help you with whatever you need, Renata."

Emmitt was relieved by his brother's intervention. He couldn't hide his excitement at the prospect of working with Renata. Of course, Andrew would be helping Renata too, and Andrew knew how Emmitt felt about Renata. Why had he told him? He knew what Andrew would say. Would Andrew trust Emmitt to act professionally? Strangely, Emmitt thought he would. Andrew allowed Emmitt far more leeway than he had expected. Even now, he hadn't stepped in as Emmitt questioned Shannon about her hoarding.

Emmitt glanced at his brother, who looked back at him with a slight frown. Andrew quickly shifted his attention to Sybil, who stood like an annoyed adolescent, sucking her teeth and crossing her arms.

"Sybil, could you please text my contact information to Renata?" Andrew asked.

Well, Emmitt thought, at least part of him is worried about me having Renata's number. *Either he doesn't trust me, or he's trying to protect me from myself. I can't say I blame him.*

Sybil plastered on a smile and uncrossed her arms. "Of course, Drew."

She grabbed her phone from the back pocket of her tight jeans and clacked at the screen with her long pink fingernails.

"Done. Now, Drew, I have so little time left today. Could we please get back to me?"

"Of course," Andrew said, smiling. "Let's get back to work."

As Sybil led Andrew back to her bedroom, Emmitt turned one last time to face Shannon. "I'm determined to work with you, Mrs. Yates," Emmitt said. "I don't exactly know what I'm doing, but maybe that's just what you need."

"How providential," Shannon replied with a smirk. "I'm still not working with you, Mr. Key."

"Not yet," Emmitt said. "But I've decided I'm not giving up on you."

Shannon shook her head as Emmitt flashed a smile to Renata and swaggered out of the room.

He followed Andrew and Sybil back to her bedroom. In the room, Sybil pointed as Andrew grabbed a box and lowered it for her to look inside. Emmitt tried to conceal the grin that lingered on his lips. He pressed a hand over his mouth as his eyes wandered in thought.

A few feet in front of him, Andrew and Sybil were speaking, but Emmitt couldn't register the words. Their voices were miles away from Emmitt's roving mind. Soon, Sybil would be gone. Soon, he would spend a day with Renata. *Soon.*

Chapter Fifteen

Three days had passed since Renata requested Emmitt and Andrew's help. Emmitt had washed and ironed his own white-collared shirt and layered it underneath Andrew's black cable-knit sweater. Like the other borrowed items from Andrew's wardrobe, the sweater was a size and a half too big. While Emmitt had never concerned himself with fashion, he had worried aloud that he looked like an overgrown toddler in his older brother's hand-me-downs. Andrew had assured him that his shirts and sweaters fit Emmitt in a relaxed style, rather than looking oversized. Emmitt didn't want to rely on Andrew's reassurances to pacify him, but the bolstered confidence the reassurances instilled outweighed the annoyance he felt toward the one who instilled it.

Despite Emmitt's embarrassment of not knowing how to properly dress himself at nearly twenty-eight years old, pride gave way to vanity, and he forced himself to ask his older brother to roll his sleeves neatly at the elbow, as Andrew sometimes wore his own. Andrew raised an eyebrow at Emmitt before exiting the SUV and walking over to the passenger side. Emmitt attempted to conceal himself from prying eyes by keeping the car door open as Andrew stood in front of him and silently folded and adjusted his sleeves and collar. Emmitt glanced down past his ironed jeans and let his eyes rest on the scuffed dress shoes he had worn to his college graduation, as well as every subsequent job interview that had resulted in failure.

A sudden flush of shame rushed to Emmitt's face as he thought of Renata Yates. Who she was, and who he was by comparison.

"Done," Andrew said, breaking Emmitt away from his thoughts. He smiled and flicked Emmitt's collar before turning to walk toward the house.

"Thanks."

As they crossed the street and entered the open driveway gate, Emmitt quickened his pace and was first to approach the front door. He reached his hand out to ring the doorbell, then hesitated and glanced at Andrew.

"Do I look like an idiot?" he asked.

"Yeah. But at least you're finally dressed well," Andrew replied, roughly patting Emmitt on the back. "I'm glad you've leveled up your physical presentation. I just hope this isn't all to impress Renata. I've already told you—"

"Unprofessional," Emmitt sighed. "I know."

"Emmitt, I'm not trying to lecture you. I know you two get along, and I understand why you're interested. Renata is kind and patient ... and attractive. She feeds you and makes sure you're hydrated while we're working. I'm sure if you bought a leash, she'd take you out for walks ..."

"Stop it, Andrew," Emmitt grumbled. "I already told you, nothing is going on."

"You don't care about looking nice for Sybil's sake," Andrew said.

"Looking nice for Renata's sake doesn't mean we're dating," Emmitt argued quietly, fearing they might be overheard.

Emmitt didn't know what he expected to accomplish with Andrew. He didn't care if Andrew knew about his attraction to Renata, but his temper flared anytime Andrew brought attention to it. Emmitt wasn't concealing anything from Andrew, and his exposed honesty made Andrew's warnings and concerns completely justifiable. He had no right to snap at his brother. But Emmitt continued to wish for the impossible: he wished Andrew would see his efforts and offer his blessing. Emmitt wanted Andrew to bend his own rules for his sake.

Emmitt reached over and rang the doorbell. His palms were sweating, and he felt a fluttering sensation in his stomach. He glanced at Andrew, who looked back at him with a concerned frown that vanished the moment he heard the squeaking turn of the doorknob. A placid look overtook Andrew's face as Renata cracked open the door and smiled up at Emmitt. Emmitt fixed his eyes on Renata and smiled back at her.

As Renata looked at Andrew, her eyes widened. She immediately turned her head to observe the narrow gap in the door.

"I know you've been coming in this way, but I didn't realize how much of a squeeze it must be for the two of you."

Before either of them could respond, Renata braced one leg on the door frame and pushed all of her weight into the door. The door didn't budge. The gap remained narrow. After a few more minutes of Renata pushing, huffing and apologizing, with Emmitt and Andrew trying to stifle their laughter at the futility of her earnest efforts, she finally gave up trying.

"Well, that didn't work." Renata quickly peeked into the house to see the potential damage she had caused. She shook her head as she reemerged. "Nothing. I didn't even dent the cardboard."

"It's no trouble," Andrew said with a wide grin. "We're used to getting in this way."

"I can let you in through the kitchen," Renata said, looking at Andrew with embarrassment.

"We'll be fine, Renata. Don't worry," Andrew said.

"It's a terrible thing to ignore," Renata argued meekly, as though she had already resigned herself to defeat. She looked at Emmitt. "If your front door didn't open more than halfway, you wouldn't ignore it, would you?"

Emmitt answered calmly, "Renata, my kitchen sink has been dripping for five months. I live in a studio apartment. The pinging sound is incessant and annoying. It's so annoying that I started using a sponge to dampen the noise. I could easily solve the problem by calling my landlord, but I don't like him, and I hate the idea of making small talk for the fifteen minutes it'll take to fix the sink. I could probably watch a video and fix it myself, but I haven't gotten around to it. Trust me, I could ignore a little door obstruction."

"You're being kind," Renata said.

"He's being honest," Andrew cut in. "You have a lot to deal with, Renata. You shouldn't feel the need to take personal accountability for every little problem."

"But it isn't little. I'm so used to going through the side yard to enter through the kitchen that I don't even think about the front door anymore. Every issue is a big issue, but there are so many big issues that it's easy to ignore them individually. I'm glad you're willing to work with my mother, but she's still refusing to participate. Even if she has a sudden change of heart, I'm worried her progress won't keep up with her collecting. The door may just be stuck like this. She may never sleep in her bed …" Renata stopped herself from elaborating further.

"You're thinking too far ahead," Andrew said. "We should focus only on what *you* want to accomplish today."

"I know," Renata sighed. "I'm grateful for the work you've done so far. I just wish my mother would accept help."

"Well, I'm sure Emmitt made a lot of headway with your mother after he verbally accosted her the other day." Andrew plastered a broad smile on his face as he narrowed his eyes at Emmitt.

Was that a joke? From Andrew? In front of a client? Andrew's cynical jab intrigued Emmitt. Emmitt considered his own behavior over the past few weeks and decided to keep his feigned shock and disappointment to himself.

"Mother can take it." There was a bite to Renata's words, despite the smile on her face. She softened as she addressed Emmitt. "She's not here today, so you don't have to worry." Her forehead wrinkled, and her smile faded. Her eyes darted to the side as if she had caused some great offense. "Oh, but I'm not saying it's your fault she's not here …"

"It is, at least, partially Emmitt's fault," Andrew insisted.

Emmitt was struggling to find any trace of Drew Key in his brother. Renata was interacting with *Andrew*. It felt like some kind of precedent was being set. No client ever interacted with *Andrew* Key.

"Yeah," Emmitt admitted. "I'm sorry I got carried away."

Renata's dark-blue eyes shone as they locked on Emmitt. "Don't be sorry. I could hear you from the dining room. You made her admit to being a hoarder."

"Yeah, but she only relented after implicating everyone else in your family. I really don't think I accomplished much." Emmitt wondered how much of the conversation Renata had heard from the dining room. Had she been hiding there the entire time? Why? Emmitt wouldn't risk embarrassing her by asking.

"You accomplished more than anyone else. You don't realize how difficult Mother is. It may have seemed like a small thing, but you were amazing with her." Renata's intensity broke as she seemed to remember there was a third party in the conversation. She glanced at Andrew, saying, "Sorry, I got distracted. I'm just wasting your time chatting at the front door. Please come in. We can start in the kitchen, if you don't mind."

Andrew smiled at Renata. "No apology necessary. We're here to do whatever you need us to do."

As Renata entered the house, Emmitt casually slid in front of his brother. He squeezed through the entry and followed Renata toward the kitchen. When they arrived, they saw two large cardboard boxes sitting on the kitchen counter. The boxes were closed and taped shut.

"Are these boxes for kitchen items?" Emmitt asked.

"Yes."

"Great!" Andrew said. "Let's open them up and start sorting."

Renata shook her head as she looked at Andrew. "Oh. No ... I've already gone through the kitchen and packed the items I wanted to donate. I separated the appliances into one box, and the pots, pans, and baking trays into the other one. They're ready to be donated. They're heavy, so I just need some help carrying the boxes to my car."

Andrew dramatically put his hands in the air. "Renata, you're doing our job for us! No sorting piles? No trash bags? I have a feeling Emmitt and I are going to be useless today."

Renata grinned. "I swear, there's more."

"We don't believe you," Emmitt teased. "If I randomly picked a kitchen cabinet and opened it, how organized would it be?"

"See for yourself," Renata said.

She ran her fingertips along the cabinets as she glided gracefully across the kitchen on dark-teal socks that matched her sweatshirt. Emmitt briefly let his eyes wander to the elaborate black calligraphy of the printed logo for the Yates Museum and Botanical Gardens, then brought his attention back to Renata's deep-blue eyes.

Emmitt scanned the kitchen and pointed to a top cabinet next to the built-in refrigerator. Renata opened it, revealing three neatly organized shelves with a matching set of dinner and salad plates, bowls, cups, and saucers.

"Wow," Emmitt said. "But you've got to have some kind of catch-all drawer somewhere in the kitchen … you know, for batteries, broken pencils, extra birthday candles, loose change …"

"That's what the rest of the house has become," Renata said soberly.

"Right. Sorry. I don't always think before I speak." Emmitt lowered his eyes and cursed himself in his head.

"It's fine. Really. Living in this mess is frustrating. I just thought …" She stopped and sighed.

"What did you think?" Andrew asked.

"It's stupid … but, I thought, if I worked with you, my mother might try to do the same. Sybil is always willing to get herself involved in things like this, and I usually try to stay away as much as possible. You two have been different. Sybil hangs on your every word, Andrew … and Mother responds well to you, Emmitt. I hoped she would trust you if she saw *I* trusted you."

"She may work with us, eventually. We still have time." Andrew was calm and reassuring. "Who knows? Emmitt's strategy of wearing her down may marry itself to your strategy of being an active participant. At the very least, you've both stirred the pot. And, more importantly, you've piqued her curiosity. She may end up surprising us all."

"Maybe … but it's not likely to happen." Renata moved to open the door that led into her sitting room. "I have more items to donate in my bedroom, if you're ready."

"Lead on," Andrew said.

The three of them moved through the sitting room to another closed door. Renata opened the door into her bedroom. Like the rest of the rooms under her care, the bedroom was warm, inviting, and spotlessly clean. The queen-sized bed had four posts that were connected at the top. White lace curtains had been drawn open on all sides of the bed. The bedspread was a crisp white cloud, and a deep-green blanket was neatly arranged on top of it. Much like in the sitting room, artwork covered the walls from floor to ceiling, but that wasn't the first thing Emmitt noticed.

"So, clearly you have too many pillows. There's got to be a dozen on your bed … and look at this bench … thing." Emmitt walked to the foot of the bed. "You can't even sit on it."

"They're decorative." Renata's eyes widened as she stared at Emmitt in surprise.

"The bench isn't," Emmitt responded. "And anyway, none of the pillowcases match."

"They're not supposed to match. They coordinate. It's the portraits on the walls I need to pare down."

"How do you sleep at night with all these pillows, though?" Emmitt asked with a teasing grin rising on his lips.

Renata narrowed her eyes at Emmitt. "I pile them up and sleep underneath my mountain of pillows. I think physically burying myself every night allows me to suppress my overwhelming desire to hoard."

"Really?" Emmitt asked.

"No," Renata smirked.

Emmitt dared to use his best Drew Key impression. It was the voice he used to chastise, motivate, and entertain himself in the bathroom mirror. "Renata, if you want to live the rest of your life as a pillow hoarder, we will not stop you. You need to be the one who decides to change. We'll be here when you're ready to admit you have a problem."

Renata giggled, then put a hand over her mouth and glanced at Andrew to gauge his reaction. Emmitt, who had never considered his brother's reaction, looked curiously at Andrew. His brother stared at him with a cocked head and a half smirk.

"That was a decent impression," Andrew finally said. "If you weren't so cynical, I would say you have some promise in life coaching."

Renata smiled softly at Andrew. "We shouldn't tease you. I'm sorry for laughing. It was an uncanny impression, though."

"Yeah. Sorry, Andrew," Emmitt asserted without sincerity.

Renata stood by the bed and carefully studied the cushions. After a moment of contemplation, she picked up three pillows and threw them at Emmitt. She then walked to the bench at the foot of the bed and grabbed two more pillows, tossing them absently in Emmitt's direction. She turned once more, moving toward a loveseat in the corner of the room. She picked up two pillows, examined them, and placed one gently back on the couch. The other pillow was flung at Emmitt's feet.

"Is six enough?" Renata playfully raised an eyebrow as she looked at Emmitt.

"You really don't need to get rid of them, if you don't want to," Andrew interjected. "Right, Emmitt?"

"Right. I was just joking ... I mean, you do have a lot of pillows ... but I can put these ones back."

"Donate," Renata insisted.

"Are you sure?" Andrew asked.

"Yes. Emmitt might be blunt ... and a little irritating ... but he makes a good point. I need to set a better example. I can let them go."

Andrew scowled at his brother. "Emmitt, don't try this technique with Shannon or Sybil. You're lucky Renata seems to be immune to your jackassery."

"Language, Andrew," Emmitt corrected innocently. He placed his right hand over his heart. "I promise, on my honor, I will only unleash my jackassery on Renata."

"Lucky me," Renata said. "Any thoughts on the art?"

"I know as much about art as I know about decorative pillows." Emmitt puffed out his chest as he spoke.

"Which means he knows nothing," Andrew said.

"Clearly," Renata agreed. "Quite a few of these were gifts from my uncle. Not the one you met. My Uncle Lucas is an ... artist. His works are ... prolific. He has a hard time selling most of his pieces, and he refuses to dispose of anything he creates, so he gives his art to friends and family. Strangely, his art is the one thing Mother doesn't mind throwing into the garbage. Even Sybil won't accept any gifts from Uncle Lucas."

"But you feel guilted into keeping his art?" Emmitt asked.

"Yes. His art has to stay. He comes over to visit his creations. I'm convinced he only visits me to make sure I haven't thrown anything away."

"Renata," Andrew began, "this scenario sounds a bit like the issue you were having when Sybil was trying to use your room for storage."

"It's not the same." Renata was surprisingly curt. Emmitt heard Shannon's voice in her objection.

Andrew softened his tone. "I'm not trying to convince you to do anything with your uncle's artwork, but I worry other people may be taking advantage of your kindness."

"It's not kindness. I'm not kind. I'm bitter. I hate it ... he knows I hate it. They all know. I'm just a pushover. I don't like confrontation ... and I especially don't like feeling guilty." Renata almost sounded petulant. Her eyes narrowed in defiance as she frowned at Andrew.

"I think you are kind, Renata," Andrew said.

"Kindness is a choice. I'm not choosing anything," Renata replied.

Andrew seemed puzzled by Renata's objections. "You can't experience guilt without empathy. I think you're an empath."

"Empath?" Renata scoffed. "In my experience, the people who try to convince everyone they're empaths are always, without exception, entitled, selfish, and emotionally unstable ... Sybil tells people she's an empath. She also likes to blame her worst qualities on her star sign. I'm not an empath."

"Got it," Andrew said. "Not an empath. You're empathetic … compassionate. Look, whatever you want to call it, you care more about making others feel comfortable than standing up for yourself and your own needs. You didn't want to help Sybil with sorting, but you ended up getting involved, anyway."

Renata seemed wounded by Andrew's insistence. "I had practical concerns. Sybil would have kicked you out if I hadn't agreed, and removing Sybil's boxes from the driveway made it less likely for the city to come in and condemn the house. By helping Sybil, I'm helping myself. None of us wants to face another eviction. It's exhausting."

Emmitt was growing concerned for Renata. She was desperate to prove to Andrew she wasn't a good person. Andrew appeared anxious to lift her up, but Renata refused to yield.

"Renata," Andrew stressed with a nearly pleading intensity, "you do so much for your family. For God's sake, Sybil doesn't even know where the trash bags are kept!"

"I don't allow Sybil in the kitchen," Renata countered defensively. "It's the one thing I won't budge on. A month after we moved in, Sybil had the brilliant idea to buy three different juicers for an internet video review. She spent five hours in the kitchen, and by the end of the day, I was the one who had to clean up the mess. I had to wipe beet pulp off the ceiling, then paint over the stain it left."

"Why did you feel you had to clean up Sybil's mess?" Andrew asked.

"I'm the only one who would do it. Sybil doesn't care. I hate living in filth. I can control the kitchen and my rooms, so I keep them clean for myself."

"Why live with them at all? Why punish yourself with the stress they cause?"

Is this what I did to Shannon? Emmitt felt a rising guilt as Andrew pressed further. He watched silently, wondering, for the first time, if Andrew was doing the right thing.

"Someone has to." Renata was almost indignant. "Their living situation isn't safe. Neither of them knows how to live on their own. We can't hire a cleaning service. Someone has to keep the hoard from completely consuming them. I take out the cups and plates from Sybil's office and clear the trash from the breakfast table where my mother sits. I feed them. I clean the bathrooms … at least the ones that are still accessible. It may not look like it, but I keep things from getting worse. I don't know what would happen if I wasn't here."

"Why is that your problem, Renata?" There was almost an ache in Andrew's gentle voice.

"Because my dad's dead. He looked out for them … now it's only me." Tears welled in Renata's eyes. She tried to blink them away as her breath quickened.

"That must be hard for you," Andrew said. There was a slight furrow in his brow. His tone was low and deeply consoling. For any other client, the sentiment might have been comforting. Touching. Supportive.

A quick look at Renata revealed to Emmitt that she had no interest in being pacified by Andrew. Renata would not be soothed.

"Stop it," Renata scowled. "That whole stating the obvious thing. Of course, it's hard. I don't need you or anyone else to tell me something I already know. It's patronizing."

"I'm not trying to patronize you, Renata. I'll stop." Andrew had a pained expression on his face as he looked at Renata. He hadn't helped her. He had offended her.

Renata turned to Emmitt. "Anything you want to add?"

Emmitt's eyes widened. "No ... I was just joking about the pillows ... I didn't expect things to get so ... intense ... I ... uh ..." he stammered, grasping for something to say. "I think we should get back on track ... We're, uh, we're not donating any of Uncle Lucas's paintings, right?"

"Right," Renata said, wiping a tear from her eye as she struggled to regain her composure.

"Okay, then," Emmitt continued, slowly regaining his own composure. "What do you want us to donate?"

Renata stared blankly ahead as though she was looking through the walls of her bedroom. She pointed mechanically. "This one ... that one ... this ... you can donate this ... and that one, and the one next to it on the right ..."

She continued to point as Emmitt and Andrew moved silently throughout the room, taking portraits off the walls. When they had finished, only half of the art remained. All the paintings she had received from her uncle were still hanging.

As Emmitt placed the final portrait on a growing stack that leaned against the wall, Renata excused herself from the room and closed the door behind her. Emmitt and Andrew watched her leave and stood motionless in the quiet room. Behind the door, they heard the faint sound of Renata's broken sobs.

"Shit, Andrew, what now? Should we comfort her?" Emmitt asked miserably.

"I think we should give her a minute," Andrew said with a tone as rigid as his demeanor.

"Do you usually make your clients cry?"

"No. Not out of frustration, at least." Andrew closed his eyes as he rubbed his forehead. "The best thing we can do is wait for Renata to calm down. We'll only make things worse if we follow her. She wants to be left alone."

"How do you know she wants to be left alone, if it's the first time something like this has happened to you?" Emmitt hissed, trying to keep his voice to a whisper.

"Would you want the person who upset you to follow behind and watch while you cried?" Andrew snapped in a low voice, still rubbing his forehead with his thumb and middle finger.

"If it was the great guru, Drew Key, I would expect him to know how to handle the situation."

"Renata doesn't want a guru. I thought I would try to vary my approach. I tried to be more casual ... like you. Clearly, that was my mistake." Andrew stopped rubbing his forehead and shook his head. "It won't happen again."

Emmitt paused. He was still angry with Andrew, but he wasn't interested in suffering the hollow positivity of Drew Key for the rest of the day, and he suspected Renata would feel the same.

"You can't act like me. You're better than me. I get away with prying because I'm an endearing asshole. When you try it, you end up sounding intimidating and mean. I'm sure you don't mean to, but it's just how things are."

Andrew raised an eyebrow at Emmitt. "You don't honestly believe that? You really think I'm intimidating ... and mean?"

Emmitt shrugged. "Sometimes."

"Do you think I scared Renata?" Andrew whispered.

Emmitt shook his head. "Nope. Renata's not scared. She's pissed."

Andrew's jaw tightened as he forced a hard exhale through his nose.

Emmitt looked at Andrew's agitation and awkwardly attempted to reassure him. "Hey, you tried something new ... and it didn't go so well. But it's not a failure, right? We don't believe in failures."

"Emmitt," Andrew groaned.

"Hear me out, Andrew. Drew Key is too composed and too perfect to play the part of the lovable fuckup. Drew isn't supposed to be sympathetic. And Drew doesn't need to pry. He already has all the answers. Andrew Key is slightly less put together, so he can get away with more. Andrew can act like an ass, but Renata has only ever interacted with Drew ... until today. That's not Renata's fault. You made her cry, but unleashing your full guru potential won't help in this situation. She's not Sybil."

"No, she's definitely not Sybil," Andrew agreed. "I know how to motivate Sybil."

Emmitt grabbed his brother's shoulder. "Then challenge yourself, Andrew. You can still be you and help. Who knows? It's possible that her breakdown is some sort of breakthrough for her ... I don't know ... I'm out of my depth here ... I didn't exactly help with the pillow jokes. You're the one who always has a solution. You caused this problem, so fix it!"

Andrew sighed deeply. "Alright. Just calm down ... and wait."

They stood quietly, listening to the muffled cries of the woman behind the closed door. After ten minutes, Emmitt moved to the loveseat and sat down. Andrew remained static with his eyes fixed on the door. Another ten minutes passed. The crying stopped. After another five minutes, they heard footsteps, and the door to Renata's room slowly opened. Her tears were wiped away, but her eyes and nose were red, and she sniffled as she breathed in.

She locked her red eyes on Andrew and surprised him once again. "I'm sorry I snapped at you. I know you were just trying to help."

The tension slowly dissipated from Andrew's face. "You shouldn't apologize. It's completely my fault. I shouldn't have pushed you so hard." Andrew's body remained frozen in place while his eyes were fixed on Renata. "But I should also say that I'm glad you snapped at me. I think you should do more snapping at people who deserve it."

"Probably," Renata sniffled. "I thought today would be easy. I know their hoarding affects me … I wasn't expecting to have to actually confront it today." Her lip quivered between a pout and a smile. She forced out a whisper, "Maybe we can ease into the discussion next time?"

Andrew nodded, then asked tentatively, "Are we okay?"

Renata inhaled a small stuttering breath as she slowly lifted the corners of her lips. "We're okay, Andrew. I'm not mad."

"Do we need to stop?"

"No," Renata said. "There isn't much left to do. I'd like to finish."

Sensing a shift, Emmitt brazenly chimed in, "Unfortunately, Renata, my jackassery is a learned behavior. You can see who taught me this terrible habit."

"Are you sure it wasn't *your* jackassery that rubbed off on Andrew?" Renata asked.

Emmitt feigned a look of shock.

She walked up to where he sat and softly patted the top of his head. "Sorry, Emmitt. I'm just trying to practice snapping at people who deserve it, like Andrew suggested."

"That's the spirit," Andrew half-chuckled as he let out a relieved sigh. "And you couldn't have picked someone more deserving. Emmitt has always been a bad influence."

Emmitt's face brightened. "So, Renata ... has Andrew harassed you into admitting you're a kind and caring person?"

Renata tilted her head and smirked as she stared at Emmitt. "Why do you phrase it in a way that makes us both seem completely unhinged?"

"It's a gift." Emmitt turned and grinned mischievously at Andrew. "Few people can pull it off. Sometimes, I don't even realize I'm doing it. So, can we say you're a good person?"

Renata relented. "You can say it all you want. It isn't for me to tell anyone what kind of person I am."

Emmitt's grin widened. "If that's the case, I'm calling you an empath."

Renata tried to stifle her laughter. "No, Emmitt. That's where I draw the line."

She shifted her attention to Andrew and addressed him with a soft smile and serious tone. "We're getting closer to the deadline. I know Sybil wants to keep working with you, but she's a flake. If I left it up to her, she'd forget to ask. I wanted to let you know, I'm going to request an extension from my uncle, if you're interested in continuing the cleanup. Sybil has been more consistent with you than anyone else we've brought in, and I'm still hoping Emmitt can wear my mother down. Plus, I enjoy having both of you around. You make me feel like I'm not alone in this." She glanced at Emmitt before looking back at his brother.

Andrew nodded as his eyes flashed. "Thank you. We would be happy to continue working with your family."

Renata studied him quietly, as though she was contemplating something. After a long silence, she spoke again. "I've also been thinking … about the waiver. You've had opportunities to leave, and we've given you plenty of information that you could've leaked to tabloids, but you haven't. Sybil hasn't been easy, but you've continued to be patient with her … and the rest of us. I've decided … I want to sign the waiver."

It was Andrew's turn to lose his composure. "You …" Andrew began with a puzzled look. "You want to sign the waiver? You're okay with being in the book? Are you sure?"

Renata giggled. "Yes. I'm willing to be in your book. I know I'm not as interesting as my mother and sister, but Mother probably won't sign, and Sybil has a habit of getting distracted."

"She signed off on the first waiver," Emmitt said. "She couldn't have been too distracted."

Renata shook her head. "Andrew got lucky. It was Sybil's previous agent who badgered her into signing the first form. Sybil will embarrass herself with or without a contract. She doesn't see the point of formalities, even when they're designed to protect her. I'm sure you can get her to sign again … she already has grand ideas of how the book is going to help her grow her empire … but it might take a bit more pestering with the paperwork."

"We can focus on the formalities with Sybil after we deal with the stress of the cleanup," Andrew began firmly, then furrowed his brow. "But I don't want to pressure you, Renata. I already made you cry. I don't want to leave the house feeling like I bullied you into signing."

"You're not bullying me, Andrew. I want to sign the waiver," Renata said.

Emmitt watched curiously as Andrew seemed to recognize that he was actively working against his own interests.

He took a deep breath and settled into his usual professional aura. "Thank you for agreeing to this, Renata. If you wait here for a few minutes, I'll grab the form from my car and bring it to you to look over and sign." Andrew headed out the door, leaving Emmitt and Renata alone.

It must have been a shock to Andrew. Within an hour, Andrew had produced defiance, tears, and an unreasonable outpouring of trust from the mildest member of the Yates family. She had disarmed both of them, but Emmitt suspected his surrender would be far more satisfying than Andrew's token victory. Emmitt understood there would be consequences, but he was eager to remain seated, rather than retreating behind his brother. He wouldn't follow this time.

When Andrew was out of sight, Renata stepped silently toward the loveseat and sat so close to Emmitt that her left arm pressed firmly against his right. So deliberate, that each of her fingers brushed slowly and gently against the back of his hand.

"May I see your phone, Emmitt?" her voice was almost a whisper. "I'd like to give you my number, just in case you need to contact me regarding the book ... or anything else that might pop up."

Emmitt sat upright and hurriedly fumbled for his phone. "Yeah, of course." He pulled it out, unlocked it, and handed it to Renata.

"Are you doing anything next week?" she asked innocently. Her eyes fixed on the screen as she added her information to Emmitt's phone.

"No. I'm totally free whenever," Emmitt replied. It didn't matter if he wasn't free; he would make himself free for Renata.

"I was thinking, maybe next Thursday, if you're available, I could show you around the museum and gardens. It's only a couple of blocks away from the house. Maybe it could help with your book." She handed back the phone as she looked up at Emmitt.

"Yeah. I like that idea. My dad and I used to visit when I was younger. I think my mom even taught a few yoga classes in the gardens before she became famous." Emmitt tried to curtail his eagerness, but it was useless.

"I'll call you Wednesday night."

"I'm already looking forward to it." Emmitt cringed at his own words.

Andrew's footsteps could soon be heard from the sitting room. Renata stood and casually walked away from the loveseat. She moved to the bench at the foot of the bed. As she sat, Emmitt let out a cackle.

"Hey! You have a place to sit now. Aren't you glad you decided to donate some of your pillows?"

Renata grabbed one of the remaining pillows on the bench and hurled it at Emmitt's face. Emmitt caught it before it landed a blow.

"This thing has beads sewn onto it, Renata. It's practically a weapon!" Emmitt teased.

As he lifted his arm to toss it back to her, Andrew entered the room. Emmitt lowered the pillow and placed it next to him on the loveseat while Andrew walked to where Renata sat and wordlessly handed her the waiver. Emmitt and Andrew kept their eyes fixed on Renata as she scanned through the pages.

At the end of the last page, she snickered and shook her head. "I can see the family attorneys were heavily involved in drafting this. There are pretty severe restrictions on what you can actually disclose about us. Severe penalties too. Why would you be interested in writing anything with all these limitations?"

"Emmitt is a competent writer," Andrew said. "And my intention is to help your family. Emmitt and I are going to focus on the positive steps we're making toward achieving your goals. If we're successful, we may help others with similar difficulties ... and with your contributions, we can explore healing and success from different perspectives. My greatest aim is to inspire others by highlighting your accomplishments."

"That's sweet." Renata looked at Andrew with a sad smile. "But we haven't achieved much. We may never be successful."

Andrew disagreed. "You've already made progress in changing your outlook. You're working to inspire your mother to accept help, and you've encouraged your sister with her progress. We're steadily working toward success, even if we haven't fully achieved it yet. That's something to hold on to."

"That's a very nice sentiment." Renata gently touched Andrew's arm. "I just hope we don't end up disappointing you. There's a lot of hurt in our family, and I'm not sure it's possible, or even healthy, for you to try to heal it. I know I get overwhelmed by it. My mother and sister are in a worse position than I am, and Sybil has a habit of developing unhealthy attachments to people who are hired to help her. You're capable … and determined, but it's still a lot of pressure to put on yourself, Andrew. I'm worried it's too much pressure."

"My brother's a perpetual optimist," Emmitt reassured Renata. "Even if you fail, he'll turn it into something positive. Right, Andrew?"

Andrew held tightly onto Renata's compassionate gaze. "Right," he said with a slight frown. "Everything is an opportunity to learn and grow."

Renata signed the waiver and handed it back to Andrew. "I have three boxes in the garage. I don't need to go through them. They're just vases and flowerpots and some old textbooks from college. If you could help me pack them into the car with everything else, then we should be finished for today." Looking back at the art that still hung on the wall, she added, "You've given me a lot to think about. There are definitely things I need to work on … but it'll take longer than today to fix."

"Yeah," Emmitt agreed.

"It was a pleasure to help you today, Renata." Andrew clasped both her hands in his, as he did on their first meeting. This time, Renata didn't shrink back from his affection. "It's nice to work with someone who is kind and … good. It's nice to work with a good person."

"It's nice to work with you too, Andrew." Turning to Emmitt, Renata reached out and squeezed his hand. "Thank you, Emmitt. I enjoyed working with you as well."

"Yeah, no problem," Emmitt replied. His smile was subdued, but he could feel his heart pounding in his chest.

After packing the donations, Andrew and Emmitt said one last goodbye to Renata and walked down the driveway and across the street to Andrew's car.

As they drove toward Emmitt's apartment in silence, Emmitt pre-occupied his mind with the anticipation of spending a day alone with Renata. He glanced at Andrew briefly and caught his brother's furrowed brow and quiet stare as he kept his eyes fixed on the road. Was he worried? Drew Key was too positive and self-possessed to be worried. Wasn't he?

Emmitt pushed his mild concern aside and stared out of the passenger window. He allowed himself to sprawl comfortably inside his head, indulging his fantasies, while ignoring his brother completely. It was probably nothing. And Drew Key was a life coach. Whatever little twinge of emotion Drew Key felt, he could easily work it out on his own.

Chapter Sixteen

Emmitt breathed deeply as he drove past the Yates house. He followed Renata's instructions from their earlier conversation and turned the corner, heading south for five blocks until he arrived at the open gates of the Yates Museum and Botanical Gardens. An overwhelming eagerness had led him to call Renata the previous morning to ask when they should meet. She had teased him for his impatience, then suggested they meet at the entrance an hour and a half before the museum's opening. Emmitt's restlessness led him through the gates two hours before the museum opened.

He pulled into the mostly empty lot and parked his powder-blue station wagon close to the entrance next to Renata's expensive black sedan. Andrew may have been embarrassed by the old station wagon, but Emmitt cherished the car his family had once piled into during summer trips (when the Key family had still been intact enough to vacation together).

He exited the car, adjusted the collar of Andrew's navy polo shirt and hastily tucked the shirt into his jeans. The almost-winter sun had been half-hidden behind a billowing white cloud. A brisk breeze blew, causing the hair on Emmitt's arms to raise. Emmitt looked through the car window at his black windbreaker, which had been balled up and tossed carelessly in the backseat. It was still covered in dog hair from his last visit to the animal shelter, and it smelled worse than it looked. No jacket today, Emmitt thought, as he rubbed his arms with his hands to keep from shivering.

He jumped up and down to pump his blood, then leaned over and smiled into the side-view mirror, making sure his breakfast burrito hadn't left pieces of cilantro or onion in his teeth. Satisfied by his spotless smile, Emmitt straightened his posture and popped a piece of peppermint chewing gum into his mouth to mask any offending odor from the cilantro and onions. With a slight sense of self-assurance, Emmitt casually walked toward the museum entrance.

As he approached the entrance, he noticed Renata was already standing by the closed gates, waiting for him. She wore a knee-length black and green plaid skirt, a tight black sweater, and a dark-green knit cardigan. Her long hair was loosely curled and tumbled in waves past her shoulders, with the ends brushing against her elbows. The headband in her hair matched the plaid design on her wool skirt.

Emmitt smiled and called out to her. "Hey! You're early. How long have you been standing there?"

Renata waited for Emmitt to come closer before she answered. "Not long. A couple minutes, maybe. Are you ready to get started? The café isn't open yet, but we can come back later for coffee ... if you want to."

"That works for me. It's been a while since I've been here. My dad took me here all the time when I was a kid. We would buy little cups of pellets and feed the ducks at the pond."

"Oh, the pond is bigger now. It's practically a lake." Renata widened her arms to illustrate. Her excitement quickly turned to consternation. "But … we don't allow anyone to feed the ducks anymore. Aunt Gracie got involved years ago. After a lifetime of avoiding any type of work with the museum, she suddenly inserted herself by insisting we use only the highest quality duck feed. Uncle James grumbled about it, but he bought the brand she recommended, which was, of course, a special brand developed by her then-boyfriend. It had the same ingredients, was manufactured by the same company, and was packaged in the same facility that made the cheaper duck feed we previously used … I guess the packaging made it healthier." Renata's voice rose in indignation. "Then, a week after dumping the premium duck feed guy, Aunt Gracie said she was concerned about a duck obesity epidemic on the premises. She may have overstated the issue to one of her animal-activist friends. A couple of weeks after complaining about chubby ducks, there were six billboards within a mile of the museum, claiming our ducks had fatty liver disease … which was untrue. Our staff vets checked them regularly and insisted they were healthy."

Emmitt stood still while his eyes widened. "What happened next?"

Renata took a breath. "I … may have overshared. We worked it out, in the end."

"Come on! Please, tell me how it ended! I swear I won't put it in the book. Please?"

Renata sighed. "Doesn't it frustrate you to find out sordid details about my family, knowing you can never repeat them to anyone?"

Emmitt shook his head vigorously. "Information is valuable, whether it's written or spoken or kept hidden. If you're the only one I can ever discuss it with, that's enough for me."

"Fine," Renata calmly relented. She took a step closer to Emmitt and lowered her voice. "My uncle brought in the family attorneys, and the billboards came down three days after they were put up. When my aunt threatened to stage a protest at the museum entrance, the museum board responded by prohibiting guests from feeding the ducks. Our family reputation suffered some damage, so Aunt Gracie suggested a large donation to an exotic bird sanctuary—"

"In Santa Barbara!" Emmitt finished.

Renata rolled her eyes as she tried to suppress a smile. "Yes. The bird sanctuary was owned and operated by the same ... person ... who put the billboards up. Aunt Gracie thought Sybil should appear at a fundraiser for the charity. It was a catered event with a meaningless awards ceremony set up by PR firms looking to raise the reputations of their wayward clients. Sybil received an award that night. Her popularity wasn't what it used to be, so she jumped at the opportunity to be at a red-carpet event and show off her beautiful, beachy waves."

Renata flicked her long hair over her shoulder as she mocked one of Sybil's signature poses. She tilted her head, plastered on a fake smile, and gazed haughtily off in the distance.

I don't think she realizes just how much she looks like her sister. Emmitt prudently kept the observation to himself.

"That sounds a bit like extortion," Emmitt thought aloud.

"Maybe," Renata shrugged. "But it's just how things work. Anyway, Sybil was happy to do it, and Aunt Gracie made sure the protesters—who had already been purchased and scheduled for delivery—never arrived at the museum gates. When Aunt Gracie ended her affair with the exotic bird guy, her concern for the ducks waned considerably ... like Mother said, she moved on to collecting dogs."

"That's ... fascinating ... and terrible."

"Yeah," Renata agreed half-heartedly.

"Why do you seem so unfazed by it?"

"I'm used to it, I guess. It's more annoying than interesting to me."

"Why do all the interesting things happen to people who don't appreciate them?" Emmitt complained.

"You should be grateful to have stability. All these fascinating things have consequences. Drama is only entertaining to hear about when it's attached to someone else."

"I don't know," Emmitt said. "Some people thrive on drama. Sybil seems to be incapable of functioning without it."

Renata narrowed her eyes at Emmitt. "Sybil could be used as a case study for clinicians and lab scientists. She's an anomaly." Another rush of wind blew. Renata clutched at her cardigan as her teeth chattered. "Is it okay if we head in?"

Emmitt turned his attention to the enormous iron gates that were closed and latched behind them. "Of course. You got a key for those?"

Renata smirked. "I have a *Key* right here, but I don't think he can open the gates. We can head in through the staff entrance."

Renata motioned to a path, surrounded by hedges that led to the side entrance of a large building. Emmitt followed closely behind. The heels of her black boots clicked on the pavement as he watched her skirt sway and bounce with her quick steps.

"You're resorting to puns, Renata?" Emmitt said.

As she stopped and spun around, Emmitt saw the hem of her skirt brush against his jeans. She didn't say anything at first. Emmitt realized, with immediate horror, she was waiting for his eyes to move up from her skirt before responding. When their eyes locked, Emmitt flushed. Renata grinned with amusement at his reddening face.

"I like puns," she said, ignoring Emmitt's wandering eyes. "Your name lends itself to a lot of future puns. It's docent humor. If I'm leading a guided tour, I stick to dad jokes and puns ... I have to be as inoffensive as possible."

Emmitt sighed out his ebbing embarrassment, then teased, "Do you also tell people about your deep, dark family secrets on guided tours?"

"No." Renata's eyes flashed. "You're getting the VIP museum experience. It's very different from what I normally do."

"I'm honored."

"You should be," Renata snickered, as she turned away from Emmitt and dug inside her purse. Finding the key, she opened the door.

The hallway they entered led to a sitting area that looked like the lobby of a boutique hotel. The sofa and armchairs were a soft white. Oversized porcelain vases held cascading bouquets that sprayed outward and spilled over in every direction. There were decorative sconces throughout the room that bathed everything in a warm yellow light. At the back of the room was a ten-foot Christmas tree decorated with white, silver, and gold ornaments. On top was a curly-haired angel with a white embroidered gown and feathered wings.

"This is where the VIPs begin their guided tours," Renata said in a hushed voice. "The main offices are in this building, and through that door—" she pointed behind where she and Emmitt stood, "—are the ticket counters for general admission. If we follow the hallway on our left, we can exit and head to the museum."

"You guys really go all-out for Christmas," Emmitt remarked.

"Uncle James and I are mostly to blame. We try to outdo ourselves each year. I can't decorate the house—for obvious reasons—so I have to limit my festive spirit to the museum grounds. Mother used to help us decorate for the holidays."

"Why did she stop?" Emmitt asked.

"She had a falling out with my uncle. She blames him for … certain things. I wish she would get more involved. She's too isolated."

"Did you decorate this tree?" Emmitt said, hoping to lighten the conversation.

"Yes." Renata's face brightened. "We have staff and volunteers who decorate different trees around the museum and gardens. Most of the decorations have been up since Thanksgiving, but the Dickens Village is only half-erected … it's taking longer than we thought to get it up."

"Is that a dirty pun, Renata?"

Renata looked quizzically at Emmitt, then considered her words. Her eyes widened. "No!" she blushed.

Emmitt smirked. "I must say, the VIP tour is absolutely the way to go for vulgar Dickens jokes."

Renata sighed as she brought a hand to her cheek. "Oh, God. This is embarrassing."

"Why? It's been a perfect tour so far, and we've just started."

Emmitt noticed Renata's eyes fix downward as her face turned a deeper shade of red. He hadn't intended to fluster her. He assumed Renata might even appreciate the joke. Emmitt's thoughts spiraled. *I'm ruining everything.* Renata was kind enough to ignore his looking … leering … earlier, and he had thanked her by pointing out a dirty joke she had not intended to make. *Jackass!* Be normal, he commanded himself.

He hesitated, then forced himself to act. He raised his left hand and lightly brushed his fingers against Renata's elbow to draw her attention. Her eyes lifted to meet his.

"I'm sorry. I'm nervous. Are you nervous?" he asked.

Renata's crimson face nodded silently.

"It's not quite the same as when we're at your house, bullshitting with each other. This feels different ... not bad different ... but, I don't know, more ..."

"Serious? Heavy? Significant?" The words poured anxiously out of her mouth.

Emmitt smiled. "Yeah. All at once. I'm sorry for making a crude joke. I'll try to be quiet."

"No," Renata said. "You don't have to be quiet. It's nerves. I want everything to be perfect. This is what I do. It's what I'm good at. I'm trying not to mess up. I'm not offended by the joke ... you made me lose my place." She twisted her mouth and admitted, "I practiced what I was going to say. It's stupid, and I don't normally do it, but I had butterflies last night. I was so anxious I could barely sleep."

"You're doing a great job," Emmitt said, then risked his own pride by attempting a compliment. "And you look nice ... pretty ... like the angel with the curly hair on the tree. You look like Christmas."

"Thanks, I think," Renata laughed. "I've never been told I look like a holiday before ... that must be why you were staring at my plaid skirt."

"I ... I deserved that," Emmitt stammered. "But it is a nice skirt. It's festive."

"Mhmm," Renata hummed with a coy smile.

She moved toward the exit. Emmitt followed behind, with his eyes fixed firmly on the back of her head. Once outside, Emmitt glanced back to see the other side of the closed iron gates.

"Is anyone else here besides us?"

Renata grinned at Emmitt's inquiry. "Well, the gardeners and maintenance staff started hours ago … security and tour guides will arrive soon … and some of the restaurant, bakery, and café staff are already prepping, baking, and brewing coffee … but, if you ignore all of them, it's just the two of us."

"Where are we headed first?"

"I was thinking we'd start with the house and galleries before the museum opens. Then we can walk through the gardens, and end with a visit to the pond. And, if you're interested, I can stop to show you some plans we have for expansion."

"I'm interested," Emmitt said.

They walked on the path through the expansive grounds with trimmed lawns of emerald grass, ornate fountains with half-dressed statues of Greek or Roman deities, and long pergolas that acted as canopies, blotting out sunlight, and sagging with the weight of the climbing pink bougainvillea, which Renata called "Rosa Preciosa." At all times, the mansion remained within view. Even in the distance, the Yates estate was colossal. As they approached, it towered over them. It looked more like a cathedral, or a governmental palace commissioned by a foreign dictator than an early twentieth-century family home built on the West Coast of the United States. It was both beautiful and garish.

"My great-great-grandfather, Thomas Yates, bought this property in 1896, which was the same year he married my great-great-grandmother. Construction of the house began in 1899 and ended in 1905."

Renata was measured as she repeated the words she had undoubtedly spoken countless times before. Emmitt held his tongue and tried not to interject as Renata continued.

"The house was constructed during the Gilded Age, and built in the Beaux-Arts architectural style, blending Greek and Roman classicism with Baroque influences, as well as elements from the French and Italian Renaissance—"

"So, rich Americans traveled to Europe, bought one of everything and incorporated it into their houses? Like if Frankenstein created a mansion instead of a monster?" Emmitt heard himself interrupt.

"Not really." Renata furrowed her brow. "While it's true that the style pulls from many periods and cultures, it's not a unique occurrence. The Renaissance itself was a revival of Greco-Roman classicism. Most architectural styles take inspiration from earlier periods in history."

"Got it." Emmitt grinned sheepishly. "I've clearly established my ignorance."

Renata ignored Emmitt and continued. "While the Beaux-Arts style originated in Paris, it became popular among wealthy Americans in the latter half of the 1800s, and it maintained its popularity into the early 1900s. The style, unsurprisingly, fell out of fashion by the beginning of the Great Depression. Thomas Yates and his wife, Mary, lived here with their three children: Robert, Grace, and Margaret. Mary died in 1939, and Thomas died the following year, leaving the entire estate to my great-grandfather, Robert Yates. Instead of living on the property, Robert maintained the estate and opened the mansion and gardens for public viewing in 1946. By 1960, he had constructed two additional art galleries, paved pathways for guests, and dug the pond at the southwest corner of the property. The house remains just as his parents left it before their passing. Nothing has been added or removed … except the rope barriers that keep people from touching the art and sitting on the furniture."

"You know a lot about the history of this house," Emmitt said.

"Well, I grew up here … I didn't live here, of course, but my family has always been involved with the museum. When my great-grandfather opened his father's home to visitors, he insisted the family be responsible for its upkeep and any future developments. My grandfather, James Sr., expanded the rose garden and added a desert garden and an atrium for tropical plants, and Uncle James has acted as his successor. Uncle James is the one who's most involved in day-to-day operations, and he still finds time to give guided tours. Mother used to plan events, and Dad worked as an appraiser and art historian. I'd follow them around on tours, and by the time I was eight, I had the whole script memorized."

"You don't have any anxiety talking in front of a tour group?" Emmitt asked, while suppressing the urge to question her about her late father.

Renata shook her head. "Like I said, I've memorized the script. I feel less panicked when I know what I'm doing. Leading guided tours is a rite of passage for the younger Yates family members. It's a pretty decent gauge for future involvement in the museum. Sybil was never interested in learning the script, but both of my parents were so knowledgeable, a guest could point to any object in the house or galleries, and they would give a detailed lecture, then transition effortlessly back to the rehearsed lines."

"So, is that your job at the museum? You give guided tours?"

"Sometimes, but it isn't the only thing I do. It's not my favorite thing to do, either. I prefer to work behind the scenes, like decorating for the holidays and setting up events ... and working in the gardens. My grandfather preferred the outdoors, and my cousins and I would always end up with our hands in the dirt whenever we spent the day with him. We're developing a new garden, in his honor. I'm excited to show you ... but I'm already getting ahead of myself."

"I'm excited to see it."

"You'll love it ... I hope," Renata said. "If you follow me, I'll take you through the house."

Emmitt had toured the Yates ancestral home several times with his father when he was younger. He remembered, vaguely, trying to speed through the labyrinthine mansion to have more time to sit at the pond with the ducks. He would rush ahead, only to have his father call him back to look at a painting or piece of furniture. Emmitt would slump his shoulders and nod mechanically, then grab his dad's arm to pull him into the next room. Even now, as an adult, Emmitt maintained his disinterest in old furniture and paintings. Despite this indifference, he decided he would study the rooms carefully. Having been acquainted with the Yates women, he'd developed a new set of eyes to look through. He was eager to see the house with this enhanced perception. It wasn't just a trip to the museum for Emmitt. It was an investigation.

Entering from a side door, they walked through a long corridor. Blue velvet ropes cordoned off the two open doors attached to the hallway. One room was an office, the other was a parlor. Both were elaborately decorated with paintings, tapestries, ornate desks and couches, and full bookcases that reached the top of the fifteen-foot ceiling. Although the rooms were large, they felt overcrowded. Cramped. A person could walk around the room if they wanted to sit in a chair, or sofa, or pick out a book from the bookshelf, but there wasn't any superfluous space apart from a designated path.

The corridor led to an open hallway, which led to more rooms congested with items. The living rooms, library, and bedrooms were all functional, but they were filled with so many pieces of fine art and furniture, they looked more like a museum than a family home. Of course, the family home *was* a museum, but Renata said nothing had been added or removed. Even when it functioned as a home for Renata's great-grandfather, it would have felt like a museum. Emmitt wasn't surprised that Robert Yates refused to live in the claustrophobic mansion.

When they reached the third (and largest) formal dining room, meant for dignitaries and Thomas's wealthiest associates, Emmitt paused.

Ten cream and gold gilded china cabinets lined the east and west sides of the room. Five towered on each wall. Behind the glass cabinets, Emmitt could see that each was filled with dishes and crystal glassware. A large triptych hung on the north wall, depicting the Virgin Mary holding her infant, with the Annunciation and Crucifixion on either side. Surrounding the triptych were other religious paintings depicting the Last Supper, the Nativity, and the Baptism of Jesus.

"You've been standing here for a while," Renata finally said, breaking Emmitt away from his thoughts.

"I think I agree with your mom," Emmitt said absently. His eyes remained fixed on the room.

"What do you mean?"

"You said the house was left exactly as it was when your great-great-grandparents died. This is how they lived, right?"

"Yes ... but I don't see the point you're trying to make." Renata leaned closer to Emmitt and followed his eyes as she peered into the room.

"Are all the rooms like this?" Emmitt scratched the back of his head as he questioned Renata.

"Decorated?"

"Cluttered."

"They were collectors ... but there aren't boxes ... or piles ... everything is organized perfectly ..." Renata stammered. Emmitt feared she might become indignant.

"It's beautiful, opulent, and well decorated," Emmitt said. "Like I said, I don't know anything about home décor or art or antiques, so I'll just stay quiet and let you continue the tour."

"No," Renata said. "Continue. 'It's beautiful, opulent and well-decorated,' but ...?"

Emmitt could feel her staring at him. He turned to face her glare. "But ... ten china cabinets? This house has more religious art and statues than your mom has piled up in your house. Are the kids' rooms also curated? There's no space to move or play or live—"

"The property is three hundred acres," Renata protested. "There's plenty of room to play outside ... and you haven't seen the children's living quarters to judge."

"Show me."

"Fine."

To Emmitt's surprise, Renata grabbed his hand firmly and walked him through a maze of hallways and rooms to a staircase that led to the wing where the Yates children lived a century prior. Her grip tightened as they ascended the stairs to view the children's rooms.

Breathlessly, Renata released Emmitt's hand and gestured at him to look through the door. "This was my great-grandfather's room. Down the hall are my great-aunts' rooms."

Emmitt peered inside. "It looks like a normal kid's room, I guess," he admitted. "It's a little stuffy ... not too many toys ... a few too many chairs and sofas ... and that ottoman seems like it would get in the way ... but I will concede that this room is maneuverable."

Renata raised her head and smiled smugly. "Do you still think my mom is right?"

"Yes."

"You think my great-great grandparents were hoarders?" Renata was incredulous.

"I don't know ... probably not. But there are more hutches in that dining room than your mom has in hers ... and we passed by two more dining rooms on the way up here. How many dining rooms does this house have?"

"Seven," Renata said defiantly.

Emmitt continued cautiously. "I'm not saying it's the same situation. I'm not saying your great-great grandparents were hoarders. I'm just saying I understand your mom's perspective ..." Emmitt held his hands out, urging Renata to let him explain.

Renata didn't give him the opportunity. "So, the rest of my family should just sit back and let my mother continue to accumulate, since, in her own mind, she's just a collector like Thomas and Mary Yates?"

"No. I know it's not the same ... but there are similarities that shouldn't be ignored. I'm trying to see what your mom sees."

"Your comparisons are erroneous," Renata declared. Her whole body stiffened in defiance.

"That's fair," Emmitt said, hoping it would soothe Renata's growing wrath. "I could be overstepping ... I am ... I am overstepping. I do that a lot. But—and don't hate me for saying this—perhaps there are legitimate comparisons that you haven't noticed."

"Enlighten me." Renata's lips were drawn, but her body had relaxed, and her tone was slightly less combative.

"No. You'll just get mad at me again. I want to continue the tour." Emmitt grabbed Renata's hands and dropped dramatically to his knees. "Don't kick me out, Renata! Don't keep me from the ducks, and the lake, and your new garden. I promise I'll be good."

Renata pulled one hand out of his and cupped it over her mouth. Emmitt wasn't sure if she was trying to suppress laughter or tears. She let out a long breath and lowered her hand as her eyes looked down at Emmitt. "You can't always use humor as a means of deflection." Renata spoke slowly and thoughtfully. "In your mind, you're just speaking casually or thinking aloud, but your comments aren't harmless. They fracture and collapse the things that have kept me protected and held me together. When I spend too much time focusing on the discrepancies, I feel like I'm unraveling."

Emmitt's heart sank as she spoke. A cold sweat beaded down the back of his neck. He released Renata's hand as he scrambled back to his feet. "I'm sorry. I'm focusing too much on the work we're doing at the house. This is separate. I need to keep it separate when you and I are out … recreationally."

Emmitt didn't want to misinterpret Renata's invitation as a date. Perhaps it was a date in her mind, but he wasn't sure enough to make any assumptions. Emmitt wanted it to be a date. He had an irksome wriggling feeling in his gut that, if it *was* a date, he had already ruined his chances with Renata at every shift and turn of the conversation.

Renata whispered, "Is this going to be a problem for us? Is it even possible to keep things separate?" All traces of anger had melted. She sounded worried.

"I think we can manage …" Emmitt hesitated to answer definitively. "I really wasn't trying to hurt or provoke you. I know I'm not saying the right things, but I don't want to lie to you either."

Renata sighed deeply. "I always thought I was fine. I thought my mother and Sybil were the dysfunctional ones, and I was the rational, responsible one who was saving them from their own destructive habits. Then Andrew exposes me for being an enabling doormat, and you accuse every Yates family member of hoarding."

"Shit. I didn't think about it that way. I'm sorry."

Renata turned her head away from Emmitt. "I know you are. I know I'm too sensitive, and I should have a thicker skin, and I should be open to constructive criticism, but this is the only place that makes me happy. It's the only place that makes me feel accomplished … and appreciated. I know you aren't trying to take that away from me. I just don't want to think about my family problems here. My home life is chaotic enough."

"I get it. Andrew said it was unprofessional for me to want to spend time with you when we're not working at the house. I had resigned myself to being professional ... but then you invited me here."

"Your resolve couldn't have been too strong, if you accepted my invitation," Renata said, eyeing Emmitt.

"I said I was *resigned* to act professionally, not *resolved* to do it," Emmitt dared to tease. "I'm glad you invited me, and I'm glad I'm here, but I'm starting to understand Andrew's concerns. It's difficult for me to fully separate our friendship from our working relationship. I want to know more about you because I'm interested in you ... I like you ... but I'm also interested in your family life, because I want to help your mom and sister fix their hoarding problem. I don't always know when I cross that line ... and sometimes I *do* know, but I push anyway." Emmitt bit his lip as he nervously tapped the side of his leg.

Renata gently placed her hand over his to stop his fidgeting. "You really told Andrew you wanted to spend time with me?" she asked. She removed her hand and studied Emmitt's face.

"Yeah, well ... I may have mentioned it. I figured we had a lot in common ... family issues, a disdain for self-help ... crushing anxiety."

"But you weren't planning to initiate anything?"

"I think I already mentioned crushing anxiety. Andrew had already said no. I didn't think I would need to defy him. I wasn't expecting your boldness, Renata. Did you agree to sign the waiver just so you could get me alone?"

Renata's mouth gaped.

Emmitt grimaced. "Shit. I'll shut up."

"No." Renata giggled nervously. "It's just ... really embarrassing."

"Got it. You don't have to say anything. I just wanted to let you know we don't have to hold you to anything. I could tell Andrew you changed your mind about being in the book. He'd understand."

"Ugh," Renata groaned. "I had already decided to sign the waiver. I didn't know Andrew would have to leave us alone to get it. That wasn't my plan."

"You had a plan?" Emmitt asked incredulously.

"I had two plans," Renata said. She winced and avoided Emmitt's eyes.

"Oh," Emmitt breathed. "Can I ask?"

Renata bit her lip. "Don't laugh."

"I won't," Emmitt whispered.

"I had a box of old clothes in my closet I was going to forget about. I would wait until you had packed everything else, then suddenly remember and ask you to go back to help me carry the box to my car. If that didn't work, I was going to ask Andrew to give me your addresses, so I could send you both Christmas cards."

"Huh … you know, you could've just waited until Sybil came back from her vacation and asked me at the trash cans. It would have saved you some stress, at least."

"I didn't want to wait."

Emmitt felt a warmth from within that filled his lungs and sighed out of his mouth. "You're brave, Renata."

"You're obvious, Emmitt."

Emmitt smiled. "Well, in my defense, I'm also pretty dense. But in the spirit of shared embarrassment, I'll admit that, including you, I only have three friends … and before you even ask, yes, I'm counting Andrew as a friend."

"Who's the other one?" Renata's shining eyes betrayed her feigned solemnity.

Emmitt felt his face flush. He breathed deeply before continuing. "My only other friend is an eight-year-old shepherd mix named Henry. I visit him twice a week at a local dog shelter ... and I read to him."

Renata's face brightened. "That's so sweet ... and kind of sad too. I don't have any friends outside of my extended family and the nuns, so I can't really make fun of you."

"Hey!" Emmitt beamed. "Something else we have in common."

"We're both losers?" Renata asked.

"No, we are both very discerning regarding the company we choose to keep," Emmitt said.

"Ah, yes. That must be it."

"Are we good?" Emmitt asked.

"We're good, Emmitt ... but I think I'm going to keep you outside for the rest of the day. We'll skip the house and galleries and tour the gardens instead."

"You don't trust me to keep my mouth shut?"

"You don't seem to trust yourself to keep your mouth shut."

"You're wise, Renata."

Emmitt and Renata descended the stairs, wound through corridors, and finally exited through the front door of the Yates mansion. As the sun shone on his face, Emmitt glanced at Renata. She wasn't smiling, but her blue eyes glimmered, and her blonde curls bounced as she synchronized her pace to Emmitt's. As he looked ahead at the path, he felt her small, warm hand slip into his. He repeated *thank you* in his head to no one in particular as he walked with Renata, hand in hand down the path.

Chapter Seventeen

The crisp breeze, soft sunshine, and Renata's warm hand momentarily broke Emmitt free from worry. At that moment, he could remember it was a nice day, and he was finally alone with Renata.

The thought was fleeting. Another caustic, burning dread seeped deeply into his mind and boiled slowly to the surface. He'd hurt Renata. He hadn't intended to hurt her, but the intention didn't matter. Unraveling, he thought. *Fracturing and collapsing.* Emmitt pictured a porcelain doll shattering to pieces. Was Renata really so vulnerable? So fragile? Emmitt's mind trapped him in a spiraling cycle of guilt and unease.

It was Renata's voice that grabbed Emmitt and pulled him out of the quagmire created by his stewing, miserable thoughts.

"So, I really don't know if I want to bring this up …" She paused for a moment.

As she walked down the path with Emmitt at her side, she absentmindedly twirled the ends of her long hair with her fingers. Just as Emmitt wondered if she had decided against telling him whatever it was she didn't want to bring up, she continued.

"Here." She pointed to a tall row of hedges which partially obscured the two large brick buildings behind them. "This hasn't been announced yet, but that's not why I'm hesitant to tell you about it."

"Okay." Emmitt wasn't sure what to say. The conversation in the Yates mansion flooded back to his mind. "You don't have to tell me." It was the safest answer he could give.

"I want to tell you, but you need to promise not to say anything. I already know what you're going to say. Just don't say it."

"I promise I won't say anything."

"Good. So, these buildings, beyond the hedges, are the on-site warehouses we use. My uncle has been building another warehouse on the southeast corner of the property to hold all the seasonal decorations. In a few years, we're hoping to knock down these warehouses and build a research library."

"That's amazing." Emmitt hoped he could prove to Renata he could keep his negative thoughts to himself.

"My great-grandfather, Robert Yates, was a book collector." Renata looked at Emmitt, waiting for a reaction.

"The son of Thomas Yates?" It was as far as Emmitt dared to go. He was determined to be less inquisitive, for Renata's sake.

"Yes. Thomas Yates hoarded artwork, furniture, and antiques, according to you. By the same measure, I'm sure you would probably accuse Robert of hoarding books and articles. He was obsessed with preserving history."

"Nothing wrong with that," Emmitt said, trying to sound casual. He was failing miserably, and he suspected Renata knew it. "How many books did he collect?"

"Three hundred thousand books. He also owned 700,000 photographs dating back to the 1860s, 500,000 historical prints from various parts of the world, and over 400,000 periodicals. These warehouses store most of them. Uncle James figured we could create an online catalog and display some of the collection, rather than keep everything hidden away from the public."

"Hmm." Emmitt tried to collect himself. "It sounds like you have enough materials to stock a research library. I'm looking forward to seeing it when it opens."

Renata laughed. "I appreciate how difficult that must've been for you."

Emmitt let out a sharp breath. "You nearly killed me, Renata."

As they continued to stroll, the path led them to the rose garden. Rows of rose bushes lined the green lawn, spanning acres. Winding, bloomless branches wrapped and twisted around trellises, gazebos, and arbors.

"The rose garden is bigger than I remember ... are they all roses? I can't tell," Emmitt said.

"Yes, they're all roses." Renata smiled as her eyes surveyed the garden. "It's underwhelming now, but by April, they'll all be in bloom. We have hundreds of varieties, and we've bred dozens of hybrids. You can usually tell which ones are ours ... they're mostly named after saints."

Emmitt gently nudged Renata with his elbow. "I guess you'll have to invite me back. I'd like to see everything in bloom."

"Of course! I can make a reservation for us at the Rose Patisserie. The tables overlook the garden, and we serve trays of little desserts and tea sandwiches." She moved closer to Emmitt and tried to stifle her laughter as she whispered, "I'm very popular with the staff at the Rose Patisserie … I can get us the best table."

"I wouldn't want anyone to think I was only using you for your pastry connections," Emmitt laughed.

"You'd be the only one *not* using me for my pastry connections. Reservations fill up months in advance. I have to guarantee a chaperone if Sybil wants a table—it's a long story that I will absolutely tell you, but not today—and Uncle James gets denied all the time. Everyone has to go through me."

"I had no idea." Emmitt smirked. "I'm very impressed by your power and influence."

Renata hooked her arm around Emmitt's as she led him further through the gardens. They wandered through the desert garden, past pink-blossomed camellia shrubs, and through a large, humid atrium with a miniature jungle of tropical plants. Despite the crisp chill of early December, the air in the atrium was thick and wet. Emmitt nodded and listened as Renata gave detailed explanations of the classifications and countries of origin. He watched with intense interest as she provided trivia from propagation to medicinal applications. He was happy seeing her happy.

When they finally exited the atrium, the cold air hit the moisture that had accumulated on Emmitt's arms. He tried to keep from shivering as he felt Renata tighten her grip and press herself closer to his side. With her free hand, she pointed up the path to a fenced-off area. Green netting obscured the view beyond the chain-link fence. Renata led Emmitt within feet of the fence and stopped.

"Okay, so I didn't think about the fence when I told you how excited I was to show you the new garden." Renata frowned as she realized her mistake.

"It's only a minor oversight," Emmitt assured. "What kind of garden is it?"

Renata released her hold on Emmitt and moved closer to the fence. "We're developing a large potager garden. It's a scaled-down replica of the Potager du Roi in Versailles." Renata's face was a beam of light. Emmitt was excited for her, but he had no idea what she was talking about.

"That's great! What is a potager?"

Renata giggled. "It's a vegetable and herb garden. We're also planting a small citrus orchard—this whole city used to be orange groves—and we're adding a farm-to-table bistro. We're going to raise chickens and quails … assuming Aunt Gracie doesn't have a hissy fit over free-range eggs. Oh, and we'll have an area to explain composting, hydroponics, and irrigation techniques." Renata's eyes were wide and shining.

"You said it was to honor your grandfather, right? Was this his idea?"

"It wasn't specifically his idea, but he inspired it. Grandpa used to teach workshops on subsistence agriculture, and he practiced homesteading in his own backyard—and front yard—then he convinced his neighbors to get involved. Grandpa had a very contagious spirit. He would have loved this garden."

"It seems like you inherited his contagious spirit. I've never planted anything in my life, but now I kinda want to get my hands in the dirt and see what I've been missing out on."

Renata's eyes glistened at Emmitt's words. "That … is one of the best compliments I have ever received. Thank you, Emmitt."

Emmitt's breath caught in his throat. "Yeah, well. It's the truth … and I'm glad you're able to honor your grandpa. So, when will it open?"

"We expect to complete everything by next October, which will coincide with our first fall festival. The citrus trees will be delivered and planted in early spring, and we're on schedule to start planting in the garden by April. I have a diagram of the garden plots, and I'm researching the best heirloom seeds for each season. The foundation has already been laid for the bistro, and the outdoor patio will overlook the orchard … and … I'm rambling. Sorry, Emmitt."

"Don't apologize for being excited. I'm wondering … with the garden … is it something I could help with, or is it better left to experts?"

Renata's smile broadened as she clasped her hands together. "Of course you can help. Once the greenhouse is up by the end of winter, I can show you all the seeds we're going to plant. They need time to mature in the greenhouse before we transplant them into the garden. It's a straightforward process, although some herbs can be a little tricky to get started."

Emmitt basked in Renata's pure joy. "I'm looking forward to seeing your garden."

Renata's bright eyes shifted from Emmitt to the paved path that wound up and over a small hill. "I've kept you long enough from the duck pond. It's this way."

They followed the path over the hill and through a woodland of native oaks, finally arriving at the pond. Renata hadn't exaggerated when she called it a lake. The new pond was at least five times larger than the one Emmitt had visited as a child.

As they approached the water, Renata noticed a member of the gardening staff driving a cart up the path. "I have an idea," she told Emmitt, as she waved her arms wildly to get the driver's attention. When he recognized the young woman, the driver stopped and waved back at her.

"Follow me," Renata playfully beckoned to Emmitt.

At the cart, Renata introduced Emmitt to the staff member, then spoke casually with the man, carefully listening to his assessment of future weather patterns and sincerely inquiring about his wife and teenage daughter.

After a few minutes of pleasantries, she asked, "Mike, do you think there's any way we can get some duck food? I know there's some in the maintenance shed, but I don't have the key to unlock it."

Mike smiled and winked at Renata. "I can open it for you. But if Miss Grace comes by, I'm denying everything."

"I promise to take full responsibility if I get caught. I think we're safe, though. Aunt Gracie hasn't visited the property in months, and she hasn't been near the ducks in years."

"Well, now you're just tempting fate," the man chuckled.

"William says Aunt Gracie will only appear on the premises if you say her name three times while staring at your reflection in the duck pond."

Mike let out a booming laugh. "Will would say that. His father's sense of humor certainly rubbed off on him. But I suspect that kind of humor also keeps Miss Shannon away. Tell her we all miss her. Maybe if she keeps hearing it, she'll start coming back."

"I'll definitely let her know," Renata said.

They walked down the path, and Mike opened the door to the maintenance shed. He entered, grabbed a clear plastic pitcher, and filled it to the brim with duck pellets.

He handed the filled pitcher to Emmitt. "Just leave the empty container by the door when you're done. I'll have someone swing by and put it back later."

"Thanks, Mike," Renata said. "And sorry for the inconvenience."

"It's no inconvenience, Miss Renata. In fact, next time you pass by my office, stop in and I'll get you your own key … just in case you want to sneak in and feed the ducks again."

"I will. Thanks again."

As Mike walked back to the cart, Renata led Emmitt to a secluded bench near the pond. She quickly rummaged through her purse and drew out her phone.

Looking at the screen, Renata said, "We have about fifteen minutes until the museum opens. We'll have to finish feeding the ducks by then."

The two of them sat together on the park bench. Emmitt grabbed a handful of pellets and gently tossed the food a few feet in front of him. Soon, a swarm of ducks began to swim and waddle toward them. As they approached, Emmitt and Renata began to feed the ducks out of their hands. The ducks nibbled and pecked contently as Emmitt and Renata continued to draw more handfuls from the container.

When the pitcher was empty, Emmitt leaned back against the wooden bench and watched the ducks waddle back to the water and swim away. "I'm glad we were able to feed the ducks without getting caught," Emmitt said casually, as he stared out at the rippling water. "Who's William?"

"My cousin. He's the oldest of Uncle James and Aunt Helen's kids. He's here almost as much as I am."

"How many cousins do you have?" Emmitt asked.

"Nine on my mother's side. Five from Dad's side."

"Do all the Yates cousins work at the museum?"

"Not all. Uncle James's children work and volunteer here. I'm closer to them than I am to Sybil. Aunt Gracie's youngest two work here during their summer break ... they're still in high school. Do you have cousins?"

"I don't know," Emmitt said.

"That's an odd way to answer."

Emmitt shrugged. "None from my dad's side. He was an only child. His parents had plenty of siblings, so I have great-aunts and uncles and second and third cousins. They all live in the Midwest, so we were never really close. I couldn't name the majority of them. We visited for a couple of weddings and funerals. There was one baptism too. My dad's cousin wanted him to be the godfather. My great-aunt Kathy had a fit."

"And your mother's side?" Renata asked.

"Mom was estranged from her family before Andrew and I were born. I don't even know her real name ... she had it legally changed before she met my dad. If he knows, he's never told me, and Andrew won't ask Mom. All I know is that her parents were both Italian—not sure if that means they're from Italy or they're of Italian descent—and Dad once let it slip that she had siblings ... I don't know how many, and I don't know if I have cousins."

"That's weird," Renata said. "And you've never pushed to find out more? That doesn't sound like you."

"No one pushes Serenity," Emmitt said in a low voice. "No one questions Serenity. No one challenges Serenity."

"Not even you?"

"Not on that. I've made her angry plenty of times, but I've only asked her about her family once. I think I was twelve ... possibly thirteen. I wasn't even being sarcastic or rude. I was just curious. She wouldn't speak to me for two months. Not one word. She wouldn't even look at me, and she'd leave whenever I walked into a room she was in. She used Andrew as an intermediary. He was furious."

"At her?" Renata asked.

"At me."

Emmitt let out a sharp exhale. "Andrew's sure her secrecy is motivated by some kind of childhood trauma. I think she experiences sadistic pleasure in using and discarding the people nearest to her. We've never been able to meet halfway on the matter." Emmitt shook his head and grabbed the empty plastic pitcher. He lifted it up for Renata to see. "Should we hide the evidence?"

"No. We'll put it back in a minute. We can relax here for a little while. I think we're safe from Aunt Gracie today ... but I expect she'll appear when we bring in the chickens and quails for the bistro. We've doubled the space needed to classify them as free-range, and we're only using their eggs for the menu, but it might not be enough. We might get lucky, though. She has her hands full with her dog rescue, and she's recently started going after 4-H kids."

"The kids that show livestock?"

"Yep. She was a bit too confrontational during a demonstration she attended. She ended up pepper-spraying a twelve-year-old."

"What!" Emmitt bolted upright. "That seems like something that would be on the news."

"The demonstration was on his parents' pig farm. Guess how much it cost the family to keep everything quiet." Renata's eyes stared out at the water as she spoke.

"She paid to keep it out of the news?"

"The family trust paid, and the family attorneys made sure it was kept out of the news. Two hundred fifty thousand dollars cash for Aunt Gracie to keep her dignity ... or whatever she has left of it. And that doesn't include the attorneys' fees ... both ours and theirs."

"Wow." Emmitt paused and considered. "I'm not sure if that's too much, too little, or just right. It's such a weird thing to have to think about fair compensation for a pepper-sprayed preteen."

"Not for my family," Renata sighed. "It's not a normal occurrence, but things like this still happen too often. Part of me wants my aunt ... and Sybil ... to have to face the consequences of their actions, but I also realize, if they actually faced those consequences, the Yates name would be negatively highlighted in the headlines. Our name is our legacy. If one of us messes up, it affects all of us, and a scathing article with the Yates name attached to it can affect the profitability of the museum. If people stop coming, we can't grow. I want to continue expanding the museum and gardens. After the research library and potager garden are completed, my cousin William and I want to focus on adding activities and exhibits for children. I don't want our hard work to be ruined by family scandals ... especially scandals involving pepper-sprayed preteens."

"I think the work you're doing here can survive any bruises or blemishes to the Yates name. If certain family members are living their lives without concern for potentially besmirching the family name, why can't the rest of you just keep doing what you're doing, and not worry about it?" Emmitt reached his arm across the back of the bench as he spoke.

"The name means something. The consequence of being born into wealth and prestige is the responsibility of living up to the name. It's a small concession. No one expects Gracie or Sybil or Lucas or Mother to be perfect. We'd all settle for mediocre. There's no excuse for their selfish behavior when they have so much to be thankful for. None of us can extract ourselves from the Yates name, and we should all bear an equal responsibility for maintaining a good reputation." Renata inched her way closer to Emmitt and rested her head against his shoulder.

"I get it. My mom and brother have created their own little legacy with the Key family name. It's nowhere near as influential as the Yates name, but their brand is tied to the self-help world. I can't change their influence. I could exploit it for my benefit, or I could actively try to work against it, but I can't ignore it."

"Do you feel you're exploiting their name?" Renata asked.

"Sometimes," Emmitt answered.

"Wait," Renata blurted. "Do you think you're the Sybil of the Key family?"

Emmitt frowned. "I hate to admit it ... but yeah. I think I am the Sybil of my family." Emmitt winced as he uttered the words. "I'm not actively trying to ruin their name, but it's my name too. It's not my fault I'm not like Andrew and Serenity. I want to have autonomy, outside the umbrella of the Key legacy. Maybe that's what Sybil wants."

"No. Sybil is awful," Renata insisted. "I understand what you're saying, but I don't think you're anything like Sybil. You're not destroying anything; you're just trying to do your own thing."

"I'm a hypocrite, Renata. I criticize Serenity and Andrew, and I hate what they do, but I'm using their name to benefit myself. I'm using my brother's name to publish a book … a self-help book. I'm only here with you because of him."

"Do you regret it?" Renata whispered.

"No. I'm glad I agreed to work with Andrew … I'm happy I'm here."

"I'm happy too," Renata said softly. She let the silence hang for a moment before adding quietly, "Do you think the stress of working with my family is affecting Andrew?"

"No way," Emmitt said. "My brother isn't fazed by anything or anyone."

"You sound certain."

"I am." A sliver of doubt pricked Emmitt. "I think I am … what have you noticed?"

"Nothing, really," Renata said. "I guess it's more of a feeling. He seemed unsure of himself while we were working in my room. He's usually upbeat and confident when he works with Sybil. I can't put exact words to it … but when he looked at me … when he held my hands, I felt sorry for him."

"He's not used to working with someone who doesn't worship the ground he walks on. You're different from his other clients. They only want Drew Key's positivity and platitudes. You prefer Andrew.

I think that threw him off." Emmitt was only partially confident this was the case, but he felt he owed it to Andrew to come up with some rationalization, while not completely dismissing Renata's concern. "I think it was a one-time calibration. You caught him in the act of tuning his frequencies … but I promise I'll watch out for him if you're worried."

"I am worried, but it's probably nothing." Renata snuggled closer to Emmitt as he slid his arm around her shoulder.

They sat silently together. For a few moments, there was nothing but the two of them sitting on the bench overlooking the pond. The breeze blew gently, the ducks quacked contentedly on the softly rippling water, and the sun shone brightly on Emmitt and Renata.

Chapter Eighteen

More than a month had passed without a call from Sybil or a trip to the Yates' house.

Despite completing her original aim of obtaining Emmitt's phone number, Renata had resolved, without Emmitt's knowledge, to meet with both brothers a week before Christmas. While Emmitt appreciated the professional pretense Renata had maintained by notifying Andrew of her desire for the trio to meet for lunch, he was slightly concerned (and equally jealous) that she had made plans with Andrew while mentioning nothing to him. His angst was ill-founded and short-lived. Emmitt's curiosity and mild agitation over Renata's secrecy dissolved when she entered the restaurant with her arms filled with gifts for him and Andrew, and a gleaming, mischievous grin adorning her face.

She presented the cards and gifts and watched with wide and eager eyes as they opened them. Each brother received a canvas bag with branded items from the Yates Museum and Botanical Gardens gift shop: a deep-green shirt and matching mug with the same ornate black lettering that embellished Renata's dark-teal sweatshirt; decorative boxes filled with rose, lemon balm, and lavender tea blends; and a jar of honey from the Yates estate's apiary. The Christmas cards were handwritten and flowing with a heartfelt sentimentality that touched both Emmitt and Andrew. The last gifts she presented were a tin of homemade cookies and candies for Emmitt and a stocking full of cured meats and jerky for Andrew.

Emmitt elevated his previous belief in Renata's spirit. It wasn't just contagious. It was exultant. Sacred, almost. Andrew seemed to sense it too. He dropped Drew Key altogether when he was around her. His lively and jovial demeanor allowed Emmitt and Renata to sneak smiling glances and nudge and tap the other's arm or hand while maintaining discretion and decorum. It was an unspoken arrangement, and not entirely deceitful in its intention. Both were aware of the boundary they were edging toward, and neither had pushed past the superficial physicality of friends who were hesitant to risk the security of their bond to explore the hazards of the unknown.

After lunch, Andrew thanked Renata for her thoughtfulness, but alone with Emmitt in the luxury SUV, cautioned his brother to avoid reciprocation.

"It may not be appropriate to buy a gift, given the circumstances. I'll send Renata a card from the two of us, but it would be inappropriate to add another piece of clutter to the house, no matter how well-intentioned."

Emmitt hadn't argued, but he hadn't obeyed, either. He had already used a portion of his paycheck from James Yates to buy several packets of expensive heirloom pumpkin seeds, hoping they would be an appropriate addition to the autumnal unveiling of Renata's potager garden. Emmitt's preliminary research opened the floodgates to a previously unknown realm filled with plant hardiness zones, soil pH levels, and light availability, which turned a simple, thoughtful gift into a panic-inducing hero's journey. Ultimately, Emmitt's efforts had the intended effect—Renata's face lit up with breathless giddiness at the unexpected present—but the anxiety it induced had cost him five pounds and five nights of sleep.

Now, with the emergence of the new year, Emmitt lay in bed, reflecting on the previous weeks, and pondering what portent they had for the future. As Emmitt continued to see Renata, he continued to keep Andrew ignorant. He assuaged his guilt by maintaining that he and Renata had remained friends. They flirted, held hands, and hugged, but they hadn't kissed. Not yet, at least. Emmitt couldn't discern if she was waiting for him to take initiative, or if she wasn't ready to further complicate their already complicated circumstances. Emmitt was ambivalent about what he should do. He didn't want to scare her off by being too assertive, but he also didn't want her to feel as though he simply wasn't interested in a relationship.

He drew his covers up to his neck as he forced the internal admission of an additional explanation for his reluctance. It was gutless, and he loathed to admit its influence over him. Emmitt realized if he didn't ask Renata if she wanted to be his girlfriend, she wouldn't have to answer, and he would save himself from having to confess anything to Andrew. He didn't *want* to care about compliance, but every time he thought about Renata, Drew Key's voice thundered *"unprofessional"* in his mind.

Despite the shattered nerves and prickling conscience he experienced in moments of solitude, Emmitt felt alive and steady whenever he was in the presence of Renata. After the long morning spent at the Yates Museum and Botanical Gardens, Emmitt drove Renata to Gigi's Beachfront Diner for lunch. A week later, she had taken him to a farmer's market. There had been coffee and dinner dates, the Christmas lunch with Andrew, and one trip to a drive-through holiday light display, where he presented his Christmas gift to Renata. She squealed and leaned over to hug Emmitt awkwardly from the passenger seat of his station wagon as he attempted to stay on the designated path. She released Emmitt and giggled her apologies after he narrowly missed an inflatable reindeer and nearly plowed into a pile of illuminated presents as the pop star on the radio trilled a nasally rendition of "The First Noel." During their last meeting, Emmitt had taken Renata to visit Henry at the animal shelter.

Emmitt could argue that all of their dates were nothing more than visits between friends. Emmitt was already guilty of complicating matters with the two people that mattered to him. At this moment, at least, he could honestly claim that he and Renata were not a couple. Not officially.

"Schrödinger's relationship," Emmitt mused to himself, as he stared at his ceiling from the comfort of his bed.

A hard knock on his apartment door startled Emmitt. He contemplated remaining silent—ignoring the visitor—until he heard his brother's voice call his name from the other side. Emmitt begrudgingly kicked off his covers, rose to his feet, and walked across the room to open the door.

Flustered wasn't a word that Emmitt would have ever used to describe his older brother, and perhaps he wouldn't have even noticed a hint of agitation now, had Renata not mentioned her concern for Andrew. Maybe Emmitt was imagining things. Andrew looked like Drew Key. His posture was straight, without being stiff. His outfit was crisp, clean, and unwrinkled, and his dark-brown hair was styled without a strand out of place. Maybe there was a hint of frenzy or a flicker of worry in his cool gray eyes, or maybe it was only the power of Renata's suggestion.

"Do I have something on my face?" Andrew asked, slightly annoyed. "Are you going to let me in, or are you too stunned by how handsome I am?"

Emmitt rolled his eyes. "I just thought I saw a new wrinkle developing under your left eye. It's deep, Andrew. Really off-putting. When's your next wrinkle treatment?"

"Next month," Andrew said casually as he brushed past Emmitt and sat on the couch. Even at Emmitt's apartment, Andrew never reclined.

"It's unsightly," Emmitt mocked. "You should move up your appointment."

"Nah. I've been thinking I'm going to let myself age from now on. I've maintained myself so well that I don't even look like your older brother anymore. If you put the two of us side by side, I could easily be mistaken for your grandson."

"Huh," Emmitt said, ignoring Andrew's insult. "No more treatments? Isn't your face your primary means of advertising?"

"My face is just fine, with or without treatments. I don't need the chemicals, and I've decided it's not something I want to invest in anymore." Andrew narrowed his eyes at Emmitt's sudden interest.

"Why?" Emmitt asked.

"Why do you care?" Andrew glared at Emmitt. Before Emmitt could answer, Andrew hastily added, "It's not important. Aren't you curious why I'm here?"

"I just thought you wanted to visit me because you love me … Andrew, do you not love me?" Emmitt clutched his hands to his heart.

"Forget it," Andrew sneered as he rose upright from the couch. "I'll go alone."

"Go where?" Emmitt raised an eyebrow and stared at his brother curiously.

"The Yates house. Renata called me."

Emmitt froze. *Renata wouldn't say anything. Would she?* Emmitt was certain she wouldn't. Mostly certain. Somewhat certain.

Emmitt cleared his throat and asked, "Why did she call you?"

"Apparently, Sybil had a large delivery early this morning. Renata and Sister Eugene scrambled to put the boxes in Sybil's bedroom." At the mention of Sybil's name, Andrew's left eye twitched.

"Oh." A rush of relief filled Emmitt. After the tide ebbed, a cold realization began to rise and take hold. "How much damage?"

"From what Renata said, almost all our progress in the bedroom is gone. They brought in dozens of boxes … apparently all of them are business-related, according to Sybil."

"So, we can't get rid of them?" Emmitt asked.

"No," Andrew said firmly. "We'll have to come up with a new strategy."

"What do we do?"

"First, you need to put a shirt on and change out of your sweatpants. It's nearly ten, Emmitt."

"I was editing a video essay all night. I just posted it a few hours ago. You still have other clients … I still have to work too. I sleep whenever I have time to do it."

Andrew nodded and sat back down on the couch. "I get it, Emmitt. It wasn't a fair criticism. Get dressed, and we'll drive over to the Yates house and assess the situation."

"Has Sybil said anything to you about the boxes?"

"No. Sybil hasn't called or texted me once. I've tried to contact her, but she hasn't responded … so I've been checking her social media to figure out when she'll be back." Andrew shifted his eyes.

Emmitt was sure he heard embarrassment in Andrew's voice. Emmitt didn't want Renata to be right about Andrew, but he had to admit something was off. He reached into his dresser and grabbed a plain black tee shirt and slipped it over his head.

"Yeah, well, that's understandable. She was only supposed to be gone for a week … then two weeks … it's been almost six weeks. You can't blame yourself for checking up on her if she isn't decent enough to let you know when she's coming back. She's still a client, right?" Emmitt grabbed a pair of jeans and underwear and walked into the bathroom to change.

Andrew responded in a raised voice from the couch. "As far as I know, she hasn't fired us. She's still a client."

"What has Sybil been doing?" Emmitt asked.

"She went on a cruise, then had a photo shoot for some new business venture. Then, she attended a spiritual detox. Then, an extended retreat in Sedona. Emmitt … it was a Rivers of Younity retreat."

Emmitt's mouth gaped. He zipped his jeans and rushed out of the bathroom. "She attended one of Mom's Rivers of Younity retreats? Those are for her distributors! Andrew, if Sybil is some kind of weird stalker or guru groupie, I wouldn't blame you for wanting to back out … I knew she was trouble."

"Don't overreact, Emmitt. Sybil's gone on retreats with Mom before."

"How many times?" Emmitt demanded.

"I don't know. Mom leads a lot of retreats. And most of them aren't connected with her business. When Mom told me about Sybil—"

"Mom was the one who set you up?" Emmitt gasped. "This is bad, Andrew."

Andrew responded calmly. "It didn't happen that way. Sybil resonated with a speech I gave at a motivational conference in Las Vegas a few months ago. After the conference, she attended one of the women's leadership retreats that Mom hosts in Santa Cruz. Sybil asked Mom if I was available to help her and her family with their hoarding issues. Sybil approached Mom. Mom gave Sybil my number, and Sybil had her uncle contact me with the details."

"You can't be serious, Andrew." Emmitt's anger was building. "You really believe Mom wasn't orchestrating this? She set you up with a lunatic! And for what? Exposure? Notoriety?"

"Legitimacy." Andrew remained calm. "My previous books have all been successful. A book featuring Sybil Yates will expand my reach and solidify my reputation. It'll also help rehabilitate Sybil's image, and it'll allow you to start your career as a best-selling author. It's a win, win, win."

"Did Mom tell you Sybil was one of her distributors?"

Andrew hesitated before answering. "No."

"Shit."

"We can figure this out, Emmitt," Andrew said. "You shouldn't assume the worst."

"And you shouldn't presume Mom's innocence. What did she say when you told her you wanted to work with me? Does Serenity even know we're working together?"

Andrew paused. "She knows," he said, then paused again, considering his words. "She didn't say it was a bad idea when I told her I wanted to work with you."

"So, she gave you the silent treatment? I know what you're saying … don't try to obfuscate an obfuscator."

"Fine. Mom didn't specifically tell me not to work with you, but she wasn't happy about it either. It doesn't matter, Emmitt. We are working together, and Sybil is our client. Not Mom's client. Ours."

"Why aren't you more worried about this?" Emmitt challenged, resisting the growing urge to lay bare Renata's concern for Andrew, which Emmitt now shared.

"Mom wouldn't have suggested helping the Yates family if she thought I couldn't handle it," Andrew insisted. His assuredness fueled Emmitt's ire.

"Bullshit!" Emmitt spat. "She threw you into the deep end of the pool to teach you how to swim. Not metaphorically. Literally. I remember Dad jumping in to save you from drowning."

Andrew chuckled. "You're exaggerating. You were only three when Mom did that. She wouldn't have let me drown. Dad panicked, which caused you to panic."

Emmitt gritted his teeth. "I know what happened. You make too many excuses for her. If we couldn't accomplish something, it was always because we didn't try hard enough, or we didn't 'manifest success,' whatever the fuck that means. She would absolutely give us something we couldn't handle, just so she could say she was encouraging us to rise to the occasion. Andrew, there are consequences if we fail at this. Even if we succeed, we don't know how things will turn out for the Yates family ... or for us."

"I know." Emmitt felt a wave of melancholy at Andrew's gentle reassurance. "But I'm not giving up. Renata was the one who called. She's the one asking for our help. She may just need us to come over to the house, nod, and say to her, 'Yeah, that's a messed-up thing that Sybil did. I'm sorry you have to put up with this.' If that's what Renata needs, that's what we'll do. Right?"

"Right," Emmitt grumbled. He couldn't argue. If Renata needed support, he wanted to be there to provide it.

In the car, they were silent. Emmitt seethed at the revelation that Serenity had been pulling the strings that impelled Andrew to work with Sybil. He was angry that Andrew refused to acknowledge the machinations of their mother. Why hadn't Andrew been honest with him about their mother's involvement?

The answer boomed in his head with stunning immediacy. *Because, dipshit, you wouldn't have agreed to work with him. And if you didn't work with Andrew, he would have to deal with Sybil alone ... and you wouldn't have met Renata.*

When Andrew pulled up to the Yates' house, Renata was already standing with her arms crossed at the front door. She quickly ushered them into the house without a greeting or pleasantries. They wound through the familiar path and stopped at the door to Sybil's bedroom.

Renata wrung her hands frantically. "She called once and said to expect a few boxes from her work. I told her I wasn't calling Uncle James to store them, so she told me to put the boxes in her room. She said she'd be home next week to sort through them, but she never said what day she'd be back."

Andrew and Emmitt peered into the room. All progress was gone. The room appeared almost the same as the first day they visited. It was nearly four months wasted.

"It's bad. You both did so much to help. I'm so sorry this happened." Renata's face was colorless. Her eyes pooled with unshed tears.

Andrew gently laid a hand on Renata's shoulder. "You have nothing to be sorry about. This is a learning process for all of us. Besides, if the boxes are for business, I'm sure there are more items for sale than personal use."

"Most of it is for personal use," Renata said, dabbing the corners of her eyes with her finger. "It's part of the marketing ploy." Renata shook her head and sharpened her tone. "Sybil joined a new pyramid scheme: Amelior Wellness. She has an entire case of laxative teas and a few boxes of herbal amphetamines she's supposed to ingest three times a day. She also received three boxes of workout equipment, four boxes of sneakers, and eight boxes filled with athletic wear ... she said they're sponsored gifts. Apparently, Sybil can't 'sell the dream' without ninety pairs of yoga pants with matching weights, shoes, and sports bras. The rest of the boxes are from the essential oils cult she's still a distributor for: Rivers of Younity." She pointed to a stack of boxes and tilted her head to read the printed lettering. "'The essence of You springs from the Rivers of Younity' ... how profound."

As Renata finished her tirade, Emmitt burst into an uncontrollable fit of laughter. Renata and Andrew stared in bemused silence as Emmitt laughed himself into hysterics. He would stifle his chortles long enough to choke out, "I'm sorry ... it's not funny ... I'm really sorry ..." Then another wave would sweep him up again. After finally settling himself to a few involuntary snickers, he turned to Renata, who looked confused and slightly worried.

"You okay, Emmitt?" she asked.

It was Andrew who answered. "Rivers of Younity is our mother's essential oils cult ... Emmitt came up with the tagline."

"As a joke!" Emmitt sputtered, trying to control a fresh bout of laughter. "I didn't think she'd actually use it ... and I haven't received any royalties from it. That's my intellectual property."

"You might not want to brag about that," Renata said with a slow smile.

Emmitt cleared his throat. "I'm good now. It's out of my system ... I think."

"So, is this some sort of coincidence? Did you know Sybil and your mother were working together?" Renata looked curiously at Andrew as she spoke.

"I don't think it's a coincidence," Andrew answered. "I didn't know Sybil sold our mother's products until I saw her posting pictures at a Rivers of Younity retreat ... but Mom was the one who gave Sybil my contact information. I knew Sybil had gone on a few leadership and wellness retreats with our mother ..." Andrew glanced at Emmitt, then looked back at Renata somberly. "I honestly didn't think there was anything sinister about their connection, but Emmitt feels differently, and I shouldn't discount his concern. Now that we know they're working together, I can't deny that their business affiliation may be the reason I was asked to come in and help. I don't work for my mother, or sell her products, but it is my duty to disclose any potential conflicts of interest—"

"Relax, Andrew," Renata interrupted. "I don't want to stop working with you, or Emmitt. I trust you. It isn't much of a shock to find out my sister is a distributor for your mother's company. Sybil has Serenity's books and goes on her retreats, and she's joined dozens of network marketing businesses over the years. If Serenity owns the company, it makes sense that Sybil would join Rivers of Younity. I don't know your mother, so I won't speculate about her intentions ... Oh, and I'm sorry I called your mom a cult leader."

"Are you kidding? Serenity Rivers-Key would be flattered to know that someone thought of her as a cult leader." Emmitt had regained most of his composure and retained all of his vitriol toward his mother.

"What are we going to do?" Renata asked.

Andrew looked at Renata apologetically. His head dipped and his eyes lowered. "The only thing we can do right now is wait for Sybil to get back home."

Renata scrunched her nose at Andrew. "I knew you were going to say that. All I do is wait."

Andrew smiled. "I understand. This isn't what any of us wanted, but it's a reality we had to prepare for." He turned to Emmitt. His eyes glared at him as if he had forgotten something important. "Anything you wanted to add?"

Emmitt's face brightened, remembering his brother's words at his apartment. "Oh, yeah." He looked into Renata's eyes. "That's a fucked-up thing that Sybil did to you. I'm sorry you're the one who has to put up with her. You don't deserve it."

Renata smiled and wrapped her arms tightly around Emmitt. "Thanks. I really needed to hear that."

"I'll keep saying it … if it makes you happy." Emmitt flushed at Renata's sudden impropriety. He stiffened and kept his arms from reciprocating the hug as he caught Andrew's eye.

Renata laughed as she let go of Emmitt. "Once is enough, but you could text me later with other things that annoy you about Sybil."

"I can definitely come up with a few things."

Andrew's eyes remained fixed on Emmitt. "Perhaps it would be better if you provided positive aphorisms to motivate Renata rather than spewing things you hate about Sybil. We all still need to work together, regardless of the challenges we encounter."

"I guess that's good advice," Renata said, as she poked Emmitt playfully in the chest. "So, think of all the things you like about me and text me … you can start with how patient and considerate I am." Turning to Andrew, she added, "I feel better … not great, but it could always be worse. I'll let you know if I hear anything from Sybil. Thanks for coming over on such short notice."

"It's never an issue. Call or text us anytime," Andrew said.

Renata led them to the front door and hugged them both goodbye. As Emmitt walked briskly to the SUV, he smiled to himself and meditated on the flurry of compliments he would rain down on Renata once he was alone in his apartment. His steps lightened as he closed his eyes and embraced her in his mind.

He was still smiling when he reached the passenger side and caught the frigid stare of his brother. Emmitt's bright mood shattered when Andrew grabbed for the driver side door handle. Andrew's cold, calm voice pierced Emmitt's heart.

"How long have you two been seeing each other?"

Chapter Nineteen

Emmitt entered the car with an agonizing anxiety that tangled in his gut. Andrew had the patience and professionalism to smile and wave at Renata, who smiled and waved back from the driveway. Once they had reached the first stop sign at the end of the street, Andrew began his monologue.

Emmitt knew he deserved his brother's admonishments, but the concession of culpability that pervaded his thoughts refused to be uttered through his lips. He crossed his arms in mock-defiance and stared out of the passenger window, pretending not to listen. Emmitt didn't justify himself. He didn't have the opportunity. Andrew never paused. There was no invitation for Emmitt to join the conversation. It wasn't a conversation; it was a lecture.

Andrew had been eerily calm. Emmitt was ashamed, but he wasn't sorry, and he didn't intend to change his behavior. He silently persevered through unyielding traffic. Emmitt would have sworn they hit every red light. Andrew circled the block of Emmitt's apartment four times to finish his frigidly serene scolding. Emmitt thought he had heard the end of it when Andrew finally stopped the car in front of his apartment building.

Five days later, they were back in Andrew's luxury SUV. Sybil had finally arrived home, and finally reached out to Andrew to continue the cleanup. Surely, Andrew would be too preoccupied with Sybil's transgressions to worry about what Emmitt and Renata were doing. Emmitt was wrong.

The first five minutes in the car were blissfully silent. Andrew's face was tight, but he was staring ahead at the road. Emmitt hoped Andrew would continue to ignore him. That hope was dashed when Andrew reached the freeway on-ramp.

Still staring ahead, Andrew began icily, "Have you thought about what we discussed?"

Emmitt rolled his eyes. Andrew's reprimand had not been a discussion. Emmitt once again fixed his gaze outside the passenger window.

"Well?" Andrew persisted.

"Maybe," he finally replied in half-hearted defiance.

"How long has this been going on?"

"What do you mean?"

"You know exactly what I mean. When did you and Renata start seeing each other?"

Emmitt shrugged as he kept his eyes fixed blankly at the passing cars. "A month ago."

"A month? You lied to me for a month!" Andrew's voice rose. "This is a serious issue, Emmitt."

"Well, ... I guess, technically, it's closer to a month and a half ... but in fairness, Renata and I haven't really done anything ... We're hanging out. We're friends."

"You're trying to lawyer your way out of taking accountability with semantics? Emmitt, you spend too much time talking to Dad. I will ask as plainly as possible: do you, or do you not want to be romantically involved with Renata?"

"What I want isn't relevant. Renata hasn't pressed the issue, so I'm not pressing either. We're friends."

"And if she does press the issue?" Andrew nearly growled.

"Maybe we shouldn't worry about things that haven't happened yet."

"Maybe you're right. You've always been too much of a coward to initiate a relationship. Renata will probably lose interest before long."

Emmitt's head reeled. "What? Wait. Do you *want* us to be together? Are you saying I should ask her to be my girlfriend?"

"No. From a business perspective, it is completely unprofessional. As your brother ..." Andrew sighed. "I wish the circumstances were different. You've made things incredibly difficult. I've never been in this kind of position before."

Emmitt cast his eyes downward and stared at his restless hands. "I'm sorry. I didn't mean for it to happen ... but I didn't stop it from happening, either. I wasn't planning on getting involved with Renata until ..." Emmitt stopped himself from elaborating. "It doesn't matter. Look, I'm trying to remain semi-professional to make you happy—"

"You can't be half-in with both of us."

"Do you really think I'm a coward?" Emmitt tried not to sound hurt.

"You depended on your past girlfriends to let you know when you were in a relationship. I don't remember a time when you asked anyone out. You've always rested on your charm, Emmitt."

"No ... that's not entirely true," Emmitt protested.

Emmitt knew it was precisely true. The women he normally want-ed to date were too shy or anxious or disinterested to approach him, so he only dated women who were willing to ask him out. All of them were extroverted. The desire for intimacy kept Emmitt involved and attentive for a while, but his interest would inevitably drift away the more time he spent getting to know them. It certainly wasn't their fault, and he certainly was a coward, but it hurt Emmitt to know that his brother had not only perceived this flaw but was eager to say it to his face.

"Who asked for a phone number?" Andrew commanded.

"Renata," Emmitt mumbled.

"So, you're planning to string us both along until one of us cuts you loose?"

"No. I'm going to help you, and I'm going to ask Renata to be my girlfriend. I'm determined to do both, and I'm confident I won't let either of you down. I'm manifesting it now." Emmitt closed his eyes tightly and contorted his face. After a moment, he opened his eyes and grinned maliciously at his brother. "There. It's manifested."

"You're really going to turn this into a joke? Especially after the amount of grief you've given me over Sybil's shameless flirting? A month and a half, Emmitt. You lied to me for a month and a half."

"I know—"

"You've blamed Mom, and Sybil, and me for decisions and dealings that might derail the job. A month and a half ..."

"Yeah," Emmitt breathed. "But it's Renata. You see it ... tell me you see it, Andrew."

"You and Renata clearly have a good rapport—"

"It's more than rapport!" Emmitt nearly choked the words out. "She's special. You see how special she is … and she likes me. She doesn't have to. Maybe she shouldn't. But she does."

"Oh God, Emmitt," Andrew sighed deeply. "You can't possibly—"

"I do."

Andrew shook his head. His tone was gentler than Emmitt expected. Gentler than he deserved. "It's an uphill battle when you start a relationship in secret. It's not impossible, but there are things you can't account for. You don't know how her family will react when they find out. I don't know where this goes. You can't ignore the fact that we're attempting to help her family through a major crisis. It's foolish to think she's immune to the trauma caused by Sybil and Shannon's hoarding."

"I know," Emmitt said in a low voice. "I know that I don't know what I'm getting myself into. I know there will be consequences. It doesn't change my resolve. I still want to pursue a relationship with Renata while working with you to help Shannon and Sybil. Can I try to do both? I promise, if this all goes to hell, I'll compensate you. If it takes the rest of my life, I'll pay you back. You can lecture me anytime you want … Please, Andrew."

Andrew stared ahead for an eternity. His breath was long and steady. The veins on the back of his large hands pulsed as he gripped the wheel tightly.

"Fine," Andrew finally relented. "I won't stop you. But this isn't a minor thing. I'm extremely disappointed in you … and I'm worried about both of you. Are you sure, Emmitt?"

"Yeah," Emmitt whispered, then resumed looking silently out the window.

Emmitt's stomach twisted. Andrew was exasperated. Emmitt wasn't sure when or where he would approach Renata, but now that he manifested their relationship in front of his brother, he knew he had to follow through. He had once again revealed too much to Andrew. He told him more than he should have, but he didn't regret it. Andrew's understanding fortified Emmitt. His brother might have been disappointed, but he wouldn't stop him.

His thoughts turned to Sybil: the woman who single-handedly ruined several months' worth of progress with one day's worth of online purchases. The woman who'd disappeared. The woman who'd affiliated herself with Serenity Rivers-Key. Why wasn't Andrew mad at Sybil? Or Mom? Emmitt wondered if he was the only one who was safe enough for Andrew to be angry with. They were brothers; they could love and hate each other simultaneously. There was a biological simplicity to their relationship. They were not completely unlike primates eagerly picking ticks and fleas off of each other after hours of flinging feces.

Emmitt buried himself in his thoughts until he felt the car stop. Andrew parked his SUV across the street from the Yates house, as he had done countless times before. Emmitt shouldered the door open and slowly planted his feet on the ground. He looked to see Drew Key striding briskly toward the house. Emmitt ambled sluggishly behind his brother.

As he passed through the gate, he straightened his posture and quickened his pace. From the driveway, his face lit, and he hastened his speed when he saw Renata open the door. Drew's arm extended to ring the bell just as her head popped out of the cracked opening. She smiled and motioned wordlessly for the two of them to come in.

Emmitt slid through the door after Andrew. He carefully avoided the towers of stacked boxes and came to an abrupt halt behind his brother. All three stood static at the end of the entryway. Sybil was blocking their path.

Sybil's newly bronzed body was clad in lavender and pink geometric patterned athletic leggings and matching sports bra. Over the bra was a loose-fitting cropped pink tee shirt that hung off her right shoulder. Her platinum blonde hair matched her newly bleached teeth. Her sneakers mirrored the exact purple and pink shades and pattern on her outfit, and the gloss on her artificially plumped lips coordinated with her bubblegum-pink top. Sybil had clearly committed herself to a new branding strategy. Emmitt questioned the influence of Serenity in shaping Sybil's metamorphosis. His mother's concerns were primarily driven by self-interest, and her rare displays of kindness and care only extended to Andrew. If Serenity Rivers-Key was indeed helping Sybil, Emmitt was certain it wasn't for Sybil's sake.

"I'm back! Did you miss me?" Sybil cooed as she reached her long lavender claws out to embrace Drew Key.

Andrew stiffened as he moved one arm to hover around her. He gently patted his hand on her upper back until she released her grip.

"We're glad you're back. We're energized and ready to get back to work," Andrew said in Drew's voice.

"Oh, me too. I'm so energized. I've started this new program—you'll see the boxes soon enough—but don't worry. They're all work-related."

A thought dawned on Emmitt. *She doesn't know we've already seen everything. Renata didn't tell her.* Thankfully, Andrew seemed to have the same realization.

"Boxes?" Andrew asked innocently. "How many boxes?"

"Oh, I wouldn't worry about the number," Sybil said. "I had a long conversation with Serenity, and she thinks I need to reorganize my goals. She said she loved all of my goals, but she thinks I should start with the office first. She said I can earn my bedroom sanctuary only after I prove my worth … and worth is manifested in the office."

"Our mother knows a lot about helping people achieve their goals," Andrew said. "If you want to reorient your priorities, we can start working in the office."

Sybil's impossible lashes fluttered rapidly as she looked up at Andrew. "Serenity was surprised that you didn't try to reach out to me more often while I was away. I was gone a long time. Only two calls, Drew?" Sybil said with an air of juvenile suffering.

Andrew appeared unmoved by Sybil's attempted criticism. "I'm sorry, Sybil. I didn't want to interfere with your trip. I'm glad you had a productive experience with my mother." There wasn't a hint of shame or animosity in Andrew's tone, but it was clear to Emmitt that Andrew wasn't planning on indulging Sybil's feigned petulance when she had refused to contact him during her extended absence.

Andrew turned and smiled at Renata. "Is it alright if we use your sitting room to sort?"

Sybil abruptly cut in. She must have sensed Andrew's disinterest, as her voice was soft and pleadingly sweet. "That won't be necessary, Drew. I don't need to use the sitting room today … and I should have contacted you while I was away. I really wasn't trying to accuse you of anything …"

"I didn't think you were, Sybil. I'm happy you were able to take time for yourself, and get away for a bit," Andrew said. He looked at her thoughtfully and continued, "So, if we don't need to use Renata's sitting room, what would you like us to do?"

"I'm clearing away all products tied to businesses I'm no longer affiliated with. Serenity hired a team with a dumpster to get rid of the junk so I can focus all of my energy on growing my empire. Serenity explained it to me. It was very enlightening. The dumpster should be here within the hour."

All traces of Drew's unflappable confidence vanished. What remained on Andrew's face was a look of puzzled incredulity. "Do you need us to do anything?"

"Of course, silly," Sybil smiled impishly. Emmitt was certain she was proud of herself for finally provoking a distinct reaction from Drew Key. "We just need to pull out anything that isn't labeled Amelior Wellness or Rivers of Younity. Every other box in the office is garbage."

"If you want to pile the boxes into the hallway with ... Drew—" Renata seemed to catch herself before calling him Andrew, "—Emmitt and I can start moving them outside."

"That sounds like a good plan," Andrew said. He flashed a peevish glance at Emmitt before resting his cool eyes on Sybil. "Does that work for you, Sybil?"

"Of course, Drew." Sybil giggled as she turned to enter the hallway.

Andrew followed Sybil, and Renata and Emmitt followed Andrew. The line stopped in front of the office. Like the front door, boxes had partially barred Sybil's office door. Andrew opened it less than halfway before it hit the blockade.

"Smaller boxes first," Andrew said, as he maneuvered into the room after letting Sybil slip through the gap.

Emmitt and Renata waited in the hallway. After a minute, the lavender claws reached through the opening with two small, stacked boxes. Renata grabbed the boxes and handed them to Emmitt. Two more boxes followed.

Renata called into the room, "We're going to take these out to the driveway. Just keep stacking boxes in the hallway. We'll be back for more."

"Will do," Andrew's voice called back.

Emmitt led the way out to the driveway. As they placed the boxes down, Emmitt leaned closer to read the label.

"'Tamed and Twisted Tresses,'" Emmitt read. "That's a tongue-twister. What is it?"

"Hair care. Shampoos, conditioners, hair masks, and styling products. That one's defunct now. Class action lawsuit. People were losing clumps of hair after using the products. Some reported chemical burns. When the company went under, Sybil took her downline and moved on to the next pyramid scheme."

"Network marketing scheme. They get around the pyramid part by actually selling a product," Emmitt corrected.

"The shape is still a pyramid, even if there is a product. Candles, makeup, ugly leggings, essential oils ... Sybil's 'network marketed' a lot of people into financial ruin." Renata shook her head and sighed. "We should probably head back. There's an entire room to clear out. I don't know what your mom did to convince her to throw everything away ..."

"She convinced Sybil to get rid of her competition," Emmitt said icily. "My mom legitimately teaches master classes in manipulation. She's perfected the jargon. Slapping a label of 'empowerment' or 'self-care' onto her lectures encourages people to feel accomplished whenever they act like entitled assholes. And who doesn't want to be told they deserve to have everything they've ever wanted?"

"Is she really that bad?"

"Yes."

Renata stroked Emmitt's arm as she moved toward the house. As the tips of her fingers brushed off his elbow, Emmitt reached out and grabbed her hand. She turned back to look at him.

Emmitt's face flushed. "Before we go in, can I ask you something?"

"Sure."

"I enjoy spending time with you ..."

"I do too, but that's not a question, Emmitt."

"No, I know. Sorry ... I'm not great at this. I'm interested in ... more than a friendship with you ... like, being a couple ... romantically ... officially. I was wondering if you feel the same way." Emmitt let out a groan at the sloppy execution of his proposition.

Renata dramatically pondered the question. She stared off to the side and scratched under her chin. "Hmm ... I guess so." She giggled as she nudged Emmitt with an elbow. "Yes, Emmitt. I thought I was being obvious. I guess I didn't realize just how dense you actually are."

"I warned you," Emmitt grinned.

With a gentle tug on his arm, Renata lowered Emmitt's head to meet hers and kissed him on the cheek. "I know you did, and it's my fault too for not being more assertive. I guess I was a little nervous with the circumstances, and I didn't want to push you if you were having second thoughts. I thought I was dropping enough hints, but hinting is an easy way to avoid being direct. It doesn't matter now. We should probably head back, though. Sybil isn't patient, and I don't trust her to be alone with Andrew for too long."

Emmitt stammered, "Do … do you … have second thoughts?"

"Do you?"

Emmitt shook his head. "No."

Renata's face shone. "I don't either. I've been waiting for you to ask."

Renata grabbed Emmitt's hand and pulled to lead him back into the house. Emmitt pulled her back to him and leaned down to kiss her lips. He gently brushed away the hair that streamed down her face as he rested his palm on her warm cheek and let his fingers slowly stroke the side of her neck. Renata relaxed into his affection and breathed out a satisfied sigh as he released her.

"We can go in now," Emmitt said.

"Well, now I don't want to," Renata said with a smirk.

"You didn't want to leave Andrew alone with Sybil, remember?"

"It's starting to come back to me," Renata said. "I guess we should go back inside." She entwined her fingers with Emmitt's and led him back into the house.

Emmitt and Renata moved back and forth, carrying boxes from Sybil's office to the driveway. After the fifth trip, Andrew fully opened the office door. As he joined Emmitt in carrying stacks of larger boxes through the kitchen and out of the side gate, a truck carrying a dumpster pulled into the driveway. A second white van followed behind and parked on the side of the street near the Yates' house. Six men piled out of the van and stopped in front of the growing stacks of boxes on the driveway. After a brief discussion with Sybil, the men began loading boxes from the driveway into the dumpster. Once the men cleared the driveway, they followed Sybil and Andrew into the office to finish the job. Emmitt and Renata stood on the front lawn and watched.

"So, we're dating?" Renata asked. Her voice was nearly a whisper.

"Yep."

"Did you tell Andrew?"

"He figured it out on his own. But he was the one who pushed me to make things official."

"Really?"

"Yeah. He said I was a coward for not taking initiative."

"Are you sure he didn't say you were an idiot for being interested in one of the crazy Yates women?" Renata looked at Emmitt with a suspicious grin.

"'Unprofessional' was the word he used. He never called me an idiot—not in this instance, at least—and he would never call you crazy."

"I'm glad he finally knows. I hated keeping it from him, but I was more interested in spending time with you, and I was worried that he wouldn't approve. Is he okay with us dating?"

"He's not thrilled with the circumstances, but he likes you. He finally yielded when I told him I wasn't backing down." Emmitt puffed his chest and raised his chin.

Renata poked at Emmitt's ribs, deflating him. "And what would you have done if he hadn't found out?"

"Honestly? Well, we probably would have bought a house together, had a few kids, and picked out matching headstones before I felt comfortable enough to ask you if we were a couple."

Renata laughed. "I'm glad he irritated you enough to ask me to be your girlfriend."

"It certainly could have gone worse. I think Andrew went easier on me because he thinks so highly of you."

"He really is a good brother," Renata said. "It would be nice to have an older brother like Andrew."

"Yeah? Well, maybe having an older sister like Sybil wouldn't be so bad, either."

"Funny."

"I'm serious," Emmitt said. "She's spontaneous ... and bold."

"She's chaotic and reckless," Renata corrected.

"I bet she's the kind of person who would get up and go at a moment's notice. I'd say 'Sybil, let's go to Roswell, or Vegas, or Amsterdam,' and her eyes would light up, and we'd pile into the car and drive to the airport as she scrambled to buy tickets ... or she'd call some old acquaintance to get us on a private jet. I'd ask if we should have packed first, and she'd wave her hand and tell me we'll go shopping when we get to our destination."

"You're right," Renata said. "But that sounds like a nightmare to me."

"You're definitely a planner," Emmitt declared. "I bet you make itineraries for every trip."

"I do. I hate surprises."

"Andrew's the same. During my last year of high school, he took me on a trip to DC. Serenity wouldn't go. She made an excuse about 'the importance of brotherly bonding,' but I know it was because Andrew planned the trip. He had a printed itinerary, he packed both our suitcases a week in advance, and he made sure I kept a printed piece of paper in my wallet with the address of the hotel ... in case I got lost."

"All of that sounds reasonable to me," Renata said.

"He had every day planned, from six in the morning to eight at night. We'd have to go to bed by eight-thirty, because we had 'a long day ahead of us.' He'd say that every night. Oh, and he'd touch every building. Every door. Every wall. 'Historical significance,' was uttered everywhere we went, or 'we're standing in the exact spot so-and-so stood when doing such-and-such.' By the end of the trip, I crashed. It took me a few weeks to recover."

"That sounds like a dream vacation. It clearly impacted you."

"Yeah. *Impact* is the key word. I felt like I'd been hit by a truck when we finally came home. Hey, you never told me why Sybil needs a chaperone at the Rose Patisserie."

"Oh." Renata glanced down and her tone became somber. "The more I think about it, the sadder it seems. It really isn't funny."

"You don't have to tell me."

"I already promised I would tell you." Renata looked seriously at Emmitt as she spoke. "Sybil doesn't like to be alone. Sometimes, it seems like she's incapable of being alone. Occasionally, she could get a person from her downline or a guy she was sleeping with to go to the patisserie with her to keep her company, but most of the time, she would end up going by herself. She wouldn't stay at her table, though. She would mingle. Most people didn't mind, but some people just wanted to eat their food and enjoy the roses in peace. The breaking point was when someone recognized her, and called her an old, has-been, D-lister as he walked past her table. She was inconsolable. She pushed everyone away, and she wouldn't leave the table. I had to be called to collect her. The manager led me to her, and she flung her arms around me and sobbed. I just held her until she calmed down.

She was back to normal—well, normal for Sybil—after I took her out for ice cream ... and let her give me a makeover."

Emmitt rested a hand on the small of Renata's back. "You're a good sister."

"It had been ten years since we hugged. I thought her meltdown would be a turning point for us. But it wasn't. We haven't hugged since ... and I still don't get why it set her off. She's been called far worse."

Emmitt thought for a moment. "It's possible she lets things build until the dam breaks. She lets everything pour out, then she builds everything back up again."

"That's ... pretty accurate, actually. She's purging everything right now. I'm not sure if I should worry about another breakdown. Maybe this *is* the breakdown. I don't know, but it scares me."

Emmitt let his hand glide to her hip as he guided her body closer to his. "I'll be here, if you need me ... just ... please, no makeovers."

Hearing Sybil's voice nearing the side gate, Emmitt quickly put his hand down and took a step away from Renata.

Sybil sang out, "I led them out from the kitchen, Renata!" Finally coming into view after opening the gate that led into the backyard, she added, "These boxes were too big to fit through the front door."

"That's fine," Renata called back to Sybil.

Sybil led the parade of men. Some had multiple boxes stacked above eye level. Andrew brought up the rear with a box that looked like it could barely fit through the kitchen door. He wore a mechanical smile and stared blankly ahead. As he noticed Renata and Emmitt standing together on the grass, his eyes brightened, and his smile softened.

"I think we should be discreet, for now," Renata said in a low voice after the parade had passed by. "Just while we're working at the house.

You don't have to keep anything from Andrew, but I don't want to put more stress on him while he's trying to deal with Sybil ... and I don't want to ruin your book by making my mother and sister suspicious of your motives."

Emmitt nodded. "I think I can be discreet."

"It'll be hard for me. They've already noticed I've been a lot happier lately."

Renata kicked off her shoes and sat down on the soft grass to watch the workers load the boxes into the dumpster. Emmitt sat down next to her, leaving enough space to imply friendship. For Emmitt, friendship meant a distance of three feet.

After two hours, the final boxes had been hauled into the garbage. On the last trip, Andrew brought out the office cot that Sybil had slept on for three-ish years. He held it out for Sybil to grab onto, and together, they heaved it into the dumpster. After she sprayed her hands with a small hand sanitizer she had pulled from a pocket in her leggings, Emmitt and Renata rose to give her a standing ovation. Sybil momentarily froze. Her eyes misted with surprise and delight as she realized the applause was meant solely for her. She smiled a dazzling, genuine smile, and took a bow.

CHAPTER TWENTY

The weeks passed quickly. After the workers in the white van left, and the dumpster was hauled away, Emmitt and Andrew spent the rest of the day removing the boxes that had blocked the entrance to Sybil's bedroom, allowing Sybil to regain access to her bed.

Days after the purging of the office, Sybil and Renata's cousin William delivered the organization system from the museum warehouse and helped the brothers and Renata install it. Sybil supervised their progress as she clacked mindlessly on her phone and swiveled around the room on her rose-gold ergonomic desk chair. The rose-gold shelves of the organization system showcased Sybil's elixirs: essential oils, pre-workout powders, herbal supplements, electrolyte replacement drinks, and packets of ground superfood meal replacements. The newly installed rose-gold drawers were used to pack away excess products. The gifted athletic wear quickly overfilled the small office closet. Renata helped Sybil hang the remaining outfits on the rolling adjustable rose-gold garment rack that matched the rest of the installed unit. Fifteen new pairs of shoes were placed on rose-gold shoe racks, and a label with the words "workout shoes" had been stuck on the bottom lip of the shelf using Sybil's rose-gold label maker. They placed a set of rose-gold weights that maxed out at ten pounds on top of a plush white rug and propped a rolled rose-gold yoga mat next to the dumbbells in the corner of the room. Once Sybil's computer, ring lights, and cameras were moved onto a rose-gold executive desk, and the rose-gold folders were placed in the matching filing cabinets, the office transformation was complete.

Serenity's influence was undeniable. By the end of the week, they had assembled the organization system. Two weeks later, they had successfully completed half of Sybil's listed goals. Now, six weeks after Sybil's return, Andrew and Emmitt focused their attention on finishing Sybil's bedroom sanctuary. With only a half-room of boxes and bins left, their work with Sybil was nearing completion.

Emmitt supposed he should be grateful for this Mater ex Machina, but he felt he knew Serenity well enough to understand her benevolence required reciprocity: if she was building up karma, it was only a matter of time before she came to collect.

Despite his growing unease, Emmitt maintained a simmering excitement. Renata was visiting his apartment, and she was bringing a surprise with her. Emmitt couldn't imagine what the surprise was, but he was glad to spend time with Renata. He waited anxiously for a knock on the door as he busied himself vacuuming crumbs off the floor. He sprayed down his kitchen counters for the third time, then rubbed at the bridge of his nose as he felt the burn from the smell of chemical disinfectant.

Hearing a knock, he quickly tossed the bottle and rag under the sink and rushed toward the door. He opened it and saw Renata's beaming face. Looking lower, he noticed the dog at her side.

"Henry?" Emmitt's eyes widened.

"Surprise!" Renata exclaimed.

Emmitt quickly ushered them into the apartment and shut the door. Henry leaned his head under Emmitt's hand for a pet. Emmitt crouched down and held the dog's head in his hands. He scratched Henry behind both ears and let out a deep sigh. It was a perfect surprise, but it was cruel. Emmitt knew the cruelty wasn't intentional, but that only made it worse. Emmitt hated that Renata would have to share in his heartbreak.

"I picked up a leash and collar for him. I had his name engraved on the tag ... oh and I have bowls and food for him in my car ..."

"Renata ..." Emmitt's voice nearly cracked. He cleared his throat and steadied himself. "I can't keep him."

"Oh, no." Renata paled at Emmitt's words. "I thought you visited him at the shelter because you wanted him as a pet. You don't want him?"

Of course, he had wanted to keep Henry, but he had deliberately hidden that fact from Renata on their visit to the shelter. He introduced the two, and he read to Henry, as he always did. Then they left. Renata said Henry was special and thanked Emmitt for taking her to visit his friend, but she never asked if he wanted to adopt Henry. Emmitt never told her he wanted to adopt Henry. Telling her would mean he'd have to explain that he couldn't afford an apartment that allowed pets, and he couldn't afford to take care of a pet, either.

"I want him," Emmitt finally said. "More than anything. But I can't ..." Emmitt couldn't finish the sentence. He cleared his throat a second time and bit his inner cheek to keep his emotions contained.

Renata frowned as she asked timidly, "Did I do something wrong?"

"No," Emmitt said in a hushed voice. "You did nothing wrong."

Renata fell silent. She looked down at Emmitt, then struggled to remain calm as her eyes settled on Henry. She hesitated as she spoke. "If it's about ... the money ... I was the one who adopted him. I can pay for all his food and any vet bills or medications ... it really isn't a problem."

Emmitt knew it wasn't a problem for Renata. Money would never be an issue for her.

Emmitt sat on the floor with the dog draped lazily over his lap. He breathed in and out deeply. He felt heavy. "My apartment doesn't allow pets."

"Oh," Renata whispered. "Well, it was my fault ... maybe ..." She paused. Sitting down next to Emmitt, she continued in a wavering voice. "Maybe I can find an apartment that allows pets ... something comparable, and I could pay any additional expenses ..."

"No, Renata." Emmitt put his hand on hers.

"But ..." she began.

"I can't accept that. It's way too much."

"It really isn't ..."

"I couldn't pay you back," Emmitt rasped more sharply than he had intended. "I'm sorry."

"You wouldn't have to ..." She stopped speaking as Emmitt vigorously shook his head.

They sat in silence. Renata rested her head on Emmitt's shoulder as they both petted the dog.

When Henry was asleep, Renata spoke again. "The money means nothing to me. It's not like I earned it ... but it matters to you?"

"Yeah."

"You know I don't think less of you ... right?"

"I know. You've never made me feel that way, Renata." Emmitt flushed at the thought of her money and his lack of it. He cursed himself for caring, but the shame persisted.

Renata sighed. "Well, I have to do something. It's such an enormous responsibility, and I just pushed it on you without thinking. What can I do?"

"We'll think of something," Emmitt said, squeezing Renata's hand.

Renata lifted her head from Emmitt's shoulder. "I can't believe I did this to you ... I'm just like my family, trying to throw money at a problem that I caused."

"You don't need to get upset about it," Emmitt said with forced tranquility, hoping to soothe Renata's guilt. "I'm not offended. I'm not angry. He really is the best gift I've ever received."

"I'm so sorry," Renata said.

"I know. But I don't want to take advantage of your generosity ... especially since I can't reciprocate. I don't want to get in the habit of taking from you if I can't give you anything in return."

Renata's face twisted in shame. "I didn't think about it that way ... I should have. My dad always felt like he couldn't keep up with my mother's spending. He didn't complain, but he didn't have to. Mother always got what she wanted. If Dad couldn't afford something, she'd go to my grandparents. They had a hard time saying no to her too. Everyone else had to shoulder the burden caused by her thoughtlessness. Now, I'm doing the same thing to you."

"You're not," Emmitt tried to reassure Renata. "I should have explained things at the shelter. I guess I was too embarrassed."

"No. I was being stupid and inconsiderate ... I should have asked first."

Renata's continuous self-admonishments concerned Emmitt. He was the one who received a dog he desperately wanted but knew he couldn't have, yet Renata was taking it harder than he was. She wasn't simply pouting or playing victim over the mistake; she seemed crushed by how much she had hurt him.

Still holding her hand, Emmitt was determined to reach a solution, both for Renata's and Henry's sakes. "I don't think I can ask Andrew right now," Emmitt thought aloud. "I already pushed past my luck when I told him I manifested our relationship."

"Manifested?" Renata couldn't help but smirk.

"Yeah. I had to speak in terms he could understand … and I was being a prick. So, he's out of the running for fostering Henry. What about your Aunt Grace?"

"No," Renata said. "She has too many animals, and she lacks the knowledge to care for them properly. Mother was right when she called Aunt Gracie an animal hoarder. I don't want to risk Henry being bullied by bigger dogs. I'm not taking him out of a shelter to put him in a worse situation."

Emmitt looked seriously at Renata. "What about you?"

Renata considered the question. "Do you think it's safe for him? I just criticized my aunt, but my house is worse than hers … it's why I didn't bother to suggest it. I didn't want to put you in the awkward position of telling me you didn't want Henry in my house. It's understandable, and I wouldn't blame you, but it would still hurt to hear you say it."

"The way you feel about the hoard is the same way I feel about the money," Emmitt said with a sad smirk. "It's hard to ignore two elephants in a room this small."

"I see your point. Maybe neither of us should feel ashamed."

"Yeah, but it's not that simple, is it?"

"No, it's not simple, but we both need to work on it. That way, in the future, we can arrive at a practical solution *before* immediately spiraling into hopelessness."

"That's sensible," Emmitt said. "But in our defense, we only spiraled a little before reaching a practical solution. We got there in the end."

"Yes. We're not getting rid of Henry. We're keeping him. And he's staying with me," Renata declared in a voice that reminded Emmitt of Shannon. Then, in a voice that was nearer to her own, she added apprehensively, "We'll still need to work out the logistics, though. I don't want Henry to get hurt in the house."

Renata's words lifted Emmitt and allowed him to consider their options. "As long as he doesn't go past the kitchen, he'll be fine. You have more space in your sitting area and bedroom than I have in my apartment, and you have access to the backyard through the kitchen. You'll probably have to use the side entrance to bring him in and out of the house, though."

"I can do that," Renata said. "Are you sure you don't mind if I look after him?"

"I'd be relieved to know that he was with you. I know you'll love him and take care of him. There is one change we'll have to make, though."

"What do you mean?" Renata asked.

Emmitt smiled. "Henry wouldn't just be my dog. He'd be *our* dog."

Renata let out a childlike gasp that sounded like Sybil. "Of course! I've always wanted a dog."

The more time he spent with Renata, the more Emmitt's heart softened for the two other Yates women. Renata's eyes and air of poised propriety were a mirror of Shannon's. In moments of pure expression, her scrunched nose and high-pitched utterances of joy were a sanctified version of Sybil's affectations. He wanted to devote himself to her. He wanted to help her family. He needed to be more than he was.

Emmitt straightened his posture to appear more competent than he felt. "I have some money saved from the work that Andrew and I have done, and if I'm a bit more consistent posting video essays and updating my website, I should be able to look for a new place when my lease is up. There's also the book ... you've done a lot, and Sybil is getting closer to completing her goals. Even if your mom doesn't get involved, there should be enough material to complete the book by the end of the year." Emmitt paused as he considered additional obstacles to their plan. "Is your uncle opposed to you having pets on the property?"

"No. He'd let me keep Henry if I asked."

"And your mom or Sybil? Would they be mad?"

"Mother won't care. She never cares what I do. Sybil will probably insist on having her own pet ... that might initially cause a problem, but she's easily distracted. Within a week, Henry will lose his novelty."

"And you're sure you're okay taking care of Henry? I don't want to put that kind of responsibility on you if you aren't interested."

Renata's tone sharpened, "I deserve the consequences for my reckless behavior. You're certainly putting more thought into all the considerations of pet ownership than I did. Plus, you already said he's *our* pet ..." She looked at the sleeping dog sprawled on Emmitt's lap, and her voice softened. "I get so mad at Sybil's impulsivity ... but God has a way of slapping you in the face when you act too high and mighty ... at least, that's what Sister Eugene says. Maybe I needed to be reminded that I'm more like my mom and sister than I would care to admit."

"Maybe a little, but I think that's true for everyone."

"Are you saying I'm not unique?" Renata pouted, trying not to smile.

Emmitt laughed. "Not in this instance. Just be glad you're self-aware enough to see it."

"And you still like me? I haven't scared you off?"

"I still like you. You haven't scared me off."

Renata grinned as she arched an eyebrow. "So, if we're all like our parents and siblings, when should I expect you to start your own essential oils cult?"

"No essential oils for me. The real money is in men's printed leggings. There's a massive demand and almost no supply. I was thinking tractors, bald eagles, hunting knives, pellet smokers ..." Emmitt's eyes lit up.

Renata stifled laughter as Emmitt's hands gesticulated wildly.

"Picture an entire collection of men's leggings depicting famous historical battles: Normandy, Gettysburg, Waterloo. You really need to get in early, and now is the perfect time to start your own business. The beginner start-up pack is only five thousand dollars. We've marked it down from twelve thousand dollars, so you know you're paying the best possible price for the highest quality items ..."

"But what about premium packages?" Renata inquired with breathless excitement.

Emmitt's eyes widened, and his smile broadened. He had never been in the presence of anyone willing to play along with his exaggerated pomposity. Andrew entertained him from time to time, but Renata was a willing participant. It fueled Emmitt further.

"I can tell, just by looking at you, that you are a woman driven by financial ascendancy. You're in luck, Renata. We've just announced the iron, steel, and titanium add-ons. The premium packages are optional, but I think you're smart enough to understand that your success as the owner of a men's leggings boutique is directly corelated with your level of investment. Of course, I'll be the actual owner of the company … but you can pretend to be your own CEO."

Renata struggled to catch her breath through suppressed giggles. "That's scary. I swear I've overheard Sybil give that exact pitch to her downline every time she switches over to a new network marketing scheme."

Emmitt shrugged. "It's in my blood. I have to fight every day of my life to suppress it."

"I admire your resolve to fight against your true nature." Renata smirked.

"I'm willing to do it for you, Renata."

Renata's smirk faded. "The thing is, I thought I was doing the same. I thought getting Henry for you was a move in the right direction … like I was finally shifting my responsibilities away from my family and solidifying my relationship with you. I normally just hide myself away. It's difficult to begin a relationship and have to explain why my family is the way it is … and why I can't just leave them living in squalor."

"I get it," Emmitt said.

"I know you do. I don't think you realize how much that means to me. It's the reason I wanted to surprise you with Henry. I couldn't think of a better way to thank you."

"Renata," Emmitt sighed, running his fingers through her hair, "I'm still helping Andrew ... and I'm still being paid. I don't think you should thank me for helping your family."

"You can't stop me." Renata smiled and leaned in so close that Emmitt could feel her warm breath on his cheek. "It's not just about the work. You already know my family is a mess. You don't treat us like we're crazy ... or sick, and you've even defended my mom and Sybil. Embarrassing things aren't as embarrassing when I tell you. And you've embarrassed yourself, more than once, to make me feel better. Even now, I royally screwed up and you're trying to help me fix the problem." She placed a hand on the side of his face and kissed him gently on the lips.

Emmitt felt a tingling heat rising through his body. He exhaled deeply as Renata slowly pulled away. He looked into her eyes. "You were the one who agreed to keep Henry at your place. You solved the problem more than I did. I just wish you wouldn't work yourself up so much."

"It was a problem I created," Renata argued.

"And it's solved now. Go easy on yourself. You can't keep blaming yourself for a problem we've already fixed."

Renata's brow furrowed. "I can't mess up the way the rest of my family does. We solved *this* problem, but what if I do something worse? I couldn't forgive myself. I can barely forgive them."

"Well, that's where we differ. I mess up all the time. The more I do it, the easier it gets."

Renata shook her head and frowned. "I don't want to end up like them."

Emmitt stroked the sleeping dog with one hand as he stroked Renata's arm with the other. His crossed legs had gone numb. He felt a dull ache in his lower back, but he didn't want to move.

It was Renata who was the first to get up. She grabbed Emmitt's hand, kissed it, and rose to sit on the faded gray couch. Sensing movement, Henry woke up, raised his head, and licked Emmitt in the face before standing, stretching, and ambling over to Emmitt's bed. The dog looked at the bed as though pondering his own agility. After a minute of mental preparation, Henry leapt up. His back legs barely cleared the two-foot gap between the floor and mattress. The dog walked to the middle of the bed and circled twice before finally laying down.

"He's made himself comfortable," Renata said. She let out a satisfied sigh as she leaned farther back on the couch.

Emmitt stood and stretched before walking over to sit next to Renata.

"Is he going to be allowed on your bed?" Emmitt asked.

"I don't mind. But I might have to get him a ramp ... or maybe an ottoman to help him step up to the bed. He barely made it onto yours. Mine's about a foot higher. I'll need to get him his own bed, too, and some blankets, in case he gets cold."

"He has a ton of fur, Renata. He's not going to get cold."

"For comfort, then. He's an orphan. He's suffered ... Emmitt, would you kill me if I got him a sweater?"

"A sweater would be undignified. He's supposed to be naked."

"I saw the cutest Easter bow tie at the pet store. It's pastel with a little bunny in the middle."

"He doesn't need a bow tie."

Renata narrowed her eyes at Emmitt. "Well … I also saw a tactical harness in camo with attachments for a portable water dispenser, a dog first aid kit, and an extra pouch for night-vision goggles."

"Yes. Get that."

"He's eight, Emmitt! Henry's not hiking twenty miles in the wilderness. He'll be going on mile-long strolls in a quiet neighborhood."

"There's no reason he can't look ruggedly handsome on his mile-long strolls wearing a tactical harness," Emmitt argued.

Renata ignored Emmitt. "I can walk him to the convent. The nuns are going to love his Easter bow tie."

"So, our dog is Catholic? That's a pretty serious commitment. Do I get a say?"

"Not while he's living in my house. He can be agnostic when he moves back in with you. But he's getting a blessing on the feast of Saint Francis, no matter who he's living with." Renata stuck her tongue out at Emmitt.

"You're baptizing him?" Emmitt laughed.

Renata giggled. "It's just a blessing. Not a baptism … Are you agnostic?"

Emmitt stopped laughing and looked seriously at Renata. "I don't really think about it. I'm okay with the idea of God … my dad is Catholic … nominally. I celebrate Christian holidays, and I like some of the Christmas songs. Is that okay?"

"Yeah," Renata said. "I didn't mean for it to sound like an interrogation … or an indictment. Would it be weird for you to go to Mass with me on holidays? Not now … but maybe in the future? I don't want you to do anything that makes you uncomfortable, but I always want you to know you're welcome to come along."

"It wouldn't bother me. If you want me to go, I'll go," Emmitt said.

"Really?"

"Yeah. I have a lot of questions. You'll have to suffer my curiosity … and probably some criticism."

"That's fair," Renata said.

She was serious. Serious about Emmitt. Serious about his soul. Serious about their future. She saw a future with him.

Emmitt shifted toward Renata and ran his fingers up her arm. "I don't think you're like your family," Emmitt said. "At least, not in any way you need to worry about."

Renata fixed her determined eyes on Emmitt. "There's more I have to do before I can be sure. I want to do everything I can to be better than I am. For you, and me, and us."

"I like who you are." Emmitt brushed a strand of hair out of Renata's face and kissed her forehead, then her nose, and finally her lips.

Chapter Twenty-One

Another unexpected call brought Emmitt and Andrew back to the Yates' house. This call was far more surprising than Sybil's impromptu business trip or Renata's concern over Sybil's backslide. This time, it was Shannon Yates who had called Drew Key in a panic. She demanded that the brothers hurry to the house, as their meddling had led to a "catastrophic dissolution of the family."

When he heard the news, Emmitt called Renata. There was no immediate answer. He frantically messaged her, asking if she was alright.

She had texted the response, *Everything is fine, mostly. We'll talk later.*

Emmitt was unnerved, but levelheaded enough to trust that Renata would have contacted him immediately had the matter truly been an emergency. Emmitt preferred to assume the situation was, as Renata said, *mostly fine.* He also knew he would be useless to everyone, including Renata, if he allowed his thoughts to burrow deeply into the sublevels of his own catastrophizing mind.

Emmitt waited anxiously for Andrew to pull up to his apartment. In the SUV, he urged his brother to drive faster, but Andrew maintained his composure and refused to indulge Emmitt's agitated demands. Despite Emmitt's insistence that Andrew was deliberately driving below the speed limit and intentionally stopping at yellow lights, they arrived at the Yates' house within the normal span of thirty minutes.

Sister Eugene met them outside the front door. "Thank you for coming. Shannon is beside herself. She's a bit temperamental right now, so don't take anything she says to heart. As you've probably noticed, some of the Yates family members have a tendency to … overexpress their emotions."

Sister Eugene's smile was subdued. Her eyes twinkled and her arms reached out so broadly to usher them in, Emmitt almost expected to be embraced by the massive nun.

"Is everything alright?" Emmitt asked. He was worried about Renata but hoped a general explanation might cover all of his concerns.

"I think so. It's certainly not as decidedly disastrous as Shannon led me to believe when she asked me to come over. I offered to wait out here to collect you boys when Shannon mentioned she had insisted you rush over. I hope she wasn't too prickly with you on the phone, Drew."

"Nothing I couldn't handle," Andrew said with a shrug and half-smile.

Sister Eugene's answer didn't abate Emmitt's growing anxiety, but he didn't want to pry too deeply. He didn't want to appear overly concerned for Renata. Shannon's dramatics may have nothing to do with Renata. Renata hadn't clarified anything to him. Perhaps she was preoccupied trying to console her mother … but it was possible Renata was at the center of the not-so-disastrous mystery.

"Let's go in. I'm sure if we work together, we can calm Shannon down," Sister Eugene said.

She wedged herself through the door. As her large bust caught in the gap, her laughter rose and filled the house.

"It never gets any easier," she boomed as her body wiggled and spasmed with her unabated laughter. "God certainly has a sense of humor when He reminds us of our excesses."

With one final push, the nun popped her way fully into the house. Emmitt and Andrew followed quickly behind. Emmitt's beating heart rose to his throat as Sister Eugene led them past the living room and into the dining room. They made their way through the kitchen to the closed door that led to Renata's sitting room. Emmitt held his breath in anticipation. He didn't know what to expect, but his mind prepared him for the worst: convulsive sobs, shouting, packed bags, and blackened eyes. The thoughts swirled in his mind until Sister Eugene opened the door.

No one was shouting. No bags were packed. There were no physical injuries that Emmitt could see. The room was still. Quiet. Renata sat on the floor near Henry's new bed, stroking him calmly. Shannon sat on the couch. Her face and eyes were red. She breathed steadily as she stared blankly ahead. Emmitt was witnessing an aftermath. He couldn't guess what happened, and he was certain he shouldn't be the one to ask.

Emmitt wanted to hold Renata. He felt like a coward, keeping his distance. And for what? *The book.* He tried to comfort himself with the fact that he and Renata had both agreed to keep their relationship hidden. But, Emmitt thought, sometimes women liked grand displays of affection. *Does she want me to rush to her, or stay discreet? What if I do the wrong thing?* Emmitt was frozen in indecision. A slight panic settled in his chest. He rubbed at the base of his neck, trying to disperse the growing sense of dread.

Sister Eugene broke the silence. "Now then," she began in a resonant voice that conveyed a compassion that reminded Emmitt of the Annunciation prayer card Renata kept as a bookmark for her Bible. He supposed if an angel came from heaven with a message, it would probably use the same tone as Sister Eugene. "Shannon, you called us here. Would you like to tell us what happened? Or should we just find a place to sit quietly with you?"

"Lucas." Shannon scowled. Her bloodshot eyes drifted slowly up. They locked unforgivingly on Andrew. "It's your meddling that caused it. She only had James and Lucas to step in after Arthur ..." Shannon drew a hand over her mouth to hide her quivering lips. She removed her hand as she steadied her voice. "They would visit and check up on Renata after her father passed. It took both of them, and they still didn't measure up to a quarter of the man he was. You took Lucas away from Renata."

"Mother," Renata said in a measured tone. "Don't blame Andrew or Emmitt. It was my decision. I'm really not that broken up about it."

"What exactly happened?" Andrew asked. "My brother and I have clearly offended you, Mrs. Yates. We can't move forward if we don't know what we did."

Renata answered, "I invited Uncle Lucas over to tell him I was getting rid of his paintings. I wrapped them up and propped them against the garage door. I told him I would donate whatever he didn't take with him. He didn't handle it well."

"That's an understatement," Shannon seethed. "His screams were so loud, I'm certain the neighbors down the block could hear them. Renata had to let the dog outside. The poor thing was trembling with its tail between its legs."

Emmitt looked down at Henry, who was softly snoring on his bed, as Renata continued to stroke his head. She focused her attention on the sleeping dog, not bothering to look up at Shannon.

"I was prepared for him to make a scene," Renata said quietly, smiling placidly at Henry. "Maybe he was harsher than I expected, but I needed to get rid of the paintings, and I needed to tell Uncle Lucas I was doing it."

"But why would you do something like that?" Shannon sounded as confused as she was exasperated by Renata's tranquility. "You know more than anyone how petulant Lucas is with his art. Why provoke his petty wrath over a few ugly paintings?"

Renata kept her eyes on the dog. "That's just it. They're ugly paintings. I didn't want to keep them. I shouldn't have to hang them on my walls just to keep the peace with Uncle Lucas."

"But you accepted his gifts … and keeping them seems like such a small thing to preserve the peace," Shannon pushed. "You've had them up for years, and it's never been a problem."

"Are you mad at Uncle Lucas, or are you mad at me?" Renata's eyes flashed up at her mother as her voice sharpened.

"Lucas, of course." Shannon leaned back on the couch as her hand reached to clutch a crucifix that hung around her neck. The tension in her face was noticeable. She rubbed the cross between her thumb and index finger as she struggled to communicate with her daughter. "I'm not mad at you, honey. This simply isn't something you normally do. I just can't comprehend what precipitated this decision."

Renata's face relaxed. "I want all of us to change for the better. We all need to make better decisions. Sybil was making progress, so I decided to work on some of my own issues."

"Honey, you're not like Sybil. You didn't have to do anything." Shannon kept her right hand on the crucifix as her left arm crossed defensively over her abdomen.

"I can't say no to people."

"So? You're polite. There's nothing wrong with that. We could have just as easily tossed the paintings without telling Lucas. Or you could have told him I tossed them in a fit of rage ... it's not like my relationship could get any worse with him. I would have taken the blame to spare you from his fury. You didn't need to handle it yourself. If you had asked for my help, I would have intercepted Lucas at the entry, told him to leave, and slammed the door in his vile, pretentious face. I would have been happy to do it." Shannon looked at Sister Eugene, hoping for some affirmation.

"She shouldn't have to be a doormat," Emmitt blurted from the open doorway. "And you shouldn't be so eager to continue isolating yourself, Mrs. Yates. I know you're trying to help Renata, but shutting yourself away and preventing her from being more assertive won't help either of you."

"Excuse me?" Shannon growled. "I don't recall asking for your assessment, Emmitt."

"Emmitt's right, Mother," Renata said. "I'm constantly worried about hurting people's feelings, while you hide yourself away and hold on to grudges. I don't want you to cut anyone off for my benefit. I need to stand up for myself. It wasn't so bad. I survived Uncle Lucas's tantrum—"

"So now you think you can do a better job putting your foot down with Sybil and me? Is that what this is about?" Shannon let go of the crucifix and crossed her right arm over her left.

"No," Renata said calmly. "I need to know that I can endure the anxiety I feel when I let people down. I hate disappointing people, but I've taken it too far. We've all gone too far. I wanted to set a good example ... but I wasn't trying to force you to do anything."

Shannon's entire body tensed. "It was completely unnecessary. You think getting rid of a few pictures is equivalent to forcing me to give away all of my belongings?"

Sister Eugene intervened. "That isn't at all what Renata is saying, Shannon. Renata is attempting to show you it's possible to change for the better. Your struggles are not the same as her struggles. You and Sybil don't have any art from your brother. Why is that?"

"Sister ..." Shannon began.

"Why is that?" Sister Eugene repeated.

Shannon sighed. "We told him we weren't interested in his ... art."

"And did you or Sybil ever experience distress when considering that you may have hurt your brother's feelings by rejecting his art?" Sister Eugene continued.

"No," Shannon answered coolly.

"Any sleepless nights?"

"No."

Sister Eugene lowered her eyes as she moved nearer to Shannon. "Then you cannot fully appreciate what Renata has achieved. It wasn't easy for her to confront Lucas."

"I won't deny the fact that I want you to change, Mother," Renata said. "But I know you have to be the one who decides to do it. If I'm ever going to help you, I have to work on becoming stronger and less timid. We've all contributed to the hoard. I need to be accountable for my part in it."

"Fine." Shannon shielded her tear-filled eyes as she launched herself off the sofa and hastened toward the door. "Then there's nothing else to discuss. Renata's fine. You can all leave now," she huffed as she hurried into the kitchen and slammed the door behind her.

Sister Eugene walked toward Renata and petted her gently on the head in the same manner Renata had been petting Henry. "I'll try calling her tomorrow after she's calmed down. Do you need anything before I head out?" Sister Eugene asked Renata.

"No, thank you, Sister. I'm fine."

"I'm proud of what you did," Sister Eugene said with a final pat on Renata's head.

"Thanks." Renata smiled as she looked down at Henry.

Sister Eugene nodded goodbye to the brothers and walked through the door, disappearing into the kitchen.

As the door closed behind her, Emmitt finally moved closer to Renata. He sat next to her on the floor and stroked her back. Andrew stood guard by the closed door.

"Do you want me to wait in the kitchen?" Andrew asked.

"No. Please stay." Renata looked up at Andrew. "I won't keep you long. It's nice having you both here."

"Should I stand in front of the door to make sure no one barges in on you two?" Andrew said.

As Emmitt turned, he braced himself for a cynical grin. Instead, the rigid and serious expression on his brother's face sobered Emmitt. A burst of self-loathing battered him as he absorbed Andrew's solemn sincerity.

Renata smiled at Andrew, softening his stern countenance. "No. If Mother finds out, she finds out. I'm not ashamed. You can sit, Andrew."

Andrew nodded. He walked to the velvet sofa and sat down. He leaned forward, placing his elbows on his thighs. His hands rested thoughtfully under his chin. The three sat in a silence that was intermittently broken by the deep snores and occasional dreaming whimpers of the old dog. It was an excruciating silence for Emmitt, who wanted to know more. He knew he should wait for Renata to feel comfortable enough to start the conversation, but as the silence dragged on, his impatience intensified. He watched the ticking seconds of the antique clock on Renata's bookshelf. After three revolutions, his impatience prevailed.

"So, you decided to get rid of your uncle's paintings, after all." Emmitt's smile contorted as he heard the tactless words come out of his mouth.

"Right to the point. Well done, Emmitt," Andrew said, rolling his eyes.

"I'm used to it," Renata said. She glanced at Emmitt before looking at Andrew. "He can't help himself. It's better to let him get it out of his system now. Once he satisfies his curiosity, his nerves settle. Emmitt can be surprisingly insightful and comforting when he's calm." Renata looked back at Emmitt and gently patted his cheek.

"I can be quiet," Emmitt grumbled.

"I'm sure you could," Renata said. "But I wouldn't want to put you through that kind of torture."

"You're too kind to him," Andrew said.

"I can't argue with that," Emmitt agreed. "Renata, you can say—or not say—whatever you want."

Renata smiled and sighed as she fidgeted with her hands in her lap. Emmitt wondered if she wanted to share the story with them, or if he was just one more person she struggled to say no to. He didn't feel like he pushed her into answering, but maybe that was part of the problem. And now, with Andrew sitting in the room with them, Emmitt felt too embarrassed to ask Renata if he had overstepped. Wasn't this his issue? Renata couldn't say no, but Emmitt couldn't stop himself when his inquisitiveness overtook him. Or could he? Emmitt had a gnawing realization that he didn't *want* to stop himself. He was fairly confident he could stop himself if he ever bothered to try. But he hadn't. It was no use now. Renata had already begun to describe the events.

"I knew Uncle Lucas was in town, so I called him over to visit. I would be lying if I said it was entirely my idea. Ever since the day we worked in my bedroom, the thought has been pestering me ..." Renata paused for a moment, considering her words. "I'm not saying I blame either of you for my decision ... I always felt anxious when Uncle Lucas came over with a new piece of art for me to display. I didn't want him to stop visiting, and I really didn't want him to be angry with me, so I kept quiet."

"What made you finally decide to tell him?" Andrew asked before Emmitt could interject.

"When you helped me take down the artwork, I knew what I wanted to keep. I was angry that I couldn't bring myself to get rid of my uncle's art, and even angrier that you called me out for it. I want to have my space and my autonomy, but I hate feeling like I have to ask for the most basic level of civility. My family shouldn't want to take advantage of me. No one has to ask me to be polite. Why can't I expect the same consideration from them?"

"You're not like the rest of them," Emmitt said. "That's a good thing."

Emmitt's answer didn't satisfy Renata. "That's what my mother keeps saying, but it doesn't amount to anything when I constantly suffer from their actions. Everything hanging here, in *my* sitting room, is my mother's. The pieces are too valuable or too sentimental to be left in her piles of clutter, so I keep them here for her. I can't get rid of them. I don't want to, because it would hurt her too much … but she never considers how much it hurts me to contribute to her hoarding."

Emmitt scanned the paintings and photographs covering the walls.

Renata pointed to a large closet. "Look in there," she said.

Emmitt stood and walked toward the closet. He slowly opened the door and peeked inside. Dozens of pieces of artwork were neatly arranged on the floor against the wall. Sheets and tea towels separated the pieces and protected the frames from scratching against each oth-er. Looking back at the room, Emmitt realized just how little Renata kept for herself. Her sitting room was hers, but it wasn't fully her own. She had conceded so much to a family who repaid her kindness by continuing to encroach.

"A month ago, my uncle joked he was giving me the rejects no one else wanted." Renata's brow furrowed. "Before that moment, I had agonized over confronting him. I thought it would crush him if he found out I didn't want his paintings, but it was all a joke to him." Renata exhaled sharply. "He wasn't laughing today."

"Was that your tipping point?" Emmitt asked.

"Sort of. It certainly made me angry enough to want to confront him, but it was already something I was becoming more determined to do. I guess I needed the push. I figured if he could be so irreverent about his works of art, then I could tell him I didn't want to keep them anymore. I didn't want to tell either of you until I actually did it … Surprise." Renata let out a melancholy sigh.

"Did your uncle really scream at you?" Emmitt rushed through his question, fearing Andrew would pounce with a vague or boring inquiry.

Renata nodded solemnly. "If you're not on the receiving end of his long-winded diatribes, he can be extremely entertaining to watch. He told me I had no taste, no decency, and he can understand why my mother struggles to love me." Renata paused as the words seemed to wash over her a second time. A small smirk rose on the corner of her lip. "At one point, he called me an 'uncultured artistic abortionist.' I think that may have been the point when I pivoted from complete devastation to the realization of how absurd it all was. I told him I would give a donation to a local arts foundation in reparation of my grave sin. And I called. Right at that instant. Right in front of his smug face. I think I surprised him. I surprised myself. It was petty and wrong for me to give a donation out of spite … but it felt like a victory. Uncle Lucas just stood like an overtired toddler, stamping his foot and balling up his fists. That's when Mother came in. She thought he was getting ready to hit me."

"He didn't hit you, did he?" Emmitt moved closer toward Renata. His eyes carefully scanned her, looking for any marks or bruises.

"No." Renata laughed, reaching for Emmitt's arm and tugging gently until he sat beside her. "Uncle Lucas is all bitchy bluster. He'll calm down, eventually. He probably won't ever apologize ... but he'll call in a couple weeks to see what I'm doing and take me out for coffee. I'm really not worried about him."

"And your mom?" Emmitt asked.

Renata rolled her eyes. "That's the last question."

"Understood," Emmitt said.

"Hmm ..." she pondered aloud, as she eyed Emmitt with a grin. "As I said, my mother burst through the door while Uncle Lucas was having a tantrum. She screamed louder than he did ... even uttered a few expletives ... she must have forgotten about that during her own recollection of events. She kicked him out and then called Sister Eugene and Andrew. Then, she broke down and started crying. I was too busy trying to calm her down to answer your calls, Emmitt. Sorry for that," she said, resting her hand on Emmitt's knee.

"May I ask one more question?" Andrew spoke calmly. He kept his hands firmly planted under his chin.

"Emmitt is really rubbing off on you," Renata said. "Sure, Andrew. Go ahead."

"You seem fairly calm about the situation, but the entire scene sounds frightening. How are you feeling?"

Emmitt silently scolded himself for being so callous. Of course, Andrew had to ask the last question, and of course, he had to be far more sympathetic toward Renata than Emmitt had been. Emmitt caught the eye of his brother and saw the smug smile set upon Andrew's lips. *Asshole*. Emmitt rested his hand gently on top of Renata's as he shot a biting glare at his brother. It flashed a moment, then relaxed as he turned his attention back to Renata. She smiled at Emmitt and entwined her fingers with his.

"I'm okay," she said. "It wasn't a best-case scenario, but it didn't make me crumble, which was a pleasant surprise. Honestly, now that it's done, I feel pretty good … mostly." Renata paused. "I'm still mad … and I still want them to change … but I understand I can't expect too much."

"Emmitt and I see what you're doing. We see the progress you're making and the example you're setting for Sybil and Mrs. Yates. Sister Eugene sees it. And I'm sure your mother sees it too," Andrew said. He slowly raised himself from the sofa and headed toward the kitchen door. He stopped to pat Renata's head in the same way Sister Eugene had. "I'll be in the car. Don't be too long, Emmitt."

When the door shut behind Andrew, Emmitt scrambled to his feet and offered a hand to Renata, gently pulling her up from the floor. Renata reached for his face and stood on her toes to kiss him. Emmitt bent his head to meet her lips. The apology he meant to give her was lost. There were no words in his head. The only image was of Renata's soft, glossy lips.

He felt her hair cascading through his fingers as her body pressed firmly against his. He breathed in and savored her scent-—sweet and floral, like candied rose petals. The feeling of comfort consumed him. Emmitt wanted to stay in Renata's embrace, but he knew it couldn't last. Andrew was waiting for him.

All at once, the words and intrusive thoughts poured back into Emmitt's mind. He thought of the hoard, the book, and the Yates family. He thought of Andrew. Then his thoughts circled back to Renata and her glossy lips. He tried to cling to the image, but the word *commitment* kept repeating in a loop in his mind. He couldn't muffle the word, and he felt a rising dread that something would eventually have to give way: the hoard, the book, Andrew, Renata, or Emmitt.

As he struggled to free himself from his thoughts, Emmitt felt Renata gently release him. She smiled up at him, and the dread subsided to a mere whisper of discomfort. She's my sanctuary, he thought. *When did that happen?* Emmitt held Renata's face in his hands and kissed her forehead, and they slowly said their goodbyes.

Back in Andrew's SUV, Emmitt tried to pinpoint what he was feeling. He loved Renata. Emmitt hated the secrecy of their relationship, but he knew it was only a matter of time before she told her family. He hated Andrew for saying all the things he should have said, but figured the feeling would pass within the hour (as it usually did). He hated Lucas, though he didn't know him, but he still felt an aching sympathy for Shannon, who he thought he should hate at the moment, for Renata's sake. He hated his own mother for inserting herself into a job that was supposed to be his and Andrew's. He loved Sister Eugene for being a mother to all of them. And despite his increased efforts to maintain his indifference toward her, he felt a rising, somber affection for Sybil, who was desperate to never be alone.

Another thought came to Emmitt's mind. There was something he hadn't told Renata. Something new. Something he needed to tell Andrew first. Before he could open his mouth to speak, Andrew broke the silence.

"I've been talking to Melody." Andrew's voice was so low, the words were almost a whisper.

Emmitt snapped out of his thoughts and perked up with the pleasant surprise. The tepid hatred of his brother lifted immediately. He smiled at the thought of Andrew rekindling his romance with Melody.

"You're back with your crazy cat lady? That's great!" Emmitt said with genuine excitement. "We can do a double date. That's a thing normal people do, right?"

"We're talking, not dating," Andrew said.

"Not dating *yet* … or not dating *ever*?" Emmitt's elation was deflating almost as quickly as it rose.

"I don't know. Forget I said anything." Andrew slumped slightly at the wheel. Drew Key never slumped.

Emmitt had successfully held back his animated interrogations while in the sitting room with Renata. Now, alone in the car with Andrew, he unleashed all of his questions in furious succession. "No. You brought it up, and I'm not letting it go. Why aren't you dating Melody? Why bother to talk to her at all if you're not planning on getting back together? You still love her, right? Wouldn't you just be torturing yourself to settle on a friendship?"

"I saw how well things were going with you and Renata, and Melody just kept popping into my mind, so I called her. I just wanted to hear her voice and see how she was doing," Andrew began in Drew's cool, unbothered tone as he spoke. But at the mention of Melody's name, his stoicism fractured and melded with an almost imperceptible trace of pained longing. Emmitt noticed. Andrew noticed Emmitt noticed.

Andrew cleared his throat and stiffened his posture. "It was just a couple of calls. Nothing more."

"You needed more than one call to hear her voice and see how she was doing?" Emmitt said with a raised eyebrow.

"Yeah. I like to talk to her. Are we done?"

Emmitt laughed. "Nope. We still have about twenty minutes until you drop me off. You're stuck with me."

"I have nothing more to say." Drew's cool insistence may have been enough for most people to take the hint and back down. Emmitt was not most people.

"Then I'll speculate."

Andrew groaned. "What else could you possibly want to know?"

"How is Melody?" Emmitt asked with a wide grin.

"She's doing well."

"Was she surprised when you called her?"

"No."

"No?" Emmitt asked. He rested his left arm on the center console and leaned closer to Andrew.

"We still text and call each other, occasionally. Birthdays ... and holidays. We're friends."

"That's what I said when I was lying to you!" Emmitt cackled.

Andrew's jaw tightened. "I'm not lying."

"So, what's the point? Why call her?"

"She's positive. She's a good listener. She isn't judgmental, and she always has constructive opinions."

"Oh," Emmitt uttered meekly. "Not like me, then."

"Not at all like you," Andrew said. He relaxed the tension in his jaw and continued. "But ... she was excited to hear that you and I were working together."

"You told her we're working together?"

"Yes."

"Did you tell her about Renata?"

Andrew paused before answering. "Yes."

"And?"

"Melody knows her. She said Renata is kind and sweet … and perfect for you." Emmitt saw a glimmer in Andrew's eyes, though his face remained relaxed.

"Is Melody dating anyone?"

"No."

"What's she up to?"

"She's starting a rescue that doubles as a cat café. The building she's renting is only a couple of miles from my place. She's working with her contacts from local fostering charities. All the cats will be available for adoption, so Melody can foster more of them without having to keep them in her house. Plus, she'll have a staff of employees to help her."

"How many cats live with her now?"

"Two." Andrew paused again. "They're both Sphynx cats."

"What does that mean?"

"They're hairless."

Emmitt's eyes widened as he tried to keep from shouting in excitement. "Andrew, this is destiny! You see it, right? Whether you want to call it the Universe, or God, or an alignment of frequencies, this is a sign that you two need to be together."

"God?" Andrew smirked.

"Yeah … well …" Emmitt stammered. "I've spent the last twenty-eight years of my life acting as though God doesn't exist. Maybe I'll spend the next twenty-eight acting as though God does exist. I'll let you know in a couple of decades if it made any difference."

"How pragmatic."

"Don't deflect, Andrew. If you can't compromise on this ..."

"It wasn't just the cats that caused the breakup, Emmitt."

"What else happened?"

Andrew was silent.

"Andrew?" Emmitt persisted. "You told me it was the cats. What else happened?"

"She wanted kids." The words nearly caught in Andrew's throat.

"That's ... a serious thing." Emmitt sighed. "You didn't want kids?"

"It's complicated."

"What's complicated? You didn't want kids then? You don't want kids now? You want to wait, but she doesn't? She changed her mind, but now you want kids?"

"You talk too much, Emmitt. You press too much. This isn't any of your business."

"You brought Melody up, Andrew," Emmitt grumbled. "Is that why you've been so bothered lately? Are you having some sort of existential crisis with Melody?"

"Bothered?" Andrew's body tensed as he glanced icily at Emmitt.

"Yeah. You've been acting weird. I only noticed a few little things. Renata said she was worried, so I've been paying closer attention. She was right. There is something off about you."

"Renata noticed?" Andrew's lips pressed tightly together. Emmitt couldn't tell if he was angry or embarrassed.

"She cares about you," Emmitt said. "That's not a bad thing, Andrew."

Andrew sighed. "I know. I appreciate how much she cares."

"You were right about Renata too. Total empath … but don't tell her I said that. She thinks you're a good brother. She wants you to be happy almost as much as I do."

Andrew looked ahead at the road. He let out a deep breath and spoke in a low, stern voice. "Despite the total mess you made with your unprofessional behavior, I can't bring myself to be angry at you for dating Renata. I want to be angry. I deserve to be angry … but I get why you did what you did. If it was anyone but Renata, I'd be furious. You should thank her for saving you. I'm going easy on you for her sake."

"I know I deserve the full impact of your wrath, and I'm grateful for your mercy," Emmitt half-joked. "But why can't you have what I have? Why can't you be happy with Melody?"

"Don't get sentimental, Emmitt."

"Why not?" Emmitt asked. "Did Melody reject you?"

"No," Andrew scoffed.

Emmitt lowered his voice and whispered solemnly, "Is it a medical thing?"

Andrew rolled his eyes and groaned. "No, Emmitt. We're both medically fine."

"Then why don't you want to have kids with her?"

"I *never* said I didn't want to have kids with her!" Andrew roared in exasperation.

"Never? Did you want to have kids with her before? What stopped you?"

"Drop it," Andrew growled.

"No." Emmitt said the word with such despondency that Andrew turned to look at him. "You two would be great parents. Why would you do that to her? Or yourself?"

"It doesn't matter," Andrew snapped. "You really need to stop, Emmitt."

Emmitt wouldn't stop. "It sounds like you want to be with Melody. You both want kids. You still talk to each other. I don't understand what's stopping you. Why are you being so cryptic and confusing?"

"Emmitt," Andrew's voice raised sharply. "Mom doesn't think I should get involved with Melody. She didn't think it was right then. She hasn't changed her mind."

Andrew shocked Emmitt into silence. As he allowed the words to penetrate, a fuming anger rose through Emmitt's chest and tightened in his throat.

"M-Mom ... this is about what *Mom* wants?" he choked.

"It's about what's best for my career. Mom doesn't think a serious relationship ... or kids ... are beneficial to my brand right now. She's put a lot of work into helping me build my business. She thinks I'm on a precipice of actualization—"

"With Sybil?" Emmitt exclaimed, nearly rising out of the passenger seat. "You'd give up Melody for Sybil?"

"It's not like that," Andrew objected. "I'm not interested in dating Sybil, but Mom thinks I can help her. And we *have* helped her. More than anyone else has ... and the job is nearly done. Sybil has a higher profile than my other clients. Having her name attached to our book will broaden my influence."

"'Broaden your influence?' So, you want to be just like Mom?" Emmitt fumed.

"Yes ... and no," Andrew said slowly. "I want to be successful, and I want to help people, but I don't know if I want Mom's level of success if it means I can only work with clients like Sybil. I'm not trying to disparage Sybil. I like Sybil, and I'm happy to work with her and motivate her, but I'm not interested in micromanaging her life. I want to help my clients set manageable, attainable goals and accomplish them. I don't want to feel like I'm relegated to the role of a parent ... or husband ... with any client." A deep line set into Andrew's forehead as he stared ahead at the road.

"So, why can't you tell Serenity to stop butting in?"

"Mom thinks she's helping."

"She's not," Emmitt snarled.

"Neither are you," Andrew argued. "Must be a family trait."

Emmitt ignored the comparison. "So, you're going to let Mom dictate every meaningful decision of your life?"

"Not every meaningful decision."

A fresh wave of anger washed over Emmitt. "If you want to let someone else dictate the most important decision of your life, you could at least pick someone who loves you and wants to see you happy. If you would have asked for my advice four years ago, you'd be married to Melody, you'd have a couple kids—"

"And I'd be struggling to grow my business," Andrew interrupted. "Mom wouldn't be speaking to me, so I wouldn't have had access to her publishers for my previous books. She wouldn't have allowed me to continue speaking at her retreats and conferences, and I wouldn't have been able to expand my clientele as quickly. Mom jump-started my career, Emmitt. I owe a lot to her."

"So, you'd be poor and happy … nothing wrong with that. It's not so bad, speaking from experience."

"You're choosing to ignore the fact that Melody isn't poor … and neither is Renata," Andrew said. "I wouldn't have been poor if I married her … and you won't be poor if you marry Renata."

"I know that," Emmitt said with a flush of shame.

"There's more to a stable relationship than just being able to provide, Emmitt. It's about being responsible. And maintaining devotion. It's sacrificing …"

"It's commitment," Emmitt said. Even now, the word overwhelmed his thoughts.

"Yes," Andrew nodded in agreement. "Exactly. Their wealth doesn't let us off the hook. But it doesn't let me off the hook with Mom, either. She put a lot of time, effort, and money into my success. I'm an investment to her. I don't want to let her down."

"Parents are supposed to put effort into their children's success," Emmitt argued. "You're Serenity's son. You're not an investment." He looked out the window as he considered Andrew's words. "I know I messed up. I really didn't intend to hurt you, and I'm still committed to working with you … but I'm more committed to Renata. Thankfully, my commitment to you isn't at odds with my commitment to her, but I know Serenity won't be as accommodating to you as you are to me. So, if Mom forces you to choose, who do you pick? Who are you more committed to, Mom or Melody?"

Andrew remained silent.

Emmitt turned his head and glared at his brother. "Seriously, Andrew? No answer?"

Andrew shook his head.

"I don't get you, Andrew," Emmitt announced, raising his hands in confusion and agitation. "You aren't struggling financially. You're able to balance your work and personal life. Your other clients admire and respect you. Melody wants to be with you. Why is it such a hard decision?"

"I don't know," Andrew breathed. "I've always wanted what Mom has. She's been mentoring me for years. She's given me solid advice and I owe my wealth and my reputation to her. It would destroy her if I suddenly said I didn't want it. It would make me ungrateful. I don't want to hurt Mom."

Emmitt couldn't tolerate Andrew's deference toward Serenity. Andrew would never see Serenity through Emmitt's eyes. He never tried. He always ignored Serenity's open contempt for her younger son. Maybe he didn't notice it. Even if he did notice, it wasn't as though Andrew could do anything about it. Still, Andrew's desire to protect their mother's feelings battered Emmitt and hardened his disposition.

"If you're so determined to keep Mom happy, why did you bring Melody up in the first place? You knew how I'd react. I'm sure you *wanted* me to react."

Andrew nodded his head and replied calmly, "You're right. I knew mentioning Melody would get a reaction from you. I realize I can't expect you to listen calmly while I try to work things out for myself. That was my mistake. I'm sorry. I shouldn't have said anything."

Emmitt had stopped listening to Andrew. His mind was already in a tailspin as he caught the words "I'm sorry." No, he thought. *Sorry isn't good enough.*

"You're not getting off that easily," he seethed. "We're visiting Serenity tomorrow."

Andrew laughed. "You never want to see Mom. Besides, we'd have to make an appointment."

"Tomorrow. We're going to see Mom. If you want to call her to warn her, go ahead. If you won't go with me, I'll go alone." Emmitt's words were sharp and determined.

Andrew stopped laughing. "No. You're riled up about something that isn't your business. I said I was sorry for bringing up Melody. I won't risk Mom's wrath over your curiosity."

Emmitt was unyielding. "I'm going. Mom inserted herself into our work. We have a right to ask her what her motives are."

Andrew was equally resolute. "You will not mention Melly to Mom ... and what motives? You're acting like Mom is some sort of mustache-twirling villain."

"And you're acting as though she's some well-intentioned saint who just wants what's best for her boys. She's castrated you, Andrew, yet you continue to defend her. We need to know what her intentions are with Sybil. She placed Sybil squarely on your lap, and now she doesn't want you to date Sybil's competition."

"Melody gave up acting years ago. She isn't competing against Sybil."

"But Sybil hates Melody. She's been tormenting you by belittling Melody for months, and her insults are only getting worse ..." He stopped himself as he glanced at Andrew. He realized he had passed the line and was now hurtling himself toward Andrew's breaking point.

Sensing the heat of Andrew's nearly unbridled anger, Emmitt shook his head and quickly shifted his argument. "Look, even if there's not a major conspiracy against your ex-girlfriend, I'm concerned about Serenity's sudden interest in Sybil. You should be concerned too. Why would Mom pry herself away from her highly cultivated cabal to give Sybil advice on goal setting? Why would she care enough to convince Sybil to abandon almost all of her other businesses to focus on Rivers of Younity?"

"I'm not sure ..." Andrew paused. Emmitt watched as his brother's expression shifted from indignation to uncertainty. "I never mentioned specifics to Mom, but she knows we're still working with Sybil ... It's possible that Mom recognized Sybil at the retreat and took her aside to give her advice. She clearly motivated Sybil ... and you can't argue with the results." Andrew's face tensed as he continued hesitantly, "I'll admit, it may have been ... improper ... for Mom to suggest that Sybil focus most of her professional energy on Rivers of Younity, but it was ultimately Sybil's decision ... and this isn't new information. You and I know they're working together. Renata knows they're working together ... and we've already cleared the office ..."

"Yeah. We emptied a room packed with unsold products. There were enough boxes to fill the dumpster Serenity provided. We threw away tens of thousands of dollars ... maybe more. I know Sybil is rich, but that's still a lot of wasted money."

"I ... hadn't thought about it that way." Andrew frowned. "You're right, Emmitt. It's a lot of wasted money. But it's also an unavoidable consequence of clearing a hoard."

"I know, but there was something else that bothered me about Sybil's business affiliations ..." Emmitt paused. He had taken on an assignment without permission and was unsure if his unauthorized research would be well-received by his willfully incurious brother. "I tried to ignore it the last couple months, but I couldn't get it out of my mind, so I did some digging about a week ago. You remember the other marketing scam Serenity allowed Sybil to promote?"

"Amelior Wellness?" Andrew asked guardedly.

"The CEO is one of Serenity's clients … It's Felix Bryson."

"Shit," Andrew groaned. "Have you told Renata?"

"Not yet. I wanted to tell you first. We need to visit Mom."

"You could have led with that revelation," Andrew scolded.

"Well, I would have gotten around to it if you hadn't brought up your deep, abiding love for Melody," Emmitt shot back. "I thought I could tell you and Renata without confronting Mom about it, but it's clear that Serenity has fully entrenched herself. She's peeking through all the cracks and fixing our failures … sorry … not failures … *opportunities*. It can't all be incidental. We need to know what she wants."

"Fine," Andrew said. "I'll go. But you need to promise to be on your best behavior."

"No."

"Please." It was halfway between a plea and a command. Andrew tightened his grip on the wheel and hardened his resolve. "We won't get anything out of her if you're screaming obscenities and calling her a terrible mother."

"But she is a terrible mother," Emmitt said.

"Regardless of how you feel, promise me you'll control your anger."

"I don't see why I should," Emmitt protested.

Emmitt could hear the forced restraint in Andrew's voice. "Because it will take all of my effort to keep Mom from losing control of *her* anger, and I can only handle one of you at a time. You meddled, like you always do, and now we owe it to Renata to see if Sybil's being taken advantage of. I would love to leave this up to you to sort out, but I know I can't let you go alone. Your mouth is a hammer, Emmitt."

Emmitt felt another hot flush of shame as he relented. "Alright. Fine. I promise to be on my best behavior."

Andrew clarified further. "We stick to Sybil. No Melody. No insults. Swear to me."

"I swear," Emmitt said with a growing petulance. "No backing down. We're definitely going tomorrow, right?"

"Yes." Andrew's body was stiff. Emmitt could see the bulging veins in his forearms and neck as he stared fixedly ahead. "We're definitely going tomorrow."

Chapter Twenty-Two

A restless night followed by the long drive with Andrew to their mother's house tested Emmitt's unwavering resolve from the day before. His intestines knotted and gurgled in the passenger seat of the SUV. Andrew would call it karma. Renata would call it atonement. Regardless of semantics, Emmitt's body was suffering from a reckoning.

Andrew pulled into gas station convenience stores and fast-food restaurants countless times as Emmitt nearly doubled over with wave after wave of intense cramping. Andrew remained quiet. He didn't question. He didn't complain. And he didn't laugh. Despite his weak nerves and weaker bowels, Emmitt remained determined to see his mother and question her involvement with Sybil Yates.

The last time Emmitt visited Serenity was five years prior. Both Andrew and his father insisted he attend a surprise forty-fifth birthday party she had planned for herself. Months earlier, he'd completed college, worked for his mother's lifestyle magazine for one week, and been fired. Emmitt expected Andrew to pressure him to attend the party, but he was surprised to hear from his father when Andrew failed to persuade him. It was an effective strategy. After Tommy Key's long-winded intercession, Emmitt finally relented. It was a decision he still regretted.

Serenity never acknowledged his presence at the party. Emmitt soon realized she only wanted him invited so she could actively ignore him. Late in the evening, a hired photographer requested a family photo to print in the magazine. She called out to Drew, and they posed together in front of the fairy-lighted gazebo in the backyard. She intentionally excluded Emmitt. Andrew said nothing. When Emmitt confronted Andrew about their mother's behavior, Andrew defended Serenity. He said it didn't matter how she acted since it was her birthday, and Emmitt was unreasonable to expect her undivided attention when there were so many guests in attendance. Andrew also argued that Emmitt wouldn't have wanted to be in the picture anyway, so Serenity had saved herself the embarrassment of being rejected. Emmitt refused to speak to Andrew for two weeks.

Five years later, Emmitt feared Andrew might turn on him again.

Serenity's forty-fifth birthday was two houses ago. Her newest home, bought from a combination of snake oil sales and scamming gullible celebrities, was the Zen retreat she had always wanted. It was a gated house in a gated community. There were no automated key codes to get in; all guests had to pass inspection by a security guard. The uniformed man sitting in the booth stopped both of the cars ahead of Andrew's SUV and required their windows to be rolled down for inquiries. Andrew didn't bother to crack open his window. Presumptuous ass, Emmitt thought. *He honestly believes he's important enough to be waved through the gates. How embarrassing.*

Just as Emmitt let the thought bubble up into a smug smirk, the on-duty guard waved Drew Key in. The guard didn't even bother to look up from his desk as the SUV drove past the ornate wrought-iron gate into the opulent Empyrean Cliffside Estates.

"How?" Emmitt demanded.

"Unlike you, I actually visit Mom. It's been busy the last few months trying to keep up with the Yates family, my other clients, and all your nonsense, but I visit often enough for security to remember me."

"What's his name, then?" Emmitt asked.

"Charles. He has an ex-wife named Denise and three kids he sees on weekends: Charles Jr., Derek, and Maggie. You want to know the kids' extracurriculars? Or Charles's hobbies?"

"No."

Andrew wound his SUV up the hill, past high fences, tall hedges, and impassable roads that led to massive hidden estates. Emmitt had always seen his mother as a self-serving, disingenuous yoga instructor. The image of Serenity as a yoga instructor was lodged so firmly in his mind that it seemed to blot out the reality of her meteoric rise. Now, winding up the unfamiliar neighborhood to a mansion he had never visited, the reality of who Serenity had become seeped into Emmitt's thoughts. She wasn't just a yoga instructor. She wasn't just a life coach or a wellness ambassador with her own magazine. Serenity Rivers-Key was a global name. She was a shaman of the stars. A business mogul. She gave keynote speeches to solidify her influence over celebrities, corporate boards, and heads of state. She had sway. Pull. She could throw her weight around in politics, if she wanted.

All this time, Emmitt was struck by the wealth and repute of the Yates family, but he had never considered how his own mother lived. He didn't really care how or where his mother lived. He didn't want to visit her, and she never invited him. They were happy living their separate lives. They only had Andrew in common. The thought of Serenity having influence over Andrew made Emmitt's stomach churn and roil. But having influence over the country? Or the world? Emmitt felt lightheaded. He rolled down the passenger window and breathed deeply.

"You okay?" Andrew asked, looking over at Emmitt.

"The winding is making me carsick," Emmitt said.

"If you have to throw up, do it out the window. I had the car detailed last week … and lean your head out, so it doesn't get on the paint."

"Got it." Emmitt gave Andrew a thumbs up and closed his eyes until the car stopped moving.

He lifted one lid as he heard Andrew's voice speaking to one of Serenity's countless employees over the intercom. A high-pitched buzz set off a motorized gate that slowly opened for Andrew's SUV to pass through. Another long road led to a manually forested area of over-grown tropical plants and trees that had no business among the rocky cliffsides and dry brush that lay just beyond the property line. Emmitt considered the amount of water required to keep up with the jungle they were currently driving through. Of course, Serenity didn't mind paying extra for the privilege. She kept her mind at ease while baking in her personal sauna, flying on private jets, vacationing on luxury yachts, over-heating her yoga studios, and importing her essential oils from India. She was financially invested in the carbon offset companies she donated to, so the money always circled back around. Her abundance was her wholeness. Andrew was driving through Serenity's self-actu-alized heaven.

After a few minutes up the long road, Andrew finally reached a driveway that was large enough to be considered a parking lot. Seven cars occupied half of the marked spaces. Emmitt was certain they belonged to Serenity's employees. Serenity always kept her own car in the garage, and none of the parked cars matched the level of client Serenity advised. Even Andrew's recently detailed luxury SUV wouldn't be mistaken for a car owned by Serenity's A-list clientele.

Emmitt took one last deep breath as he shouldered open the car door.

Standing in the driveway parking lot, Emmitt couldn't see the mansion. A dense foliage hid the house from view. The brothers followed a path that led to yet another closed gate. A slight young man with glasses and a gaunt muscular frame opened the carved wooden gate. He politely welcomed them into an expansive outdoor courtyard.

As Andrew slipped off his sandals, the man smiled and asked Emmitt to take off his shoes. Emmitt fought to control his indignation. He couldn't bring himself to smile back at the man, so he resigned himself to silent compliance. Emmitt shifted his eyes away from Serenity's assistant and barely acknowledged his presence. Once Emmitt's shoes and socks were off, the man guided them past a large koi pond to a secluded area.

Tropical bushes, trees, and climbing vines surrounded and strangled a latticed wooden pergola. A long, carved wooden bench and two hanging rattan chairs created a sitting area within the wooden structure. A muted beige cushion had been placed on the hard bench, and matching cushions and pillows lay inside the egg-shaped hanging chairs. There was a large stone fountain installed behind the pergola.

Emmitt noticed the sound before he noticed the source. He only realized what it was after he saw the large boulder spitting water up from a hole in the top of it. Other than the strange geyser that erupted from its center, the dark-gray rock blended into the other gray rocks within the dense tropical jungle Serenity had constructed.

The man gestured for Emmitt and Andrew to sit, assuring them that Serenity would be out to visit them shortly.

Emmitt waited for the man to leave before daring to speak privately with Andrew. Sitting next to his brother on the wooden bench, Emmitt leaned in and whispered, "Do you always talk to Mom out here?"

"No." Andrew wasn't whispering. "Forrest usually lets me into the house."

"Forrest?" Emmitt continued to whisper. "Is that his real name or his cult name?"

"I don't know, Emmitt. I didn't ask if it was his cult name. Honestly, it's no wonder Mom doesn't want you in her house. You're socially feral."

Emmitt chuckled. "Yeah. I've got too many ketones or candida ... I forget what Serenity said last time I actually visited her ... you know, besides her birthday."

Andrew rolled his eyes. "You'll never have too many ketones with all the carbs you eat, and candida is a fungal infection. Maybe she said your ketones were too low. That's probably why you're so nervous and tired all the time."

"My God, Andrew. That was a joke. If you want me to be nice to Mom, you need to meet me halfway. You're clearly not going to say anything negative toward her, so you need to be nicer to me to compensate."

Andrew sighed. "Okay. I hear you, Emmitt. I understand you're frustrated, and I will do my best to validate your feelings—"

"I don't want *Drew*. I want Andrew. Okay?" Emmitt snapped.

"Okay, Emmitt." Andrew looked at his brother with uncertainty.

"I'm serious. I don't want Drew. Drew and Serenity are always a team. I need you to be Andrew, my brother. You can be Serenity's protégé some other time. Preferably when I'm not here." Emmitt locked eyes with Andrew as he spoke.

Andrew nodded solemnly. "I get it, and I'll do my best, but it's not like Drew is a completely separate person. He's still me."

"He's not enough like you," Emmitt grumbled.

"Like hyper-neurotic, blurt-everything-out Emmitt isn't part of you? You can't divide me into pieces and just take the parts you like. Part of me is Drew."

"Then part of you is Andrew too. Mom only wants Drew. I, at least, am willing to suffer Drew to spend time with you. Would Mom suffer Andrew?"

Andrew didn't answer. They listened to the splashing and spluttering of the fountain until they heard faint footsteps on the stone path leading toward the pergola. Serenity's yoga pants were an ombre of oatmeal fading into cream. Her loose tunic was a soft ivory. Her long, chestnut-brown hair draped over her shoulder in a loose braid, and her loving eyes were fixed on her favorite son.

"Drew, darling. It is so auspicious for you to come here to see me. I was telling my team I had envisaged you coming over for a visit, and I immediately began to manifest the image into reality. And now, here you are! Of course, my ability to bring thoughts into existence may be a bit too powerful ... I set the intention for you to come over next week. Unfortunately, I am just so busy this week. I'm afraid our visit will have to be brief." Serenity's words flowed thick and sweet.

"Hi, Mom!" Emmitt called out boldly to Serenity with a wide grin. "Looks like your power to manifest is so great, that both your sons came to see you. How *auspicious* for you!"

Serenity let her honey-brown eyes fix on Emmitt. He had always hated seeing his own eyes staring back at him through her face. Her smile was soft, but her glare was venomous. "Emmie, I'm overjoyed to have you here."

"It's like a family reunion," Emmitt brayed, still grinning broadly while trying to contain the nervous, hateful laughter that was rising to meet his fury.

"Yes, I suppose it is." She broke eye contact with Emmitt and focused her attention on Andrew. "So, why do I have the pleasure of seeing *both* of my darlings today?"

Andrew cleared his throat. "Do you want to have a seat, Mom?"

"Oh, no Drew. I spent the last two hours on a conference call with manufacturers ... I won't bore you or Emmie with the details. I desperately need to root myself. It really is the best medicine."

Always an exit strategy. I guess I inherited something from Serenity, after all. Emmitt considered that both Andrew and their father were prone to hour-long goodbyes at parties. They were always the last guests out the door. Serenity was so practiced and adept at making excuses, the host would usually apologize to her for the inconvenience of inviting her over. On those occasions, Emmitt would sneak out the door after Serenity and beg her to take him home with her. Sometimes, she would relent. It was one of the few pleasant memories he had with his mother. Emmitt knew the sentiment wasn't mutual. *I was happy to go home with her, but she never seemed to enjoy the drive when I was in the passenger seat. And she was always annoyed when Andrew stayed behind with Dad.*

As Emmitt momentarily sank into his thoughts, Andrew spoke to their mother.

"I wanted to thank you for the help you gave Sybil Yates. She took remarkable initiative when she came back from your retreat."

Serenity's soft smile widened. "Is that why you're here? Well, that is so sweet, darling, but it didn't require you to come all this way. And I didn't do much. Sedona does most of the work for me. The mystical cosmic energies are so healing. Just physically being there made Sybil more pliable to manifesting positive changes in her life. You should thank the desert, and the mountains, and the convergence of electromagnetic energy rising from the earth."

Serenity's condescension only seemed to increase the longer she spoke. With a mock-sympathetic look, she said, "I was debating whether I should say something Drew, but I have to admit, you gave me a bit of a scare. You seemed rather unlike yourself when you called me last night. Is Emmie's anxiety affecting your vibrations? It is always going to be difficult to coalesce two very disparate frequencies. I was hoping Emmie's frequency would rise to match yours when you said you were planning on working together."

Emmitt stirred in his seat.

Perhaps sensing an outburst, Andrew said, "Emmitt has been working hard with the Yates family. He's built a great rapport with Shannon Yates ... and he's been especially adept at connecting with Renata Yates." Andrew glanced at Emmitt, who struggled to feign innocence in response to his brother's covert teasing.

Serenity kept her eyes on Andrew while speaking about his brother. "I'm glad to hear it. Emmie has the potential for greatness, but he constantly stands in his own way, and he refuses to listen to the wisdom of his mother. I'm grateful he's been gaining insight from you, Drew. You just need to be careful that he's building and strengthening his own vitality, rather than siphoning yours."

"We've been working well together … but we can't ignore your contribution." Andrew struggled to maintain his measured tone. The hair on Emmitt's arms raised as he heard the fear that seeped through Andrew's deference. "I was wondering … why did you hire a crew with a dumpster for Sybil?"

Emmitt's eyes widened at Andrew's question. There was a certain finesse to starting a conversation with Serenity. One couldn't immediately say what they wanted to say. Emmitt assumed it was the main reason his mother hated him. There were no pleasantries with Emmitt. If he had a pressing question, he would ask it, regardless of how tactless he was in the asking.

Serenity was equally direct, but far more callous in her delivery. She spoke with unwarranted confidence on almost every topic, but she shielded herself by disallowing others to be direct, forthright, or critical of her. Over the years, that shielding had expanded to envelop Andrew, but it never extended to Emmitt. He was always outside of it. Now, Emmitt sat in astonishment as Andrew asked the question. Usually, a flurry of compliments and circumlocutions would be required to ease Serenity into any semblance of a mutual conversation.

"Why? Well, to help you, of course. Isn't that obvious? Darling, you mentioned how slow the process was going, so I helped you speed it up." Her smile remained, but her head cocked slightly at the indignity of being probed.

"We really appreciate it, Mom," Andrew said. "When I mentioned it was a *gradual* process, I wasn't trying to complain. I'm sorry if it came across that way. You certainly worked a miracle by motivating Sybil, and Emmitt and I are grateful … but you didn't have to intervene. We know how busy you are—"

"It wasn't an inconvenience, darling," Serenity interrupted. "I was happy to help."

"Thanks," Andrew said. Emmitt watched as his brother forced out another inquiry. "Why didn't you tell me she was going to your retreat? Sybil was gone for over a month … closer to two, actually. We had to pause everything to wait for her to return, and she never gave us any updates."

Serenity kept her head tilted as she furrowed her brow. She spoke with a tenderness that was bathed in condescension. "Drew, you undermine your own authority when you blame others for your mistakes. A client like Sybil needs extra attention. Two missed calls. No voicemails. No texts. Sybil showed me your lack of dedication. You, of all people, should know that you can't allow your level of care to slip with Sybil. You need to stay on top of her."

"I get it," Andrew sighed.

"Drew, I really think you need to realign yourself after spending so much time with your brother. You seem a bit off. Why are you bringing any of this up? Did you lose money? Is Sybil threatening to fire you?"

"No," Andrew said. "We have Renata to thank for agreeing to an extension. I can take responsibility for my lack of care with Sybil. I can try to encourage her to be more honest in the future, but we can't keep asking for more time if we're not actively working with Sybil. It's not fair to the Yates family."

"You'll try? Not fair?" Serenity tittered resentfully. "It sounds like you need a retreat more than Sybil. We don't *try*. We do. We accomplish. Darling, the Yates family can afford to keep you indefinitely. You take what you can get from them. Nothing is fair. You need to fight for your livelihood. If the uncle cuts you off, you get cozier with Sybil. I really shouldn't have to be this blunt. It should be obvious. Sybil has her own money from acting, sales, and sponsorships. She may not be as rich as her uncle, but she certainly has enough money to keep you as a full-time advisor and mentor ... if you maintain her interest. It isn't difficult to know what Sybil wants. Her eyes light up every time she utters your name, darling. Believe me, those are the easiest clients to keep."

Emmitt closed his eyes and rubbed his brow. As he shielded his face from Serenity, he whispered to Andrew, "They're cash cows to her, and she's pimping you out to Sybil."

Serenity narrowed her eyes at Emmitt. Her tone was sharp. "Don't be crass, Emmie. At your age, you should know how to conduct yourself. Drew's concern and compassion are enough to keep Sybil interested. I wasn't suggesting anything more than professional attention. But Drew can't ignore the fact that Sybil is a reliable source of income. She doesn't depend on the allowance she gets from her uncle, but that money is nothing to sneer at. Sybil's monthly allowance is higher than what you make in a year, Emmie. I'm only guessing, of course ... it may be closer to what you make in *two* years." Serenity looked at Emmitt's silent glare and shook her head. "I'm stating it as a matter-of-fact, darling. You could do more to pull yourself up ... a lot more."

"Did Sybil tell you about her finances?" Andrew cut in.

Serenity shifted her attention back to Andrew. "No. Their trust attorney keeps pestering me to take him on as a client. He's not my type, but he is a chatterbox. Most of what he says is gossip, but some of the information is useful. For instance, I found out that Sybil and her mother were written out of the Yates Trust. Sybil's uncle gives them an allowance out of pity. Apparently, her sister offered to split her own inheritance evenly between the three of them, but the uncle wouldn't allow it. Could you imagine? The girl's either stupid or a living saint. Stupid is my guess."

Emmitt felt a burning rage rise from his chest into his throat as he fought with himself to stay silent.

Andrew again inserted himself, clearly hoping to deescalate the rising tension. "Renata Yates is very kind and generous. She's kept us in the Yates house and helped with Sybil's progress."

"What an angel." Serenity sighed contemptuously, then turned the conversation back to the Yates Trust. "The attorney said Sybil's mother realized what was going on immediately. She hates her brother, but she needs his money. Apparently, Sybil still thinks she's receiving an inheritance from her grandfather, rather than an allowance from her uncle. I suppose it doesn't matter. Money is money, regardless of the source, but the attorney thinks Sybil may be close to outpouring, rather than the trickle she gets now. He said her uncle set up an account for her, and he plans to give her the same inheritance the other grandchildren received as a lump sum once she gains control over her hoarding. I don't know if it's a stipulation in the will, or if the uncle is as overgenerous as Sybil's sister."

Emmitt's confusion briefly overtook the intense anger he felt toward his mother. "So, you're trying to help us expedite the process, so Sybil can receive more money? Why does it matter? We're being paid by James Yates. We don't need to use Sybil or her money ... and she's almost finished cleaning and organizing her rooms. Once the book is complete, it'll generate its own revenue ... eventually. If what you're saying is true, Sybil won't get any of the trust's money until after we've finished working with her."

"Emmie, you haven't been listening. I don't blame you. You've always lacked acumen in financial matters, so I'll speak as plainly as possible: the Yates' home cleanup and your little book are jobs. Sybil Yates is an investment." Serenity's sweet tone dripped with disdain for her short-sighted son.

Andrew shifted uncomfortably on the bench. "You mean a long-term investment? You think I should continue mentoring Sybil after the cleanup is done?"

"Of course. Drew, that woman is the perfect steppingstone for you to progress to the next level. A client like Sybil can be kept in perpetuity. She'll always be in need. She'll always require guidance from a higher authority, and she'll always have the money to pay for the privilege of being in the presence of a gifted motivational expert. Sybil was born into wealth. People like Sybil don't internalize cost or value. You could double your prices within the first year, and she wouldn't care or complain. Darling, you are more than ready to be a guiding force for Sybil."

And there it was. Emmitt glanced at his brother's expressionless face. That's what it took to be Serenity. Andrew knew Serenity encouraged Sybil's interest in him, and he knew Sybil's notoriety would increase his reputation. But he didn't know the metamorphosis that would be required to transform into Serenity. No butterfly. Only leech. Andrew wanted to be a household name, like his mother. Could he force himself to operate in the same manner? Could he live with himself, if he did? Would he be willing to play her games and use people to build his legacy? Emmitt studied Andrew carefully as he spoke.

"What about Renata and Shannon?" Andrew asked somberly. The initial shock had dissipated, but Emmitt could tell Andrew's heart was on the verge of breaking. "Our commitment included all three of the Yates women. We've made progress with Sybil, but Renata has also worked hard, and Emmitt is so close to a breakthrough with Shannon—"

"If Shannon Yates is connecting with Emmie, there really isn't any hope for her. Like attracts like, I'm afraid. She'll never listen to you, Drew."

"But Renata—" Andrew began.

"She's a nonstarter," Serenity interrupted. "No problems. No media presence. She's rich, but she lacks any meaningful influence. If she has any amount of common sense, she's useless. Sybil is the only one who matters. She is practically begging for someone to coach her into a fuller state of being. That's the type of client you need, darling."

Andrew frowned, but his voice managed a strained calm. Emmitt could see his throat tense as his words released. "I already have clients."

"Are you referring to the chain-smoker with the pug? Or the binge-eater who broke her water fast by eating an entire jar of mayonnaise? Drew, you need to increase your quality so you can decrease your quantity."

Andrew seemed almost despondent as he tried to reason with his mother. "To me, they're all quality clients. Cynthia allowed her ex-boyfriend to keep the pug and ended up adopting a Labrador. The puppy won't leave her side. She had to quit smoking to keep up with the constant walks she has to take with her new dog. I've been recommended to several of her friends, and I've gained three new clients because of her. She also gifted ten sessions to her brother. He's a Marine veteran. We've worked together to find him a therapist, we go to the gym together, and I've been helping him with breathing exercises and guided meditations."

"And what happens when his ten sessions are up? How will he compensate you?" Serenity asked calmly.

"He completed his sessions two weeks ago. I've discounted the price for him. The money I receive from my new clients more than makes up for the few hours I spend with him."

"Drew, darling ..." Serenity sighed. She stopped and considered. "Actually, we could make that work to our advantage. I would just need to whisper a few things into the right ears, and it could be all over social media. 'Drew Key: Hero to Disenfranchised Veterans.' Perhaps we could even let Emmie write the article." She smirked at Emmitt. "But we still need to build a higher quality of clientele for you. We don't want people to think that you need to take on a charity case. The public needs to see just how far you have to lower yourself in order to pull someone up from the gutter."

Emmitt had heard enough. His eyes fixed maliciously on Serenity. "Why are you working with Felix Bryson?"

Serenity's lip twitched as she tried to maintain her arrogant smile. "How do you know that name?"

"Research. Didn't he just get out of jail?"

Serenity's jaw tightened. "He's reformed. He's learned his lesson, and his new business is above reproach. Amelior Wellness supplements have gone through rigorous, court-ordered testing. Everything he sells is FDA compliant."

"No amphetamines this time?" Emmitt snarled.

"I would never align myself with an active drug dealer. And I would never subject Sybil Yates to selling amphetamines ... though I doubt she would care."

"But you trust a reformed drug dealer who sells the same products that previously landed him in jail?"

Serenity's smile twisted and tensed. "I'm a firm believer in rehabilitation and metaphysical metamorphosis. Felix Bryson is a changed man ... but even if he wasn't ... even if he was the same insufferable snake as before, he's more confined now than he ever was in prison. Felix is indebted to me, and it would be unwise for him to reject the path of redemption I've paved for him."

Serenity's manufactured intrigues appalled Emmitt. Whatever she had planned for Felix Bryson would undoubtably affect Sybil.

The flash of sympathy for Sybil unleashed a protective anger in Emmitt. "Why are you using Sybil? Why did you force her to ditch her other businesses to devote herself to Rivers of Younity and Amelior Wellness?"

"You think these businesses are all scams, right?" She didn't wait for an answer. "You should thank me for saving Sybil from a dozen network marketing businesses. Most of them were failing, by the way. In fact, Sybil was the only one keeping them afloat. She was overextending herself and wasting her time and money. Now, she's only committed to two businesses. We're well-established, highly profitable, and we're committed to taking care of her. We recognize her value."

Emmitt's lip curled spitefully as he spoke to his mother. "If Sybil is so profitable for you and Bryson, why would you allow her to be Andrew's investment?"

Serenity drew a hand up to her chest with a feigned look of hurt. "Where is this hatred coming from, Emmie? I only wanted to help. I'm not taking anything from Sybil, and Sybil wants Drew to mentor her. Where is the conflict? Darling, you can't be angry at me for helping Sybil become even more financially independent ... especially when you yourself are profiting off the Yates women. At least I provide Sybil with financial compensation. Honestly, Emmie, when you really think about it, which one of us is worse?"

Emmitt bit the side of his cheek. He clenched and grated until he tasted blood. A hot flush of shame burned through his body as Andrew grabbed his arm and squeezed.

"Calm down, Emmitt." His voice was low and stern. "You swore to me."

Emmitt's eyes locked furiously on his mother. "You already think the worst of me. You're only insulting yourself by comparing us. Is it because you know you're taking advantage of Sybil? I'll admit it. I'm taking advantage of her. Will you admit it, Mom?"

Serenity rolled her eyes. "Why are you getting emotional about Sybil Yates? I understand you're new to our line of work, but we have to maintain an emotional distance from our clients. You're the last person I thought I would have to reprimand for being too sentimental, Emmie. Do you honestly care about Sybil, or are you just directing all of your misplaced anger and frustration at me?"

Emmitt swallowed hard. His mouth was dry and metallic. His cheek throbbed from the pain.

Andrew intervened once more. "Emmitt is a little worked up. He's very dedicated to helping the Yates family. He isn't angry with you, Mom—"

"Yes, I am!" Emmitt snapped.

"Emmitt," Andrew said in a grumbling sigh.

Emmitt's shame and pain fused and surged through his body. "So, we're all making money off of Sybil, and none of us should feel bad about it, because Sybil's loaded?"

"We're helping Sybil, Emmitt." Andrew still held firmly to Emmitt's arm. "If Sybil wants to work with Mom, that's her business. We have our own business with her."

"How do we know Mom didn't just manipulate Sybil like she manipulates you?" Emmitt yelled. "And are we really helping Sybil if she's just mindlessly obeying everything you or Mom tell her to do?"

Emmitt had reached the point of shattering. He would have to break his promise for his brother's sake. Andrew would never ask the question, but Emmitt had little to lose. What was one more reason to justify Serenity's disappointment in her younger son when she already loathed him?

"What about Melody?" Emmitt thundered.

"Who?" Serenity asked.

"Andrew's girlfriend. Why won't you let him date her again? Why can't he be happy? Why can't they have kids?"

"Emmitt," Andrew snapped, as he dug his fingers deeper into Emmitt's arm. "Stop trying to help."

"Emmie, I'm not forcing Drew to do anything. I advised Drew to put his own personal development first. Lovers come and go. Kids can wait. But some of us are destined for greater achievements. Drew could change the world. He could carry on a legacy."

"Your legacy," Emmitt muttered.

"Yes, Emmitt. My legacy. I've worked hard. I've suffered. I've sacrificed. I'd like to pass my accomplishments down to Drew. The cat woman isn't worth his time ... and her idiosyncrasies might reflect poorly on him once he reaches his professional apex. She's a detriment to his brand. He can have children, if he wishes, once he's fully invested and established ... and once we've vetted a suitable partner."

Andrew softened and released his grip on Emmitt's arm at Serenity's mention of Melody.

"So, *you* determine when he's ready to start a family and who he's going to marry? Andrew doesn't have a say?" Emmitt seethed.

"What's a few more years? You don't know how difficult it is to build an empire. He deserves a woman who's sharp and determined. Someone who knows what they're getting themselves into. I'm giving Drew all the advice I wish I had when I was his age. At thirty-one, I was still an unknown yogi raising two children and nearing an uncoupling with my husband. Drew doesn't have the same distractions ... neither do you. Drew can see the financial success that materializes when following my advice ... and I'm sure you can see the consequences of actively ignoring my advice. I don't know what to tell you, Emmitt. You clearly have no interest in learning from my experience. If you want to squander your own potential, I can't stop you, but you shouldn't try to bring your brother down to your level. You can either follow in Drew's shadow, eking out a living from his generosity, or you can stay out of his way." Her feigned sweetness had been stripped away. Serenity's face was naked malice ... and hurt.

Emmitt tried to disregard it, but it was too late. He had seen it. Felt the weight of it. It was all too much for him to take in.

"He deserves better than both of us," Emmitt whispered. He stood to leave. "I'll be in the car, Andrew." He put a hand on his brother's shoulder. Leaning close, he whispered, "I'm sorry. I really did try not to cause a scene."

Serenity sidestepped to let Emmitt pass. He could feel her silent rage as he passed by her wordlessly. No goodbye. No hug. It was a normal parting for them. He grabbed his shoes and socks and walked barefoot toward the car. When he reached the driveway, he realized Andrew still had the keys. Emmitt walked to a large stone, sat, put on his shoes, and waited for his brother.

Twenty minutes passed before Andrew emerged. He carried himself with his usual quiet composure, but his face was pale. He looked tired and undone.

In the car, Emmitt was the first to speak. "How much trouble did I cause?"

"I don't know," Andrew answered. He closed his eyes and rubbed at his temples. He opened them slowly and started the car. "I calmed her down. I told her I would consider taking Sybil on as a permanent client."

"You're not really going to do it, are you?"

"I don't know. She thinks Sybil needs me. I like all my clients, but Mom thinks I can have a better impact by becoming more exclusive. If I up my prices, I can take on fewer clients. If I have fewer clients, I might have more time to volunteer with people who need help but can't afford the higher prices." Andrew shook his head as the words came out of his mouth. "And maybe we can fast-track a few things so I can eventually focus on starting a family." Andrew didn't sound convinced by any of it. He was merely parroting Serenity.

"Celebrity clients demand more than the ones you already have," Emmitt said. "They'll expect to get more than their money's worth. They'll bleed every penny. If you follow Mom's advice, you'll be watching Sybil sort her curling irons by order of importance until you're dead."

Andrew stopped the car in the middle of the driveway. He turned to Emmitt. "You drive. I've got a splitting headache."

Emmitt nodded and traded places with Andrew. Emmitt adjusted the seat and rearview mirror.

"Do not touch the side mirrors. I don't believe in violence, but I will kill you if you do it today, Emmitt." Andrew's eyes were closed. His right thumb and index finger began applying pressure on the web between his left thumb and index finger. He breathed in evenly. Held. Exhaled. Then began again.

"Sama Vritti," Emmitt said.

The corners of Andrew's lips raised slightly as he kept his eyes closed. "Box breathing. Surprised you remember the pranayama."

"Yeah, well. I listened to Mom sometimes ... and some words are bound to get lodged in your brain if you hear them often enough." Emmitt yawned as Andrew continued his rhythmic breathing. "Morning yoga and evening meditations. Every day. You, at least, enjoyed it. I still shudder when I hear the word *vinyasa*."

Andrew chuckled, then winced. "Don't make me laugh. It hurts too much."

"Sorry," Emmitt paused. "Are you going to see Melody again? Wait. Sorry. Don't answer that. I need to try harder not to pry."

"Thanks," Andrew breathed.

"No problem." Emmitt willed himself to worry about Andrew. "You want me to stop somewhere for medicine, or just get you home?"

"Home."

"Got it. I'm sleeping over at your place tonight. Partly to take care of you ... but mostly because I'm terrified to drive your car any farther than your house. Oh, and I'm taking the nice guest bedroom—the one with the jet tub in the bathroom—and I'm turning on the jets. Just letting you know. I'll shut up now so you can rest."

Andrew gave Emmitt a thumbs up and continued breathing. The rhythm of Andrew's breath lulled Emmitt into a quiet calm as he drove to Andrew's house.

Chapter Twenty-Three

In the morning, Emmitt busied himself in Andrew's kitchen. It wasn't going well. Andrew's oversized refrigerator was nearly empty. Six reusable alkaline water bottles were neatly arranged on the top shelf. A glass bottle of whole milk and a carton of two dozen organic eggs were the only food occupying space in the cavernous refrigerator. Emmitt grabbed a handful of eggs and placed them carefully on the slate-gray quartz countertop then pried his way into each of the walnut cabinets to find one of Andrew's nonstick pans. There was no butter, oil, or cooking spray anywhere in his brother's spacious open-concept kitchen.

Emmitt's disappointment increased when he opened the pantry and discovered it was more barren than the refrigerator. Peering in, Emmitt noticed a half-eaten bag of hickory smoked beef jerky. As he glanced at the packaging, he realized it was the sole remaining snack from the overfilled low-carb Christmas stocking Renata had given Andrew. On a shelf above the jerky, Emmitt spied the only seasonings his brother owned: salt and pepper.

Emmitt mumbled under his breath, "What's the point of having a kitchen this size if you don't cook? Does he ever eat at home?"

To Emmitt's growing dismay, he noticed Andrew had rid himself of his usual coffee maker. A bulky espresso machine took its place (and now monopolized a fifth of Andrew's kitchen counter space). He glared at the taunting mechanical behemoth, but ultimately decided, if Andrew wanted his morning espresso, he would have to make it himself. Breakfast was an apology, after all. Emmitt had no desire to add to the list of things he needed to apologize for by inadvertently breaking Andrew's new (and presumably prized) possession. Besides, Emmitt thought, *he probably enjoys making his own espresso.*

"I'm sure the process grounds him ... I should tell that joke to Renata. She'll appreciate the pun." He chuckled to himself as he broke the eggs into the pan. He extracted several pieces of shell with his fingers, poured the salt and pepper, scrambled the eggs with a spatula, and tried to keep them from burning while waiting for Andrew to wake up.

Andrew eventually walked casually down the floating walnut steps of his black cable-railed stairs as Emmitt was plating his breakfast. He wasn't wincing or squinting from a headache. He wasn't smiling or scowling, either. Andrew had already showered and dressed, and he appeared to be operating at his baseline functionality as he sat on a swiveling black and walnut barstool at the kitchen island. *Thank God,* Emmitt thought.

"I made breakfast. It's just eggs with salt and pepper. Nothing fancy. I would have made you coffee too, but that thing is way too complicated," Emmitt gestured toward the espresso machine with his left hand still clutching the spatula. He grimaced at his own carelessness as he watched little bits of egg slide off the silicone and splatter on the floor.

"Sorry. I'll clean that up."

Emmitt crouched down and picked up the pieces of egg that had fallen and threw them and the offending spatula into the sink with the pan.

Looking at the burnt egg residue still stuck to the pan, he added, "And I'll clean up my mess. I'm just letting the pan soak."

Emmitt quickly filled the pan to the brim with hot water and generously squirted a quarter cup of dish soap. He shifted back to the kitchen island and slid the plate of eggs in front of his brother.

"Thanks," Andrew said without looking up.

"No problem." Emmitt waited for Andrew to say more. When silence followed, he continued, "I wanted to fix breakfast to apologize for yesterday."

"You sure you didn't fix breakfast to pry more information out of me?" Andrew held his attention on the plate of dry scrambled eggs as he slowly put a forkful into his mouth. He frowned as he chewed.

"No," Emmitt said. "This breakfast is strictly an apology breakfast. I shouldn't have pushed for us to see Mom. And I shouldn't have lost my temper. And I shouldn't have stormed off and left you alone to deal with her."

"Nothing to do but move forward." Andrew glowered at the eggs as he took another bite. After a pained swallow, he lowered his head and attempted to clear his throat.

"Are they that bad?" Emmitt asked.

"They're a bit dry ... and bland ... and crunchy."

"I must've overcooked them while I was waiting for you to come downstairs. I know I missed a couple tiny pieces of eggshell ... but *bland* isn't my fault. The only seasonings you have are salt and pepper."

"I've been getting a lot of my meals delivered over the last few months. I usually pick up breakfast after I have my espresso." After a minute of serious deliberation, Andrew set the fork down and looked at Emmitt. "Thanks for not trying to figure out the espresso machine. I like to make my own."

"I figured." Emmitt resisted the urge to unleash his coffee pun upon his uncharacteristically contemplative brother. "Can I pay for your breakfast, then?"

"No." Andrew stood and stepped toward the imposing espresso machine.

"You making espresso?" Emmitt asked.

"Yes."

"Does that thing make cappuccinos?"

"Yes ... Emmitt, do you want a cappuccino?"

"No. No, I was just curious," Emmitt lied. "You don't have to make anything for me. Besides, I don't deserve it. I'm being penitent."

"I'll make you a cappuccino."

"If that's what you want to do, I won't stop you ... but I still want to pay for your breakfast."

"Emmitt, the protein bowl I normally order is almost twenty dollars, and the place doesn't sell pastries for breakfast, so you probably won't find anything to eat. I'll pick something up after I drop you off."

"I don't have to eat there. I can pay for your breakfast, then you can stop at the donut shop by my apartment, and I'll pick up my breakfast. Will you please let me do that for you?" Emmitt attempted a forced smile, but Andrew's detached civility unsettled him.

"Alright."

Andrew immersed himself with grinding beans and tapping the grounds into a little cup. Emmitt waited silently for him to finish.

Emmitt's cappuccino was first. He sat on a swiveling barstool and sipped as he waited for Andrew to speak. Andrew remained fixed to the machine. When he finished brewing his espresso, he turned and stood near the island counter, across from where Emmitt sat. He stirred the contents of the little cup and put it to his lips. Emmitt stared and tried to bite back laughter as Andrew sipped.

"What?" Andrew said, annoyed at Emmitt's expression.

"You look like you're playing with a five-year-old's tea set holding that tiny cup."

Andrew stared at Emmitt for too long. His silence was reflective, but his glare was accusatory. Emmitt didn't know what to expect next. He'd never seen Andrew like this. Andrew would sometimes play along, sometimes rebuke him for being stupid, and sometimes lecture him in Drew Key's voice. This interaction was new. Andrew wasn't as long-winded as Emmitt, but he wasn't usually this laconic, and Emmitt had never seen him brood over anything. Emmitt's anxiety loosened his lips, and the words poured out.

"I'm trying to show I'm changing for the better, Andrew, but you're not making it easy for me. Look, I get it. I messed up trying to talk to Mom. I already apologized for that. If you need me to say it again, I will: I'm sorry. I don't know what I need to do for you to start acting like yourself again. Tell me what to do, and I'll do it. You can get mad at me ... or tell me how low my vibrations are ... but don't act like this. It's weird."

"It's weird …" Andrew allowed his eyes to wander as he seemed to ponder the words carefully. He finished his espresso and set the cup down gently on the counter before fixing his frigid gray eyes on Emmitt. "You need me to be normal. You need me to act a certain way for your comfort. But you also blame Mom for expecting me to act a certain way for *her* to be happy. How are you any different from her?"

The words battered Emmitt. He leaned back in his chair as though Andrew had struck him. "I … I didn't mean it like that," Emmitt stammered.

"You don't think, Emmitt. You say impulsive things, you apologize, and everyone is supposed to ignore the devastation left in your wake. I know you mean well, but that isn't enough. Mom means well too."

"You know how hard it is for me …"

"It's hard for everyone, Emmitt. Keeping our mouths shut when we want to butt in, being polite to assholes, refraining from asking prying questions. Do you know how easy my job would be if I required clients to reveal all their problems, family secrets, and bad habits so I can berate them for their poor decisions and arrogantly explain what they need to do to solve all their issues?"

"I get it—" Emmitt began.

Andrew ignored him. "And do you know how many clients I would have if I actually took that approach? None."

"Mom seems to get plenty of clients using that approach," Emmitt grumbled.

"And you, inexplicably, won over Renata and Shannon using a similar approach. Even Melly thinks you're charming," Andrew said, shaking his head. "But that isn't my approach. That will never be my approach. You and Mom are given a lot of leeway to bulldoze through conversations. Mom does it through sheer force of will. She's commanding and unapologetic, and there are people who will let her lead them by the collar. You ..." Andrew broke off.

"What about me?" Emmitt didn't want to know what Andrew thought about him, but he wouldn't stop himself from asking the question.

Andrew continued to stare at Emmitt. "You make yourself small. You trick people into thinking you're inconsequential. I don't think you manipulate people on purpose. I think you feel justified because a part of you honestly believes you're insignificant ... but a part of you knows you're not. You play at being a wounded animal, but, inevitably, you pounce. You catch people off guard, and you force them to reveal things they may not want to reveal ... or confront truths they're not prepared to confront. You get the information you want, then you feel guilty, and you apologize."

There was no malice as Andrew spoke. Emmitt felt the color drain from his face. He couldn't bring himself to argue.

"Why would you want to work with me?" Emmitt pushed the words out. He felt nauseous.

"You're capable of more," Andrew said. "I've tried to help, but your cynicism makes you believe I'm only helping because you think I'm ashamed of you. Emmitt, Mom knows publishers that were willing—and are *still* willing—to look at your novels. I have former clients with large followings on social media who will promote you. You barely acknowledge Renata's wealth, and you still don't seem to factor it into any life you may have with her in the future. You take any offer of goodwill as a sign of pity."

"Do you really think I could trust Mom to offer me help with no strings attached?" There was petulance in Emmitt's cracked voice.

"It doesn't matter. I would have helped you. I'll always help you. But you act like I'm trying to taunt you with my success."

Emmitt tried to keep upright as he felt the urge to sway. "You still didn't explain why you wanted to work with me."

Andrew shrugged. "You're my brother. I thought it would be good for us to spend more time together … and it has been good … mostly. You're insightful and you genuinely care about the Yates family. You've even taken initiative a few times … but you need to stop hiding behind me."

"Mom thinks I should stay completely out of your way."

"When have you ever listened to Mom?" Andrew smirked.

"I don't. But you do. Do you think I should stay out of your way?"

"No," Andrew said somberly. "You really shouldn't worry about what Mom thinks."

Emmitt bit his lip. He didn't want to risk an argument or an outpouring of grief and resentment over their mother. Andrew didn't deserve it, and Emmitt wasn't ready to elaborate. Even if Emmitt wanted to elaborate, Andrew may never be capable of consoling him. And why should he? Each brother was an unwitting source of suffering for the other. Emmitt wished Andrew would know how worthless he felt in Serenity's presence. He wished Andrew could understand and articulate Emmitt's pain and humiliation so Emmitt wouldn't have to speak of it himself. Wishing only elevated Emmitt's distress.

"What about Dad?" Emmitt asked. "If Mom and I are so aggravating, why do you hate him so much?"

Andrew sighed. "I don't hate Dad. I'm angry at him because he left me alone to deal with you two."

While Emmitt could wallow comfortably in his emotions, and was fond of the occasional dramatic outburst, he rarely cried. He could allow himself to be riled into theatrics by people he loved or hated, but he wouldn't allow anyone to move him to tears. His mother had taken particular pleasure in making him cry as a child. He hated the power she had over him.

As Emmitt's eyes filled, he bit his already raw cheek and felt the blood draw into his mouth once more. He sniffed and rubbed his eyes viciously until all he could feel was the deep cut in his mouth. The sudden burst of pain shocked Emmitt out of his lightheadedness. Pain gave rise to anger.

"So, you admit," Emmitt began with rising indignation, "you feel obligated to 'deal with' me."

Andrew was calm, yet stern, in his reply. "Yes. You and Mom are both difficult. Neither of you will talk to the other. You both want validation while insisting I take sides. It never ends. You both think you're always right and you both think you know what's best for me. The most aggravating thing is you both have a complete disdain for anyone you think is above you by your own arbitrary metrics, and you both use those arbitrary metrics against each other. You only hate each other because you intimidate each other."

"And you're a joy?" Emmitt scoffed as he grabbed one of Andrew's unused napkins to dab at the blood in his mouth.

"I didn't say I was perfect … but you're the one who needed to apologize. You also need to understand that the impact of every apology diminishes when you don't change your behavior."

"You don't think I'm sincere?"

"I do think you're sincere. That's part of the problem. You're sincere every time, but sincerity isn't enough if you continue to pry, or snark … or make emotional outbursts and leave me to deal with the aftermath."

Emmitt's head fell as he lowered his eyes. "You mean, with Mom?"

"Yes, Emmitt. It wasn't fair for you to use me to get to Mom, then leave me after accusing her of controlling my reproduction." Emmitt sensed the agitation in Andrew's controlled reprimand.

Emmitt raised his head and looked at his brother. "I know … but she shouldn't control your reproduction."

Andrew's palm squeezed into a fist on the counter. His calm voice had developed an edge. "You're not listening, Emmitt. Melody is not the issue. I don't need or want you to get involved. I will decide whether or not I pursue a relationship with her. Not you, or Mom."

"So, it's okay for you to push me to better myself … like offering me a job or offering your clients' business expertise … but it isn't okay for me to try to help you?"

Andrew growled, "It isn't remotely the same. Dating or not dating Melody has nothing to do with bettering myself."

Emmitt lowered his voice. "I disagree. I think you were better with Melody. If you weren't sure what you wanted to do, you could have easily kept it to yourself, and I never would have known. Now that I know, I want to help, but you won't let me."

Andrew stayed silent and contemplated a response. When he finally spoke, his anger had ebbed. "Melly is at the back of my mind right now. I don't want her to be stuck at the back of the line, but there isn't any time for me to pursue anything. I need to cool Mom's expectations, maintain focus on my current clients, figure out what I'm going to do with Sybil once the cleanup is done, get her to sign off on the book, help you write the book, and keep your relationship with Renata discreet ... I hate being deceptive."

Emmitt's body sank with the realization of just how deeply he had hurt Andrew. "I know I messed up, but I guess I didn't think about how much it affected you. I'll stop talking about Melody. I really am sorry, Andrew."

"I know you are," Andrew sighed. "But I'm not ready to forgive you yet. You need to give me more time. I'm still angry."

"I understand," Emmitt said. He breathed out a sharp laugh. "The way you are ... the way you carry yourself ... it's like you're not human. Like you're more than human. Renata calls you my 'backup guardian angel.' She says I need extra help, because my actual guardian angel is already overworked dealing with my shenanigans. That's the word she used: *shenanigans*." Emmitt smiled as his mind settled on Renata. "She knows how to conduct herself. I still struggle. She prays for both of us ... a lot."

Andrew offered a melancholy smile in return. "You both think too highly of me. I'm grateful for the confidence, but the foundation still cracks every so often."

"Well, I'm glad you decided to stop filling your cracks with neurotoxins."

Andrew's soft smile lifted at the edges. "It's impossible to hate you. There are times I've wanted to, but I just can't commit to it."

Emmitt balled the bloody napkin in his hand and rose to throw it in the trash. As he passed by Andrew, he grabbed his shoulder and squeezed.

"You've got a good heart, Andrew. Better than mine … which isn't really saying much, now that I think about it."

Chapter Twenty-Four

As Andrew drove past the weathered white brick apartment building where Emmitt cloistered himself on days when he wasn't spending time with his brother or Renata, Emmitt noticed something that caused him to grab Andrew's arm and shout at him to pull over. Emmitt knew he risked reigniting his brother's anger, given the tense exchange that was only an hour behind them, but a mixture of excitement and worry overtook him. Renata's car was parked in front of the entry door of his apartment. As Andrew passed by, Emmitt could see Renata sitting in the back seat of her black sedan.

"Why is she in the back seat?" Emmitt worried aloud. "Why didn't she call?"

Andrew remained calm. "I'll pull into the parking garage, and we'll see what's going on. You'll need to calm down, Emmitt. She's probably fine, but if she's not, it won't help anyone if you're both hysterical. Check your phone again. Make sure you didn't miss a call or text from her."

Emmitt forced himself to breathe as he checked his phone. As he tapped, scrolled, and studied the screen, he heard his own voice raise in panic. "Nothing. Shit. What if—"

Andrew stopped him from completing the thought. "No what-ifs or what-abouts. Look, I'm parking now. When you exit the car, don't run. We're going to walk over calmly and see why she's visiting."

As he shut the car door, Emmitt suppressed the urge to run. He walked beside Andrew, forcing himself to keep his brother's pace. When they reached Renata's car, Emmitt tapped gently on the back passenger window. The sound startled Renata, who was in the throes of a meltdown. Tears streamed down her face as she frantically turned her head and looked through the window. She wiped away the tears and squinted her eyes. Finally, her face showed a look of recognition. She opened the door and rushed to embrace Emmitt. Henry, who had accompanied Renata, sat patiently in the back seat, waiting for an invitation to exit. Andrew grabbed the leash and led the dog out of the car.

Renata gasped for breath. "I ... forgot ... my phone ..."

Emmitt hushed her and led her into his apartment. Andrew and Henry followed.

Once inside, Emmitt held Renata in his arms. He soothed her as she continued to choke back sobs. After a few moments, he released her and led her to the bed to sit.

"I think she's panicking, Andrew," Emmitt tried to sound matter-of-fact like his brother, but he could hear the wavering cracks in his voice as he petitioned Andrew for help.

"Renata, you need to regulate your breathing. Emmitt is going to guide you through it. Is that alright?" Andrew had taken a seat on the couch and was casually scratching Henry behind the ear.

Renata nodded her head as she fixed her reddened eyes on Emmitt. The tears had stopped, but her breaths were quick and stunted. Emmitt knelt down at the foot of the bed and covered his hands over hers in her lap. Kneeling on the ground, he was at eye level with Renata. He kept his eyes focused on her and guided her through a breathing technique his mother taught him to use as a child whenever his nerves took over. Emmitt led her gently, counting to four as she struggled to breathe in through her nostrils. He counted to seven as she held the breath. Then counted to eight as she fully released. Again. And again. And again.

Within a minute, her nasal passages began to clear. In five minutes, her breathing had slowed.

"She's gone," Renata choked.

Emmitt didn't understand. "Who's gone? Did Sybil leave again?"

"My mother," Renata replied. "I don't know where she went." Her vacant stare extended indefinitely.

Emmitt felt compelled to reel her back to reality. He looked over at Andrew, whose expression suggested he had no intention of offering help. Henry now sat beside his brother on the couch, propping his front legs on Andrew's lap. He sniffed and nuzzled Andrew's neck while Andrew lovingly scratched behind Henry's shoulder. Andrew remained on the couch with the dog, too contented to be stirred. As the smile built on Andrew's relaxed lips, Emmitt realized the dog's simple outpouring of affection was filling the cup that Emmitt and Serenity had emptied. Emmitt felt a pang of guilt for his part in Andrew's languishing. The guilt settled into his thoughts and fortified him. Andrew wouldn't be his shield.

Emmitt moved his head closer to Renata's, forcing her to meet his gaze. With their eyes locked, Emmitt asked with forced tranquility, "When did she leave?"

Renata furrowed her brow and looked off to one side, as though struggling to comprehend the question. After an extended pause, she answered slowly, "Two nights ago. It was a couple of hours after you left. She yelled from the dining room that she was going to the nuns' retreat house for the weekend. I figured Sister Eugene had offered for her to stay and cool off for a couple of days, but when I called Sister yesterday to see how my mother was doing …" Renata's voice cracked. Hearing Renata's renewed anguish seemed to pry Andrew from his complacency. He gently lifted the dog from his lap and rose from the couch.

"Where are your tissues, Emmitt?" Andrew asked.

"I don't have any."

Andrew stepped into Emmitt's kitchen. "Napkins, then. Or paper towels."

"I'm out of those … there's some toilet paper …" Emmitt trailed off shamefully as Andrew sighed.

Andrew opened Emmitt's kitchen drawers until he found a clean tea towel. He stopped to glance at the still-dripping sink and shook his head as he walked to Emmitt's bed. Andrew handed the towel to Renata, then sat back down on the couch and lifted the dog onto his lap.

"Thanks, Andrew," Renata said, dabbing her eyes and nose before continuing. She breathed in deeply and exhaled fully. "Sister Eugene said there wasn't a retreat scheduled for this weekend, and she hadn't seen or spoken to Mother since her outburst the day before."

Remembering his brother's prior admonishments, Emmitt tried not to pry further than he had to. "I'm assuming you've reached out to other retreat houses …"

"And hotels, hospitals, antique stores, shopping centers, and family members. Everyone is calling and driving around, looking for her. I know she's an adult—and it hasn't been a full two days—but this isn't like her. She doesn't always say where she's going—usually when she spends the day shopping—but she's always back within a few hours. And when she actually goes on retreats, she lets me know when and where they are ... she schedules months in advance."

"Okay." Emmitt squeezed Renata's hands. "It sounds like everyone is doing all they can right now. What do you need me to do?"

"Just be with me. Sybil thought I was overreacting yesterday—and I didn't want to worry you during your visit with your mom—but when Mother still wasn't home this morning, I got worried and drove to your apartment. Then I realized I left my phone at home ... Then I noticed you weren't here ... Then I worked myself into tears and couldn't drive back to the house. So, I waited."

"Are you okay to drive now, or do you want me to drive you home?" Emmitt asked.

"Could you drive, please?"

"Of course. My car ... or yours?" Emmitt hesitated to ask. His stomach dropped at the prospect of having to drive yet another borrowed luxury car onto the freeway.

"Would you mind driving my car?"

"I don't mind, if that's what you want," Emmitt lied. He put enough force behind his words to beat out the worry that threatened to unmask him. He was determined to remain artificially composed. Emmitt supposed, with enough practice, he might one day attain genuine composure. The idea of effortless confidence momentarily bolstered Emmitt.

He held Renata's hands firmly, rose to his feet, and lifted her up from the bed.

Andrew called from the couch, "I'll head back to my place. You can call me if you need anything." His words shocked Emmitt, who assumed his brother would follow them to the house. He wasn't being unkind, but it was clear he expected Emmitt to assume control. At this moment, Renata would have to rely solely on Emmitt.

Makes sense. Renata's my girlfriend. This is her crisis … our crisis.

Emmitt recognized his actions played a part in the chain of events that resulted in Shannon's disappearance. When he chose to pursue a relationship with Renata, he understood there would be unforeseeable consequences. This was an unforeseeable consequence. Andrew had warned him, but Emmitt's desire clouded any sense of caution. Emmitt hadn't intended to overcomplicate matters, but it was becoming an ongoing habit. He couldn't fix the habit instantly, but he could start by letting Andrew go without an argument.

"Alright," Emmitt said. Turning to Renata, he asked, "Do you think we'll need to do any additional driving today, or are we staying at the house to wait for her?"

"I'm not sure … Sybil is home now, but she isn't reliable. I think we may just wait at the house to see if Mother gets home … but if Sister Eugene comes over, she can watch Henry, and maybe we can drive around a bit …"

"I can take Henry. He can spend the night at my house." Andrew hadn't raised himself from the couch. The dog had fallen asleep on his lap. Henry's head rested heavily on one of Andrew's muscular thighs.

Renata smiled as she looked at the pair. "Oh. I thought you were allergic."

"Only to cats. Dogs don't bother me. But I have some antihistamines at home, so I'm safe either way."

Renata's bloodshot eyes lighted. "Does that mean you're dating Melody again? You know, she used to color with me and help me put puzzles together when Mother would drag me to Sybil's auditions. And Sybil hated when I tagged along with her to Melody's house as kids. She would always end up playing dolls with me instead of gossiping with my sister. Melody has always been very kind ... even to Sybil. Emmitt says you're perfect for each other."

"Emmitt says a lot of things. Too many things. He doesn't know when to stop saying things," Andrew said, while staring at his brother.

"He means well." Renata sniffled, squeezing Emmitt's hand. "And he loves you. He looks up to you."

Andrew grumbled, "It doesn't seem like it."

Renata clearly sensed the growing tension. She smiled sympathetically at Andrew. "I think we're alike, Andrew. You and I have to keep things calm and stable. That's our role within our families. I sometimes get weepy, and I'm sure you get frustrated, but ultimately, we have to persevere and do what's best for everyone's sake. Our families can't function without us."

"It's not easy," Andrew whispered hoarsely.

"No, it's not," Renata agreed. "But Emmitt's willing to hurl himself into danger to defend our honor. That's his talent. I know I could never get away with saying half the things he says, but he gets through to people in a way that we can't. Every blow he lands creates a breach. It's never comfortable, but sometimes—maybe most times—it's necessary."

Emmitt felt the warmth rising into his face as Renata effortlessly smoothed the sharpest edges of Andrew's stern exterior with words Emmitt would never think to utter.

"I wish I had a better relationship with Sybil," Renata continued solemnly. "If we were closer, or she was different, we could've worked together to find Mother ... but we don't have that kind of relationship. You should both cherish what you have."

Andrew lifted one corner of his mouth. "I needed to hear that. Thank you."

Renata smiled at Andrew. "And I'm grateful you didn't force Emmitt to stay away from me. I know our relationship has put you in a difficult position, and I'm sorry for my part in it."

"You don't need to apologize. I'm glad he has you. I see how happy you are together." Andrew let out a sigh and smirked at Renata. "Besides, Emmitt was determined to be with you. Nothing was going to stand in his way."

Renata squeezed Emmitt's hand and looked up at him. "We should probably head out."

Emmitt nodded silently.

Her eyes drifted back to Andrew. "Thank you for watching Henry. I'll send you the name of the food he eats ... and I'll pay you back for any supplies. Hopefully, we can pick him up tomorrow morning ... when ... if ..." Renata crossed herself as her bottom lip trembled. "I hope she comes home soon."

"I'll take care of everything. And don't worry about reimbursements. I should have supplies on hand if I'm going to babysit my nephew." Andrew flashed a teasing smirk at Emmitt. He gently woke the dog and raised himself from the couch.

Before Andrew led Henry out of the apartment, he gave Renata a hug and a "good luck" while aggressively ignoring Emmitt.

Once Andrew was gone, Emmitt stood with Renata at the door. "We had a bit of an argument this morning. He chewed me out. I deserved it. I'll tell you more about it after we find your mom, okay?"

"Did you yell at your mom?" Renata asked.

"Yep."

Renata sighed. "Well, given how bad things are with my mother, I really can't scold you. I'll take back my moral high ground when we find her. And I'll try to help you fix things with Andrew, if I can."

"I think you've already breached his defenses," Emmitt said, smiling at Renata. "Are you ready to go home?"

Renata nodded. "I'm ready."

Chapter Twenty-Five

Emmitt cautiously scanned the road as he entered onto the freeway. His grip tightened as he kept the speed limit in the slow lane. Although he wasn't a bad driver, he had the nagging fear that if he was to be involved in an accident, it would have to be while driving someone else's car, because that would be the worst-case scenario, and Emmitt had always braced himself to be the recipient of a worst-case scenario. Renata wasn't helping. She sat in the passenger seat with her head lowered, clutching a silver rosary with sparkling amethyst beads as she murmured the prayers that accompanied each gemstone.

"My driving isn't that bad," Emmitt joked nervously.

Renata stopped murmuring but didn't look up. "The prayers aren't for your driving. They're for my mother, and to fix your relationship with Andrew and your mom, and for courage for me."

"Isn't that cheating? Shouldn't you have to do one full rosary for each of us?" Emmitt tried to keep his eyes on the road, but he couldn't help but dart them to steal glances at Renata.

He noticed a small smile lift on her lips. "I can make my intentions for anyone I want. But if you keep interrupting me, I won't even be able to finish the one I'm working on by the time I get home."

Relieved that Renata's prayers weren't a passive-aggressive indictment of his driving, Emmitt left her to offer her intentions to whomever would listen. At the end, she recited a prayer she hadn't repeated in the endless list of Hail Marys, Our Fathers, and Glory Bes. He caught and reflected on a portion of the verse. "*To thee do we send up our sighs, mourning and weeping in this valley of tears.*" The words repeated in his head, then tumbled out of his mouth.

Having completed the rosary, Renata looked up at Emmitt.

"The Salve Regina is my favorite. I love saying the words. It sounds more like a poem than a prayer."

"It's appropriate, given the circumstances," Emmitt decided. "You Catholics don't seem to mind steeping yourselves in sorrow. And I can appreciate the inherent belief that life is miserable."

"That's only part of it, though. There's more than sorrow and misery. You're missing the hope. The mercy. Having someone to advocate for you and watch over you and care about your suffering."

"It's a nice thought, Renata."

"Even if you don't believe that God or the Blessed Mother look after you and care about you, you still have Andrew ... and me," Renata's voice softened to a whisper.

"I know." Emmitt dared to pry one hand off the steering wheel to find Renata's. She raised his hand to her lips, kissed it, then released it.

She remained silent in contemplation. Emmitt turned his head, catching occasional glimpses of her, waiting for her to speak.

As they exited the freeway, she finally shared her thoughts. "You don't have to believe what I believe. The rosary helps me when I have problems with my mother ... which is often. It's nice to have someone to turn to that fills in the gaps when our own mothers fail us. It's comforting."

"Would you like me to say rosaries with you?"

"Not if you don't want to." She scrunched her nose, furrowed her brow, and looked out of the passenger window. After another minute, her face finally softened, and she attempted to clarify. "I'm going to pray for you because I love you, and—"

"I love you too," Emmitt rushed to assert himself after hearing Renata's profession.

"Did ... did I say it out loud? Did I really say it first? So casually?"

"Yep. You said it like you've already said it a million times before. To be fair, though, I've been thinking about it too. Constantly. It could have just as easily been me saying it first."

"So, you could have said it first, but waited for me to say it?" Renata's eyes fixed mock accusingly on Emmitt.

"I could have said it a month ago ... but I knew earlier than that. Loving you is the one thing I'm confident about. The logistics are a mess, and I know I've complicated things for you ... and Andrew ... and your family. I should feel guilty, but I don't regret it."

Renata sighed dreamily. "I knew pretty quickly too. I'm glad I said it, and I'm glad you feel the same. If you didn't, it would have been an awkward car ride home."

"Renata, I'm a gentleman. I would have pretended I didn't hear you say it, and saved you from total, excruciating humiliation."

"What did I ever do to deserve you?" Renata giggled.

"Must've been one of your rosaries."

"You can joke, but I'm not discounting it. I know we're both nervous and pessimistic, but I feel calmer when I'm with you, which is really something, since you don't have a naturally calming demeanor. I guess it's more of a deep, internal calm ... You calm my soul, Emmitt."

Emmitt flushed as he struggled for words. Finding none to satisfy the way he felt, he whispered, "I should have said it sooner. I should have said it first."

As Emmitt pulled into the driveway of the Yates' house, he and Renata noticed the car parked ahead of them.

"She's home. Thank you, God." Renata breathed out in relief. Then, in a sharper tone, she added, "Where was she all this time?"

"I guess we're going to find out," Emmitt said.

As Renata reached to open the car door, Emmitt rested a hand on her shoulder. "So, is this the part where I tell you to breathe and try not to lose your composure when you talk to your mother?" Emmitt asked with a sincerity that surprised both Renata and himself.

Renata looked at Emmitt defiantly. "Did that work when Andrew tried it on you before speaking to *your* mother?"

"No, but I only made things worse when I didn't listen."

Renata's mouth tensed. "I'll try not to lose my composure."

"I tried too ... and failed spectacularly."

"I guess we'll see what happens, then." As she spoke, she flung the car door open and hurried toward the house.

"Okay," Emmitt groaned as he exited the car and followed Renata.

Once inside the house, Emmitt tried to keep up as Renata darted along the path to the breakfast nook. Shannon sat at the table, meticulously searching through a mountainous pile of full plastic, paper, and canvas shopping bags. She was so preoccupied sorting through her various treasures that she didn't notice her daughter hovering over her.

Renata gently tapped her mother on the shoulder. Shannon bolted upright in the chair and turned to see her daughter standing behind her.

"Oh, I didn't see you, Renata. I have something for you," Shannon said absently.

Shannon turned back to the assortment of bags and began opening each one, pulling out items, shaking her head, and shoving them back in. She moved on to the next bag. And the next. And the next. She sifted through seven bags and still hadn't found what she was searching for. Emmitt could see Renata steadily losing patience with her mother's antics.

By the eighth bag, Renata had enough.

"Where were you? Everyone was worried about you." There was a tightness in her voice.

Shannon answered casually, still searching distractedly through her things. "Sybil wasn't worried. Honestly, Renata, it's not like I was gone for a week. I'm just glad you had enough sense to keep from declaring me a missing person." Shannon chuckled to herself at the mention of Renata's overreaction.

Renata wasn't laughing. "Sybil doesn't worry about anyone but herself, but this isn't like you. You've never been gone this long without telling me where you're going. You lied about going on a retreat, you didn't answer my calls, and you still haven't told me where you were." The strain was tightening. Renata's voice was thin and sharp. It would only take one more flippant remark from Shannon for her to snap. Shannon didn't seem to be intentionally provoking her daughter, but her intense preoccupation with her new possessions had made her indifferent to any suffering she incited through her actions.

"I'm a grown woman. I don't have to tell anyone what my plans are or where I choose to go. But, if you must know, I took a drive to Monterey to clear my head. I turned off my phone notifications to tune out any unnecessary distractions—"

"From your *family*?" The intensity of Renata's incredulity matched the pained look on her face.

"Yes. My family was the source of my frustration, so I took a break from everyone. I'm not sure why you're angry, honey. You're always pestering me to leave the house and have more meaningful experiences. So, I did. Once I felt better, I came back."

"You could have told me."

"I thought I would spare myself a lecture until I came back from my trip. I must say, I didn't expect you to get so worked up over my absence. Renata, you really need to stop projecting your worries onto other people. When I checked my phone, there were dozens of missed calls and messages. You didn't answer when I called back, so James had to notify everyone to end the search party. Honey, I don't want to admonish you, but you caused a considerable amount of stress on our family with your hysterics ... ah, found it."

Shannon held up a navy-colored sweater with the word *Monterey* printed in large white letters and turned to hand it to Renata. "This one is yours. They didn't have yellow or green, but I thought the navy would complement your eyes. It's a small, so it should fit you, and just feel how soft it is! I bought the same sweater in a light pink for Sybil."

Shannon was too enchanted by her treasures to register the visible enmity on her daughter's face. She smiled happily, looking back at the dozens of shopping bags on the table.

"There's a little porcelain pelican I wanted to give you, but I'll have to keep searching for it, as it seems to elude me at the moment. It's just darling, and it's a tiny thing, maybe only three inches high—"

"Mrs. Yates?" Emmitt tried to interject, before Renata's frustration erupted. "Renata was concerned about you. She was really upset. I don't think it's fair to call her hysterical."

Shannon stood from her chair and turned to face the voice that interrupted her. "Ah. I see Emmitt has tagged along. Where's the other one? Too busy? Or was he smart enough to see there was nothing to worry about?"

"I asked Emmitt to be here," Renata snapped.

"Why? Was he going to help you clean while I was away?"

"He was going to help me call and drive around to find you. He was here to support me ... he's been supporting me for a while." Renata paused and closed her eyes. "We're dating."

Shannon's eyebrows raised as she moved her eyes from Renata to Emmitt. "I see," she intoned. "Well, Emmitt, now I understand why you agreed to be part of your brother's little scheming venture. I'll admit, I thought I had to worry about the big one going after my Sybil ... she is so shamelessly impressionable ... I never thought I would have to worry about Renata. I apologize, Emmitt. If Renata would have told me earlier, I could have bought a matching sweater for you. What are you? Medium? With your height, maybe large?"

"I'm not stupid, Mother," Renata seethed.

"I never suggested you were. I'm just surprised you can't see that this man is clearly a grifter."

Emmitt's mouth gaped as the accusation sank in. He had worried about this, but it still stung hearing Shannon say it. He hadn't expected to be accosted once—let alone twice—in such an aggressively direct manner in one day. Even Serenity hadn't wounded Emmitt as deeply as Andrew, and now Shannon.

He struggled to explain himself, but every justification that whirled through his mind felt like an excuse a grifter would give. He resigned himself to silence for the time being. *"To thee do I send up my sighs."* He wasn't sure if it was an intrusive thought or a genuine prayer. He supposed it might be both.

Renata didn't notice Emmitt's shock and horror. Her burning eyes were laser-focused on her mother. "He hasn't asked me for anything. He hasn't taken anything from me. He insists on paying when we're out together. He supports me. He's defended you. He's helped Sybil—"

"And he's being paid by your uncle." Shannon was calm and detached as she interrupted her daughter. "And a book. If he convinced you to sign away your right to privacy with his little waiver, I'm sure he's siphoned a host of anecdotes and dirty secrets he will most certainly use for his book. He's using you. I don't want to see you get hurt."

"Hurt? You don't want me to get hurt?" Renata fumed. "You hurt everyone who tries to help you. You push us all away, but we can't just leave you alone. You'll die in here—or in some other lair ... with only your hoard to comfort you—but you don't care. You don't even have a bed to sleep on, but you don't care. You don't care how everyone else is affected by your selfishness. You are mentally ill."

Shannon's face paled at her daughter's words.

Renata persisted. "You shield yourself with it and use it as an excuse to guilt the rest of us into backing down. Every time. How many houses have you ruined with your hoarding? How many times do we all have to pack and move your junk to one more house? When have you ever thanked Uncle James for all the help he's given us?"

"I never asked for James's help. And, as I have always said, you don't have to live here." Shannon's voice was frigid and sharp.

Renata's voice broke. "I do, Mother. I have to live here to make sure you don't end up like Dad."

Shannon's eyes flashed. "What exactly have you told him?" she demanded, pointing at Emmitt.

"Nothing yet. But I will tell him."

Emmitt stood frozen in place. He didn't know if he should try to excuse himself for Shannon's sake or suffer through it for Renata's sake. Should he remain silent? Should he try to deflect? Or intercede? Or was this the conversation Renata and Shannon needed to have at this moment? Emmitt didn't know. Renata's father was a portrait hanging on the wall with the collage of framed photos on the Windsor chair and the sprays of dead flowers and lit votive candles surrounding it. He wasn't real to Emmitt. He was like the portraits of Renata's other nameless ancestors at the Yates Museum.

Emmitt suddenly wished the man would remain cordoned off. He wished he could continue to exist as nothing more than a decoration.

An uncomfortably restrictive warmth enveloped Emmitt. He hated himself for wanting to know about the man. *Arthur. Mrs. Yates called him Arthur.* The casual jokes he told Andrew. The not-so-casual glances at the shrine, trying to decipher some clue as to the manner of death. He didn't want to know now. Knowing would change things.

Emmitt's vision tunneled as his eyes remained on Renata and Shannon. He tugged at his tee shirt collar, hoping the gesture would give him more room to breathe. It didn't. Their obscured voices entered his ears through a tin can. He swayed, then caught himself, without either of the women noticing. Shadowed spots blurred his view. He felt hot. Dizzy. Everything slowed down. He was floating. Or falling. Then, there was nothing but black.

Chapter Twenty-Six

In the novels Emmitt read and movies he watched, he had developed an expectation for the aftermath of unconsciousness. The fainter bats their eyes open dreamily, finding themselves in a comfortable bed with a plush white pillow. Perhaps a lover or doctor has carefully placed a cold compress on their head. Fawning friends and family surround the swooner. They smile encouragingly and gently explain the events leading up to (and often including) the fainting spell. Emmitt had been deceived.

The black faded quickly—quickly for Emmitt, at least, as he had no sense of time—and he could feel himself come back to consciousness. He woke dazedly with Renata screaming half at him to wake up, and half at her mother to "Call an ambulance! And get some water!"

He felt a surging pain in his lower back before his vision was fully restored. When the blurry static dissipated, Emmitt noticed he was lying on his back on the floor. Renata was sitting cross-legged on the ground with his feet propped up on her lap. Her face was red and wet. Even her nose was crying. He eventually realized, as he tried to prop himself up to a seat, that his belt was undone, and his jeans had been unbuttoned and unzipped.

"He's awake!" Renata screamed at her mother, then abruptly shifted into soothing reassurances toward Emmitt. "Don't get up too soon. Let me get on the other side of you, and I'll help lift your head when you're ready."

Renata eased Emmitt's feet from her lap and carefully maneuvered herself to sit by Emmitt's head. Emmitt turned his head and saw the destruction his body had wrought on the stacked boxes. He had caused an avalanche. He noticed one box with a corner completely crushed in. *That explains the back pain,* he thought.

"Am I still calling an ambulance?" Shannon's voice called out from another room.

Emmitt and Renata shouted simultaneously, "No!" and "Yes!"

Sybil, who must have heard the commotion and decided to stay for the entertainment, sat cackling on a dining chair. Emmitt noticed she was holding a small pink porcelain flamingo in one hand. *To go with the pink Monterey sweater.*

He couldn't resist asking, "Did you find Renata's porcelain pelican?"

Renata let out a sniffling sigh. "Don't call an ambulance," she shouted to her mother. "He's fine. Just a glass of water and a bag of frozen veggies, please."

"It's right … here." Sybil moved her fingers over almost a dozen unwrapped bird figurines before lifting the pelican to show Emmitt. "Are you going to have Renata put it in her will for you? It's the only way you're getting anything, you know. My uncle will make you sign a prenup … been there, done that." Sybil continued to giggle to herself. "Twice. Neither amounted to anything, though. The acupuncturist never divorced his wife … so I was a polygamist for an entire week.

The other one didn't count because it was done by an Elvis officiant impersonator."

Emmitt's head hurt, trying to make sense of Sybil's statement. Sybil grinned as Emmitt's eyebrows raised and contorted in confusion. It must have been the intended effect, as she seemed eager to explain.

"I hired an Elvis impersonator to officiate, but he was rushed to the hospital with a burst appendix the night before the wedding. He called up his friend, who was also an Elvis impersonator—it must be some network or club they all belong to—anyway, he thought it was no big deal, but it turns out his friend never took the certification course to become an officiant. He didn't have a license, so the marriage didn't count.

"Did you get married at one of those chapels in Vegas?"

"Pasadena … I met the impersonator at a friend's birthday party … he really looked like Elvis. That's where I met the guy I married too. Josh? Jason?"

"Justin," Renata said. "He had a tattoo on his neck that said 'Angela.'"

"Well, he said he was going to remove it. I think there might have been a stipulation in the prenup … but I guess it doesn't matter now."

Emmitt looked up at Renata, who had carefully helped him raise his head onto her lap.

"How long was I out?" he asked.

"Out cold? Maybe a little over a minute. Sybil helped me drag you out of the boxes. And Mother couldn't wait to tell her about our relationship."

"I was scandalized! Appalled!" Sybil exclaimed dramatically.

Renata rolled her eyes. "You were incoherent for a few minutes after that. Are you sure you don't want us to call an ambulance or a doctor?"

"He probably doesn't have insurance," Sybil said, peeking into shopping bags and pulling out anything glittering and shiny.

Three tennis bracelets with various colorful gemstones were clasped around Sybil's wrist, and she was currently sorting through sunglasses. Although Sybil's disinterested assertion was true, Emmitt had no desire to affirm it.

He attempted to raise himself up to his elbows, only to have Renata grab him firmly and pull him further into her lap. Emmitt could feel the back of his head pillowed by her breasts. He tried to distract himself, and remembered, in shame and horror, that his girlfriend had already partially undressed him in front of her mother and sister. His face reddened as he fumbled with his fingers to quickly zip, button, and fasten his jeans and belt.

"I remembered that you're supposed to loosen anything that might be too tight." Renata was apologizing almost as much as she was attempting to explain. "We took your shoes off too ... they're around here somewhere ..."

We? Terrified at the thought, he whispered to Renata. "Who unzipped me?"

Another roaring cackle came from Sybil in the breakfast nook. "He's just too cute, Renata."

"I did," Renata soothed, gently stroking Emmitt's head and trying desperately to suppress a giggle.

"She was quick too. It was surprising, with those virginal fingers. She must really like you, Emmitt." Sybil grinned as she tossed an empty shopping bag onto the floor. "I was starting to worry where she might try to perform CPR. I almost felt the need to remind her it's called mouth to *mouth*. But I'm sure you wouldn't have minded either way."

Emmitt tried to turn his head and shoulders to look at Renata, but she tightened her hold around his chest and wouldn't let him budge.

"Sybil, please don't," she murmured.

"I was just joking … He knows, right?" Sybil raised an eyebrow and tilted her head curiously at her sister.

"I know," Emmitt asserted.

She never said the words, but it didn't need to be spoken to be understood. Renata was affectionate, but she had never spent the night with Emmitt, and she was always careful where she put her hands. She was earnest in her faith, and though she wasn't prudish or detached, she always seemed to pull away before their affections could escalate. Emmitt followed her lead and didn't push. He wanted Renata, but if having her meant waiting until she was ready, he was willing to wait.

"Good," Sybil said, narrowing her eyes at Emmitt. "Do you love her?"

"Yes," Emmitt said. "I love her."

She shifted her eyes to Renata. "They say that sometimes, to get what they want. I think he means it, but you don't have to believe it."

"I believe it, Sybil," Renata said in a low voice. "He means it. He hasn't pressured me. He's safe. Okay?"

Sybil's lips twisted and tensed as she nodded at Renata. "Cuz I have more experience with how they operate."

"I know," Renata soothed gently. "He's not like that. You don't have to worry."

Emmitt heard footsteps and watched as Shannon walked silently from the archway into the breakfast nook. She held a glass of water in one hand and a bag of frozen broccoli in the other. Shannon bent down and handed Emmitt the glass of water. Her eyes studied him with suspicion, though the stony look of disdain had subsided.

"That certainly is one way to de-escalate a conversation. Is that one of your brother's new-age tactics?" Shannon's voice was steady, but her legs and hands were trembling. She handed Renata the frozen bag of broccoli and quickly stood upright, crossing her arms.

"I've never passed out before," Emmitt confessed. He sipped at the cold water as Renata gently pressed the icy bag to his forehead. "I'm sorry I messed up your boxes, Mrs. Yates. I'll put them back, if you like. Or I can leave them completely alone, if you prefer. And I'll pay you for any damages—"

"No, you won't," Renata insisted. "You did nothing wrong. Mother, tell him he doesn't have to reimburse you for anything."

There was no fight left in Shannon. "No, Emmitt, you don't have to pay for anything that might be damaged. And I would prefer to put everything back myself. Thank you for offering to help." She moved to the table and sat next to Sybil.

Renata continued to hold the frozen bag on Emmitt's forehead. "How do you feel? Does anything hurt?"

"I think my back hit a corner of a cardboard box, so that's a little sore. But I'm fine. I can probably get up on my own."

Renata cooed lovingly, "Are you sure? Your skin feels clammy ... and you still look a little pale ... and it's only been a few minutes." As Renata spoke, Emmitt could hear Sybil's taunting giggles from the breakfast nook.

"I'm sure," Emmitt asserted with feigned confidence. "I don't feel lightheaded or dizzy anymore."

"If you're sure, then I'll help you get up," Renata said.

Emmitt tried to protest, but Renata was determined. She allowed Emmitt to sit up on his own as she stood. She took the cup of water from Emmitt and handed it and the wet bag of partially thawed broccoli to her mother. Renata's distraction allowed Emmitt to get up on his own. His body felt heavy, but he was steady enough to pull himself upright.

Renata looked over and gasped. She rushed over to him and let out little cries of "Careful!" and "Slow down!" as she wrapped her arms around him and attempted to direct him to an empty chair next to Shannon. Renata's petite frame attached to his waist was far more of a hindrance than a help to Emmitt, but she was determined to care for him, and Emmitt had no desire to thwart her compassion. He stayed silent, allowing her to believe she was guiding him to the chair.

When he sat, she took the cup of water from her mother and handed it to Emmitt. She retrieved his sneakers from the living room floor and brought them back to the table. Emmitt's eyes widened as she crouched down by his side with one of his shoes.

"Renata, I can put my shoes back on," he whispered as he felt his face heat. He glanced up and caught the amused stares of Sybil and Shannon.

"Are you sure you want to risk bending over? You may pass out again." There was a solemn earnestness to Renata's ridiculous act of benignity. She wasn't teasing. Emmitt loved her for it, but he still felt uneasy being subjected to that immensity of affection in the presence of her family.

"Let Emmitt put his shoes on, Renata. Look how red he is. He's more likely to faint from embarrassment than from bending over to tie his own shoes." Shannon was shaking her head at her daughter, but her eyes were gentle, and her voice was tender.

Renata reluctantly handed Emmitt the shoe in her hand. She picked up the second shoe and placed it gently on Emmitt's lap, then kissed the top of his head and offered him a popsicle from the freezer. Emmitt was both charmed and humiliated. He supposed, had Renata's family not been there to see her take care of him, he wouldn't feel humiliated at all. But they *were* there. He had fainted in front of them. Been unzipped in front of them. *Oh God. She'll probably want to call my big brother to come pick me up.* Emmitt had never felt so embarrassed, or so unabashedly loved in his life.

As Renata left the cramped room to put away the broccoli and find a cherry popsicle for Emmitt, he found himself alone at the table with Sybil and Shannon Yates.

Emmitt quickly slipped on his shoes and silently sipped his water as he watched Sybil continue to hunt eagerly through Shannon's treasures. A dozen empty plastic and paper bags were now on the floor, which Renata would undoubtedly clean up later. Knickknacks, jewelry, scarves, and sweaters were sorted into piles on the table and draped over empty chairs.

Emmitt's eyes casually scanned the table. They stopped on a small mound of refrigerator magnets. He saw words and scenic images of various locations: Santa Barbara, Monterey, San Simeon, Big Sur.

"You went up PCH? That's a five-hour drive ... and that's assuming you didn't hit any traffic," Emmitt said.

"Why wouldn't she? It's way prettier than staying inland," Sybil said while studying herself in a pink mother-of-pearl compact mirror she had discovered.

"I don't think I could make that drive up and back in two days. Ten hours is a lot of driving," Emmitt replied.

Sybil smirked without looking up from the mirror. "Ten hours of driving might seem like a lot for someone who has a hard time standing upright. You might have an electrolyte imbalance, Emmitt. You know, I have some new supplements you could try out. I have electrolyte powders in harvest apple, mango sunset, and lavender lemonade. They're all delicious ... although some people with unrefined palates have claimed lavender lemonade tastes like soap ... but I'm sure *you* wouldn't think it tastes like soap, Emmitt. I can get some for your water, if you're interested. I won't charge you, either. The first one is always free. Oh, and for any future purchases, you should know, you get the family discount now."

Emmitt shook his head. "Thank you for the offer, but you're busy, and I don't want to force you to get up."

"Suit yourself," Sybil said as she puckered her lips and tilted the mirror to view her side profile.

"I prefer the scenic drive," Shannon said. Her arms crossed around her body as though she was cold or desperate for comfort. She was staring blankly at the piles on the table. "As Sybil mentioned, the view is stunning. Beautiful is too small a word. There is something sacramental about it. It calms my nerves and allows me to clear my head, but it also makes my prayers feel like they have more weight. More ... impact. I wasn't lying to Renata. It felt like a retreat. I have a program that recites all the mysteries of the holy rosary from my phone. Renata showed me how to connect it all to my car ... then Sybil explained it again in a way that I could understand. Now, I'm able to listen to all my devotions while I drive."

"Shopping also helps you unwind, right, Mommy?" Sybil was still preening in the little mirror.

"Yes," Shannon said. "But I don't intend to keep anything. Everything here is a gift."

"These are amazing gifts, Mrs. Yates. You seem to put a lot of effort into choosing them. You even considered the color of sweatshirt for Renata and Sybil ... I don't think my mom knows my favorite color ... or cares enough to tell me what color would complement my eyes."

Shannon paused and frowned, as though Emmitt had revealed a great injustice. She stared thoughtfully at Emmitt, then addressed him with a tenderness he wasn't expecting. "Navy. Or a deep-hunter green. Those would suit you well. You have warm eyes, Emmitt."

Emmitt smiled bashfully and stammered, "Thanks ... Mrs. Yates."

Shannon's eyes softened and pleaded for Emmitt's compassion. "Renata doesn't understand. Every item has a purpose. Everything is so darling, and I know many people who would appreciate my gifts. You can clearly see I have impeccable taste, Emmitt. Nothing on this table is cheap. And Easter is coming up. I can assemble little baskets for some of my nieces and nephews ... and the nuns usually organize silent auctions for the local Catholic schools, hospitals, and food banks. They take donations several times a year. All of this *can* be used."

"But *will* it be used?" Renata cautiously challenged her mother. She handed a cherry popsicle to Emmitt and sat on the dining chair next to him. "You do have good taste, and there are exquisite and expensive items here, but they're rarely given away. I just walked past a dozen half-completed gift baskets intended for the sisters' Christmas boutique left on top of piles in the dining room. Very few of your treasures leave the house. You get overwhelmed trying to sort through everything, so you store items in boxes and bags, and it all just ends up being tossed onto the towers and piles. No one benefits."

A rising panic ignited Shannon's defiance. "I'll admit, sorting the gifts can be overwhelming, but you don't know how daunting it is to accomplish something when everyone is constantly looking over my shoulder and expecting me to fail."

Emmitt felt compelled to soothe the agitated woman and ease the growing tension between mother and daughter. "What if we helped you, Mrs. Yates?"

He immediately felt three sets of eyes looking at him. Even Sybil had pried herself away from her own reflection to stare at Emmitt with curious suspicion.

"How can we help?" Renata asked.

"Yes, Emmitt. How?" Sybil mockingly chimed in.

"Well," Emmitt began, trying to push through the heated stares of the Yates women. "We could all help Mrs. Yates sort through her gifts ... if she'll allow it. Sybil has made good progress unwrapping and organizing everything into piles. We can organize the gifts by their intended recipients, then Renata and I can mail them out tomorrow."

"That isn't a bad idea," Renata said. She looked past Emmitt to gauge Shannon's reaction. "Does that work for you, Mother? Would you allow us to help you organize all your gifts?"

Shannon lowered her eyes to the table. She studied the gifts with intense focus. Finally, she nodded her head. "But I will have the final determination of the gift recipients? No arguments?"

Emmitt was quick to answer. "You're in charge, Mrs. Yates. Whatever you say is canon."

Shannon smiled at Emmitt. "I may not totally despise this one, Renata. But that doesn't mean you've earned my blessing, Mr. Key."

"Not yet, ma'am," Emmitt said. "But I *will* earn it."

Shannon raised an eyebrow at Emmitt. "We'll see."

"What am I doing?" Sybil asked eagerly, not wanting to be left out.

"Exactly what you've been doing so well: unwrapping and organizing the gifts," Emmitt said.

Sybil scanned Emmitt's face for any hint of ridicule. When her eyes determined he was being genuine, she flashed a self-satisfied smile and continued to pull souvenirs out of shopping bags and place them alongside similar items on the table.

Emmitt turned to Renata. "Do you have a notepad so we can keep track of the names of gift recipients?"

"Yes, in my desk drawer. I'll be right back." Renata rushed out of the room.

He waited for her to return with the paper and pen before turning his attention to Shannon. "Where would you like to start, Mrs. Yates?"

They worked from early afternoon into the night, sorting through Shannon's gifts. Renata and Sybil were each given sweaters, bird figurines, and matching bracelet and earring sets. Sybil further coerced her mother into giving her the mother-of-pearl compact mirror and a glittering pair of rhinestone-studded, pink leopard-print sunglasses that were clearly intended as a gift for a preteen. After Sybil had continued to pry additional presents away from her mother, Shannon felt compelled to offer Renata more items to add to her gifts. Renata politely declined. Shannon divided the remaining gifts amongst one sister, nine nieces and nephews, twelve great-nieces and nephews, twenty museum staff members, fourteen nuns, and the convent where the sisters lived.

The nuns received the most practical gifts: a pair of warm socks made of alpaca wool and a small wooden box with rose-scented sachets to be hung in their closets or placed in their dresser drawers.

The convent itself received the most expensive gifts for the upcoming spring auction: a bottle of hundred-year-old wine from a maker Emmitt hadn't heard of (though Renata and Sybil seemed impressed), a foot-tall porcelain statue of Our Lady of Sorrows dressed in an ornate black velvet mantle with seven pewter swords piercing her heart and a pewter halo of stars surrounding her head, and a first edition of John Steinbeck's *Cannery Row*, which impressed Emmitt.

The hours flew by. By nine thirty, they had finished sorting. Sybil, having nothing left to unwrap, raised herself from the table and left with her arms full of treasures. Emmitt noticed an extra bracelet, a lavender scarf, and a tie-dyed baseball cap had been added with no effort of concealment. Renata and Shannon watched her leave the room without a word of protest.

After Sybil left, Shannon took a fountain pen from a small pile intended for one of her nephews. She handed it to Emmitt. "You may have this. You deserve proper acknowledgment for the help you've provided. Besides, William has too many gifts on his pile. I wouldn't want him to think he's my favorite. He isn't."

Emmitt hesitated to accept the gift. "I was hired to help you, Mrs. Yates. I'm already being paid."

"Were you hired to seduce my daughter, as well?" Shannon asked.

"No, ma'am," Emmitt sheepishly replied.

"You and Renata have changed the dynamics of our working relationship. That isn't my fault, but it is something that I may be willing to adapt to. So, you may accept the pen as a sign of my appreciation for your hard work, or you may accept it as a sign of my willingness to trust your intentions ... though I will say you have a very long way to go before I'm able to wholeheartedly assert that you are not, in fact, a grifter." She held the pen out further to Emmitt. It felt more like a threat than an olive branch.

Emmitt took the pen and thanked Shannon.

"Please don't scare Emmitt," Renata said.

"Why not?" Shannon said. "I'm never allowed to play the part of the vicious mother-in-law. Sybil has a revolving door of boyfriends, fiancés, and fraudulent husbands. And she doesn't care what I say. In one ear, out the other with that one. There's nothing staunch about her. This is the first boyfriend I've had the opportunity to scare. Let me enjoy it, Renata."

Renata's face reddened in embarrassment as Emmitt laughed in amusement. Noticing Renata's flushed face, Emmitt abruptly halted his laughter. "Sorry, Renata."

Shannon smirked. "I must admit, he surpasses all of Sybil's paramours. Better a solid one than a hundred zeros, as your father would say."

Renata nodded.

Emmitt tried to change the subject. "So, all we need are the addresses, and Renata and I can mail everything out tomorrow."

Renata let out a relieved sigh at the shift in conversation. "I can type up the addresses. Mother, would you like to drive to the convent tomorrow and deliver the gifts to the sisters?"

Shannon considered the idea before answering. "Yes. I think I would like to surprise them."

"Would you like me to come with you?" Renata asked.

"No, honey. I think I can manage alone. You and Emmitt can send out the other gifts." Shannon was studying the items on the table, running her fingers along the line of woolen socks.

"Alright." Renata's eyes fell as her lips struggled to maintain a placid smile. "I'm going to take Emmitt home. Do you need anything before I go?"

"No, Renata. I'm going to head to bed soon. Drive safe."

Shannon sat back down in the dining chair. Her focus remained on her treasures. Tomorrow they would be released from her guardianship. Tonight, they were still hers. They were still within her sight. She could touch them. Rearrange them. Emmitt wondered if she would actually part with them in the morning.

He said goodbye to Shannon, and Renata drove him home. The drive was silent. Emmitt was collecting his thoughts, and as he watched Renata's face in the flashing glow of the streetlights, he could see her brow furrow in silent rumination.

When she parked the car, Emmitt spoke first. "Do you want to talk here, or in the apartment?"

"Apartment," Renata said. "I love you," she added hastily.

"I love you too. Today was a lot."

"Too much." Renata's hands tightened on the steering wheel. "But I want you to know everything."

Emmitt didn't know how to respond. What was "everything"? He didn't know if he wanted to find out, but he understood it was a consequence of loving Renata. His father had advised him on the responsibilities required to attune himself to her faith and family. Their love had to be selfless and steadfast and suffering. Each would have to endure the other's injuries. If Renata was ready to tell, Emmitt had to be ready to listen.

He opened the car door and walked with Renata into his apartment.

Chapter Twenty-Seven

Renata entered first. Emmitt flipped on the light switch. As he closed the door and turned to move toward the faded gray couch, he stopped, startled, as he came chest to face with Renata. Before he could ask what was wrong, Renata put her hands on either side of his face and gently pulled his head down to meet hers. Emmitt thought she was pulling him in for a kiss, but when he reached her eye level, she held his face inches away from hers and stared at him with serious concentration.

"What's wrong?" Emmitt asked.

"I'm just checking to make sure you don't have a concussion." She paused, then frowned. "But now I'm not sure if it's dilated or un-dilated pupils that indicate head trauma."

"As long as they're the same size, I think I'm alright. No headache. No dizziness or vomiting. I'm not in a drooling stupor. I'm not in a fog, or confused ..."

"Okay," Renata said, releasing her warm hold. "But you shouldn't be alone tonight. Someone needs to make sure you don't slip into a coma or aspirate on your own vomit."

Emmitt cocked his head and smirked. "Renata, that's the sexiest way any woman has invited herself to spend the night."

Renata looked down and struggled for words. "I'm ... my faith ..." She fell silent and fidgeted with her fingers.

"It's alright, Renata. You don't have to spend the night. And I get it. We'll go at your pace. You don't have to explain anything."

Renata seemed frustrated by her own bashfulness. "I should be able to say I'm a virgin without getting flustered. You've been more than patient with me. I'm glad you told Sybil you knew ... and it's sweet that you haven't guided things to a point where explanations would be necessary, but I should have been clearer from the beginning. I'm not ashamed ... but it's hard to say out loud. It's not like I'm not interested ... I enjoy kissing you and being held by you ..." Renata blushed as the words left her lips. She let out a sharp breath and forced herself to continue. "It's not that I don't think about it, but I'd like to save the main event for marriage. Sex, I mean." She raised her eyes and looked at Emmitt. "I don't want you to feel like I'm teasing you or leading you on. But I don't want you to feel any pressure to speed things up, either."

"You mean marriage?" Emmitt asked.

"Yes ..." Renata hesitated. "Emmitt, I don't want to push my beliefs onto you, but there doesn't seem to be any way to escape it. There are some things I can't compromise on, but it's not fair for me to expect you to adhere to my faith. There are a lot of future implications ..."

"I know," Emmitt said. "You don't have to compromise your faith. I love who you are, and I would never expect you to change. I want to be with you. I want a future with you."

Tears welled in Renata's eyes as she smiled up at Emmitt. "Really?"

"Of course." Emmitt beamed. "You calm my soul, Renata."

Renata squeezed Emmitt tightly around the waist. He winced, then, struggling to recover, wrapped his arms around her and held her close to him.

Renata pulled back. "Oh, I forgot about your back. Let me check it."

Before Emmitt could protest, she maneuvered behind him and lifted the back of his shirt to examine him. He could feel her warm breath on his lower back and her soft touch around the affected area as she scrutinized the injury.

"It's already red. It's huge!" Renata gasped. "Do you think the box hit anything vital? Like a kidney? Emmitt, are you sure you don't want to go to the hospital?"

Emmitt tried to ignore her soft breath and the gentle strokes of her fingertips on his back, while simultaneously suppressing laughter at Renata's exaggerated concern. In her mind, he was sure, there was no exaggeration. She was seriously worried.

He was as reassuring as he could be, despite his amusement at her overreaction. "I'm not coughing up or pissing blood. Nothing is numb. I'm not short of breath ... though I will be if you don't stop touching me like that. I promise, Renata, it's just a bruise."

Emmitt could hear Renata let out a long sigh. "Are you sure?"

He turned around and softly placed his hands on her shoulders. "If it makes you feel better, I'll lie on my left side tonight. That way, I elevate the bruise, and I won't aspirate if I vomit."

Emmitt was smiling. Renata wasn't.

"Am I overreacting?" she asked nervously.

"Yes," Emmitt answered. Seeing her rising horror, he added, "I'm not complaining, Renata. It's overwhelming in a good way. Like you can't contain all your compassion, so it just spills out everywhere. I'm not used to that. I love your compassion, but I don't want you to worry yourself sick."

He'd never uttered the phrase before, though there were several occasions when others had said it to him. Renata's demeanor fit the idiom. She was pale with fervent distress. Emmitt motioned to the couch for her to sit.

"All this worry isn't just for me. I'm missing something, right?" Emmitt asked as he sat beside her.

Perhaps it was a compounded issue, he thought. Everything was stacking up, and she had wanted to tell him *everything*.

"Yeah." Renata looked at Emmitt with the same contemplative face she had in the car. She was looking at him, then through him, then at him once more. "I worry about losing you. I worry about my mother. And Andrew. And Sybil. I just ... worry."

"I'm here. I'm fine. I'm not going anywhere," Emmitt said.

"I know," Renata said. "You're not him. But you're like him in some ways, and I don't want the same thing to happen to you."

"Your father?" Emmitt knew he needed to proceed with caution. He would crack open the door for discussion, but he would press no further. His inquiry was enough of a breach for Renata to burst through.

"Yes. I didn't know anything was wrong. He never told anyone anything was wrong ... but he and I were so close. I should have been able to see what was going on."

He tried to console Renata. "Whatever it was, you couldn't have known."

"I was the one who found him," she whispered.

"I'm so sorry." Emmitt didn't know what else to say.

"Do you hate your mother?"

The question caught Emmitt by surprise. He considered it thoroughly but found it hard to articulate a straightforward answer.

"Sometimes ... most times," Emmitt began tentatively. He felt a needling urge to qualify his meaning. "But even though I think of it as hate, it's not like it's an all-consuming thing ... well, sometimes it is, but I don't want her to be hurt or ...." Not knowing the details regarding Renata's father, he hesitated before saying *killed* or *dead*.

He began again. "I'd be upset if something terrible happened to her, like a car accident or cancer ... but I would probably be happy on a sadistic level if she suffered financial ruin or public humiliation. I don't know if that's hate or hurt, but that's the best way I can think to describe it. I want her to face consequences, but I want those consequences to morph her into a better person. It's not likely to happen, but I can still hope."

Renata sat quietly for a long time. Emmitt sank his body into the couch, considering his own words and trying to make his feelings clearer. He wanted to find some sliver of insight that may help Renata. It was useless. He was too tired to think clearly. Too tired to even be anxious.

As his body melted further into the worn couch, the throbbing ache in his lower back was building in intensity. Renata sank herself down to meet him. She nestled her head onto his shoulder and closed her eyes.

"I think I may hate my mother," she confided in a hushed voice, as though someone might be listening in. "I try not to, but I have to confess it to the priest almost every month. I can't confront her, because it might make her worse. I can't leave because it might make her worse. But if I can't talk to her, and I can't distance myself from her, I can't forgive her. The priest says it sounds more like anger and frustration … and hurt … like you said. I don't want to hate her. I want to love her. I try to love her, but I think she avoids me because she can feel my hatred … It's possible I'm just projecting, and she really doesn't care about me."

"I'm sure she cares," Emmitt said.

"She cares about herself … and Sybil. She's always given more love and attention to Sybil. There are always excuses; Sybil is lost, or wounded, or misguided, and she always requires more attention because of it. Mother doesn't even want me in the car with her for the three minutes it takes to drive to the convent." Renata sounded bitter and wounded.

"It's possible she didn't know. You may have to tell her you want to go with her."

"But I don't want to have to tell her. I want her to want me to go with her." Renata scoffed at her own words as soon as she spoke them. "It's stupid. I'm being stupid and petty. But she could have done more."

"She probably could have," Emmitt said. His eyes were getting heavier, but the pain kept him awake. "My mom never hid the fact that Andrew was her favorite. I guess I always thought it was my dad and me against Serenity and Drew. Andrew knocked me back to reality. Turns out, the divorce affected him too. I hadn't considered that. Pretty selfish, huh? I blamed Mom for mistreating me and pushing Dad out. Andrew blamed Dad for leaving him in charge when he was only twelve."

"Do you hate her less or more, knowing Andrew suffered too?"

Emmitt closed his eyes and forced himself to concentrate. He contemplated the question before answering. "Less. I guess there's more of a distribution of hatred to go around, or maybe it's a vindication to know someone else noticed how overwhelming she could be. Andrew doesn't normally say he's suffering, and I wasn't willing to read between the lines. I didn't want my dad to take any of the blame, because he was the only one who ever defended me. He never called me a failure or a screw up ..."

Emmitt stopped and breathed deeply. "But when I see Andrew's perspective, I think I have to admit—for his sake and mine—Dad wasn't perfect. He had his own flaws, and he made selfish decisions that negatively affected us. I'm not defending Serenity, and I still love my dad, but Mom and I were stuck with each other. We couldn't take a break from each other. Dad could have stepped in—if he stuck around—or he could have stayed closer to keep me away from Mom without taking me away from my brother."

"What if ...?" Renata paused as her voice wavered. She breathed in slowly before continuing. "What if your mother had affected your father so deeply that he couldn't ... go ... on ..." Her voice broke.

"God ... I'm so sorry ... I had no idea."

He held tightly to Renata as she sniffed back tears.

Clearing her throat, she continued steadily through her sniffles. "Would it ... be impossible to ... to love her? Could ... could you ever ... forgive her?"

"I don't know. I'm so sorry you have to live with that."

A thought struck Emmitt like a crowbar to the head. *She found him. Oh God, she found him. How old had she been? Ten? Twelve?* Emmitt held her tighter.

"She kept the chair!" she nearly choked. "It was in the basement … with the other clutter … he used it … to stand on … the beam cracked … but it held … and he was gone … but still swaying." Her sobs were louder, and her words disjointed. "It's below his portrait … the chair … I see it … walk by it … every day. She fought to stay. I had nightmares … hid in my room … terrified … but she … she didn't … want … to leave … her house! Two years, Emmitt! And only … because she … she was forced out."

Emmitt held her as her body convulsed in sobs. He breathed deeply and steadily, with her body clutching to his chest. His back was on fire, his eyelids were leaden, his shirt was wet with her tears, but he held her firmly and quietly until she was calm.

After nearly an hour of silence, Renata spoke. "That's everything."

"It needed to be said, and I'm glad you trusted me enough to tell me."

"Is it okay if I stay the night?" she asked, still clutching at Emmitt's chest. "I still need to make sure you don't die in your sleep … and I don't want to be alone."

"Sure. You can have the bed. I'll take the couch."

"No." Renata's protestation was limp and tired. "It's your apartment. I'll take the couch."

Emmitt stretched his arms above his head and yawned. "Nah, I'm already comfortable."

Renata dabbed at her cheeks with the sleeves of her sweater and gently kissed Emmitt. "I love you."

"I love you too. Go rest."

Renata raised herself up slowly from the couch. She walked over to the bed and sat on the edge, looking thoughtfully at Emmitt. "I … don't think I want to be alone right now. Can you resist me if we sleep in the bed together?" Her words were seductively teasing, but her tone was earnest, and her face was somber. Her cheeks were red and stained with tears, and her dark-blue eyes were bloodshot, but she was Venus to Emmitt.

Emmitt winced as he sat upright. Renata rushed back to his side on the couch.

He grinned mischievously, despite the pain. "I can control myself, Renata. Even though you are the most beautiful woman I have ever known, and it wounds me terribly to know I cannot have you, I swear I will act professionally."

"Not too professionally," Renata cooed softly, kissing the smirk off Emmitt's face. "Will you hold me?"

"Yeah." Emmitt nodded and tried to stifle his eagerness as he stood.

As they lay together, Emmitt held Renata. He relished the feeling of her body pressed against his for only a moment before he sank into sleep.

Chapter Twenty-Eight

Emmitt woke to see Renata sitting on the bed beside him. She had propped herself up with a pillow and was looking placidly at her phone. Emmitt yawned, stretched, and rubbed his eyes. As he turned to face her, he let out a small groan. His lower back was stiff and aching.

He smiled drowsily as he laid his hand on Renata's thigh and squeezed. "Morning," he said with another yawn. "Did you sleep okay?"

Renata shifted her eyes away from the screen and smiled at Emmitt. The red in her cheeks had faded to a rosy pink. "Yes. Once I hit the bed, I was out."

"Are you okay?"

"Yes, and no. My problems aren't solved, but I'm relieved I finally told you about my dad. I've been holding it in like a secret. It didn't feel right."

She looked back at her phone and giggled. Before Emmitt could ask, Renata tilted the screen to show him an image of Henry.

"Andrew took Henry for a walk this morning. And look! He bought him a tactical harness." The words bubbled out of Renata's lips.

"I told you he'd look good in a tactical harness."

The mention of Andrew sparked a realization in Emmitt's mind. He quickly reached for his phone on the nightstand beside his bed.

"Shit," he groaned, while blindly scanning the surface of the nightstand with his palm. Remembering he was still dressed from the night before, Emmitt immediately abandoned the search, reached into his back pocket, and pulled out his phone and the fountain pen Shannon had given him. He laid the pen gently on the nightstand beside him, then turned his attention back to the phone.

"What's wrong?" Renata asked.

"I forgot to tell Andrew what happened."

A rising eagerness lifted Emmitt. If he told Andrew about his harrowing experience and the unprecedented progress made with Shannon Yates, perhaps his brother would be proud of him. Perhaps he would even forgive Emmitt. Emmitt struggled with his frantic fingers to unlock his phone.

"I already let him know," Renata said.

Emmitt looked up from the screen. "When?"

"When I was getting your popsicle. I texted him to let him know you fainted."

Emmitt looked back at his phone to see if he had missed any calls or texts from his brother. He breathed out his hope of reconciliation in a sharp huff. "Nothing. Asshole. He knew and didn't even bother to see if I was okay." He looked at Renata. "Did he respond to you?"

"Yes," Renata answered hesitantly.

"What did he say?"

"Verbatim?"

"Yes, please." Emmitt attempted to keep his tone stable. He didn't want Renata to think her helpfulness had caused his irritation.

"Alright," she said. She scrolled through her messages and recited her conversation with Andrew from the day before. "I texted, 'We found Mother. She's fine, but Emmitt fainted at my house.' He replied, 'Hahahahaha.' All one word. No spaces. Then, I asked, 'Should I take him to see a doctor?' He asked, 'Did he hit his head?' I replied, 'No, but he hit the edge of a box on his way down, and a stack of boxes fell with him.' He laughed again." Renata looked up, trying to gauge Emmitt's reaction. She frowned at his poorly masked annoyance. "Then he said, 'It would be an exercise in futility to try to force Emmitt to go to a hospital if he's coherent.' He said some other things ... Do you want me to continue?"

"No," Emmitt grumbled, despite his effort to remain calm. "I get the idea. Thanks for contacting him."

"I could ask him to call you," Renata said.

"No," Emmitt pouted. "It's like you said with your mom. I don't want him to be forced to contact me. He should want to do it on his own."

"Why is he so angry with you?"

Emmitt thought back to the conversation with Serenity and Andrew. "I told you Andrew and I were visiting Serenity the night before our trip to her house, but I wanted to wait to see what I could get out of her before I shared any details. I forced us to meet with Mom to figure out why she was so invested in Sybil ... and to figure out why she wanted to pry into Andrew's relationship with Melody. A lot happened. I riled her up, then I left Andrew alone to deal with her. He was upset, and now he's ignoring me."

"What did she say about Sybil?"

"Quite a bit. I wanted to tell you after I smoothed things over with Andrew, but that didn't go so well. Then your mom left on her impromptu road trip, and I didn't want to add more stress to an already stressful situation."

"I think the worst of it is over. I'd like to hear what happened during your visit with your mother."

Emmitt frowned as he looked away from Renata. "I gave in to my curiosity. I didn't know why Serenity would allow Sybil to sell Amelior Wellness products when she convinced her to drop everything else besides Rivers of Younity. It didn't make sense. So, I looked into it."

"What did you find out?"

"Amelior Wellness is owned by one of Serenity's clients ... Felix Bryson."

Renata's eyes widened. "Felix Bryson owns Amelior Wellness? How? His last supplement company went under ... Nostrum Vitae, I think it was. He was selling amphetamines. We removed Sybil from his distribution line just before the company went under, but it nearly ruined her. It took weeks for her to detox from the so-called supplements. I'd like to say she got what she deserved, but she didn't know what she was selling any more than the other distributors."

"Once Bryson was released from prison, Serenity helped him set up a new network marketing scam. He was required to contact the FDA to verify his supplements weren't laced with anything this time. Mom ran three articles about his new business in her magazine ... I'm so sorry, Renata."

As Emmitt shifted his eyes back to Renata, he was met with a look of curious fascination. She didn't blame him. She wasn't angry. Her eyes twinkled and a soft smile built on her lips. "And you wanted to confront your mother, for Sybil's sake?"

"Partly," Emmitt admitted. "Sybil doesn't deserve to be used by Serenity or Bryson. I wanted to protect her. I wanted to help Andrew too."

"Did you find out Bryson was connected to Serenity *before* or *during* your visit?"

Emmitt grimaced. "Before."

"It sounds like you had enough information to avoid visiting Serenity." Renata shook her head as she smirked at Emmitt. "But that wouldn't have been enough for you. You need all the details, don't you, Emmitt?"

"You know, Renata, it's difficult for me to be repentant of my sins when you don't discourage my meddling behavior. I was hoping you would be a bit more disappointed in me."

"Okay ..." Renata paused, then tilted her head and narrowed her eyes seductively at him. "You're a bad boy, Emmitt."

Emmitt breathed out heavily. "That's ... not helping."

Renata put a hand over her mouth to stop herself from snickering. When she had calmed the urge to laugh, she lowered her hand. Her eyes still twinkled as she spoke. "Andrew might be justifiably angry, but I'm happy you cared enough to investigate. You could have ignored your mother's financial dealings with my sister, but you and Andrew let me know they were working together. When you found out about Bryson, you confronted Serenity. I can't help but love you for that. If Sybil is putting herself in a dangerous situation, I want to know about it."

Emmitt nodded. "Mom told us about some rumors. I don't know if they're true, but she claims to be friends with your trust attorney."

"Which one?"

"Don't know. It's a man, though, and my mom has him wrapped around her finger."

Renata pressed Emmitt intently with her eyes. "What did she say?"

Emmitt tried to remember everything. "She said your mom and sister were written out of the Yates Trust, but your uncle still gives them money. She said your mom knows about it, but Sybil doesn't. Sybil thinks she's getting an allowance from your grandpa."

"Crap."

"What?"

"I'll need to talk to my uncle. I won't implicate you or your mother, but this needs to be dealt with." Renata's eyes wandered pensively as she seemed to process the information.

"Andrew didn't know any of this," Emmitt said. "That's why he's mad at me ... well, it's one reason ... there are other reasons. Serenity expects Andrew to keep Sybil on as a permanent client, even after the cleanup. I don't think he was prepared to hear that revelation. There were quite a few revelations he didn't want to hear about. I deserve Andrew's anger ... and yours. I kicked a hornet's nest trying to help. I made everything so much worse."

Emmitt watched Renata's eyes wander back to his. She gently touched his cheek. "You can't force me to be angry, Emmitt. I don't blame either of you, okay?" Her tone was tranquil and reassuring. "If one of our attorneys is divulging private information to your mother, he may be talking to others. We know lots of people who say lots of things. I can pass it off as gossip I overheard. I'll think of something."

Emmitt grinned nervously. "I thought you said you don't like secrets."

Renata shrugged. "Then I'm a hypocrite. I can live with that, if it means protecting you and Andrew ... I wonder ..." She shook her head. "No. Never mind."

"What?" Emmitt asked. "What do you wonder?"

She hesitated, but then said, "I don't know your mom and I don't want to ask something that may be offensive to you."

"Ask. Please, ask. There is nothing you could say about Serenity that would offend me."

"Okay ... is it possible that your mother would leverage Sybil's ignorance to exploit my family financially?"

"I ... don't know. She's definitely an opportunist, but I never thought ..." Emmitt trailed off, uncertain of what to say. He didn't understand his mother's motivations well enough to wholeheartedly accuse her of extortion, but he couldn't rule it out completely.

"It's probably nothing," Renata said. "Really. Please don't worry about it. We'll figure it out."

"I don't know how to fix this."

Emmitt's soul ached. He deserved an admonishment for the chaos he'd unleashed, but Renata was unwilling to grant him anything but love. The sharp sting from Andrew's scolding had already dulled, and in retrospect, seemed almost palliative when Emmitt considered the cancer his curiosity had created. Emmitt couldn't force them to hate him. His only option was to strive to be deserving of their love.

"You don't have to fix anything." Renata soothed Emmitt by stroking his arm. "I hear a lot of weird rumors about my family. It's only unnerving when the rumors turn out to be true."

"Sybil really doesn't know about the trust?" Emmitt asked, still hoping some of what Serenity said was exaggeration.

Renata shook her head. "We haven't told her, but Sybil never asked questions, either. She prefers to remain ignorant."

"Has she always been like that?"

"Yes. Sybil's had a string of assistants, agents, gurus …" Renata smirked cynically. "Not Andrew, but others have been more than willing to take advantage. The money she makes from her acting career, brand deals, and pyramid schemes are her business. Sybil's not stupid, but she is short-sighted, gullible, and shallow. She'll hire people based on looks, or vibrations, or intuition. She hired her newest agent after a recommendation from her psychic. My uncle had to get the family attorneys involved to sort out invalid marriages—as Sybil herself pointed out—and three separate instances of embezzlement."

"She must keep the family attorneys busy."

Renata nodded and rolled her eyes. "It's expensive, but it's the only way to make sure she's protected. The trust pays for the attorneys, so Uncle James and I always know what kind of trouble she's in. Two years ago, he sent them after a celebrity psychiatrist who tried to force Sybil into a conservatorship. She's lucky to still have her own money. Her monthly allowance ensures that she'll always be able to support herself, even if she squanders her personal wealth."

"But why does she need to believe she's receiving money from your grandfather instead of your uncle? Either way, she's getting an allowance. Why hide the fact that she was written out of the trust? Why is it necessary for her to be kept in the dark?"

"We did it for Sybil," Renata sighed. "It was my grandfather who set up the trust. He lived through my father's passing … suicide." She grabbed Emmitt's hand and squeezed it tightly. "Grandpa died two years after Dad's suicide. He saw the pain it caused. He knew Mom's hoarding was a factor. I remember the look on his face when he visited my parents' house before the city condemned it. It was just before he died. The whole time, he just kept mumbling under his breath, 'Oh, Shannon.' He looked old and lost as he shuffled through the ruins of our home. He saw how obsessive Mother was about keeping the house Dad died in. Sybil wasn't as bad, but she was wasteful and impressionable. At sixteen, there were already people trying to attach themselves to her who knew exactly what to say and were desperate to take advantage. He didn't think it would get any easier for her when she became old enough to access the money. He was right."

"Your grandfather knew the rest of you would provide for your mom and Sybil."

Renata nodded solemnly. "He didn't want the money to ruin their lives, so he left Uncle James their share and told him to take care of them. Mother figured it out immediately, and my uncle wouldn't lie to her. There's not much she can do, except complain. Unlike Sybil, Mother needed the money." Renata frowned and looked down.

Emmitt remained silent and waited for Renata to continue.

After a moment of contemplation, she raised her eyes and pressed on. "Dad made a good living, but it was never enough to keep up with Mother's spending. We were never destitute. Sybil and I never worried about money growing up. Looking back, I think my grandparents and Uncle James always made sure we were okay. After Grandpa died, my uncle paid off my parents' debts, paid the city fines, cleaned the house, sold it, and gave Mother the profit. Mother still thinks the decision to omit her from the trust was a deliberate act of punishment and humiliation."

"And Sybil?" Emmitt asked.

"Sybil just accepted the monthly allowance as her inheritance. She never complained. Every check she gets, she smiles, looks up, and says, 'Thanks, Grandpa.' My sister doesn't know the truth because the truth would crush her. My uncle sees it as a kindness toward Sybil. Even Mother thinks it's best not to tell her. Sybil doesn't need the money. She needs to feel appreciated and adored. There's no nuance with her. If Sybil finds out, she'll think Grandpa never loved her. I know it sounds like a terrible reason to keep a secret from her ..."

"It doesn't. Not after seeing how easily my mom manipulated her ... or seeing the way she fawns over Andrew. I understand wanting to protect her."

"Sometimes I don't even know why we bother. Sybil doesn't extend that kind of empathy to the rest of the family, but there are certain people who are sacred to her. She practically worshipped our grandfather." A small smile lifted Renata's lips. "Sybil Felicity and Renata Dolores. We were his little sunshine and little rain. He used to say, 'Joy is sunshine, and sorrow is rain, but both are necessary for growth.'" Her smile faded as she looked somberly at Emmitt. "Sybil was inconsolable for months after he died. She grieved more for him than she did for Dad ... and she talks about Serenity with the same reverence."

"Is she that impressionable? I understand why she would have that kind of love for your grandpa, but why Serenity?"

Renata shrugged. "You really want me to explain the inner workings of Sybil's mind? As if I could untangle the mess between her ears?

I don't know, Emmitt. It's not like we talk to each other. Every time I make an attempt, she always circles back around to herself … and she can talk about herself for hours. I can be kind and tell you she attracts the worst people because she's desperate for unconditional love and acceptance stemming from the tragic events of our childhood, or I can be cynical and say she's an opportunist who's just smart enough to be a low-level manipulator, which has the consequence of making her a susceptible target for master manipulators. Somewhere in the middle is probably the truth."

"Fair enough," Emmitt smirked. "There was another thing I remembered. Serenity said your uncle planned to set aside a lump sum to give to Sybil if she could prove she wasn't a hoarder. I'm not sure if that was the exact wording she used, but that was the gist."

Renata's lips curved into a smile. "That is untrue. But I know which attorney suggested that exact idea to Uncle James. My uncle told me about it a few months ago. He would never agree to it, and he thought the suggestion was strange and inappropriate." She leaned down and kissed Emmitt. "That saves me a lot of trouble. Thank you."

Emmitt lifted his hand and gently ran his fingers through the dark blonde strands that cascaded down the side of Renata's face. "I'm happy to help." He stopped and lowered his hand. "But if it was the attorney's suggestion … and if it happened recently … then there's a possibility that my mom was involved in formulating that suggestion."

Renata interlaced her fingers into Emmitt's. "It's possible, but I won't speculate on an empty stomach. You probably shouldn't suspect the worst, either."

Emmitt tightened his grip on her hand and pulled her closer to him. He gently kissed her neck and buried his fingers in her hair as she grabbed tightly to his shirt and let out a small moan.

"I can stop," he whispered, before licking the nape of her neck.

She giggled breathlessly. "No. Just keep your hands—and other appendages—out of the cracks and crevices. And mind the gaps."

Emmitt stopped what he was doing and broke out into roaring laughter. "Should I keep my hands, arms, feet, and legs inside the bed at all times? I want to be as safe as possible."

Renata shut him up with a kiss on the lips. She moved down to his neck, softly kissing behind his ear, then down the nape, then further down the base of his neck, where the collar of his shirt met his skin. She lifted his shirt and kissed his chest, then drifted down to his stomach. As she moved to kiss his belly button, he panted for her to stop.

"I can't take much more … I mean, I can. I'm more than willing. But if you keep going, it might require a change of pants … and I'm not sure of your moral stance on something like that."

"Sorry," Renata said, hastily pulling down Emmitt's shirt. "I didn't realize you were that close. I thought … " Her glittering eyes arrested Emmitt as she put a hand to her cheek and shook her head. "Honestly, I don't know what I thought. I mean, I know in theory, but clearly not in practice."

A sudden thought rose to Emmitt's mind. "Will your mom be worried about you?"

"No," Renata said, moving toward the edge of the bed. "She doesn't notice me. If she goes to the kitchen and realizes I haven't started a pot of coffee or made her breakfast, she'll think I got up early and went out to run some errands. In fairness, I do have to pick up Henry before I get back ... and you promised to help me mail gifts."

Emmitt grinned. "Will she notice you're wearing the same clothes as last night?"

"No ... but Sybil will. We have to enter through the side gate with Henry anyway. It shouldn't be a problem for us to keep out of sight until I can change clothes. It's not like Sybil would care, but it won't stop her from harassing me if she finds out."

"I think she would care," Emmitt argued. "She's more protective of you than you realize."

Renata rolled her eyes. "I don't see it. I think she just likes to tease me."

Renata walked to the refrigerator and opened the door. Scanning the contents, she raised an eyebrow and turned to look at Emmitt.

"I haven't had time to go shopping lately," he said.

"There's only lunch meat and cheese sticks in here."

"There's also milk and creamer," Emmitt corrected. "And I have cereal in the top cabinet next to the fridge."

Keeping her judgmental eyes on Emmitt, she closed the refrigerator door and moved to the cabinet. She opened it and peered in.

"Do you have any cereal without marshmallows?"

"No," Emmitt answered defiantly. "But I have powdered donuts, if you're not in the mood for cereal."

Renata closed the cabinet and grabbed a plastic-wrapped cheese stick from the refrigerator. She opened it and sat at the small kitchen table.

"I'm buying you groceries," Renata said decidedly.

"I'll make some coffee … and I'll get my own groceries. Tell me what you want stocked, and I'll have it ready for you the next time you decide to invade my sanctuary."

Renata grinned. "Coffee and cheese. Never had them together before."

"I like the fact that I'm broadening your horizons," Emmitt said, as he lumbered his aching body out of bed. "And I'll call Andrew. I'm sure he'd be willing to bring Henry here. It would save us a trip out of the way before heading back to your house."

Emmitt yawned as he walked to the kitchen cabinet and grabbed the box of donuts. He set the donuts on the kitchen table and leaned down to kiss the top of Renata's head. Walking back the ten steps to the cabinet, he grabbed the container of coffee and a filter.

"How do you feel? Does your back still hurt?" Renata asked.

"A little sore," he said, measuring a scoop of coffee from the container. "I'm fine."

"Can I see the bruise?"

Emmitt lifted the back of his shirt with one hand as he grabbed the coffee pot and shifted toward the sink.

"Ouch. That looks painful," Renata said. "It really is black and blue."

Emmitt nodded silently as he filled the pot with water and poured it into the coffeemaker. As the coffee brewed, Emmitt turned to see Renata reach into the box and gently tear off a small piece of a powdered donut. She popped it into her mouth, unaware of Emmitt's attention. The cheese stick laid next to her on the table, wrapped in plastic with only a single bite taken out of it. Emmitt sat next to her and grabbed the cheese, pulled back the plastic, and took a bite.

"I was saving it for later," Renata said without conviction.

"Too bad," Emmitt replied. "Eat your donut. I'll finish the cheese."

Renata propped her feet on Emmitt's lap as he ate the rest of the cheese stick. After the last bite, he grimaced. "You made a terrible choice, Renata."

"I know," Renata admitted. "I thought it would be better than sugar for breakfast, but I just couldn't stomach it after smelling the coffee grounds. Guess I won't be broadening my horizons after all."

Emmitt rubbed her feet on his lap. "It's okay. Sometimes boring is best."

Renata sighed and smiled. "I agree. I'll probably always complain about Sybil, but I would never want to live like she does. I could barely handle the chaos from yesterday. *This* is nice. Being boring with you makes me happy."

Chapter Twenty-Nine

Andrew refused to answer his phone. Emmitt called twice before texting a polite request to drop the dog off at his apartment. As Renata looked carefully at the request, she told Emmitt it read more like a demand. She suggested he try to be more polite. He texted again, telling Andrew that Renata had insisted he be more civil. He urged his brother to be equally civil in his response, since every word would be relayed back to Renata. Feeling confident that he had successfully blackmailed his brother into a well-mannered response, Emmitt set his phone down on the kitchen table. Within seconds, the phone rang.

"Yes?" Emmitt answered.

"Why is Renata at your apartment? Did she spend the night, Emmitt?" the cool voice questioned.

"I ... well, she ... uh ..."

"What's wrong?" Renata asked, looking puzzled.

Emmitt promptly hung up on his brother. "I may have told him you were with me at the apartment with my polite text. He asked me if you spent the night."

Renata's confusion transformed into a knowing grin. "I already told him I was going to stay with you to make sure you were alright.

He even asked for an update this morning … I would have told you, but you didn't want me to continue reading through our messages."

"That shit," Emmitt muttered. He reached for his phone and called his brother again. He put the phone on speaker for Renata to hear.

As the phone rang, Renata whispered, "Be nice. He may be mad at you, but he still loves you."

"Yeah?" Andrew answered.

"You could have called me directly, instead of relaying messages through Renata," Emmitt said.

"I prefer communicating with Renata. With Renata, I don't have to endure mean-spirited jokes and half-cocked tirades."

"You're being petty and childish." Emmitt let out a grunt as he moved from the uncomfortable kitchen chair to the couch.

"Are you on the toilet? You sound like you're straining," Andrew said.

Emmitt could imagine his brother smiling gleefully at his expense on the other end of the phone.

Renata chimed in, "He has a large bruise on his lower back. He's trying to get comfortable on the couch." She moved to Emmitt's side and ran her fingers through his hair as she massaged the back of his head. "Oh, that reminds me. I was so distracted by everything, I forgot to put ice on it last night."

Andrew answered back, "If you still want to try icing it, Emmitt always has far too many pints of ice cream in his freezer."

"I'm on it." Renata bounced off the couch and opened the freezer. "What flavor?" she asked, grinning impishly at Emmitt.

"Vanilla. It's my least favorite."

Renata raised an eyebrow. "Then why buy it?"

Andrew answered again, "He thinks of it as a side dish for other desserts. He really has a problem, Renata."

"Shut up." Emmitt rolled his eyes as Renata giggled from the kitchen.

She grabbed a pint of vanilla and sat back down on the couch. She lifted Emmitt's shirt and pressed the container against his back.

Emmitt breathed in with a sharp hiss. "That's cold!" he unsuccessfully tried to whisper.

Andrew laughed.

"I'm in pain. If you want to count it as karma, then you could at least tell me I'm getting closer to being forgiven."

Renata continued to stroke the back of Emmitt's head with her free hand. "Andrew, I know there may need to be some time for Emmitt to atone, but could you just let him know that it's possible for him to earn your forgiveness? It really is eating at him. I can see it."

There was silence on the other end of the phone.

"Andrew? You still there?" Emmitt asked. "Hello?"

Renata whispered, "Did I make things worse?"

Emmitt shook his head. "No. You never do."

They heard a thud, followed by an expletive Emmitt had never heard Andrew use. After a few more seconds of silence, Andrew finally answered.

"I'm still here. I had to get Henry into the car ... He can walk three miles and get up on his hind legs for a treat, but when it's time to get in the back seat, he's suddenly a bag of cement."

"What was the noise we heard? Are you okay, Andrew?" Renata's compassion was a soothing balm for the injured brothers. Her intercession kept them at equilibrium.

"I'm fine. I smacked the back of my head on the frame after picking Henry up and putting him in the car."

"I'm glad you're alright. I guess you and Emmitt were both smacked by car-ma." Renata laughed at her own joke.

Andrew politely chuckled. "That's a pretty good assessment of the situation. I'm working toward forgiveness, Renata, but Emmitt needs to be patient. I'm not as angry as I was yesterday. That's an improvement, at least."

A buoyancy lifted Emmitt. He couldn't contain his hope for an expedited reconciliation, and he was bursting to share his recent accomplishments with his brother. "Hey! Did Renata tell you I finally got through to Mrs. Yates? I mean, I had to pass out for her to forget she called me a grifter, but after the initial awkwardness, we sorted through all the stuff she bought during her trip to Monterey. She made a lot of progress. We're going to go back to the house to see if she's actually willing to part with anything. I've got a good feeling about it. I really think she can do it."

"That's good work, Emmitt. Look, I've got to let you go—I'm getting a call from a client. See you in about twenty minutes."

"Bye," Emmitt said and hung up. He reached behind him, took the container of ice cream from Renata's hand, and set it on the coffee table in front of them. He leaned heavily onto the couch and breathed deeply. "Well, that went better than I thought it would."

"I don't understand it. Even when you two argue, you're a lot closer than I could ever hope to be with Sybil. It seems more like petty bickering than an actual fight. I'm not sure why you're worried."

"Andrew isn't acting like himself. That's what worries me. We're both usually consistent. I get upset. I rant. I calm down and apologize.

Then, I feel better. That's how I operate. Andrew is always Andrew. He's unchanging."

"Immutable," Renata said. "That's an attribute of God. Has Andrew always been that stabilizing for you?"

Emmitt shrugged, embarrassed by the comparison. "I mean, yeah, kind of. It's not like I'd compare him to God … Please, Renata, don't tell him I even came close to comparing him to a deity. He'd never let it go. I do like 'stabilizing,' though. That sounds fitting."

"Neither of your parents provided you with any stability?"

"Not really. Dad tried, but he was in another state. Mom was too busy building her legacy. Andrew was always there. He was always encouraging me or pushing me or infuriating me with his platitudes and unsolicited advice. He would get frustrated, but never angry. And he'd always forgive me. I really disappointed him this time."

"I'm sure he'll forgive you," Renata said.

Emmitt sighed. "Yeah … but that's not the only thing I'm upset about. Honestly, I've always wanted to get under his skin, and now that I have, it kills me that it kills me. I don't want to care about making him angry or hurting him. He's made me angry. He's hurt me. Andrew has always been the favorite … and not just Mom's favorite … Dad's too … but he's never acknowledged it. The jealous, bitter little brother in me has always wanted to cause him pain, but now I hate myself for doing it. I really wanted to revel in it."

"I'm sorry you turned out to be a good person. It must be truly devastating to realize you have an active conscience."

"I get what you're saying, and I know it's petty, but I really am upset about it. I didn't expect Andrew's disappointment to shatter me. It makes me worry about other things. I mean, what if my mom is exposed for being a con artist, and I end up feeling sorry for her? Can't I have one moment of smug satisfaction?"

"Believe me, it's better to pity your mother than hate her. And what if you did feel good about hurting Andrew? That kind of self-satisfied cruelty only ever spirals downwards. It never raises anyone up. I'm glad you're a good person. I'm glad you feel guilty. It's sanctifying."

Emmitt looked doubtful. "I wouldn't go that far. I'm admitting to being a shitty person who feels shitty because of my own shitty behavior. There's no sanctification in that."

"I disagree. You know what your flaws are, which means you take the time to reflect on them. Most people don't know themselves well enough to articulate their fundamental faults and failings. I like your honesty, even when it's hard to bear."

"That ... is very sweet ... and I love you for it ... but it still makes me feel like an awful person," Emmitt said.

Renata smiled at Emmitt. "Maybe knowing you're an awful person is the first step toward recovery."

"So, you'll help me get better?"

Renata vigorously shook her head and laughed. "No way! I'd be a terrible mentor. I still hate my mom and sister. I'm way behind your progress."

Emmitt reached for her hand and kissed it. "Then I'll try my best to elevate you to my level."

"I'll definitely need your help ... I might need Andrew's help too. Having a stable brother might soften the deep disappointment of having Sybil for a sister. I think I could learn to love her in a general sense ... like as a child of God. Or a fellow human. Mother might take more effort. She likes you, at least."

Emmitt blinked incredulously. "Who, me? The grifter? She tolerates me."

"It's more than she does for just about anyone else," Renata said. "Mother only allows you and Sister Eugene to oppose her. Even Dad didn't cross her. It's why Sybil and I are Yates instead of Abbott. Mother too."

"Arthur Abbott." As Emmitt heard the name leave his lips, he immediately felt the physicality of the unknown specter. Arthur Abbott was Renata's father: the man who gave museum tours, with Renata trailing behind him, memorizing every word he uttered. The name gave the man more substance than the framed portrait above the altar or the agonizing account of his death.

Renata nodded somberly. "Dad has Yates on his tombstone, even though he never legally changed his name … Mother didn't endear herself to the Abbott side of the family with that decision. As far back as I can remember, he never corrected Mother when she referred to him as Mr. Arthur Yates. He never complained about anything …" Renata bit her lip to keep it from trembling. "I thought about legally changing my name, but I ultimately decided not to."

"Why didn't you?"

"Because I would have done it out of spite … and Dad wouldn't have wanted that. He loved my mother. He never thought he was good enough for her."

"What would it take for you to forgive her?" Emmitt asked. "I can't promise anything, but you helped lessen Andrew's anger toward me. I can try to help you."

Renata thought about it. "I'm not sure if I can forgive her. It's possible she doesn't deserve to be blamed, but she never tried to get better. Sybil and I needed more from her. I understand it was ultimately Dad's illness and his decision, but Mother's illness and her decisions didn't make things easier. He hid his suffering while she made everyone deal with hers. After he died, she insisted on the shrine ... and the chair ... but she rarely speaks his name. If the police would have allowed her to keep the rope, she'd probably want to display it ... or carry it around with her. Thank God, they wouldn't let her have it." Renata shuddered at the thought. "I'm the only one who visits him at the cemetery. I'm the one who puts flowers on his grave. I clean his tombstone ..." Renata halted as she looked at Emmitt's widening eyes. She breathed deeply. "And now I'm working myself up again."

"It wasn't a fair question, now that I think about it."

"It's a fair question, Emmitt, but there isn't a simple solution. There may never be a satisfying resolution. There are too many broken pieces, and I can't focus on all of them at once. Besides, I'm already tired, and it's not even nine o'clock. You need to save your energy so you can be nice and apologetic to your brother, and we still have to get back to the house to help Mother mail her gifts. Let's table the family talk for now. I can feel myself getting grumpy. I need another cup of coffee, and you need to change before we leave."

Emmitt squeezed Renata's hand and kissed each of her fingers before releasing her. He let out an exaggerated groan as he lifted himself from the couch and grabbed a change of clothes from the dresser. Renata let out a sighing yawn and moved toward the kitchen counter. As Emmitt took off his shirt, he paused and looked across the room at Renata.

"Should I get changed in the bathroom? I have to put new underwear on, so ..."

Renata stopped pouring her coffee and pondered the question. "Hmm. I think I'll just keep my back turned, and you can get dressed. Just let me know when you've covered your lower half."

Emmitt undressed. As he grabbed the clean pair of underwear, he stopped again.

"Pants and underwear?" Emmitt asked earnestly.

"Just underwear is fine. Wouldn't want you to think I'm too puritanical."

"You're living on the edge, Renata … I'm gonna tell Sister Eugene!"

"Don't you dare!" she squealed, stopping herself before fully turning around. "My God, Emmitt, you almost tricked me into getting an eyeful. You nearly seduced me!" She lifted one hand over her forehead, pretending to swoon.

"Don't be insensitive, Renata. You shouldn't pretend to pass out, given the medical trauma I suffered last night. Okay! I'm decent," Emmitt said, pulling up his jeans.

Emmitt sat back down at the table with another exaggerated groan. Renata sat beside him and apologized profusely for her insensitivity toward Emmitt's suffering. Emmitt lifted his head haughtily and refused to forgive her. They continued their teasing shouts and raucous laughter until they were interrupted by a knock on the door.

"Shit," Emmitt chuckled in a half-whisper.

He let out a grunt as he bolted from the kitchen table and nearly slid with his socks as he rushed to the closet. He tried not to wince as he threw on another borrowed polo. It was a warm, dark green. Shannon had said the color would complement his warm eyes.

As Renata took a last sip of coffee and moved toward the front door, she tilted her head and scanned Emmitt flirtatiously. She bit her lower lip and told him he looked handsome, which firmly proved Shannon's assertion in Emmitt's mind. As Renata reached for the doorknob, Emmitt quickly grabbed his discarded clothes from the floor, balled them up, and threw them into the bathroom, closing the door behind him.

Renata opened the door and reached to pull Andrew down into a tight hug. "Thank you for watching Henry. I hope he wasn't too much trouble."

"No trouble," Andrew answered. "He's good company. I'd be happy to watch him again for you."

Henry wagged his tail as he ambled toward Emmitt. The dog leaned his body into Emmitt and looked up at him. Emmitt knelt and vigorously scratched Henry's side and petted his head.

"Is that a satchel attached to his tactical harness?" Emmitt asked, reaching to open the bag fastened to the dog.

"Yeah," Andrew said. "It has training treats, plastic bags for cleaning up his messes, a travel water bottle designed for dogs, some antiseptic wipes, gauze, and a can of bear mace."

"That's awesome," Emmitt said.

"What would you ever need bear mace for?" Renata asked.

"Bears," they responded in unison.

"Right." Renata rolled her eyes. "I guess we'll be fine, as long as no one stops Henry on the street to thank him for his service to the country."

The dog wagged his tail at the sound of his name.

"He's a force to be reckoned with," Emmitt said with pride.

The dog's tail wagged faster.

"It certainly improved his confidence. The right harness really defines the dog," Andrew said.

Renata smirked. "I get what you mean. He really came out of his shell when I brought him to visit the nuns with his green top hat and matching bow tie for St. Patrick's Day."

Emmitt stared in horror. "But ... he's German."

"Only partly. We don't know what else he is. It's possible there's some Irish setter in him. Besides, you don't have to be Irish to celebrate St. Patrick's Day," Renata playfully argued.

"I hate to agree with Emmitt," Andrew said, "but dressing Henry as a mascot can really harm his psyche. The tactical harness increases his self-respect. Anything else you put on him will probably erode his dignity."

"You're both joking, right?" Renata's brow lifted in bewilderment.

"He's your dog, Renata. You can raise him the wrong way if you want to." A slight smile broke through Andrew's restrained calm.

"You're *both* ornery," Renata asserted, as though uncovering a secret. "You're as bad as Emmitt."

"Don't tell anyone," Andrew whispered, lifting a finger to his lips.

"I'll keep your secret, Andrew," Renata said. Shifting topics, she added, "You were up pretty early this morning with Henry. Do you have a busy day?"

"I'm catching up with clients, mostly. Actually, Henry helped with one client. He's preparing for a half-marathon ... the client, not Henry. We went on a hike this morning to warm up. We're supposed to meet up later for a jog."

"Sounds like a pleasant change of pace. It must be difficult being bogged down with one client. I know my family isn't easy to deal with, but I appreciate all the work you've put in."

Andrew let out a deep sigh. "You've been wonderful to work with, Renata, but it honestly has been more difficult than I expected. I'm not used to feeling rattled and unsure of myself. I'm happy you and Emmitt are together ... and beyond all odds, Emmitt has made headway with your mother ... but *my* mother has created complications between Sybil and me. I'm sure Emmitt has told you about our visit." He looked at Renata for confirmation.

Emmitt stood motionless as Andrew spoke. His brother had never been so vulnerable or candid with a client. But Renata was much more than a client now. Perhaps Renata wasn't the only one who had yearned for—and finally found—a stable sibling. Emmitt felt a sense of pride as he observed the unflappable Drew Key break character in front of his girlfriend.

Renata nodded at Andrew. "You were told about Sybil's finances and the family trust, and you learned that Serenity expects you to take Sybil on as a permanent client. I want you to know that I trust you and Emmitt. I won't say anything."

"I'll have to tell Sybil." Andrew was insistent and stern. He let out a curt breath and began again, "It isn't right for me to hide this information, now that I know it. And the only reason I know it is because of him." Andrew's jaw tightened as he pointed at Emmitt.

"I understand. Serenity and Emmitt put you in an unwinnable situation." She kept her eyes fixed sympathetically on Andrew. "If you say nothing, you're intentionally withholding information, which makes you a liar. But, if you say anything even remotely the wrong way … or even the right way … you risk exposing your mother as a con artist, damaging your own reputation, and possibly jeopardizing my relationship with Emmitt. I can promise you won't have to worry about Emmitt and me, but every other risk is serious. I'm sorry you've had to shoulder that stress."

Andrew's eyes glistened. He turned to Emmitt with an air of smug triumph. "See? Renata gets it. How is that so hard for you to understand?"

Emmitt continued to look at his brother in startled silence.

"Nothing to say?" Andrew sneered, then turning back to Renata, he asked, "What's your take on the situation with Melody?"

"Emmitt didn't say anything about Melody," Renata replied.

"Nothing?"

"He said that he wanted to speak to Serenity regarding Melody, but he didn't elaborate."

"Did you ask him to elaborate?" Andrew scowled at Emmitt, anticipating Renata's answer.

"No," Renata said. Her eyes darted anxiously between them. "It isn't any of my business."

Andrew continued to narrow his eyes on Emmitt. "There it is! I can always count on you, Renata. I knew you wouldn't pry … Though I'm surprised Emmitt didn't blurt out my business the minute he was alone with you."

"Andrew," Renata's voice was low and gentle. "Why would Emmitt want to confront Serenity for Melody's sake? Who told him there was an issue?"

Andrew's mouth opened wordlessly. He stared at Renata as though she had uncovered some hidden motive. Emmitt was too nervous to smile. He could only stare at what was unfolding.

"Andrew?" There was a quiet strength buried in Renata's tone. She stared at Andrew, waiting for an answer.

"I ... may have told him," Andrew admitted with a look of boyish embarrassment that was alien to Emmitt. "But I didn't tell him so he could try to fix things. I just needed a sounding board. He talks at me all the time, working out *his* problems, airing *his* grievances, trying to figure out *his* issues. I just needed him to listen and sympathize for once."

Renata nodded, but she continued to push. "Why did you agree to go with Emmitt to visit Serenity?"

"He would have gone without me." Andrew seemed to be taken aback by Renata's boldness. "He would have made things worse. He's lucky I was there to calm things down."

Renata eyed Andrew with teasing suspicion. "Serenity probably wouldn't have let Emmitt visit unless you were accompanying him, Andrew. Even if she let him in alone, he would have only embarrassed himself. You could have stayed out of it."

Andrew fixed his eyes on Renata and smiled. "I see you're ornery too, Renata. You hide it well." He chuckled. "I'll admit, I told Emmitt too much about Melody and me. But I didn't realize how riled up he would get."

"That can't be true," Renata argued. "I've been his girlfriend for a few months, but you've been his brother his whole life! He gets riled up over everything ... I once asked for olives on my tuna sandwich, and he practically accused me of committing a war crime."

Andrew tried to stifle his laughter. He exhaled and stiffened his posture. "Fine. I knew Emmitt would get riled up, but I didn't realize how determined he was to visit Mom. When I couldn't talk him out of visiting, I went with him. I hoped I could temper his anger and keep him and Mom from erupting at each other. I failed."

"So, Emmitt and Serenity blow up at each other. Why is that your problem?"

Andrew shook his head and smiled somberly. "Because my dad left us. He can't look out for them, so the responsibility falls on me. I keep things in order. I have to protect them. They both need me, and I need to keep them from tearing each other apart ... I couldn't bear to see our family fractured any more than it already is."

Emmitt's breath caught. He pressed his lips together and tried to breathe out the tension constricting his throat.

Renata placed her hand on Andrew's arm. "I understand how that feels. But when you visited your mother, did Emmitt ask questions you would have never dared to ask?"

"Yes."

"Did he uncover anything important?"

Andrew breathed deeply. His whisper was nearly inaudible. "Yeah."

"Like I said, there are some things you and I can't do ... but he can." She looked at Emmitt with a pride that made his heart swell. "Emmitt's love isn't mild. It's obstinate and relentless and overwhelming. He isn't always tactful, but I don't doubt his love for me ... I felt it long before he said it out loud. You shouldn't doubt it either."

"Emmitt's a hammer," Andrew sighed.

"Sometimes we need a hammer to knock a few dents into our ironclad mothers," Renata said. "Our disappointed glances and gentle scoldings certainly don't have the same impact as Emmitt's unbridled blows. It's good for my mother to encounter some resistance. It might be good for your mother too. We can't always hold things together, Andrew."

Andrew sniffed and cleared his throat as he nodded his head in wholehearted agreement. "That's the truth."

Renata faced Andrew and Emmitt with her head raised. "You two belong together. You're better together. You complement each other. You need to work this out." There was an authority in her voice that made both of them stare at her in awe and fear.

Andrew groaned guiltily and looked at Emmitt. "You shouldn't try to stick up for me when I tell you not to."

"I know," Emmitt admitted.

"I'm more furious at Mom's antics … but I'm still mad at you."

Emmitt nodded silently.

"I don't know how things will turn out when I talk to Sybil, but we have to prepare ourselves for the worst," Andrew said.

"You can say whatever you need to say. I'll accept the consequences. Andrew, I'm sorry."

"I know … I forgive you."

Renata gently touched Emmitt's arm. "I'll help, however I can. I want to be in this with you."

"You're already in this, Renata," Emmitt said. Turning to his brother, he whispered loudly, "What do you think, Andrew? Is having a sister better than having a brother? Because she seems a little bossy to me."

Renata poked Emmitt in the ribs with her elbow, prompting an exaggerated gasp from Emmitt.

"She certainly fits in," Andrew said. "She won't put up with either of our bullshit."

"Conduct yourself, Andrew," Emmitt scolded.

Renata's smile shone. "Andrew, you're the life coach. Do we end with a family hug?"

Emmitt and Andrew grimaced at the suggestion.

"No? Okay. I'll just hug you separately then."

She squeezed Andrew tightly around the waist as he gently wrapped his arms around her. He turned and directed his gaze forcefully at Emmitt.

"You need to keep this one," Andrew commanded.

Emmitt nodded seriously. It was an oath he knew he could commit to. He was determined to keep his word. "I swear, I will."

CHAPTER THIRTY

Renata parked in the Yates' driveway and hurried ahead of Emmitt and Henry to "freshen up" and change her clothes. Emmitt followed with Henry through the side yard, then closed the gate and removed the dog's leash and harness, allowing him to roam freely on the grass in the backyard. Emmitt walked to a deck chair on the patio and carefully lowered himself. The grass had been recently cut and the spring air was crisp. Emmitt breathed it in deeply. He watched the dog wander past the shade of a large oak and pause on a patch of grass soaked in sunlight. Henry circled and lowered his body heavily, letting out a satisfied grunt as he laid on the soft grass.

Emmitt tried to lower himself further onto the uncomfortably firm deck chair, but a fresh pain began to pulse and radiate from his lower back. He winced and quickly repositioned himself, pressing his forearms firmly against the arms of the chair and straightening his back until he was seated fully upright.

"How the hell does Andrew sit like this all the time?" Emmitt grumbled under his breath as he struggled to maintain perfect stillness.

Emmitt closed his eyes and forced himself to focus on the sound of his breathing. He tried to count on the inhale, but his restless mind immediately wandered away from the numbers. When he was alone,

Emmitt often allowed his thoughts to sink and fester. There was an aching comfort to his melancholy. His mother had always hated his brooding, but his head was the only place he could ever find refuge … until now. The isolation was less soothing to him now. He had no use for it presently. Not with Renata. Not even with Shannon.

Emmitt opened his eyes and stretched his back. He felt another sharp surge of pain wash over him. He slowly breathed it out. It was a small blessing to endure the annoying, yet not unbearable, discomfort from his fall. It was, at least, a welcome distraction from the habitual scratching and picking at internal lesions that only ever tore wider from too much introspection. The word *sanctifying* came back to mind, then left his thoughts as quickly as it had entered.

The soft creak of the kitchen door's hinges pulled Emmitt back to the Yates' house. He turned his head and smiled as Renata leaned out from the kitchen and called to him.

"I'm dressed. You ready to come in, Emmitt?"

"Yeah. I'm coming." Emmitt raised himself gingerly and walked through the kitchen door, with Henry trailing behind.

As he entered the kitchen, Emmitt eyed Renata in her navy Monterey sweatshirt, tight blue jeans, and white tennis shoes.

"Your mom was right. That shade of blue really makes your eyes pop."

Renata looked down at the sweater and smiled. "It really is soft. I almost wish I had told her about us sooner … we could have coordinated with matching outfits." She grinned at Emmitt with her darker, bluer eyes, then shifted them downward to look at Henry.

"Naptime, buddy," Renata said sweetly to the dog, patting his head.

Henry looked up at her with pure adoration, then obediently walked through the open door to Renata's sitting room and laid down on a pile of soft blankets that covered the large dog bed.

Emmitt grinned at Renata's excessive show of love. "Exactly how many blankets does Henry need? I think you've been adding more to his bed."

"I want him to be comfortable." Renata side-eyed Emmitt and placed her hands on her hips. "I don't want to hear anything about making him uncomfortable to help him build character. He's my dog too. I'll spoil him if I want to."

"You take good care of Henry ... and me. We're both lucky to have you."

"I know," Renata said with cheery confidence. Then, far less confidently, she added, "We're stalling."

"Yeah," Emmitt agreed. "You ready?"

"No. You?"

"Nope," Emmitt said.

"Great. Let's get this over with."

Renata walked listlessly through the kitchen and dining room to the breakfast nook. Emmitt followed. When they reached the table, Shannon was already sitting in her usual dining chair, sipping her coffee while she fixed her attention on the sorted gifts.

"You were out early this morning," Shannon said dully, without looking up.

"Andrew dropped off the dog at Emmitt's apartment. I drove them both here this morning," Renata said innocently.

That wasn't technically a lie, Emmitt thought.

"Ah, yes. And how are you feeling today, Emmitt? Any permanent injury or emotional distress? Are you planning to sue us?" Shannon smirked. She slowly looked up at Emmitt, noticed his hunter-green polo, and softened her smile as she met his warm, honey-brown eyes.

"No, ma'am," Emmitt said. "Just a bruise. It'll heal in a few days. Plus, my dad's a corporate attorney. He instilled an unjustifiable hatred of personal injury lawyers when I was a kid … I distinctly remember being on the receiving end of a thirty-minute lecture when I ran through the kitchen singing the jingle of a slip-and-fall attorney. I was seven."

Shannon put her hand over her mouth to subdue a snicker. Quickly regaining her composure, she said, "I'm pleased to know you have someone of substance in your family."

"Mother, please be kind," Renata said.

"I have said nothing unkind. Do you think I'm being unkind, Emmitt?"

"No, ma'am. Not unkind. Just a little … captious." Emmitt smirked.

Shannon narrowed her eyes at Emmitt and sharpened her tone. "Do you think you'll win me over with a broad vocabulary, Emmitt? Or do you believe I'm too stupid to know what captious means, and in my ignorance, take it as a compliment?"

Undaunted by Shannon's frigid façade, Emmitt widened his playful grin. "The former, ma'am. I didn't think cranky, or cantankerous, or irascible were fitting. Captious fits. You don't seem to be malicious or cruel. You just have high standards."

"That no one can live up to," Renata mumbled.

"I heard that, Renata," Shannon said coolly. Turning to Emmitt, she let out a deep sigh as her eyes once again softened for him. "It gives me no pleasure to admit it, but you've charmed me, Emmitt. I'm not sure if I mean that as a compliment or as an indictment. I still haven't ruled out the very probable scenario that you and your brother are con artists. You need to provide me with some peace of mind on the matter. I believe I'm entitled to that much. How long have you been dating my daughter?"

Before Renata could object, Emmitt eagerly poured out the answer. "About four months, Mrs. Yates. Renata invited me to the museum for our first date. She's a fantastic tour guide. She said she learned a lot from you and your husband. She told me about the new research library and the potager garden. We even fed the ducks ... but please don't tell your sister about that. The staff misses you, Mrs. Yates. They want you to come back ..." Emmitt stopped abruptly as he noticed both Renata's and Shannon's eyes widen at his unconcealed enthusiasm. "Sorry," he whispered.

"I ... appreciate your candor, Emmitt." Shannon tried to collect herself, but Emmitt had cracked her stony veneer. "Please tell me, what are your intentions with Renata?"

"Mother, these aren't appropriate questions to ask," Renata snapped.

"I'll answer," Emmitt said. "I love Renata. I don't like the idea of being apart from her. I intend to be with her for as long as she'll have me."

"Why do you love her?" Shannon asked. There was a hopeful reticence in her tone that further softened Emmitt's already melted heart.

Emmitt smiled, turning his attention toward Renata. "How can I not? She's perfect. She makes me feel better than I am. Sometimes she even makes me *believe* I'm better than I am. She's devout and charitable without being sanctimonious. I want to do everything I can for her. I want to make her happy. I'll love you, Mrs. Yates, and Sybil, for her sake. I know she wants a better relationship with you and Sybil, and I'm determined to make that happen for her. She deserves to have someone who's devoted to her, so I think you're going to have to deal with me for a long time."

Renata's eyes welled as Shannon sat in silent contemplation.

After a reflective pause, Shannon lifted her eyes back to Emmitt. "That's acceptable, for now, I suppose. Though I don't appreciate the indictment of myself and Sybil as being ... difficult to love." Emmitt thought he heard a pang of hurt in Shannon's stern voice.

"It can be terrifying to love someone who wants to be unlovable. I don't think you're unlovable, Mrs. Yates, but you try very hard to be. It isn't fair to the rest of us. I already like you better than *my* mom. I don't think it would take much effort for me to love you if you allowed it. And I'm sure Renata wants the opportunity to love you."

"Renata hates me," Shannon sulked.

Emmitt glanced at Renata nervously, not knowing how or if to respond. He looked at her intently, seeing if she meant to answer.

Renata opened her mouth as if to speak, then closed it. The silence hung, while Renata seemed to struggle with what to say.

"I told you she hates me," Shannon said, breaking the silence.

"That's not fair." Renata's low voice was almost a whisper. "You never let me talk about anything important. You get angry, or upset, or you ignore me."

"There's only one thing you ever want to discuss. Your grandfather and uncle have already blamed me for what happened to Arthur. I still feel the looks of disappointment from the rest of our family. Your father's side won't even speak to me. I couldn't endure accusations coming from you. It hurts to hear it from them, but it would be devastating to hear it from you. But that's what you want to do, isn't it? Place all the blame for your father's death at my feet."

"No," Renata said, casting her eyes downward. "Not all the blame. Dad made a choice. It's possible he was too sick for it to feel like he had a choice. That's what Sister Eugene says. I don't know, but it still makes me angry. He left us, then whatever was left of you was gone too. I needed you."

"You think I was in any frame of mind to actually help? I surrounded you with people who could help you heal: Sister Eugene, the grief and family counselors ... James. Even while he was berating me for my selfishness and clutter causing Arthur's death, I still allowed you to spend time with him and your cousins because it gave you a sense of normalcy. You were always happiest when you were away from me. You deserved to have some peace, even if I couldn't be the one to give it to you. I thought I spared both of us by keeping my distance."

"You pushed me away. If I could have spoken to you, we could have worked things out, but you isolated yourself from everyone. You kept collecting and hoarding instead of trying to fix the problem. You chose your *stuff* over your kids. Sybil may not have minded, but I did ... I still do." There was a forced tranquility in Renata's soft voice. She pointed at her father's portrait. "I walk by this every day. I light the votive candles in the morning and blow them out before bed. I clear the path around the altar, and I check multiple times a day to make sure the house doesn't catch on fire." The calm in her voice cracked as she asked her mother, "Why do you keep the chair?"

Shannon stiffened as her body leaned away from the question. Her lips pressed tightly together, and a tear blinked down her cheek. "It was the last thing he touched. If I part with it, I would be throwing out a piece of him."

"Do you feel that way about all your treasures, Mrs. Yates?" Emmitt asked.

Shannon nodded. "Everything has a memory attached to it." She ran her hand along the plastic-covered book on the table. "Steinbeck was Arthur's favorite author. We used to take the girls to Monterey when they were little. Renata and Arthur would sit at the shore and watch the dolphins and pelicans for hours. Sybil wasn't interested in any animal unless it was pink. She always adored flamingos." Shannon's eyes lovingly examined the treasures on the table before they wandered up to Emmitt. "Everything I have is important to me. I can give certain items away if I know they'll be kept and appreciated, but if I get rid of my possessions, I fear I may lose my fond memories. Those memories are all I have left."

"You still have your daughters." Renata walked to the dining chair where her mother sat and wrapped her arms around her.

Her physical affection overwhelmed Shannon. She gripped Renata's arms and wept. Between the sobs and gasping breaths, Emmitt could hear Shannon choke out the words, "I'm sorry."

Renata held her mother in her arms as Emmitt stood silently and waited.

When Shannon had fully recovered, she clasped her daughter's hands in hers. "I love you, honey … I think I'm alright now," Shannon whispered.

Renata squeezed her mother tightly before letting her go. Shannon took a tissue from a packet she kept in her sweater pocket and dabbed gently at her eyes and cheeks until they were dry. She folded the tissue and placed it back into her pocket.

With a steady voice that showed no sign of sadness, Shannon said, "Well, do you still plan to mail the gifts today?"

"Yes, Mother," Renata whispered.

"And Emmitt is going with you?"

"Yes, Mrs. Yates," Emmitt said.

"Then he can assist me in loading the gifts for the sisters into my car."

"The expensive ones?" Emmitt faltered. "Can I get the socks and perfume packets? I don't want to break or drop anything."

There was a slight agitation in Shannon's tear-stained face. Emmitt realized an inconvenient emotional outburst wouldn't hinder her determination. "You're capable, Emmitt. I have an empty box ready to be filled … just here. See?" She pointed to a brown cardboard box on the floor. "We can place the socks and sachet boxes in first, then the auction items on top. You can carry one box to my car, can't you?"

"Yes, ma'am," Emmitt said.

"Good," Shannon said. She stood and turned her attention to her daughter. "Now, Renata, I have plastic bags and plastic cushioning wrap to keep the fragile items from breaking. You put the items into bags, and Emmitt and I will join you after we pack my car."

Emmitt flashed a look of terror at Renata. She widened her eyes and shrugged. Shannon had spoken. She was determined to part with her treasures. They couldn't argue with a woman who was accomplishing the impossible.

Emmitt wordlessly placed the nuns' gifts in the bottom of the box, then grabbed the Steinbeck novel and placed it on top. Shannon wrapped the bottle of expensive wine, then turned and took another bottle of the same wine from a gift pile intended for her sister, Mary. She flashed a mischievous smile to Emmitt, then wrapped it and snuggled both bottles upright, deep into the soft woolen socks. Next, she lifted the statue of the mournful Mother of Sorrows and gently placed it on top of the packed gifts, next to the plastic-wrapped first edition.

Looking at the half-filled box, Shannon frowned. "It should be full," she said sharply.

"Mother, that box is easily worth ten thousand dollars," Renata said.

"It appears to only be half full. This will not do."

Emmitt dared to offer a suggestion. "Is there a smaller box we can use?"

"No. It has to be this box." Shannon looked around the table, then shook her head. "This will not do," she repeated stiffly.

She turned and disappeared into the formal dining room. After a few minutes, Emmitt sat on the dining chair next to Renata and joined her in wrapping bird figurines and packing the shipping bags and boxes that would soon be mailed to Yates family members and museum staff.

Emmitt leaned in and whispered in Renata's ear. "Should I go see what she's doing?"

"Better not," she whispered back. "Whatever she's doing, she's determined. I don't want to say or do anything that might break her concentration."

"Good thinking."

"Thanks." Renata leaned her head closer and kissed Emmitt on the cheek.

Ten minutes passed before Shannon came back into the breakfast nook with her arms full. Emmitt quickly raised himself from the chair and helped her place the items on the table.

"Help me wrap these, Emmitt," Shannon commanded, breathless and triumphant.

Renata stared at the items, then at her mother. "Are you sure?" was all she could utter.

"Yes," Shannon said decidedly. "These will fill the box. Besides, I specifically purchased these items for the convent auction ... I've just never had sufficient help to assemble and deliver the items in a timely manner. I suppose now is better than never."

Emmitt's hands trembled as he wrapped a light-blue porcelain vase that Shannon said was worth "roughly the cost of a compact car." When Emmitt had asked, "luxury or economy?" and "new or used?" for clarification, Shannon only tittered as if he was joking.

Shannon wrapped a framed vellum page of an illuminated manuscript taken from a medieval book of hours. She added several small, embroidered pouches containing diamond- and pearl-studded earrings, bracelets, and brooches to the box, alongside several more statues of the Virgin Mary. When they finished packing, the box was filled to the top.

"Now, Emmitt, you need to be very careful," Shannon teased.

"Mother ..." Renata began, but glancing at Emmitt's pale face, she stopped and focused her attention on him.

"Just remember, most of the expensive items were laying in piles on the floor. You'll be fine. I promise," Renata soothed.

Emmitt nodded nervously at Renata's assurances. He gulped and said, "I'm ready, Mrs. Yates."

Emmitt held tightly to the box as he followed the winding path and exited the house. He cautiously walked to the driveway, with Shannon leading the way. She pointed to her car as she unlocked it. Shannon opened the trunk, and Emmitt gently lowered the box.

Sighing in relief, Emmitt brandished a self-satisfied smile and turned to head back into the house. As he walked past Shannon, she firmly grabbed his arm and stopped him.

"You seem to be certain about your feelings for Renata. Do you plan to take care of my daughter, Emmitt?" Shannon's tone was surprisingly affectionate. Her eyes showed her eagerness to hear his answer.

"Yes, Mrs. Yates."

"And what exactly do you do? Are you a full-time assistant to your brother, or is there some other career that allows you to clock out any time we Yates women are in need?" She studied his face carefully.

"I'm ... uh, self-employed, ma'am," Emmitt stammered. Immediately angered by his fear and shame in the face of Shannon, he steadied his nerves and continued. "I run a website where I publish study guides and plot summaries of classic literature. I also post videos on the internet where I give in-depth analyses of themes, plots, and characters in fiction."

Shannon grinned. "Sounds like something Sybil would have used for her high school English classes."

"Probably," Emmitt agreed without embarrassment. "Teens are my primary demographic for the website. The video essays usually draw an older audience. The videos attract people who scanned through the book summaries in high school and college, then decided to actually read the novels as adults. I'm double-dipping, I guess. I offer a way out of reading the material while they're young and lazy, then I create a three-hour video that their older selves will appreciate. I prefer the videos—it feels like hosting a book club for anti-socials. I've been recording and posting more videos the last few months, and I'm putting almost everything I earn into savings ... including the money from your brother."

Shannon nodded, then tried to encourage Emmitt. "Renata is quite thrifty, you know. She spends money on others, but she doesn't buy much for herself. And she isn't one to complain." She gazed at him sympathetically. "Her inheritance can support both of you indefinitely ... you understand that, don't you?"

"Yes, ma'am," Emmitt whispered. "I know she doesn't worry about money ... but I do."

"Oh, Emmitt," Shannon sighed with a compassion that immediately comprehended the source of his shame. "Of course, she'd fall in love with someone like you. I should be grateful. You worry your finances won't be enough to take care of her?"

Emmitt nodded his head. "She deserves more than what I can give her now. The videos are doing well, and I'm pushing myself to be more consistent. My income has been increasing, but it's still not enough."

"Not enough for what?" A smile built on Shannon's lips and her eyes seemed to flicker with understanding. "A family?"

Emmitt flushed as he struggled to maintain eye contact. "Eventually ... if Renata wants to ... in the future ... yes."

"Do you wish to continue this line of work?" Shannon asked.

"No," Emmitt said. He was already a disappointment to one mother. He didn't want to disappoint Shannon, but her gentle eyes and maternal tone compelled him to divulge everything. "I need to drop the website. The financial return doesn't match the effort I put into it, and if I pivot away from the website, I can devote more time to other things. I enjoy filming video essays, but I would prefer to do it as a hobby ..." Emmitt paused, then lowered his voice, "I have a hard time saying this out loud, because it may never happen ... I want to earn a living as an author. I don't know if it's possible, and if I earn a better living with my videos, I can live with that. I have a few unpublished novels ... and ... the book with Andrew."

Shannon nodded silently.

Not knowing how to interpret the silence, Emmitt nervously tried to clarify. "My finances are my responsibility. I'm taking things seriously, but I know I have to do more. I need to figure it out, and I need to do it soon. I don't want to let Renata down, and I don't want you to worry that she made a terrible choice."

"I see," Shannon said. "It's important to have something of your own, Emmitt. Something that sets you apart. Renata won't care about your finances, just as I didn't care about Arthur's. Our circumstances were different, but Renata and I are similar in that regard. What's hers will be yours, without question or resentment."

"I don't want to take from her. I want to contribute and take care of her," Emmitt said somberly.

"I know, honey." Shannon said the words with such warmth that Emmitt had to fight to keep his eyes from misting over. "My husband felt the weight of it, as well. I found out too late, but Renata doesn't have to. May I impart some advice, Emmitt?"

"Yes, please," Emmitt said.

"I'm confident that you will become successful in whatever you choose to do. I can see in your eyes, you're a man of purpose, and I'm convinced nothing can stand in your way. You've certainly shown yourself to be capable. You mustn't doubt yourself. But you cannot ignore Renata's wealth. She will always be rich, and she will always want to share her abundance." Shannon let out a deep sigh before she continued. "I think my family's wealth consumed my husband. When we were living on Arthur's salary, I overspent. My father always had money to relieve our debts. He always came to our rescue, and we never worried ... well, *I* never worried. This is what I will impart to Renata: she needs to allow you to contribute. And I'll give this advice to you, Emmitt: you need to allow her to spoil you. It's in her nature. It's how she shows her love, and it would be a pity for anyone to stifle her kindness. I'm willing to wager her affection and generosity had something to do with the dog she's now taking care of. Am I correct?"

Emmitt smiled and nodded. "He was a gift. But he couldn't live with me. She offered to pay for an apartment that allowed dogs."

"But you both worked it out?" Shannon asked.

"Yes. She's taking care of Henry until I can afford a new apartment."

"Promise me you'll continue to work things out. Promise you'll compromise, and allow her to be generous, and never allow conflict between you to go unsaid … you mustn't neglect each other or ignore the other's suffering …" Shannon's voice broke.

"I promise," Emmitt said. "Thank you, Mrs. Yates."

Shannon closed the trunk of the car. Her glistening eyes smiled sweetly at Emmitt. They were Renata's eyes. They were older. Sadder. But still full of love.

"Tell your brother to bring the consent form for your book. I'll sign it the next time he visits."

Emmitt's eyes widened. He stammered, "I … I wasn't trying to guilt you into anything, Mrs. Yates. That's not … I mean … you don't have to feel sorry for me."

Shannon cackled at the suggestion. "Emmitt, honey, you can't guilt me into anything." Her eyes twinkled. She leaned closer to Emmitt and lowered her voice. "I'm going to tell you something, but you must keep it a secret. Do you promise?"

"I promise to keep your secret, Mrs. Yates."

"Good … Emmitt, I like you."

Emmitt's face lit. His smile radiated. "I like you too, Mrs. Yates."

"Yes, well." Shannon stiffened her stance and fixed her face back into a haughty smirk. "That's enough of that. I still expect you to be respectful of me in your book, but you must write. And if you need help, ask. I know plenty of publishers. I'm willing to strong-arm any of them into working with you. There's no shame in getting a leg up. You need to be confident in your creativity. Your talent is a gift, and you must share your gift with others."

"Yes, ma'am," Emmitt said, with a lump building in his throat. "Mrs. Yates, can I … shake your hand?"

"Yes," Shannon said, reaching out her hand and clasping Emmitt's firmly. "I believe this is appropriate for now." Before releasing her grip, she brought her other hand to Emmitt's shoulder and patted it gently.

Chapter Thirty-One

A month passed without Andrew visiting the Yates' house. Sybil departed for another impromptu team-building retreat. She had traveled to Hawaii with her Rivers of Younity downline and Serenity. Andrew hadn't bothered to check up on Sybil. Emmitt feared the reprimand Serenity might unleash on Andrew when the trip was over, but he couldn't ignore his brother's remarkable relief. Andrew was far less irritable, and his cool, confident demeanor returned without the freezing edge.

Andrew took advantage of Sybil's absence by devoting his attention to other clients and—as Emmitt discovered accidentally during an unscheduled visit with Henry—Melody Boutroux.

Emmitt had deliberately overstayed his welcome, which had been easy, given Melody's excitement to reconnect with Emmitt and her instant infatuation with the quiet, geriatric dog. Melody was as bubbly and chatty as ever, and as she offered Emmitt a seat next to her on Andrew's curved black sofa (which was now overly adorned with colorful tiger- and cheetah-themed pillows), she had quickly divulged every detail of their rekindled romance.

"Andy and I had our annual gift exchange last Christmas. I was really surprised he'd agree to be anywhere near me, considering one of my rescue kittens gave me a pretty severe case of ringworm."

"Of course he'd risk a fungal infection for you, Melody. My brother has never stopped talking about you!" Emmitt's smile beamed as he glanced at Andrew. His brother's smirk displayed the smug irritation of an older sibling acquiescing to a younger sibling's teasing. Emmitt had earned the right. Andrew was graciously allowing him an opportunity to savor the moment.

"With all the multivitamins, organic meat and produce, and positive thinking, nothing could take Andrew Key out," Melody asserted with confidence.

"Where'd you find the kitten?" Emmitt asked.

"In a dumpster. I spotted two kittens next to the dumpster in a strip mall ... they weren't any trouble. They came right to me, and I popped them in the cat carrier I keep in my car for emergency rescues. The third one was stuck and meowing pitifully in the dumpster. The poor thing was so terrified, he ended up scratching me on the cheek when I reached in to grab him ... and I may have snuggled him too close to the scratch before putting him in the carrier with his sisters ... but he was just so cute, Emmitt."

"Melly can't help herself around stray cats ... or dumpsters," Andrew chuckled.

"It's true! The vet even suggested I get a medical bracelet so she can make sure I'm up to date on all my shots!" Melody laughed, then breathed in deeply to calm herself down. "Anyway, the right side of my face developed a huge red ring around it. It was bad. I went through three tubes of antifungal cream. Then it spread to my neck and back, and I had to get a prescription … I warned Andy I was contagious, but he still insisted on dinner and our gift swap. He came over and cooked for me, then he made me some hot cocoa with marshmallows. After we opened our gifts, we sat on the couch and watched old Christmas movies together. Isn't he so sweet?"

"The sweetest." Emmitt darted his eyes and grinned at Andrew.

Melody gazed at Andrew with shameless affection. "My mom said he was the one. The first year after our breakup was hard. Really hard. But after a while, Andy started calling again. And after he started, he never *stopped* calling me … or coming over to visit … and Mom kept telling me to be patient and let things work themselves out, so I never really lost hope." Her smile was tender as her eyes shifted to Emmitt. "I could tell the last few months were leading to something big … our conversations were getting serious. You know how he gets when he's *manifesting* something consequential. You can hear it in his voice. Then, a few weeks ago, he told me we were supposed to be together. Well, *I* could have told him that!" She laid a hand on Andrew's thigh and squeezed. "But I guess he needed more time to realize it. He's so kind, and he always wants to make sure he can provide the highest level of attention and care for others, but Andy deserves to be happy and cared for too."

Emmitt nodded seriously. "He does. I'm trying to better myself, so he can have one less person to worry about. I'm glad you're back together."

Melody reached out her free hand and grabbed Emmitt's. "I need to thank you, Emmitt. Andy said you were the one who encouraged him to stop dragging his feet."

Andrew lowered his head and focused his attention on Henry as Melody continued to shower unabashed praise on him. Occasionally, Emmitt would notice Andrew lift his eyes to look at Melody with an adoration so pure that Emmitt couldn't help but love the woman who loved his brother.

Melody spoke of their daily communications and the unfaltering friendship that eventually led them back together. She said it was inevitable. Emmitt dared to call it "destiny," and Melody sighed dreamily and wholeheartedly agreed.

Eventually, Melody raised herself from the sofa to offer Emmitt a can of soda from Andrew's remarkably well-stocked refrigerator. She then asked innocently if he could come back in a week to help his brother install the wall-mounted cat playground they ordered online. Emmitt nodded with a wide smile, and Andrew finally decided that Melody had overshared enough. He politely shooed Emmitt out the front door and firmly cautioned him to be discreet.

"Mom doesn't know yet?" Emmitt asked.

"No. I'm still relegated to courtyard visits after the mess you made. I'll tell her when she invites me back into the house. Then, at least, I'll have the courtyard to fall back on."

"Can I tell Renata?"

"If you don't tell her, I will," Andrew said, clapping Emmitt on the shoulder. "Melly wants to have you both over for dinner."

"Before or after we install the cat playground?" Emmitt asked with a teasing smirk.

Andrew smiled and rolled his eyes. "Neither of you is capable of restraint. It's cute when Melly gets excited and overshares. It's still annoying when you do it."

When he reached his car with Henry, Emmitt immediately called Renata, and the two agreed to keep the secret together.

Shannon's decision to sign the waiver further eased Andrew's mind and renewed their hope of completing a book together. Andrew insisted Emmitt present the form to Shannon as a reward for his persistence. Emmitt thought it was more likely that Andrew suspected Shannon would change her mind when presented with the waiver. Despite their apprehension, Shannon had signed without hesitation or protest. It was a moment of triumph for Emmitt, and Andrew congratulated him upon receiving the second signed form.

"Two for two, Emmitt!" Andrew had shouted as Emmitt laughed to distract himself from the exhausting ecstasy he felt in achieving the impossible.

With all the elements aligning, and an ocean separating him from Sybil and Serenity, Emmitt dared to hope that everything would work out smoothly.

During Sybil's second extended absence, Emmitt increased his own efforts in all things that mattered to him: he visited Renata, he helped Shannon sort through and mail out the trove of gifts she had accumulated, he filmed more video essays, and he finally began to work with Andrew on their book. Emmitt also visited the Yates Museum with Renata, surveying progress on the new garden and bistro, categorizing seeds, putting up spring decorations, and filling plastic eggs for the upcoming Easter egg hunt.

On Easter Sunday, Emmitt attended Mass at the convent chapel with the extended Yates family. He received little more than a side-eye from Renata's Uncle James, but James's wife, children, and grandchildren were enthusiastic and welcoming. As the service began, three of Renata's young cousins crawled over the other adults to sit by Renata. A four-year-old with a cherubic face, deep-brown eyes, and dark-brown curls looked up at Emmitt from Renata's lap and scrunched her nose at him. It was apparently a Yates family trait, passed down generationally.

After sizing him up, her sour face brightened. With a beaming smile, she squealed, "Are you gonna marry Auntie?"

Her little voice echoed, and he could feel the heads of Renata's family turn one by one down the church pew to look at him. His face reddened, and he could hear Sister Eugene try unsuccessfully to stifle a laugh in the pew in front of him. Renata leaned down and whispered into the child's ear. She seemed satisfied by the answer her "auntie" gave. The girl sat wordlessly for the rest of the Mass, but kept a fixed, wide-eyed gaze in Emmitt's direction, and giggled uncontrollably any time he glanced over at her.

After the Mass, he joined the family at the museum for Easter brunch in the rose garden. He watched as the children gathered for the Yates Museum's First Annual Egg Hunt. Renata was radiant in her pale-yellow dress, and she was warm, confident, and relaxed, even when corralling the children for the hunt. This is what she's meant to do, Emmitt thought. *The museum is her sanctuary.* Emmitt grabbed a seat next to Shannon as Renata reveled in her joy.

When the egg hunt was over, Emmitt noticed Renata pull her uncle aside to speak to him before returning to the table. They had enjoyed the day, and Emmitt had a taste of what it would be like to celebrate holidays with in-laws. It wasn't unpleasant, in his assessment. He only wished he had invited Andrew and Melody.

"Next year," Renata said with a rosy, sun-kissed smile.

Now, as spring had reached its midpoint and the heat of summer was already palpable, Andrew and Emmitt were ready to end their financial ties to the Yates women.

When Sybil came back, they would secure her signature, and Andrew would finish what he started. Only eight boxes and containers remained in Sybil's bedroom. It was clear to both Andrew and Emmitt that Shannon would require an ongoing endeavor of devotion outside the confines of the cleanup effort. When the official job was over, Emmitt and Renata would continue to work together to help Shannon. Emmitt couldn't accept payment for helping her anymore. Sybil was still a client to Emmitt, but Shannon was family. Once they cleaned Sybil's room, the brothers' official job would be complete. All that would remain was the book.

Months ago, it was the only thing that mattered to Emmitt, but now it was in the middle of a list of intentions and imaginings with far greater importance. Renata would forever rank first. Shannon was nearing second, which made a sliver of Emmitt's heart ache for his own mother. He pushed the thought aside, and for the first time, allowed himself to focus with hopeful anticipation on the life that lay ahead of him.

Emmitt had lost himself in these gently rippling thoughts in the Yates' dimly lit breakfast nook until Sybil crashed in like a tidal wave.

"I'm home!" Sybil shouted to no one in particular.

Emmitt lifted his head from his laptop and stopped typing. He yelled back, "Hi, Sybil! We're all at the table!"

Shannon shook her head at the indecency of the screamed exchange, while Renata poked Emmitt's arm with her sharp elbow to shush him.

"Is that Emmitt's voice?" Sybil asked, still yelling from the entryway. Before he could answer back, she added, "I have so many suitcases. Could you give me a hand?"

Emmitt lifted himself from the chair and walked to meet Sybil at the door.

"Is Drew with you today?" Sybil asked as Emmitt approached.

"No, just me, today. Sorry, Sybil."

Sybil frowned. "Oh, well. I have two suitcases that won't fit through the door. I had hoped you and Drew would get the entry cleared before I got home, but I guess we don't all have the same work ethic."

Emmitt forced a smile. "I'll take the suitcases through the kitchen. You want them in your bedroom or office?"

"Bedroom," Sybil said, squeezing through the door with two pink carry-on bags. She brushed past Emmitt and knocked carelessly into boxes on her way past the entry and into the hallway.

Emmitt moved the two over-packed pink suitcases through the side yard and into the kitchen. He stopped to pet Henry on the head and let the dog outside to sun himself on the grass. Emmitt carefully maneuvered each suitcase through the house and into Sybil's bedroom. When he placed the second suitcase into her room, Sybil uttered a distracted "thanks," without looking at him. She scrolled mechanically through her phone with her newly painted coral-pink nails.

"Is there anything else you need?" Emmitt said with stiff politeness.

"Are you on the clock?" She glanced up from her phone and looked at Emmitt with a bored expression.

"No. Just trying to be nice."

She looked back at her phone. "I've got a team meeting in five minutes. I don't need you for anything."

"Already?" Emmitt couldn't help himself. "You just got home!"

"Some of us don't take breaks, Emmitt. Some of us are supposed to accomplish great things. That takes effort, and sacrifice ... and a guru who won't flake out." Sybil's words were taken from Serenity's mouth. Her eyes were determined, but there was a strained panic in her voice. Her bronzed skin pulled tightly across her skeleton; she was lean and hollow. Too lean, Emmitt thought. *Too hollow. What did Serenity do to you?*

"Can I listen in?" Emmitt asked.

"Why?"

Emmitt shrugged. "I don't know. I'm curious. Hey, is your meeting with the essential oils team or the nutritional supplements team?"

"Essential oils." Sybil sounded confused by Emmitt's sudden interest.

Emmitt wasn't entirely sure what propelled his motivation to make the request. Part of him wanted to witness a team-building meeting for a network marketing scheme firsthand. Part of him wanted to know what it took to sell essential oils for Serenity's Rivers of Younity. The smallest part of him worried about Sybil's fanaticism toward his mother and brother, and he hoped sitting in on her meeting would allow him to better understand her zeal.

"Is this for the book?" Sybil asked.

"No ... unless you want it to be in the book. Rivers of Younity is my mom's ... business."

He stopped himself from saying "multi-level marketing scheme" or "recruitment scam." Both were true, but he found that most people who sold products through multi-level marketing ventures were usually hesitant to admit they were part of one.

"We're not close," Emmitt said, "but you two seem to have a good working relationship."

"Oh, Emmitt. How sad for you." Sybil pouted. Her eyes were glittering steel on his face. "Really, though, is this to make fun of me? I understand you don't have a lot of options for a good time with my sister, but it would be pretty pathetic if you wanted to listen in just so you could gossip about me later."

"That never crossed my mind," Emmitt argued. "Honestly, I'm trying to figure you out, Sybil … and … I'm a little jealous of your relationship with Serenity. I want to understand what it is you see in her."

"You mean what she sees in me?" Sybil snapped.

"No," Emmitt insisted. "I didn't misspeak."

The steel in Sybil's eyes melted. She bared a haughty smile that reminded Emmitt of Shannon's. "Fine. But you need to be quiet. If you laugh at me, or smirk, or roll your eyes, you're out."

"I'll be good," Emmitt promised. "Let me tell Renata. I'll meet you in the office."

"One more thing." Sybil flipped her curled platinum hair over one shoulder and smirked. "Try not to fall in love with me. I know you have a weakness for rich, emotionally damaged blondes."

Emmitt smiled cautiously. "I'll try, Sybil. Hey, can I laugh if you're joking? You've got some pretty good zingers."

"Emmitt, old men say 'zingers.' Don't embarrass yourself in front of my team, please."

Emmitt nodded seriously. "I'll go tell Renata. Be right back."

Emmitt's legs took him down the path, back to the breakfast nook. Renata and Shannon looked up at him from their work. Renata had convinced Shannon to help with table arrangements for the upcoming Mother's Day brunch at the museum. On the table were shopping lists for flowers, diagrams for table arrangements, and drawings of floral centerpieces. They were debating between pink and peach roses when Emmitt stood in front of them with a nervous grin.

"What's up, Emmitt?" Renata asked when he didn't sit next to her to resume his typing.

"I'm going to sit in on Sybil's team meeting," Emmitt said.

"Why?" Renata asked with an expression that mirrored Sybil's when Emmitt had proposed the same idea to her.

"I'm curious," Emmitt answered with a wide grin.

Renata sighed. "That does sound like you. Fine. Just promise you won't join her downline."

"I promise ... oh, I forgot. I left Henry outside too." He kissed the top of Renata's head and turned away to avoid the annoyed glare that was certain to follow him.

Emmitt was quiet as he entered Sybil's office. Sybil pointed to a fuzzy white chair outside the field of view of her elaborate camera setup. She turned on two ring lights and adjusted her camera before sitting down at her computer. She took one last look at herself in a lighted mirror she kept in her top desk drawer, and then began her meeting.

Within the first ten minutes, Emmitt began to regret his decision. He watched as her team trickled into the meeting. Some showed their faces on video, while most commented in a column next to the boxes of faces on the screen. Emmitt couldn't read the text or names, but the comments scrolled past at a feverish pace. Sybil's face featured most prominently, taking up the top left quarter of the screen, with a few dozen tiny faces filling in the mosaic. She shifted effortlessly from prattling to the faces to simultaneously addressing the faceless commenters. Emmitt could feel the tension in his clenched jaw as he listened to the empty words spew disingenuously from Sybil's mouth.

"Hi, Stacy! ... Hey, Lauren! ... Oh my God, Madison, I love your hair! With those green eyes, you were born to be a redhead. Yeah, we're gonna start in a minute ... Just a few more minutes ... Yeah, just waiting for a few more people to get on before we start. Oh, Jennifer's here. Hey, girl!" Eventually, enough of the team was present for Sybil to start the meeting.

Sybil quieted everyone and began. "Okay, everyone! Namaste and thanks for being here! I wanted to thank everyone who attended the ten-day wellness and renewal retreat with Serenity Rivers-Key in Hawaii. We had a lot of fun, a lot of bonding, and a lot of inner healing. Honestly, anyone who joined us on the Hilina Pali Trail ..." Sybil paused for effect. Her eyes welled and her voice broke. "The power ... the majesty ... and the insane amount of inner peace that came from that experience ... I can't even put it into words."

There was a rush of eager agreement and support. Sybil allowed her team to share their own spiritual awakenings while hiking the trail as she composed herself and scanned through the comments.

After the fifth team member gushed, using Sybil's similar utterances of "inner power and majestic peace," Sybil interrupted.

"That's nice, Amy ... Jennifer, I know it was a tough trail. It was tough for a reason. Hawaii didn't become a stunning island overnight. It took millions of years of erupting, and growing, and reshaping itself.

Serenity talked about the fire and passion that burns in all of us. Perhaps you missed the lecture, but you wouldn't have a problem hiking the trail if you would just sign up for Amelior Wellness. I've already told you their supplements and electrolyte powders are life-changing." Sybil was sharp, and Emmitt straightened himself in the chair with a growing interest.

After a few more members gave their own accounts and chastised Jennifer for good measure, Sybil continued.

"So, I know *most* of us had a great time, and I was so happy to pose for pictures, and provide guidance to help all of you grow your businesses ... Meghan, I cropped you out of the beach pictures because your pubes were growing out of your bikini. Had you gone with the rest of us to the group Brazilian wax—which I paid for, by the way—I wouldn't have to crop you out. I tried to post them, but the pictures kept getting taken down for indecent exposure. Next time wear some board shorts or trim yourself ... don't blame me. Oh, God, Jennifer, how many times are you going to complain about missing Easter? It was an optional retreat. You didn't have to come. Jennifer, do you know how difficult it is to schedule with Serenity? Even her own sons have to make an appointment to see her."

Emmitt was at the edge of his seat. He wondered if all of Sybil's meetings devolved into this level of chaos. After two enforcers—who Emmitt guessed were in Sybil's immediate downline—intervened and calmed the rabble, Sybil once again tried to hold court.

"Okay, everyone, we got a bit off track, but I wanted to start doing team affirmations. Serenity helped me with the first one, so I want you all to think about this and share. Fill in the blank and type your answers into the comments. 'I honor ... blank.' What do you honor? There are no wrong answers. Type it up now, and I'll read the comments. Let me see ... 'Myself.' Yes, that's good. Wow, I see a lot of you typed that in. I love to see self-love, ladies! 'Prosperity.' That's another good one ... oh, 'Inner peace.' Yes! 'Our Rivers of Younity community.' Excellent! Totally agree. I love the community we've built together ... Jennifer, I can't tell if you're being passive-aggressive by typing 'family.' Is this about Easter, again?"

Sybil's tone continued to ebb and flow. One moment, she would be ebullient and gracious, the next she would be testy and lash out. Every time Sybil reached her limit, her closest minions would step in and smooth things over, only for the cycle to repeat. It wasn't clear to Emmitt if Jennifer had a vendetta, or if she had simply reached her limit with the business.

As Sybil's downline disciples stepped in again, she began clicking furiously on her phone with her long, coral nails. Emmitt strained his eyes at the screen to see if any of the miniature faces were looking down at their own phones, but the images were too small for him to discern who was part of Sybil's inner circle. Emmitt thought there were four or five voices who kept speaking up in defense of her, but their voices all sounded so similar he couldn't be sure how many were committed devotees.

When the conversation circled back around to a new line of products, Sybil took the lead once again.

Sybil's forced effervescence fizzled. "Alright, so, we have a new line for Mother's Day. Serenity put a lot of effort into the designs for the new essential oil diffusers. We still have the original diffuser design, which is perfect for someone who wants something that's understated. The original is a classic for a reason: it blends in seamlessly with any room. Serenity's new designs are gorgeous statement pieces that are eye-catching. They are truly captivating. They're made of colorful, hand-blown glass, and there is a special Mother's Day discount if you purchase this week. There is no better way to earn someone's business than by giving quality products that you yourself stand by and believe in. I recommend giving all the moms in your life a little embrace from the Rivers of Younity family."

Sybil smiled serenely at the end of her pitch. She tapped back to the comments. Scrolled. Stopped.

When Sybil spoke again, her voice was venomous. "Okay, sorry, Jennifer, I'm going to block you from the conversation. To answer your first question: No. The new essential oil facemask diffuser is not just an expensive washcloth. It is spa quality, super absorbent, hypoallergenic, and one hundred percent bamboo. It will not scratch or itch, and Serenity guarantees it will hold the scent of any oil for up to ten hours longer than a normal washcloth. As to your second question: No, again. It isn't predatory or insincere to give sample-sized oils for holidays. Rivers of Younity is the definition of luxury. You shouldn't keep these amazing products, or a one-of-a-kind business opportunity for yourself. And even if your mom *doesn't* want to join our team, you've still exposed her to the brand. She may tell her friends about the products, which will help your business grow. It's not like you're a font of positivity, Jennifer, and your sales are abysmal. Last question: No, again, Jennifer. It's not a pyramid scheme. I make more money from sales than I do from any distributors below me. That's the difference. If you all quit tomorrow, I'm still making money ... a lot of money. Look, I wasn't going to bring this up to anyone, but I just stepped through my front door, and I immediately hopped onto this call—because I care. And unlike Jennifer, I hustled in Hawaii. I stayed past the retreat, past the wellness conference, past the sacred plant ceremony, and past the sound healing workshop. I hit spas, boutique hotels, and yoga studios. I did photoshoots, shot a couple of commercials, had a long meeting with Mr. Bryson, and I secured long-term clients. You know what I'm not complaining about? Serenity's cut of my sales. She made the product. She gave me the tools to better myself. She allowed me to be part of this community, and I am grateful to be in this business. You think it's a pyramid scheme? Then stop trying to recruit. Try busting your ass. Try making the sales I make. You have dignity? Reputation? You don't want to be degraded? Leave it at the door or get the fuck out of this community. We are manifesting prosperity and influence here. If you don't have the stomach for it, leave."

There was silence from the faces on the screen. After a minute passed, one enforcer dared to speak. "It totally needed to be said. I'm glad Jennifer's gone. She really brought down the meeting."

A few more of the same voices chimed in, praising Sybil for her tenacity and willingness to speak the hard truths in such a "real" and "authentic" way. Emmitt kept from rolling his eyes at the meaningless compliments Sybil's employees poured onto her. Despite the constant starts and stops to stroke Sybil's fragile ego, Emmitt had to admit, this was far more interesting and illuminating than he had expected.

Sybil ended with another push for her team to take advantage of the Mother's Day sale, then signed off. She stood and turned off the ring lights, then plopped hard into her rose-gold desk chair.

"Assholes," she muttered. "Emmitt, you still there?" she asked without turning from her desk.

"Yep."

Sybil let out an audible sigh and swiveled her chair to face him. "Well?" she asked, surveying his expression.

"Was that a normal meeting? It seemed to get a little heated." Emmitt had no sense of what Sybil considered normal, in business, or in any other aspect of her life.

"No. Not normal. It could have gone smoother without the constant comments from the peanut gallery."

Emmitt grinned. "Sybil, old men say 'peanut gallery.'"

"I'm not joking, Emmitt," Sybil snapped.

Emmitt realized the magnitude of the divide that separated them. He loved Renata, and he was closer to Shannon than he was to his own mother. Sybil was different. Almost everything she said grated on Emmitt, and he suspected Sybil felt the same way about him. He resolved to at least try to understand her, even if he could never bond with her.

He immediately stopped smiling. "Okay. No jokes. Can I ask you a few questions? It's not for the book. I just want to understand what happened."

"It's pretty clear what happened. Jennifer got angry about her failing business and lack of discipline and took her frustration out on me." Sybil sucked her teeth and glared off to the side.

"That's ... possible. But I'm still not sure why you think you need Serenity to sell essential oils. I know you have a strong work ethic. You definitely have a commanding way of expressing yourself, and you're a savant at sales. Why don't you create and sell your own products?"

"Because it's not about the products. It's about the community. You saw how sweet my girls were. They always look out for me."

Emmitt hesitated. Her "girls" were drones. Ass kissers. They were only telling Sybil what she wanted to hear. Could he tell her that? Could he be honest at all? He thought not. He decided on a round-about approach.

"I'm not sure how the business works. Are they friends, coworkers, or employees?"

"Friends. I view myself more like a mentor than a boss. And Serenity is kind of like a mom ... Oh, sorry, Emmitt."

He wasn't sure if the words slipped out, or if Sybil was trying to hurt him. Her expressions were unreadable, and he was too busy trying to keep the conversation flowing to take any personal offense. *Sybil is sick*, he repeated in his mind.

"Do you think they'd still be your friends if you weren't in the same business?"

"No," she said flatly. "Lots of people make friends during a particular chapter of their life. Things fall apart. People grow distant. It happens."

"Not always," Emmitt said.

"It's always for me." Sybil swiveled side to side in the chair while staring at Emmitt. "Best to enjoy it while it lasts."

"Do you spend time together outside of cruises, conferences, and retreats?"

"That's not enough?" Sybil laughed. "When I add up all the cruises, conferences, and retreats, I end up spending more quality time with my team than I do with my family."

"It doesn't feel like work?"

"Of course, it feels like work ... it *is* work. I was lucky to have extra time to bond with Serenity. She talked about being an island; the forces and pressures beneath you can build you up, but in the end, you really only have yourself."

"Then what's the community for?"

"That's who does the building up ..." Sybil paused. She looked to the side as though trying to resolve the discrepancy. "Serenity explained it better. She said the people beneath you build you up, like lava erupting ... then ... well ... you become a bigger island."

Emmitt's eyes softened. "That doesn't sound like a good way to maintain your community if Serenity is suggesting that your downline exists solely to serve you and help with your personal growth."

Sybil groaned dramatically. "Tell me about it. I've dealt with a lot of people like Jennifer lately ... but I also have more distributors under me now than ever before. Serenity says it's natural for lower frequencies to flake out and fall away. I can't argue with the results. I'm making more money, and I've gotten some promising calls to come back to television. It's just reality show offers, so far ... but it's better than nothing."

"Do you want to do a reality show?" Emmitt asked.

"Serenity says it's an effective way to relaunch my career."

"But do *you* want to?"

"I don't know," Sybil said with an air of feigned indignation.

"Does being an island make you feel isolated?"

"Yes, of course it does, but I'm pretty sure that's the point, Emmitt. I have to make sacrifices to grow my brand. Your mom is a monolith. Why wouldn't I try to absorb her wisdom and experience? Who wouldn't want to be her?" Her worried eyes mirrored her frenzied tone. Emmitt noticed the corner of her lip twitch.

Emmitt couldn't compel himself to care about the disciples and enforcers in her downline. They all parroted Sybil, who parroted Serenity, and they were as disposable to Sybil as Sybil was to Serenity. Part of him understood why. What redeeming qualities did they have? Who were they outside of the collective? Sybil was an amalgamation of a lot of terrible traits, but she was also entertaining and surprisingly productive. And she was Renata's sister. He cared about her for that simple fact. The rest of them were nothing to Emmitt, but Sybil was Renata's sister. She didn't deserve to be an island. And she didn't deserve to be a chunk of useless rock attached to Serenity's expansive island continent, either.

"You said you had a meeting with Bryson." Emmitt tried to sound casual, but he could hear the contempt in his own voice. "Was he at the retreat?"

"No," Sybil said. "There's no privacy in direct sales. Felix figured out where I was going and decided to fly over and touch base. He stalks me on social media."

"Isn't that dangerous?"

"If it is, there's not much I can do about it. Everywhere I go, and everything I do has to tie back to the business. There are no incidental posts. Everything is calculated and curated. Do you know how much planning, setup, and editing it takes to manufacture a single spontaneous moment? It's worse when you're working with amateurs who keep looking directly at the camera ... but I have to share nearly every day of my life with my followers. I can't hide from anyone. I certainly can't hide from Felix. He's my boss."

"Bryson is a creep. I don't like him."

Sybil leaned toward Emmitt and lowered her voice. "He's worse when you get to know him."

Emmitt sniffed indignantly. "If he did anything—"

"Relax, Emmitt." Sybil leaned back in her chair and took in his fury with a look of amused curiosity. "Serenity went to the meeting with me. She stayed the whole time ... Felix is afraid of her."

"You don't need him," Emmitt said.

Sybil's mouth twisted as she glanced away from Emmitt. "I might," she whispered.

Emmitt swallowed his anger and pressed on. "Do you feel closer to Serenity than your own mom?"

"What are you, my shrink?" Sybil grinned. "Yes. I'm closer to Serenity. She has all the answers I need to level up my life. I've never heard her say 'I don't know' to anything. Mom likes to exude confidence, but she's always struggled. She struggled to help launch my career after *Raising Rosie* was cancelled. She struggled with her marriage. And Dad's money. Obviously, she struggled with cleaning and organizing. She may appear to be poised and proper, but she's always been a mess. Plus, she thinks I'm stupid and impulsive. It's the same with the rest of my family. Stupid is a hard thing to shake off."

"But your team supports you?"

"Yeah ... well, mostly. It feels good to have people who look up to me ... but a lot of them end up turning on me. I know it's jealousy, but it still hurts. Before Serenity, I only ever felt close to my grandpa. He always loved me unconditionally, he always had time for me, and he never made me feel stupid."

"I'm glad your grandpa made you feel special, Sybil."

Sybil studied Emmitt seriously before speaking. "Thanks. My family thinks I'm naïve, but I've been good with the allowance Grandpa gives me. I think he'd be proud of me. He always told me it was important to spend money on experiences rather than things. That's what I do with my inheritance. It's why I go on so many retreats and cruises. I've seen most of the world with Grandpa's money. Mom won't go anywhere anymore, and Renata hates me, so I have to do things with my work family."

Emmitt's grief was sudden and severe. "That's a beautiful thing to do to remember him."

Sybil's face relaxed. Her smile was soft and genuine. "Thanks, Emmitt."

"Were you being serious when you talked about not having any dignity or respectability?"

Sybil's mouth tensed again, and her eyes fixed on Emmitt. "You seem like the kind of person who would make that sort of comment about me. Are you surprised I feel the same way you do?"

"Why not change it? Why do you keep leaning into it?"

"It doesn't matter what I do. My image is shit. Even if I tried to repair it, I can't escape criticism. If I actively tried to change my life, there would be articles condemning me for being manipulative, desperate, or disingenuous."

"I'm not talking about how other people view you. I'm talking about your own sense of self-respect. Forget your image. Forget fame. Forget everyone else. You can reclaim your dignity for yourself."

Sybil pressed her lips together tightly. "I don't know if that's possible anymore," she mumbled. "Even if it is, I don't know if I want it."

"Why wouldn't you want your dignity?" Emmitt asked. "Is this about being famous? Or a 'global entrepreneur'? You really have to give up your dignity for that? Doesn't that tear you up?"

"I don't know. Why do you care?"

Emmitt's voice faltered. "It's a sad way to live. I know you've profited from Serenity's guidance, but her connections and influence might be more harmful than helpful. You shouldn't have to sacrifice yourself for Bryson's or Serenity's bottom line."

Sybil rolled her eyes. "Right. I just need to stop caring about what everyone else thinks and start believing in myself. Is that really your solution, Emmitt?"

"No ... maybe. I really don't know, Sybil. I know I'm upset for you, but I have no clue what you should do."

"That's not helpful."

"I know. Sorry."

"Anything else you need to say?" Sybil asked with a rising impatience.

"Just ... one more question: do you ever think you'll be close to Renata or your mom?"

Sybil thought before answering. "No. I think we're too different. Maybe we can learn to tolerate each other, but I think Dad's death broke things too much. It took his suicide for us to realize he was the glue. It doesn't seem fair."

"You're right. It doesn't seem fair." Emmitt felt defeated as he stood and turned to leave.

"You're kind of like him," Sybil said to his back as he reached the door. "You talk more than he did, but you try to figure us out, and you try to fix things. It's annoying, but I'm sure it's why Mom tolerates you

... and why Renata loves you. If you stick around long enough—and you don't kill yourself—it's possible the rest of us might learn to stand each other's company."

Emmitt felt one last effort rise within him. He turned to face Sybil.

"I think you can do more for yourself than my mom could ever do for you. She gave you terrible advice. You shouldn't lose yourself trying to be like her. I'm sorry that you've been taken advantage of. I don't know when it started, and I suspect, with your wealth, it'll always be a struggle for you to know who to trust. But you're capable of making decisions for yourself. You don't need a guru to tell you what to do ... and you're not stupid, Sybil."

A nerve had finally been struck. Emmitt directed his eyes away from Sybil's stunned face as he turned and walked out of the door.

Chapter Thirty-Two

"Are you sure you want me listening in?" Renata asked.

"Yeah. I may need moral support. I really don't want to do this."

Renata squeezed Emmitt's hand in the front seat of his parked station wagon. He had joined the Yates family again for Mass. This time, the curly-haired cousin told Renata to scoot over so she could sit next to Emmitt. When she demanded he go up with her to receive communion, he had informed her of his ignorance of what to do. The child assumed he was joking, but when Emmitt assured her he wasn't, she became an eager authority figure. She carefully explained—in surprisingly pretentious preschooler terminology—how to cross his arms over his chest to receive a blessing. As they walked down the line toward the priest for communion, the four-year-old frequently glanced behind to be sure Emmitt was crossing his arms correctly.

After the Mass, Emmitt drove Renata to the museum for Mother's Day brunch. As they sat in the parked car in the museum parking lot, Emmitt knew he had to make the call. The Yates' brunches would often carry over into dinner at a cousin, aunt, or uncle's house. After the celebrations of Easter and Divine Mercy Sunday, Emmitt realized Yates family gatherings were lively affairs that lasted the entire day.

There was quiet in the car. Emmitt and Renata were alone, and he had to call Serenity.

"And you're sure you want me to stay quiet? What if she says something nasty to you?" Renata said as Emmitt reached for his phone.

"She probably *will* say something nasty. I don't want you to intervene or try to reason with her. She's not Andrew. I don't want to argue with her. I just need to get the words out, and I need to sound polite and unbothered."

"No tag teaming, then?" Renata said. "Because I'm prepared to step in and give her a piece of my mind. I think I could do it. I've been channeling my inner Emmitt."

"You've really blossomed, babe."

Renata laughed. "No. I still hate talking to strangers, but I'm willing to defend you to prove my love, *babe*."

Emmitt looked down at his phone and frowned. "Okay. I've gotta do this."

Emmitt dialed the number, then put the phone on speaker for Renata to hear. It rang. Then rang again. On the third ring, Serenity answered.

"Emmie? Why are you calling?" Serenity's voice was cool and unconcerned.

"I wanted to wish you a Happy Mother's Day ... and say I'm sorry about our last conversation." Emmitt tried to remain vague. He wasn't sorry for what he said, but he was sorry for the suffering Andrew endured because of his outburst.

"That's nice, Emmie. Are we done? I'm having lunch with your brother right now. I'd like to enjoy it." Serenity didn't bother to hide her disinterest.

"Yeah … well, not completely. I was talking to Sybil, and I don't think you should tell her about the inheritance stuff. It would crush her if she found out that her uncle was the one giving her money. And it would hurt her even more if you were the one to tell her. She respects you … more than respects … she idolizes you."

There was a long silence. Emmitt waited, wondering if she had hung up on him.

After a full minute, Serenity finally spoke. "Emmie, I don't care about Sybil. I gave Drew a golden opportunity, but he's decided to steer his business in another direction. I don't agree with it, but I held her on the line as long as I could for his sake. I spent over two months with Sybil Yates during your little job. It's a testament to my devotion as a mother, though neither of you seems to appreciate my sacrifice. If Drew doesn't see the value of holding onto a long-term client, there's nothing more I can do. And, while Sybil is replaceable, it's disheartening that you think I would be bothered enough to blackmail one of my distributors. It's all so disappointing … but I'd prefer not to dwell on it."

Emmitt sighed. "I'm not trying to accuse you of anything. You have a reach and an influence bigger than just about everyone, so I can see why you don't concern yourself with those of us who aren't on your level, but Sybil adores you. I don't know if you understand how devastating—"

"Emmie, I hate to interrupt you, but as I already said, I don't care. If it makes you happy, I'll promise not to do or say anything to Sybil. I'm not planning on blackmailing her or sabotaging your relationship with the other one—which, by the way, is news I had to hear from your father. If you didn't care enough to tell me about your extracurriculars with the Yates sister, then I can only assume this so-called relationship is nothing more than a fleeting affair for one or both of you." There was a growing petulance in Serenity's voice.

Emmitt remained calm. "It's serious. Her name is Renata. I love her."

"Good for you, Emmie. I suppose I should congratulate you for finding a way to bypass hard work and dedication in order to manifest wealth into your life, but it is *my* day today, and I really shouldn't have to concern myself with any of this nonsense. It would misalign my chakras, and I would hope even you wouldn't be so cruel as to cause a misalignment on Mother's Day."

"I'm not trying to misalign your chakras, Mom."

"Good. Anyway, Sybil is a liability for someone like me. She's far too impulsive. She would have made a good steppingstone for Drew, but he doesn't think she's a good fit for him … It is curious. There are times I wonder how much influence you've had over him, but it isn't in my nature to be confrontational on a holiday." Serenity's annoyance overtook her attempt at casual indifference. "Anything else?"

"One more thing …" Emmitt realized he had to be quick to avoid the growing ire of his mother. "Sybil said you kept her safe during her meeting with Bryson. Why do either of you need to affiliate with him? He's gross."

There was another protracted pause. Serenity's tone softened slightly. "Emmie, if Sybil wants to rehabilitate her acting career, she'll have to deal with serpents. There's no way to avoid it. Felix Bryson is well-connected to people who can find legitimate work for Sybil. He may be 'gross,' but he's controllable. Believe me, there are people who are far worse than Felix. If Felix is ousted or imprisoned, there will always be someone more disgusting and depraved to take his place."

"There has to be another way."

"Most of us can't live in a world where we ignore reality. Sybil can only go so far with her acting talent. There aren't a lot of options—and she isn't my responsibility—but I did my best to shield her from the worst kinds of people. Do you understand now why someone like Sybil might need a long-term mentor? Someone I can vouch for? Someone who can attend private meetings and look out for her?"

"I ... don't know," Emmitt whispered. The exploitation was inexcusable, but he supposed Sybil's desire to act may have precipitated Serenity's callously pragmatic solution. Emmitt spoke calmly and firmly to his mother. "What about me? If Sybil needs someone to monitor Bryson, can I go to her meetings? Can you vouch for me?"

Emmitt heard a surprised laugh that almost sounded genuine. "Emmitt Thomas Key, when have you ever needed me to vouch for you? You barge in everywhere you go." As his mother's laughter tapered off, she let out a sigh. "May I eat lunch now?"

"Okay, Mom. Sorry to bother you. Happy Mother's Day ... I love you."

Emmitt could hear the shock in Serenity's voice. "Okay, Emmie ... Thank you." There was an audible exhale. Then she hung up.

Emmitt put away his phone and looked at Renata. "Well, I didn't lose my temper. That's progress."

Renata leaned in and kissed his cheek, then licked her thumb and rubbed the imprint of her rosy-pink lipstick off his face.

"I love you," Renata declared with a sharpness that almost sounded like defiance. "She should have said it back to you. You're lovable."

Emmitt smiled. "She won't say it if she doesn't mean it. Mom doesn't seem to care about the trust. She's fine using Sybil for Rivers of Younity, but I don't think she'll go any further … for now, at least."

"Serenity doesn't want Andrew's castoffs. Sybil was a good mark for Drew Key, but Serenity wasn't interested." Renata frowned. "I'm glad Serenity didn't completely abandon Sybil to Bryson, but she's the one who set her up with him … and Sybil is still selling their products. She's still being exploited by both of them."

"Yeah," Emmitt sighed.

"As much as I hate to admit it, Serenity isn't wrong. It doesn't matter who they are, or how they manipulate and belittle. They're all like Bryson and Serenity. Tyrants and monsters and manipulators. I wish Sybil could see what she's gotten herself into. She's getting so thin with the supplements from Bryson's racket. She's too nauseous to be hungry, and the meager amount she gets into her system runs right through her. I hate that she's killing herself for people who think she's disposable."

"I know. I'm sorry she's caught up in this. At least my mom can't be bothered to blackmail her," Emmitt said. "And I promise to barge my way into any meeting Sybil has with Bryson."

Renata smiled at Emmitt. "I know you will … I guess I should also be grateful your mother acknowledged your relationship with 'the other one.' It doesn't sound like Andrew told Serenity about Melody yet. That has to be hard for him."

Emmitt couldn't continue discussing Serenity. It was enough for Emmitt to have a phone call that didn't end in a screaming match between himself and his mother. He proved to himself he could be civil, and he hadn't needed Andrew to mediate. Emmitt didn't want to keep Renata from enjoying the day with her family. For now, his family could stay a mess. Hers was only beginning to heal. He wanted her to savor that minor triumph.

"Whose house are we going to after brunch?" he asked casually.

Renata's face brightened. "Uncle James's. After we eat, I have to swing by the house and pick up Henry ... oh, and we need to get you swim trunks. My uncle had a lazy river installed. I think he meant for it to be for the grandkids, but the adults are just as excited. It's the only reason Sybil agreed to go to Mother's Day Mass and brunch."

"That's understandable," Emmitt laughed. "Hey, your uncle actually made eye contact with me today. He even shook my hand at the 'peace be with you' part of Mass."

"I saw that. He's warming up to you," Renata said.

"Did you wear him down with hyperbolic praise of me, or does he genuinely like me?"

"Both," Renata laughed.

"You ready?" Emmitt asked, opening the car door.

"Not yet," Renata said, casting her eyes downward. "I ... I have something I wanted to tell you."

Emmitt closed the car door and looked anxiously back at Renata. "Good news?" he questioned hesitantly.

"Yes. I think you'll be happy. I hope you'll be excited," Renata said, still looking downward.

"What is it?"

"I've been talking to my uncle ... and he really does like you ... and I've been thinking about the future ... not the immediate future ... but ... eventually ..." Renata stammered as she spoke.

Emmitt lowered his head and leaned closer to coax her eyes to meet his own. She slowly shifted her gaze.

"I've been thinking about getting my own house."

Emmitt smiled. "That's great! It'll be good for you to have your own place."

"It would still be in the same neighborhood. I can walk to my mother's house every day to visit and help her clean, and she can use my current bedroom and sitting room. She'll finally have a clean space to live in, and a comfortable bed to sleep in. If she's safe and comfortable, we won't need to rush to finish cleaning the rest of the house. We can keep going at her pace."

"That all sounds perfect. Why do you seem so nervous?"

Renata blushed. "I know we hint at things and joke around, but this is a big step toward the future. It could be a home to start a family in ... not this instant, but possibly within the next couple years ... and ... I want you to look at houses with me. I just don't want you to feel like I'm pressuring you. I want to do this together, but if you want me to do this by myself, I understand."

"You're not pressuring me. I'll look at houses with you," Emmitt said. "I saved all the money your uncle gave me for the job. It feels wrong keeping it for myself. I don't think it'll be a big enough contribution toward the down payment, but you can have all of it."

"I've been thinking about that," Renata said. "Mother brought it up when I told her I wanted to get a house for myself ... Emmitt, I know it isn't fair for me to ask you to move into a neighborhood you can't afford. I would be happy to pay for it myself, but ..."

"But your mom knows I want to contribute," Emmitt finished.

"Yes. So, I may have come up with a compromise for you, if you'd like to hear it."

"I'd like to hear it, Renata." Emmitt placed his hand over hers.

Renata sighed and giggled. "I'm sorry. I'm nervous ... not because of you ... it's just a big step. My uncle owns the properties we're going to be looking at. He owns most of the properties in this neighborhood. They're already paid off, and he agreed that I ... *we* ... when ... *if* we get married ..."

"*When* we get married and I move in, right?" Emmitt asserted.

"Right." Renata's eyes twinkled as she looked at Emmitt. "My uncle said we can live in the house while only paying the property tax and utilities. We've had the same arrangement for all the other houses we moved into after Dad's death. Some of my cousins have the same arrangement—and Uncle Lucas and Aunt Gracie live on Uncle James's properties without paying for anything—so it's not a special case for you and me. There's no special treatment. You won't have to pay anything until we're married, and when you move in, we'll split the cost of the monthly bills and taxes ... oh, and when your book gets published, and you become a famous author, we can purchase the house from Uncle James. How does that sound?"

"It sounds like you put a lot of thought and consideration into it ... my part in it, especially. That plan works for me. I'm all in."

"Are you sure? Because I can pay for the house myself ... all of it. I feel so guilty asking you to pay for something that isn't economical. I know it's not a normal situation. I've been worried that I'm forcing you into something you don't want."

Emmitt was firm. "I want to be with you, Renata. I want to take care of you, but I know there will always be a disparity ... I understand why you're worried, but I'm not your dad, and you're not your mom. What happened wasn't her fault, and I don't want you to spiral thinking you need to prevent some calamity that isn't going to happen. I know what I'm getting myself into. If I didn't die from embarrassment when you exposed me in front of your mom and Sybil, then there is absolutely nothing you can do to kill me. I'm emotionally invincible."

Renata laughed as the tears streamed down her face. "I panicked when you passed out. And I never exposed you! I just unzipped you." Renata opened her purse and grabbed a tissue. "I know I worry too much … I just don't want to lose you."

"But you won't lose me. I don't know if you've noticed, but I'm kind of an open book. You're always the first to know when things annoy me. Complaining is my love language. I accused your whole family of hoarding on our first date, so you know I'm not subtle. I'm not stoic … I grumble and groan about everything—"

"You're perfect," Renata interrupted, dabbing the tears from her eyes.

Emmitt shook his head. "Even on a good day, I'm just okay."

"You're perfect for me."

Emmitt smiled. "I won't argue with that."

Chapter Thirty-Three

"You think we can get it all done by the end of today?" Emmitt asked, sipping his coffee in Andrew's SUV.

"I think we can, if we push," Andrew said, grabbing his phone from the center console.

"Are you gonna tell Sybil now, or wait until the end of the day?"

"End of the day. It might be too much now."

"For her or you?" Emmitt smirked.

"For both of us."

"Procrastinating? Mom was right. I *have* rubbed off on you."

Andrew laughed. "I suppose it's not that bad to be a little like you. It's not just me, though. You've been turning into a bit of a life coach. Guru Emmitt."

"Me? No way."

"Don't deny reality, Emmitt. You've made more progress with the Yates family than I have."

Emmitt shrugged. "It's been a team effort. You and I have been working well together, despite some minor hiccups. And Renata's definitely helped."

Andrew boomed, "Selfless too! Man, Emmitt, you're almost a total package. All we have to do is ween you off sugar and get you lifting weights, and we'll be twins!"

"What, no arm and chest waxing?" Emmitt grinned.

"Nah. Melly wants me hairy, like you."

"Now we'll both be ruggedly handsome."

Andrew nodded and looked seriously at Emmitt. "Hey, I realize I don't compliment you as often as I compliment my clients. It feels weird. It's not really our thing. But I've noticed you evolve. You're more confident and you really have a knack for helping people."

Emmitt's face reddened. "Nah. I'm still shitty. I just hide it better."

"No," Andrew insisted. "It's the other way around. You only have a shitty veneer. Underneath that is a solid human being. You're a good person."

"I'm just glad you're not mad at me anymore."

"I'm proud of you, Emmitt."

A burst of heat warmed Emmitt's already flushed face. He managed a forced, "Thanks," then cleared his throat. "Ready?"

Andrew patted Emmitt on the shoulder. "Not yet." He took a deep breath. Held it. Then, let it out. "Now I'm ready."

"Asshole," Emmitt chuckled.

"Yeah," Andrew agreed.

Emmitt led the way up the driveway and into the Yates' house. He opened the gap in the front door and called out into the entry, "Sybil! Drew's here!"

Another reinvented Sybil entered from the hallway to greet them. Sybil's hair was a warm light brown, with soft waves that brushed lightly over her shoulders. Her gaunt face was gaining fullness, and her tan was fading. While her makeup was far less severe, she still wore a bubblegum-pink top and tight lavender jeans that cropped at her ankles. She looked youthful and spirited, and her hazel eyes were bright.

"I've got a surprise!" Sybil bubbled. "Follow me!"

Emmitt and Andrew shared a questioning glance, then followed Sybil down the hallway. Andrew stopped at the doorway to Sybil's room.

"You're … done?" Andrew's eyes were wide with shock.

"Yep," Sybil said. "I finished it myself. It took me most of the weekend, but I did it. It's even decorated! Renata said she's going to give me some plants I can't kill. I just need you to unroll the new area rug, and I want the bed moved from the corner to the center of the room … please."

"Sure thing," Emmitt said.

Hearing the words, Andrew snapped out of his astonishment and wordlessly followed Emmitt. They placed the fluffy pink faux-sheepskin rug in the center of the room, then centered the gold-framed, queen-sized bed against the wall.

When they were done, Andrew looked disappointed. "I was ready to work," Andrew said. "It's over before we've even broken a sweat."

Emmitt wondered if Andrew was stalling. His brother confirmed his suspicion when he spoke again.

"Anything else you need help with, Sybil? Or is it possible your mom or Renata need help?"

"I'm good," Sybil said, studying herself in her lighted vanity mirror. "Mom is in the sitting room with Renata and Sister Eugene."

Andrew nodded as Sybil shooed them away from her preening.

As they walked down the hallway and into the breakfast nook, Emmitt pointed out the empty patches of hardwood floor that were now visible in the living room.

Walking into the formal dining room, Andrew let out an audible "wow" under his breath. "This is incredible! Where'd the couches go?" Andrew asked.

Emmitt stopped and turned to face Andrew. He leaned in and lowered his voice. "It was a pain in the ass, but Renata and I cleared a path to move the couches into her mom's new sitting room. We put Renata's moving boxes and furniture into storage for the next couple of weeks. We're doing everything we can to keep from losing momentum with Mrs. Yates."

"Good thinking. Your strategy seems to be working."

"We're trying to be as accommodating as possible. Mrs. Yates doesn't like to clean room by room, but if we concentrate on one type of item or specific groupings, she's really focused. It's slower, but she's making progress. There's a ton of extra space already."

"The paths are wider too," Andrew said.

"Yeah. A couple of days ago, Henry walked into the breakfast nook for the first time. He slept on a blanket while the rest of us worked at the table. It was nice. If Mrs. Yates continues at the same pace, Renata and I think we can have him walking through the front door in a couple of weeks."

"We have the rest of the day. Do you think she might let us clear the entry? We don't have to get rid of anything. You and I can move the boxes from the entry into the open areas of the living room."

Emmitt contemplated the suggestion. "We can try, but she doesn't respond well if she feels like she's being pushed."

"It's weird taking advice from you," Andrew said.

"You think I enjoy giving advice? If things go wrong, it's all my fault," Emmitt jabbed.

"That's true. I hope they don't hate you if I make a mistake," Andrew said with a wide grin.

Emmitt turned abruptly and muttered something under his breath.

Behind him, he could hear Andrew whisper loudly, "Conduct yourself."

As they entered the kitchen, they both grew silent. Andrew reached to knock on the closed door to Shannon's new sitting room.

"Come in," Shannon said.

Inside, there were stacks of books on the floor. The three women were diligently sorting, categorizing, and placing the books on the wall of shelves.

"What can we do?" Andrew asked immediately upon entering the room.

Shannon pointed to the books. "You may help us place books on the shelves, but only if you commit yourselves to following my explicit instructions on how they are to be sorted."

"Yes, ma'am," they both said in unison.

"Be careful what you agree to," Sister Eugene said with a heavy breath. Her smile broadened as she looked up at them from the floor. "Shannon's already reprimanded me twice. Now that there are more workers, perhaps we can unionize and stop her tyranny."

Renata laughed as she climbed a stepladder to place an armful of large hardcover books on a top shelf. Emmitt rushed to her and grabbed a brick of a book that threatened to slip from her arm. He then steadied her on the stepladder as she laughed harder.

"Do you see the insubordination I have to deal with?" Shannon asked, placing her hands on her hips and glaring at the spectacle.

As Shannon fixed her full attention on Emmitt and Andrew and explained her method of organizing, their increasingly dumbfounded expressions caused her to let out an exasperated sigh. "You're no better than the other two. I will point. You will fill the shelves."

The sorting took three hours, following Shannon's incomprehensible sorting system. When they had finished, she inspected their work. She double, then triple, checked, verifying the precise placement of each book.

Finally, she stood back and allowed herself to smile. "Breathtaking," Shannon whispered. "Everything is perfect."

Shannon lowered herself onto one of the antique sofas that Emmitt and Renata had moved from the dining room and stared admiringly at her new library. She then asked Emmitt to retrieve her phone from the breakfast table. When he brought it to her, she stood and walked methodically around the room, taking photos of the filled bookshelves from different angles. After she had taken over two dozen snapshots, she placed the phone down on a carved cherry wood coffee table that Emmitt had previously transported (along with two matching side tables) from the living room. Emmitt allowed Shannon to finish marveling at the accomplishment before he gently nudged his brother.

"Mrs. Yates," Andrew said respectfully. "I have a proposition for you."

Shannon still smiled, but her eyes sharpened mischievously as she looked at Andrew. "I'm flattered, Mr. Key, but you're about twenty-five years too young for me."

Andrew narrowed his eyes and smirked. "That's too bad, Mrs. Yates. We could have made an attractive couple. Could I ask you for a minor consolation since you refused my advances?"

Shannon blushed. "What kind of consolation?" she asked.

"The entryway is still blocked. Emmitt and I can move the boxes into the living room. If you agree, you would have complete control of where we put them. If you need to open them up before moving them, we can bring each one to you for inspection, and you can tell us to stop at any time. What do you think?" Andrew's warm confidence radiated.

"Please say yes, Shannon," Sister Eugene broke in. "You and the girls are little wisps. The boys and I are far more substantial. It takes a bit of work for us to squeeze through."

"We can have our family visit the house," Renata said wistfully. "Maybe not the little ones, just yet, but some of your siblings and the older nieces and nephews can come over to see you again."

Shannon looked from Andrew to Emmitt. "I have complete control?"

Emmitt nodded. "Anything you say goes. I promise."

Satisfied, Shannon looked back at Andrew. "Fine. I will agree to your proposition, Andrew."

As they moved into the entry, Shannon surveyed the boxes that blocked the door. Emmitt scanned the towers of stacked boxes, seeing just how many they needed to move for the door to open fully.

"Fourteen," Emmitt finally said aloud. He pointed to three large stacks of containers. "If we move these fourteen boxes and bins, we can open the door."

Shannon shook her head. "If we're clearing the entry, I think we should clear it completely."

All eyes fixed on Shannon.

"Are you sure, Mother?" Renata asked. "There are easily forty boxes here."

Shannon looked at Andrew. "Will you and Emmitt be able to move forty boxes if I look through them and tell you where to put them?"

"Yes, Mrs. Yates."

"I'll help," said Renata.

"We all will," added Sister Eugene. She cupped one hand to the side of her mouth and bellowed, "Sybil! We need your help, sweetie!"

Sybil shouted back, "Coming!"

Sybil bounced in buoyantly from the hallway. Once the plan for clearing the entry was explained to her, she grimaced.

Renata attempted to coax some enthusiasm from her sister. "Mother's going to open the boxes before we move them."

The coaxing worked. Sybil's curiosity was piqued.

"All the boxes?" she asked.

"All of them," Shannon confirmed.

Andrew carefully lowered a large plastic bin on the open space that served as a pathway for the family. He lifted the lid, and Shannon peeked inside.

"Oh," she gasped. "These are Great-Grandmother's dolls. You don't know how desperate I was to find them. I've wanted to give all the girls in the family one of her dolls as a keepsake. I have been praying to St. Anthony to find them … and here they are." Tears welled in her eyes. She impulsively grasped Andrew's hand. "Thank you for suggesting this." She gently sifted through the dolls and smiled as she took one out. "Marie Antoinette. She's perfectly painted, her curls are impeccable, and she's arrayed all in pink. She even has a confident little smile. Sybil, this doll is perfect for you."

She handed the doll to Sybil, who squealed in excitement and bolted to her room to put the doll away. She was back within seconds, gazing fixedly at the opened box. Shannon continued to look through the dolls, then instructed Andrew to close the lid and place the box in the breakfast nook. The second, third, and fourth plastic containers in the stack held similar dolls.

In the fifth box, Shannon found the doll that was meant for Renata. "Catherine of Aragon. A strong Catholic queen and Henry VIII's one and *only* legitimate wife." As she said the words, her eyes fixed on Emmitt.

Anxiously, Emmitt blurted, "Heretic!"

Sybil and Renata giggled.

Sister Eugene chastised Shannon. "You can't terrorize him into converting, Shannon. If he's going to do it, it has to be his decision."

"Don't forget our prayers, Sister," Renata asserted.

"I don't think Emmitt could resist any of your prayers, Renata," Andrew said, nudging Emmitt with an elbow to the ribs.

"I'm praying for you too, Andrew," Renata said with gentle determination.

Emmitt chuckled as Andrew's face reddened. He didn't think it was possible for anyone to make Andrew blush. It was one more reason to love Renata. But so was her faith. It was an inextricable part of her. Like Andrew, he couldn't separate the parts from the person.

As his laughter subsided, Emmitt had to admit to himself that Andrew was right. He couldn't resist Renata or her prayers. The seed was sown into his soul, and Emmitt wouldn't uproot what she had planted. Renata's sunshine and Sybil's rain—for Renata would always be his joy, and his affection for Sybil was born out of sorrow—had mixed with the salt and earth of Shannon and Sister Eugene, and the seed had already sprouted. Emmitt had no desire to make any public declarations, and he wasn't quite ready to make a firm profession of faith, but he would never refuse the fruits of Renata's entreaties.

"Fine," Shannon relented. "But Queen Catherine was a staunch woman. Capable. Devout. Despite experiencing intense suffering, she showed extraordinary resilience. I think you should have her, Renata."

She handed an elegantly dressed doll with a sad smile to Renata, who politely accepted it.

Shannon continued. "I'll pull out the ones I'd like to give to my nieces later ... and I may hold on to a few more. One never knows if there will be any more grandnieces ... or granddaughters." Shannon stunned Emmitt with a playful glance. "The rest will be donated to the museum. James has asked several times to display the collection."

"He'll love that," Renata said. "They're too beautiful to be kept in boxes."

Emmitt and Andrew stacked the boxes in front of one of the hutches in the breakfast nook, and the work continued. Every box was opened, scanned, closed again, and sent to a new location to be stacked.

Several times, Sybil and Renata were offered items from the opened bins. Sybil always accepted. Renata refused most of the items but kept four objects that were sentimental: a painted wooden cuckoo clock she had begged her father to buy at a cheap souvenir shop on a family trip to Germany, a stone garden statue of Saint Francis, a framed photo of the four members of the Yates family smiling in front of the Lone Cypress at Pebble Beach, and a vacuum-sealed plastic bag labeled "Renata's christening gown and bonnet."

One by one, they moved the bins and boxes into other rooms. After an exhausting six hours, they finally finished clearing the entry.

"You did it, Mrs. Yates," Andrew said.

Shannon smiled somberly. "There is … something else that needs to be done."

She grabbed Sybil's and Renata's hands and led them into the breakfast nook. Sister Eugene and the two brothers followed. Shannon stopped in front of the shrine to her husband. Arthur Yates. Arthur Abbott. She clung to her daughters.

Shannon struggled to keep her voice from trembling. "Toss the funeral wreaths in the garbage … and the chair."

Hearing the last words, Renata wept. Sybil stood still, stunned. Emmitt could see her eyes well, but she held in her tears as she clutched her mother's hand to her chest. He moved to grab a funeral wreath, but Shannon stopped him.

"Emmitt, you take the chair. I know it shouldn't matter … but it does to me."

Emmitt nodded silently. His hands shook as he slowly removed the framed photos from the seat. Emmitt breathed and steadied himself. He picked up the chair with solemn reverence and transported it carefully, never scraping or bumping into the clutter that still towered around him. He carried the chair out of the kitchen door and gently set it by the trash cans. Andrew and Sister Eugene followed with three long-dead funeral wreaths. A second and third trip brought out more wreaths and almost a dozen candles. When they were finished, all that remained was the portrait of Arthur.

"I have a place for him above the dresser in the bedroom," Shannon said, wiping tears from her eyes.

"I'll put him up on the wall tonight," Renata sniffled. "I'll put a new votive and a vase with some flowers on my dresser ... your dresser. I'll make sure the room looks perfect for you before I move out."

Shannon leaned over and kissed Renata's tear-stained cheek. They stood in quiet repose, staring at the portrait. Sybil was the first to leave the silent vigil. She squeezed Shannon's hand, then released it.

"I'll be in my room," she whispered.

Renata hugged her mother, then looked back at Emmitt and Andrew. Still sniffling, she said, "I think we've reached our limit for today. I'm going to get Dad's portrait up in the bedroom and sit with Mom for a while."

Renata slowly released her hold on her mother and hugged Emmitt and Andrew goodbye. She whispered her thanks to Andrew, kissed Emmitt, and promised to call him later in the evening. Sister Eugene put her arm around Shannon and walked with her while Renata followed the small procession holding Arthur's portrait.

Emmitt and Andrew waited for Renata to disappear into the formal dining room before turning to exit through the unobstructed front door.

Back in the car, Emmitt was the first to speak. "This day was not what I expected."

"No," Andrew agreed soberly. "I'll need to find another time to meet with Sybil."

"I'll talk to Renata about it. She'll have a better idea of how long you should wait."

Andrew looked at his phone. "Only six o'clock. You want to go to Gigi's?"

"At the beach? Now? Won't Melody miss you?"

"I'll call her on the way. She won't mind, especially after the day we've had. Plus, she'll want me to bring her back a slice of pie."

"Are *you* going to have a slice?" Emmitt asked.

"Stress eating isn't healthy, Emmitt." Andrew grinned. "How do you feel now that the job's almost over?"

"It isn't over. Not for me, at least." Emmitt smiled. "After today, I think I could love all of them … even Sybil."

"I think you already do," Andrew asserted.

"Yeah," Emmitt agreed.

As they drove to the beach, Emmitt's thoughts circled. The thought of Renata turned his mind to Shannon. Shannon to Arthur. Arthur to the chair. As he thought of the chair, the image of Sybil clutching her mother's hand flashed in his mind. The thought of Sybil returned him to the job. Then the book. His stomach knotted and tightened. He fought the rising lump that gathered in his throat and choked it down with a gulp.

It's not a job, he thought miserably. *They're not a job.*

Chapter Thirty-Four

Renata called Emmitt as Andrew was nearing his apartment. After a brief conversation regarding Sybil, she suggested Andrew wait a week to speak to her sister.

"She seems fine," Renata said cautiously. "I made dinner and offered her a plate after you left. She ate, and she hasn't been crying, but I can never tell with her. It might be best to hold off a little while."

As Emmitt hung up the phone, Andrew nodded and sighed. "I shouldn't have procrastinated. Sorry, Emmitt."

Emmitt stretched and yawned as Andrew pulled up to his apartment. "Don't worry about it. We've got time. No need to apologize."

When Emmitt entered his apartment, he didn't bother to flip on the light, undress, or turn down the covers. He lumbered heavily onto his bed and slept deeply. The following day, Renata visited his apartment and made lunch for him. They sat and ate at his kitchen table while watching a half-dozen instructional videos on sink repairs. After lunch, they drove to the hardware store for parts, then drove back to the apartment with Emmitt's back seat loaded with unnecessary supplies that Renata had purchased for Emmitt as "an investment for the future."

A simple, step-by-step instructional video that promised "a drip-free sink in fifteen minutes" took three hours for the pair to achieve. Emmitt glanced at the clock on his oven before looking back down at the dripless faucet.

As he admired their achievement, he considered how quickly the time passed. Working with the Yates family had altered Emmitt's sense of accomplishment. Every minor success now felt like a major victory. He held Renata tightly, kissed her, and took a moment to savor their triumph. As Renata spent the rest of the afternoon and evening napping on his bed, Emmitt sat at his laptop and concentrated on his work. When she finally woke up, she yawned deeply and slowly rose from the bed. She hugged and kissed Emmitt goodbye and promised to come back to visit him the following evening after work. The following evening, she arrived with enough groceries to stock Emmitt's fridge. She didn't give him an opportunity to protest. She looked up at him with her captivating blue eyes and told him to sit down while she cooked dinner. Emmitt smirked and complied. The evening after, Emmitt reciprocated by taking her out to dinner. The following day, Emmitt took a break from his work and accompanied Renata as she toured several of her uncle's properties.

Since his conversation with Shannon in the Yates driveway, Emmitt approached his work with an unyielding sense of determination. He wrote scripts for his video essays at night and filmed early in the morning. He increased his output to two videos a week, which was a considerable improvement from the bimonthly videos he posted at a leisurely pace before his involvement with Renata. As Emmitt increased his earnings, he placed most of the extra income into savings, which built on the forty thousand dollars he had accumulated from the eight-month cleanup. As the checks from James Yates came in the mail, Emmitt self-consciously squirreled the money away. He decided he would spend it when he felt less guilty. The guilt hadn't subsided. Aside from purchasing Renata's Christmas gift months ago, the money remained in his account, untouched. Andrew had already set the end date with James, and Emmitt felt relieved when the last check was delivered.

While Emmitt was motivated and enthusiastic about creating his video essays, he struggled with the book. It was easy for Emmitt to immerse himself in reading and writing fiction, but there were far more considerations when writing reality. Emmitt agonized as he tried to determine what to incorporate and what to cut out. He desperately wanted to honor the Yates women, but it felt like an impossible task. It was as though he had found Renata's hidden diary and was transcribing passages for public consumption. He would sometimes sit for hours, writing, deleting, then rewriting a single paragraph.

Now, five days after their last official day of work, Emmitt found himself weighed down again to his laptop, staring at a single sentence when he received a text from Andrew.

Are you home? Called Sybil. Need to talk to you ASAP.

Emmitt looked at the text and wondered what it meant. He texted back, *I'm home. You can call, if it's easier.*

No. Need to talk in person. Be there in a few.

The last text was from Emmitt. *Good news or bad?*

Andrew hadn't responded. Emmitt closed his laptop. The vague exchange was too unsettling for Emmitt to concentrate on his work. Unable to calm his growing restlessness, he stood and walked to the bathroom. Emmitt washed his face and brushed his teeth. He put on a clean shirt and jeans and looked around for something to keep him busy while he waited. His eyes finally settled on the dripless kitchen faucet. He had almost finished washing and drying his dishes from the previous night's dinner when he heard the knock.

"It's unlocked," Emmitt said in a raised voice as he quickly dried his hands.

Andrew entered with his eyes downcast, as though trying to make sense of some great, distant tragedy. Emmitt didn't expect to see an existential look on his older brother's face.

"Bad news," Emmitt said.

Andrew walked over to the couch and sat. He leaned back with a deep sigh, fully sinking his weight into it. Andrew never reclines, Emmitt thought nervously.

"I messed up," Andrew said. "Spectacularly."

"How?" Emmitt asked. He walked to the kitchen table, grabbed a chair, and moved it across from where Andrew sat.

"It should've been the first thing I did. Before introductions. She already signed the first one ... but I can't make excuses. I waited too long."

"What happened?" Emmitt sat and looked worriedly at his brother.

Andrew's voice was ice. "She texted me at three a.m. saying she's done."

"Okay? You're talking about Sybil? But that's what you were going to tell her. Why does it matter?"

"I would have told her to her face." Andrew scowled. Looking at Emmitt, he shook his head and spoke apologetically. "I'm not mad about that. Emmitt, I called her. She won't sign the updated waiver. She won't be in the book. God, I'm so sorry."

Emmitt's mind flashed back to his father, who had powerlessly uttered the same words in his childhood bedroom.

"Don't," Emmitt said, more sharply than he intended. "Don't apologize."

"I owe it to you," Andrew insisted. "I shouldn't have ignored your concerns about Sybil. You were right to doubt her."

As the words sank in, Emmitt's mind wandered. He contemplated the impact of Sybil's refusal.

Disregarding—or possibly worried by—the prolonged silence induced by Emmitt's internal preoccupation, Andrew continued his tirade.

"She had the nerve to blame it on you!" he thundered, startling Emmitt back to attention. "Sybil said you convinced her to believe in herself and make her own decisions. She said she was breaking free from any commitments that didn't serve her. God ... I never saw this coming. I should have. You warned me. I should've had her sign in the beginning. If she refused, I could've saved you the time and effort—"

"If you had done that, I wouldn't be with Renata," Emmitt quietly interjected.

"That's true," Andrew said tentatively. "But if I had convinced Sybil to sign earlier ..."

"No what-ifs. No what-abouts. No failures. *You* said that." There was a serenity that Emmitt didn't quite recognize in himself.

"Yeah," Andrew conceded. "But I'm worried about you. I'm not used to failing you."

Emmitt smiled. "You're used to me being the fuck-up. Well, I'll help you out, Andrew: I told Sybil she was smart. I told her she was capable of making decisions for herself. I told her she didn't need a guru. So, it *is* my fault. If I hadn't sat in on her video call with her essential oils team, and if I hadn't been so determined to figure her out, she probably would have signed. Don't apologize."

Andrew raised himself upright on the couch. "Why are you so calm? I came here to commiserate with you, then cheer you up afterwards. I guess I should be happy. You're taking the news a lot better than I expected. You're not mad at me … It's commendable, of course. Very mature. But now I feel like I have to calm *myself* down. I worked myself up for your sake, only to have you act like … well … me."

Emmitt looked at Andrew for a long time. A swell of uncontrollable laughter bubbled up and burst forth so violently, neither Andrew nor Emmitt could tell if he was laughing or crying. As the tears fell in giant drops on the coffee table while he doubled over in a fit of cackling sobs, Emmitt felt the cleansing rush of a full release.

Andrew dashed to Emmitt's side. "Emmitt! What the hell is going on with you? How can I help? What do you need me to do?"

Emmitt tried to stifle another surge of laughter. He shooed Andrew away and sobbed, "I'm fine … give … me … just a sec …"

"Are you … crying?" Andrew asked. His eyes widened in horror.

"A … little …" Emmitt choked.

Andrew tried to be reassuring. "Let it out, Emmitt. Release whatever you need to let go of."

At the half-strained, half-comforting tone of his brother's words, a fresh wave overtook Emmitt. "Shut up!" he laughed. "You're not helping."

Andrew briefly left the room, grabbed a roll of toilet paper, handed it to Emmitt, then sat back down on the couch. He stared at Emmitt with a look that fluctuated from concern to confusion, then finally settled on fascination. He watched quietly, allowing Emmitt to calm down.

The laughter tapered off long before the crying ended. Wads of toilet paper were torn off, used, then discarded on the coffee table.

When the crying subsided, Emmitt attempted levity. "I know … couples sometimes … take on … personality quirks … but … but I didn't think … I'd be bawling like Renata."

The words only set him spiraling into another fit of laughter. After a few more minutes of total silence on Andrew's part, Emmitt had calmed himself enough to breathe.

"It's been exhausting. Overwhelming. Heartbreaking," he said slowly and deliberately. "But I'm happy. I wouldn't be happy if we hadn't done it. I wouldn't have Renata. You wouldn't have Melody. We wouldn't be as close." He wiped at the tears that stained his cheeks and still threatened to trickle from his eyes. "I haven't spent the money James gave me … I tried to give it all to Renata to help with the down payment for her house. It didn't feel right to spend it on anyone but her. The book didn't feel right, either. There's too much pain in it. Even the triumphs are bittersweet. And how many people will buy the book out of morbid curiosity? I don't want anyone to get so caught up in the hoard that they miss the hope. Shit, I don't want to sound like you, Andrew …" Emmitt narrowed his glistening, bloodshot eyes at his brother.

After a brief pause, he grinned wildly. "Fuck it. I'll say it. This isn't the book we're supposed to write together. It isn't the story we're supposed to tell. I'm glad Sybil didn't sign. This isn't a failure. It's an opportunity."

"You honestly feel that way?" Andrew asked.

"Yeah," Emmitt said. "I don't want to write about them. I don't think I could do it."

"Then what story are we supposed to tell?" Andrew asked.

Emmitt stared at Andrew seriously and considered the question. As he continued to look at his brother, a slow smile built from the corners of his lips.

"Clearly, you've come up with something. Let's hear it, Emmitt," Andrew urged.

"What about *our* story?" Emmitt said. "It's half of what we've already written. It's the most enjoyable part of the draft to read through. And it means we don't have to rely on anyone else's suffering."

Andrew smiled. "You and me?"

"Why not?" Emmitt sniffled. "We've struggled. We've overcome. That's the entirety of a self-help book, right?"

"There's more to it … but it isn't a bad idea. My publisher knew it was a long shot to get all three to sign off on the book, and Shannon and Renata were always an afterthought. She was only interested in Sybil's story. Since we can't write about Sybil, she may be open to other suggestions. I can bring in some sample chapters to persuade her to change topics. If she isn't interested, we can always self-publish. It may not sell as well as a book about hoarders, but it's achievable."

"Then let's make it happen, Drew Key," Emmitt smirked. "A book about brothers."

Andrew smiled back with unflappable certainty. "I've already manifested it."

Chapter Thirty-Five

As Emmitt unlocked the door and entered Renata's house, Sybil was the first to greet him. She waved to Emmitt, looked him up and down, then immediately turned to her sister with a wide grin.

"You gave Emmitt his own key, Renata? How scandalous of you!" She giggled as Renata approached Emmitt and kissed him.

Two French bulldog puppies yapped ceaselessly, eagerly wagging their tails and jumping in place until Emmitt came over to greet them. Henry lay on his bed by the fireplace, with a *kill me* expression on his discontented face. Clearly sensing Henry's anguish, Renata walked over to the old dog, sat beside him, and gently stroked his head.

Sybil playfully eyed her sister. "Well, I suppose I should leave you two alone … to knit, or pray, or whatever you do when no one's around."

"We're going to the plant nursery after furniture shopping," Renata said.

"You know, Renata, it's no fun for me if you don't react," Sybil said. "Not even a blush?"

Renata shrugged her shoulders and smiled. "We've been spending a lot of time together, now that you've quit everything. We're getting comfortable with each other, Sybil."

"I hate it," Sybil said with a smirk.

"You can go shopping with us," Renata offered.

"No, thanks. But, before I go, you need to open the housewarming gift I brought you."

Sybil walked over to the front door and retrieved a large box from a nightstand that Renata was using as an entry table. The box was covered in vibrant floral gift wrap, with pink, yellow, and peach roses, and a bright-yellow ribbon had been tied around it. She walked back to where Renata sat and handed her the box.

"Here," Sybil said. "Open it!"

Renata untied the ribbon and delicately unwrapped the paper, being careful not to tear it.

Sybil leaned into Emmitt and whispered loud enough for Renata to hear. "Christmas is awful with her. She takes forever to open just one present."

Ignoring Sybil, Renata opened the box and peered inside. "Sybil!" Renata gasped. "I can't. You shouldn't ..."

"What is it?" Emmitt asked.

Renata reached inside the box and pulled out a teacup with gold trim and yellow roses.

"Grandpa mixed up our colors," Sybil said. "I broke the pink one—which should have been mine—but the yellow one should have been yours. I want you to have it."

"But ..." Renata began.

Sybil put her hands on her hips, lifted her nose, and smiled haughtily. "Don't be rude, Renata. You have to accept my gift ... it's good manners. You don't want to have bad manners in front of Emmitt, do you?"

Renata stood and wrapped her arms tightly around her sister. "Thank you, Sybil."

Sybil's eyes widened at her sister's unexpected display of affection. Her lip quivered momentarily before she composed herself. "You're welcome." She gave Renata a quick squeeze before pulling back. "Oh, and there was one more thing," Sybil said, turning to Emmitt. "I need to show you my books."

"What books?" Emmitt asked.

"I put a pile over there. You need to read them for me and tell me what I need to do to fix myself."

Emmitt suppressed the urge to laugh as he glanced at Sybil's serious expression. He smiled tenderly as he spoke to her. "That's not how it works, Sybil. It defeats the purpose of doing things for yourself."

"But you're supposed to be an expert!" Sybil whined. "You write book summaries, right? You can read these for your summaries, then I'll read about them on your website. When you think about it, I'm really doing you a favor."

Emmitt shook his head. "I'm not updating the website anymore. I'm focusing on writing and video essays."

"Then do a video essay," Sybil demanded petulantly.

Emmitt sighed and smirked at Sybil. "One book. I'll read one and give you a summary, but only if you read one too, and give me a summary. Then, we'll have read two books together ... more or less."

Sybil scrunched her nose. "Fine."

She scanned through the pile of books that had been dumped carelessly on the floor. She bent down and picked up the thickest one and handed it to Emmitt. "This is yours." She next picked out a thin booklet and waved it in the air. "I'll do this one."

Emmitt didn't bother to argue. "Alright, Sybil. I'll get you a summary by next week."

"You're the best, Emmitt."

Sybil kissed Emmitt's cheek, tossed the remaining books into an oversized pink purse, then reached down to grab a puppy in each arm. Emmitt unzipped the protective netting on an expensive dog stroller, and Sybil popped the puppies in, zipped the netting, and headed out the front door.

"Sybil's been surprising me lately," Renata said. "Sometimes I think there are hints of a soft, gooey human being beneath her sharp, rhinestone crust." She was back on the floor, petting Henry, and shifting her eyes between Emmitt and the box with the yellow rose tea set.

"I'm glad you two are getting along."

"She's pretty fond of you too, Emmitt," Renata said. "Are you really going to read the book she gave you?"

Emmitt placed the book on top of an unpacked moving box. He walked toward Renata and laid down on the wooden floor, resting his head on her lap. He looked up at her. "Yeah. It's a fair trade. She's reading a book too."

"It looked more like a pamphlet to me," Renata said, gazing down at Emmitt.

"She still has to give me a summary. That, in itself, is worth the trade."

"Only you would think so, but I appreciate how kind and patient you are with Sybil. You really have a surprisingly calming presence ... most of the time."

Emmitt smiled self-consciously at the compliment. "Nah. Sybil's family now. I have to be kind and patient and calming ... most of the time." He winked at Renata, then let out a groaning sigh. "Anyway, are you ready to go shopping? It'll be nice to have a couch to sit on ... and you definitely need more tables and shelves, so you can have a place to put the plants after we pot them."

"Eventually." Renata yawned. "I'm not in any rush today."

"Works for me," Emmitt said, closing his eyes. "Wake me up when your legs fall asleep."

"No napping, yet. I still need your input on the office. I've nearly finished decorating, but it's your workspace. Sybil helped me move my old sofa into the room so you and Andrew can be comfortable when you work on your book."

"You moved the sofa again? I just helped you move it from the guest bedroom into your bedroom three days ago."

"I decided it would look better in the office ... I may change my mind again, after we go furniture shopping."

Emmitt grinned. "How many decorative pillows?"

"Only six," Renata assured him. "If the pillows get in the way, you can move them. They have a designated basket."

"How many blankets?"

Renata laughed. "Three. One for you. One for Andrew. And one for Henry. I have your names embroidered on them."

"That's smart. None of us likes to share."

"I figured as much."

"I'll take a look at the office, but I'm sure it's perfect. You make everything perfect, Renata. Besides, I'm not particular, and it's your house until we're married."

"About that," Renata said coyly. "I need to talk to you about something."

"Yeah?" Emmitt opened one eye to look at Renata.

"When the time comes, I don't want you to buy an engagement ring. It's a family tradition to pick one of my great-grandmother's rings. When you ask permission from Mom, I'll tell you which ring to pick. I know it's old-fashioned, but she'll be happy to have someone who respects her enough to ask."

"The art deco emerald with diamond clusters around it?"

"How?" Her mouth gaped as her mind processed wildly behind her sparkling eyes.

"Your mom waited a week after we cleared the entry to call me and tell me about the ring. Sybil took it to get cleaned and polished before they gave it to me. I've been keeping it in a safe at Andrew's house."

"So, everyone already knows? Even Sybil? No one told me anything," Renata pouted.

Emmitt smirked. "I think you're supposed to be the last one to know … and I've already said too much, but I think it's pretty obvious where we're headed. Just don't ask when I plan to do it. Let me have one secret."

Renata leaned down and kissed Emmitt deeply. As she lifted her head, she let out an audible exhale. "Okay. I'll allow one secret. Oh … wow … and Andrew proposing to Melody in a week. Do you have our tickets?"

"Yeah. Andrew dropped them off a couple of days ago. He invited Melody's parents and brothers too. He's waiting until the fireworks go off at the game to do it, then we'll all go to Gigi's Diner to celebrate. Mom … isn't coming. But I'm picking Dad up from the airport Saturday morning. He'll be staying in town for a few days after the proposal. He's excited to meet you."

"I'm excited to meet him too," Renata said. "But I'm a little nervous."

"Don't be. He'll love you."

"I hope so," Renata said dreamily. Her lips were softly upturned, and her eyes still glittered at the thought of a proposal.

"So, today: lunch, furniture, plants?" Emmitt asked, hoping to lull Renata out of her enchantment.

Renata paused and considered. "Coffee, furniture, plants, lunch. I need to caffeinate you first. And you tend to get sleepy after eating."

"Alright," Emmitt said, slowly rising to his feet. "Should we check out the office now?"

Renata shot a playful glance at Emmitt as he grabbed her hands and pulled her to her feet. "I don't know now. Maybe I'll keep it a secret."

Emmitt shrugged. "I can wait. Can you?"

Renata grinned. "No. I'm too excited to wait."

She lovingly slipped her hand into Emmitt's and together they walked to his office.